"A sparkling, heartwarming novel with all the elements of a can't-put-it-down read—a heroine you'll root for, unexpected plot twists, and dangerously good descriptions of food!"

—Sarah Pekkanen, author of *The Best of Us*

"A funny and heartfelt tale of friendship, food, and how difficult it can be to open yourself up to love . . . This is Stacey Ballis at her witty and chef-tastic best."

—Amy Hatvany, author of *Safe with Me* and *Heart Like Mine*

"Ballis delves again into foodie women's lit with flavorful results . . . Honest and touching."

—*Kirkus Reviews*

Off the Menu

"Readers hungry for cleverly written contemporary romances will definitely want to order *Off the Menu*." —*Chicago Tribune*

"Another fabulous and soul-satisfying meal . . . With the perfect blend of humor and heart, Ballis's writing is powerfully honest and genuinely hilarious."

—Jen Lancaster, *New York Times* bestselling author of *Twisted Sisters* and *The Tao of Martha*

"Enticing. Ballis writes a bit like Emily Giffin and Isabel Wolff, and the recipes will please gal foodies as well." —*Booklist*

"Smart, sexy, and delightfully buoyant . . . In a word, scrumptious."

—Quinn Cummings, author of *The Year of Learning Dangerously*

continued . . .

"Interesting characters and a satisfying plot . . . Fans of Stacey Ballis will devour her latest book." —Examiner.com

"A great contemporary romance about a chef striving to find balance in her life and enjoying both her man and her career."
—*The Parkersburg News and Sentinel*

Good Enough to Eat

"*Good Enough to Eat* is like a perfect dish of macaroni and cheese—rich, warm, nuanced, and delicious. And like any great comfort food, Stacey Ballis's new book is absolutely satisfying."
—Jen Lancaster

"Witty and tender, brash and seriously clever . . . Her storytelling will have you alternately turning pages and calling your friends urging them to come along for the ride. And in Stacey Ballis's talented hands, oh what a wonderful ride it is."
—Elizabeth Flock, *New York Times* bestselling author of *What Happened to My Sister*

"A toothsome meal of moments, gorgeously written, in warmth and with keen observation, *Good Enough to Eat* is about so much more than the magic of food; it's about the magic of life. Pardon the cliché, but you'll devour it and wish there was more to savor."
—Stephanie Klein, author of *Straight Up and Dirty* and *Moose*

The Spinster Sisters

"Readers will be rooting for Ballis's smart, snappy heroines."
—*Booklist*

Sleeping Over

Inappropriate Men

Room for Improvement

continued . . .

Recipe for Disaster

STACEY BALLIS

BERKLEY BOOKS, NEW YORK

THE BERKLEY PUBLISHING GROUP
Published by the Penguin Group
Penguin Group (USA) LLC
375 Hudson Street, New York, New York 10014

USA • Canada • UK • Ireland • Australia • New Zealand • India • South Africa • China

penguin.com

A Penguin Random House Company

This book is an original publication of The Berkley Publishing Group.

Library of Congress Cataloging-in-Publication Data

Ballis, Stacey.
Recipe for disaster / Stacey Ballis.—Berkley trade paperback edition.
p. cm.
ISBN 978-0-425-26550-5 (paperback)
I. Title.
PS3602.A624R43 2015
813'.6—dc23
2014043350

PUBLISHING HISTORY
Berkley trade paperback edition / March 2015

PRINTED IN THE UNITED STATES OF AMERICA

10 9 8 7 6 5 4 3 2 1

Cover design by Rita Frangie.
Cover photo composition by S. Miroque.
"Woman cooking pizza at home" by Hasloo Group Production Studio / Shutterstock;
"Schnauzer" by ARTSILENSE / Shutterstock.
Interior text design by Laura K. Corless.

For Bill.

*Because my house wasn't complete till you moved into it,
and now wherever you are is home to me.*

Acknowledgments

This book is dedicated with much love and gratitude to the people who have most informed my sense of home. My dad, Stephen, who taught me that it is always okay to over-improve a property if it comes from a place of love and passion. My mom, Elizabeth, who has devoted her entire professional life to finding people their homes, and her personal life to making a loving and happy home for our family. My grandmother Jonnie, for teaching me that the kitchen is the heart of a home, that it is always preferable to be fearless there, and if the fudge doesn't set, call it fudge sauce and buy ice cream. My sister, Deborah, who keeps any home she is in full of laughter.

For Lew Coulson, who trusted us to take care of our house with the same loving commitment that he did, and made one of my biggest lifelong dreams possible.

For Bill and Colette Rodon-Hornof, who listened to twenty years' worth of ideas for our dream home, and heard what we needed, and designed something that exceeds every one of those dreams.

For Patrick King and Dennis Leary, for working so hard to make it all come to life, and for being excellent recipe tasters.

For Penny, who suffers endless hours of discussion of all the minutiae that goes into the design of every space. Whatever style and beauty our house contains always has her magical input and impeccable taste.

For Amy and Wayne, and Lisa, who are so generous with their own homes and make us feel like family when we are with them.

For Leslie Gelbman, Wendy McCurdy, Katherine Pelz, Caitlin Valenziano, Craig Burke, Brian Wilson, and everyone else on the Berkley team, for giving me such a wonderful professional home, and for Scott Mendel, who got me into their hands to begin with.

For my extraordinary friends, each and every one of them, you know how much I treasure you all.

For Quinn, who not only gave me some of the initial inspiration for this book, but let me borrow her daughter's name to boot.

And in loving memory of Molly Glynn, who was a bright light snuffed way too early. We're all stepping through it. Love hard. Be kind. Always remember.

Also a small shout-out to the person who invented central air-conditioning. Seriously, like the fifth best thing to happen in my life. Not kidding.

I slip the dress over my head. I can't remember the last time I was actually in a dress. It's definitely been over a year. I'm not big on dresses in general; it can be hard to find them for my shape. If they actually fit over my substantial boobs and wide hips, I lose my waist entirely and become a blob. Or they make me look like the mother of the bride. I was just going to wear the charcoal gray wrap dress that is always my fancy-night-out go-to, but the girls pitched a fit. And when I told them we were just going to go to city hall and then maybe have a really nice meal somewhere, you'd have thought I suggested we sacrifice puppies. On a burning altar of rare oil paintings. In the middle of the Vatican.

So my wedding gift from them turned out to be the wedding itself, and everything that entails. Caroline took charge of the whole thing, refusing to let me decline either her generosity or her good taste. It was a relief. I'm just not your girly girl dreaming of a foofy dress and bells and whistles. For most of my life I presumed that marriage itself was not for me, so now that I'm actually taking the plunge, handing over the endless details to people who think these things matter was a huge weight off my shoulders, and allowed me to keep my focus on my work while they pulled the thing together with my gratitude and carte blanche to make the decisions. Best kind of wedding? The one where you just have to show up.

At least the wedding planning gave them a chance to bond a little bit with my groom, who did have some things about the day that were important to him, and if it didn't fully solidify their connection to each other, it at least appears to have created an atmosphere of respect and the beginnings of acceptance.

Caroline, in addition to being the wedding planner and hosting the whole shindig at her beautiful house, found the dress for me, her taste in all things being impeccable. It's a wonderful shade of medium gray with a lot of green in it that makes my skin look creamy, and my auburn hair sparkle, and my hazel eyes pick up the green in fiery flecks. It's made of some kind of heavy matte silk, with a sort of an early 1960s vibe, a wide scoop neck that shows off my shoulders and my décolletage, very fitted to the waist, keeping everything locked and loaded, and then a wide sweep of skirt over an actual crinoline. I'm making kind of fun rustling noises, and for once it isn't just my ample thighs rubbing together. With the sparkly gold kitten heels I borrowed from Hedy, the effect is just perfect. The wide skirt masks my hips and substantial butt, the skirt hits just at the bottom curve of my muscular calf, giving the illusion of a slender ankle; the whole effect makes me look like . . .

"You look like a brickhouse," Hedy says, whistling under her breath.

"I know. It's weird." Even when I do wear dresses, I never feel beautiful or sexy, I just feel dressed up.

"It's not weird, it's fantastic." This, for her, is a statement of fact, an approval of the costume, if not the circumstance.

"Well, you don't look so bad yourself." She's wearing a stunning deep eggplant shift dress with a wide gold architectural necklace and chunky gold bracelets. Her chestnut hair is pulled back into a bouncy ponytail, shiny and subtly highlighted. And she's wearing a killer pair of black cage heels that I'm sure cost more than a mortgage payment, and in which I would be on my ass in less than four minutes.

"Here, let me put this on you." She comes forward with a beautiful bracelet, an art deco design in diamonds and sapphires. She clasps it on my wrist. "Perfect."

"Hey, you guys almost ready in here?" Marie pokes her head around the corner. She's wearing a fun vintage strapless dress on her voluptuous figure, in pale violet with a delicate rhinestone belt. Her long curly brown hair is twisted up into a loose bun with little ringlets escaping.

I always marvel that my three best friends in the world, as different as they are from each other, are all on the same page when it comes to dress and hair and special occasions. They like to put themselves together, to shop, to plan parties, to celebrate milestones with pomp and circumstance. Caroline likes to host at home, to show off her cooking skills, to arrange the flowers and make the little takeaway gifts by hand. Hedy is a restaurant girl, she loves a private room with a specially chosen menu, leaves the flowers to Cornelia McNamara, Chicago's florist to the stars, and has one of her many personal shoppers decide on the trinkets. Marie bops back and forth between funky venues like the Diversey River Bowl or a road trip to a drive-in movie at the McHenry Outdoor Theatre, and casual parties at the Wicker Park loft she shares with her boyfriend, John. Marie leans more toward potlucks, chili cook-offs, dogs and burgers on the grill. All different, but the impulse is the same. To gather those you care about for joy and conviviality. My best guess is that it's because they all had mothers who taught them how.

I should be flattered that they even deign to hang out with me, since my idea of shoe shopping involves steel-toed work boots, yesterday was my first manicure in nearly a year, and I almost always forget not only their birthdays, but my own too. Also? I never host a party. Ever. Occasionally a casual girls'

night, involving ordering in pizza or Thai with plenty of beer.
My idea of hors d'oeuvres involves opening a cellophane bag or
two and perhaps popping the lid off some dip.

"What do you say, lady? You ready?" Hedy asks me. Her
voice is friendly but her mouth is a thin line. She looks at best
resigned, and at worst pissed off, but I can't even think about
that today. Your friends have to forgive you eventually, and
even if they don't approve of the marital adventure I am about
to embark upon, they'll get over it once they realize that I'm
just being true to myself.

"Yep. I'm ready." I do one last check in the mirror. My usually unkempt frizzy mass of hair is tamed into gentle waves,
pulled back off my face with an antique silver clip, and my usually bare face is accented simply with very natural blush, a
swipe of shimmery gold eye shadow, mascara, and a pale pink
lip gloss.

"Okay, let's go, gorgeous." Marie reaches out and takes my
hand like she used to when we were kids. Her eyebrows are
knitted together, and she doesn't make eye contact with me at
all. "Caroline went insane down there, just so you know."

I laugh. "I never suspected anything else."

"Okay, stop gabbing, there is a party downstairs that is happening without you, and you are the main attraction." Hedy
scoots us all out of Caroline's bedroom and we go down the
wide staircase. When we get to the second floor, Caroline, looking perfect and radiant in a Tiffany-blue swirly chiffon number,
claps her hands.

"You're spectacular! Here." She reaches forward and hands
me a bundle of deep purple and mauve calla lilies. She looks me
dead in the eye. "You ready?" she asks pointedly.

"Ready."

"And you're absolutely sure?"

"I'm sure."

She nods, her forehead furrowed in query, her mouth a wan half smile. "Okay, then."

We head down the second flight of stairs. When we get to the landing, I can see all the people, about twenty of them, looking up and smiling at me. Caroline's husband, Carl, has his big camera, the one he uses when they travel, and he's taking pictures of me as I come down the stairs. The whole thing is surreal, and shocking, yet I'm feeling weirdly really happy. And light for the first time in forever. Whatever my best friends think they know, no one knows my heart the way I do, and this feels right, and safe, and shockingly real. Caroline has filled her living room with flowers and candles, all of the antique chairs from her dining room are swagged in wide ribbons, and I'm genuinely happy as I float downstairs to meet my future.

1

————

"We can't thank you enough, Anneke, it's just perfect," Claire says, her eyes sparkling.

"Really, Claire is understating, we're over the moon!" John pipes in, sliding an arm around his wife, and pulling her close to him. "It's a dream come true for both of us." Their easy affection speaks to a lifetime together.

"It was my deepest pleasure, I'm just glad you're happy." I'm keeping things professional and calm on my surface. "Live a very happy life here." I hand John the keys, on a custom titanium key ring engraved with their address, accept awkwardly the hugs they both offer, and quietly head out the front door. As soon as it latches behind me I hear a loud whoop from inside the house, followed by effervescent giggling. I turn and get a peek through the window, John is spinning Claire in the living room in a jubilant waltz, her head thrown back in laughter, and I'm able to let go of the tears that I was suppressing.

I'm not generally demonstratively emotional; in fact my girlfriends tease me about it all the time. Hedy will call me Iceberg Anneke or Proud Stroudt when she thinks I'm being distant or unaffected. Marie will shake her head and sing "It's All Right to Cry" from *Free to Be ... You and Me* with a smirk. Caroline will just reach over and squeeze my hand. Whatever. I can't help it that my besties are all sappy and tenderhearted and can produce a flood of tears at a goddamn AT&T commercial. Whenever we have chick flick night and the three of them are unabashedly weeping, they all look over to see me on the couch, dry-eyed and skeptical as Bette Midler sings about the wind beneath her wings to her best friend's orphan.

For me, I can't really understand why they are so upset at the fictional death of an actress on-screen. I just saw Barbara Hershey in *People* magazine four days ago, for chrissakes. I can't get it up for what is basically a decent makeup job, some convincing coughing, and swelling strings in the background. It's just not how I'm wired. Which, while it may occasionally be a pain in my personal life, is a good thing in my line of work. The design/build industry is still very much a man's game, and they can smell weakness from ten miles off. I know that tears are not in and of themselves a sign of weakness, but the boys I work with do not. So my ability to keep it together is very important to me professionally. It doesn't matter what happens, if the cabinets show up the wrong size or the painter drops a full bucket of Magnolia White down the newly carpeted stairs, my response at best is pragmatic and at worst is pissed off. I will cajole. I will swear. I will yell. I will question the fidelity of one's mother specifically, and the relative intelligence of the human race in general. I will punch something hard, or laugh like a hyena, or go into total crisis control mode. But I will not cry.

Except on days like today.

Despite my inner stoicism about life globally, I almost always let myself shed a tear or two on key days. When you get to look at the people for whom you have sweated over the course of months, or sometimes even years, and hand over the keys to their personal kingdom, that hits me where I live. It doesn't matter if it's just a small bathroom remodel, or a complete empty-lot-to-dream-home build from the first shovel to the final nail. The satisfaction of getting the job done, of making dreams come true for people, of creating *home* for them, it makes the long hours, the lost weekends, the damage to personal relationships completely and utterly worthwhile. Even though I've effectively been doing this for over half my life, it never gets old. It's always worth a quiet moment of self-satisfaction and a tear or two for someone else's joy that you made possible.

This had been an especially fun project. John and Claire lived in their bungalow for over twenty years, saving their money for a complete renovation, which happened to coincide with their twenty-fifth wedding anniversary. It included finishing both the basement and attic, effectively tripling the square footage of the place. We created a wonderful, bright master bedroom suite in the former attic space, with his and hers walk-in closets and a spa-like bathroom with a steam shower for John and a huge tub for Claire. In the basement, we gave them a large comfortable space for entertaining, a small office for John, an updated laundry room, and a guest room with an en suite bathroom. On the first floor, we renovated their 1970s-era kitchen, opening it up to their formerly cramped dining room and living room for a large, open-concept space. We were able to honor and highlight the Arts and Crafts details they loved about their 1919 house, while making all of the systems pure twenty-first-century functional.

My favorite kind of project, to be honest. The kind of thing that has spoken to me ever since I was thirteen and my stepdad, Joe, took me to one of his work sites, the renovation of an old Victorian brownstone, showing me the magic in how houses used to be constructed. I thought the intersection of architecture and artistry and archeology was extraordinary, the perfect arrangement of imperfect stones to create the foundation, old solid bricks supporting wooden lath and hand-applied plaster. I came home with sawdust in my hair and cement crusted on my sneakers, and new love in my heart. Both for Joe, who was the only thing I ever had in my life that could be considered family in a positive and rational way, and for old houses that needed to find their full potential.

I jump into my 1967 Ford F-100 pickup, formerly Joe's and part of my inheritance from him. Lola is a classic, with the original turquoise paint, now pitted and scratched and dulled from the years, and an engine that purrs like a lion cub. She's hauled endless loads of drywall and lumber, schlepped salvaged bathtubs and brand-new dishwashers with ease, and despite her nearly 250,000 miles, has never let me down. Plus, I get major street cred with the subcontractors. They're used to women architects and designers teetering around job sites on inappropriate shoes, and trying to climb ladders in miniskirts. I am, it goes without saying, not that kind of girl. I usually have paint on my face and grout under my stubby fingernails, and 94 percent of my wardrobe is covered in permanent filth.

I steer Lola through the icy streets of Chicago, heading back to the MacMurphy offices for a final debrief with my bosses. As much as I love the work? The job itself is craptastic on a good day. I knew when Joe retired that I wasn't ready to go out on my own. I didn't have enough experience under my belt. I knew I needed to work for a firm where I could get a wide variety of projects, where I could build relationships with subcontractors and tradesmen and suppliers. MacMurphy seemed like the perfect place. They do everything from small single-room projects to quick and dirty house flips to multimillion-dollar custom-home builds. They appreciated that I'm a general contractor who is also an architect, since they can charge the client for the two separate services but just pay me once. I sometimes think that one of the reasons I cry on key days is because it means I have to briefly spend some quality time at the office instead of out on the job site, and I hate the office.

The day is typical blustery December, overcast and dreary, with a biting wind. I pull into the lot on Clybourn, parking next to Liam's brand-new F-150. He gets a new one every other year. Always shiny, showy red, always completely kitted out with bells and whistles and every possible add-on. In-dash GPS navigation screen, upgraded Bose sound system, custom leather interior. Mud flaps with chrome shamrocks. They shouldn't say it has EcoBoost; they should say it has EgoBoost.

Liam? Is a total douche. In case that is unclear. I'm sure he thinks the slight lilt of an Irish accent makes him charming, but I like to remind him that he hasn't set foot on the olde sod since he was six, and it just makes him sound stupid and affected.

Liam is the first cousin of Brian Murphy, one of the company owners and my direct boss. Brian, Murph to his friends, runs the build side, while his partner, Marcus "Mac" McPherson, runs the design side. Liam and I have the same title, senior project manager, but somehow he always gets his pick of choice jobs and cool clients. Which is why I loved working with John and Claire so much. Usually I get the problem children, the cranky, the indecisive, the ones with questionable taste or insanely limited and unrealistic budgets. This one was just fun and easy and a real treat. Joe always said that if you love what you do, you never work a day in your life, and while it always still feels like work to me, there was much happy in the last nine months.

"Hey, Anniekay!" one of the Barbies says as I come in the door. Mac and Murph hire an endless series of buxom blondies with limited vocabularies to man the front desk and do basic secretarial work. There are usually three or four of them teetering around on those platform stilettos that look like high-heeled hooves. They all get titles like customer relations specialist or office manager. I'm always eye level with a wall of silicone and perpetually erect nipples. None of them lasts much more than a few months, and none of them can ever pronounce my name, Anneke. Ann-uh-kuh. How hard is that?

"Hi. Is Murph ready for me?"

She grins a blinding smile, veneers sparkling strangely bluish behind thickly glossed and plumped lips. She looks like a deranged grouper. "He said to give him fifteen minutes," she says breathlessly, bosom heaving, nipples aimed at me in a shockingly accusatory fashion, with the top button of her tiny shirt straining against the effort. I better extricate myself from this conversation before it gives way and blinds me. I would not be cute in an eye patch.

"Great. I'll be in my office."

I head down the hall to my tiny windowless closet of an office, barely big enough for my desk and one chair, books and floor plans and blueprints scattered everywhere. Stacks of finish samples teeter in the corners, and empty plastic water bottles are erupting out of the wastebasket. I'm something of a slob. But messy, not dirty, I like to tell myself, as if this is better. Liam? Has an office three times this size. With a window. And a private bathroom. Apparently the previous office occupant was a three-man law firm, so there are three offices with en suite baths. It was empty when I started, but I still got the "one step up from coffin" all the way in the back near the alley where I get hot-garbage scent all summer, and Liam, who started after I did, slid right into the choice digs like shit out of a goose.

"How'd it go with the Osbornes?" Liam arranges his lanky frame in my door, dark curly hair artfully rumpled, piercing green eyes shining behind long, thick, dark lashes.

"Great. They couldn't be happier, the place really turned out even better than expected."

"Good to hear. You must be glad to get that one put to bed."

"Always bittersweet. Glad to have a job finished, sad to let it go. But I'm happy that they're happy. How are things over on Fremont?" Liam is in the middle of my most hated kind of project. A wonderful old building with clients that are keeping the façade and doing a complete gut on the inside. All the original hardwood floors, beautiful cabinets and built-ins, claw-foot tubs, mosaic tile work, even some historic hand-painted silk wall coverings, all ripped out in favor of new new new everything. The couple, young trust fund babies both, wanted to build from scratch, but couldn't find a double lot on one of their seven preferred Lincoln Park streets on which to erect one of those horrible places that all look like banks, so they settled for mangling this beautiful turn-of-the-century brick home instead. I'm grateful for only two things. One, they didn't decide to tear it down completely, and two, I was able to spend a long, exhausting weekend with some of my guys salvaging everything that was salvageable and moving it to my storage unit. If I don't use it myself, I'll be sure that it all finds future useful life.

"You know. Couldn't be more generic. Open-concept main level, eat-in family room slash kitchen with homework station blah blah blah. It's going to look like a Restoration Hardware catalog." I give Liam credit for only two things. He does appreciate the old school and old world and hates to see people destroy things as much as I do. And he's as big a perfectionist as I am in terms of quality. Joe's first lesson to me was to focus my energy on doing everything the right way. "*You know what I call the building codes?*" he used to say. "*A start.*" I've spent the better part of my career convincing people to spend more money than they want to on infrastructure, and micromanaging subcontractors who insist that something is just fine "at code."

"At least you won't have budget issues," I say to Liam, wishing he would put his arm down so that I can stop staring at the swath of exposed six-pack where his thermal shirt is hiked up, stop wondering about how he might have gotten the thin white vertical scar below his rib cage. I'd love to tell him to go away, but it's become clear that Murph fully intends to hand him the management when he retires, which he threatens to do more and more, and while I'm far more qualified for the job and should be considered, I know it won't happen. I'm not enough of a suck-up. I like to think of my style as honest and straightforward, but apparently, according to my annual reviews, I'm "abrasive" and "disrespectful." At least once every few months Murph calls me in for a dressing-down because I've pissed somebody off. I can't help it if I'm going to call his buddy the plumber out on reusing pipes from a previous job and charging for new, or if I tell a client that I absolutely will not come back after inspection to build out a bonus mudroom that they can't claim on the permit drawings because it adds illegal square footage.

"True. That is something. You ready to jump onto the Manning job?" He smirks.

"Please. Don't remind me." The Mannings, new-moneyed distant cousins to a storied Chicago scion, with all of the entitlement that implies, are my next primary clients. And the design for their new dream home, an up-from-the-ground build in Bucktown, looks like Carmela Soprano decided to buy a place in Connecticut and hire Dolly Parton and Ralph Lauren as her decorators. Waspy, but with weird spangly twists. Never thought I'd see design plans that included both a room upholstered in padded tartan-plaid silk with a gargantuan gold-plated chandelier dripping crystals, AND a custom-paneled library with leather-tile floors and a window seat covered in magenta ponyhide. The whole place smacks of Martha Stewart's Acid Trip Dream House. The budget is pretty astronomical, but they still want to score a bargain wherever possible, and seem to always have a "contact" who can "get a better deal." Warren Manning, who seems to have made his money in a strange combination of flatbed trucking and school buses, is a squat, sweaty man with a badly dyed comb-over and a permanent sneer. His wife, Susie, is a pinched little round woman, who crams herself into ill-fitting designer suits, which she pairs with cheap shoes and expensive handbags. They both like to bark orders and make grand pronouncements, and they name-drop like Perez Hilton has them on retainer. I hate them and their stupid house already.

Liam grins. "Yeah, have fun with that."

Barbie Two peeks under his arm, platinum blonde extensions tipped in hot pink, because her colors are Blush and Bashful, and a skirt short enough to see her daddy issues. "Hey, um, Annamuk? Brian will see you now."

Liam shakes his head and smirks. "Better not keep him waiting, um, *Annamuk*."

S eems like everything is in order," Murph says.
     I've long ago given up on getting actual praise from him for a job well-done. And I was really good on this one. No fights with subs, no complaints from clients, no reprimands at all.

"Keys handed off today."

"You got the pictures for the portfolio?" Mac asks, always wanting to pad out the website content.

"Yes, and the testimonial sheet." I preempt the next question.

"Good," Murph says, turning his attention to his cell phone for something terribly important, like a "Which car would you be?" quiz or something.

"And you gave them their handbook?" Mac says, conveniently forgetting once again that the handbook was my idea, and is the only thing I brought with me to MacMurphy that they have adopted. Whenever I finish any build, I put together a three-ring binder for the owners. It contains manuals and warranties for all of the appliances, care instructions for fixtures or finishes, and a one-year calendar cheat sheet for upkeep schedules. Mac and Murph thought it was such a great idea they insisted all the project managers start to do it, and even printed up custom binders to contain the paperwork. I think they just like to slap their logo on anything that isn't nailed down.

"Of course. They're thrilled."

"Good. That should pretty much clear your schedule for Manning?" Murph looks at the master calendar.

Shudder. "Yep. The closet project on Maplewood is pretty much in the hands of California Closets for installation; I'll do a walk-through tomorrow to check up, and again when they're done. The bathrooms at the new Rick Bayless restaurant are just waiting for the stall doors to come back from the refinisher, and the footings are in for the sunroom project up in Park Ridge, so I've handed it off to Clark; he says it should be about a month."

"Sounds good, Anneke. Looks like everything is in order, then. Anything we need to know about Manning?" Mac asks.

"Not really. Plans are pretty much done; they are still tweaking some interior spaces, but not in a way that will impact structure, they're just finalizing some decisions that really only affect the electrical plot in small ways, so we've got time. Permit application will go in this week; my best guess is that we'll be good to go in about eight weeks. I've got plans out to the usual suspects for bids; we'll see how they come in and what the scheduling looks like and see if we need to go wider." This is my least favorite part of the job. It is very rare that a client will just trust me to hire the best guys, the ones I know will do the best job; they usually assume there are kickbacks and dirty politics involved, so you always have to get three to five bids from subcontractors for every aspect of the project. It's time-consuming and annoying, and then you have to hope that the people you actually want to work with come in at a decent price AND are available when you need them. And my favorite guys aren't always the guys Murph owes favors to, and since I don't get final approval on my teams, it is all up in the air anyway.

"Okay, sounds like that is in order, keep us posted," Murph says, by way of dismissal.

"You're welcome, I think it turned out great too," I mutter to myself under my breath as I head back to my office. On my way down the hall I see Liam talking to Oliver Jacobsen, one of Chicago's top architects, and someone I respect and admire enormously. His projects are just spectacular, Frank Lloyd Wright meets Louis Sullivan with just a hint of whimsy that is all his own. I'd give my left ovary to work with him. Actually, I'd give them both; lord knows I don't plan on using them. Murph and Mac come out and join them, with lots of back-patting and manly joking. It's clear that there is a new project in the offing, and Liam is essentially pissing all over Oliver to stake out his territory. I can feel my heart sink, because with this one simple tableau, I can see that I will never be able to fully break into this stupid boys' club, and my chances of working with Oliver Jacobsen are about as good as getting struck by lightning. Twice. In my living room. On a sunny day.

As I pass by the employee lounge, I notice that someone has left a box of doughnuts on the table. I wonder who got laid. It's an old tradition, the camaraderie of the job site; if you get lucky, you bring doughnuts in for everyone. And of course Murph started doing it at the office too. Usually they just appear anonymously. But this box? Has a note on the lid.

Enjoy! Liam

Of course he did.

I grab a napkin and a chocolate frosted, and then I pause. What the hell. I add a vanilla crunch on top. I'm heading out with my bounty when I bump into the current third Murph's Angel in the hallway. This one is a tiny little thing, shorter than me, except for the platform boots, and I've heard Liam and Murph refer to her as a spinner behind her back.

"Oh, hey, America!"

Seriously? I just give up. "Hi."

"God, I'm so jealous!" she says, looking down at my plate. "I wish I didn't care about my figure. You're so lucky!" And she hobbles past me into the bathroom, completely unaware that she's said anything offensive.

I go back into the lounge, debate putting both of the pastries

back, think "Fuck it," grab a raspberry glazed for a Neapoli-
tan doughnut bonanza, and head back to my hovel to eat my
feelings.

M ost people would leave a long day of paperwork and
phone calls and emails and go straight home, heading for
a cocktail and something to eat, needing to get home and walk
and feed the dog. And that was certainly my intention as well,
when my phone rings.

"You on your way home?" my fiancé, Grant, asks.

"Just leaving."

"I'm going to be stuck at the restaurant till close, but I stopped
home and walked and fed the beast, so the night is yours. How
was the day?"

"Up and down. Finished the Osborne house and they love it."

"Congrats, baby, that is fantastic! I'll bring home a bottle of
bubbles. What about the down? Hack and Smurf being their
usual charming selves?" I am always tickled at his nicknames
for Mac and Murph.

"Yep. And it looks like Liam probably just snagged my
dream project right out from under my nose."

"I'm sorry. I hate that for you."

"Oh, and apparently my name is now America."

"Nipple Barbie or Pinky Tuscadero Barbie?"

"Spinner Barbie."

"Wow. You have got to start thinking about an exit strategy,
that place is a toilet bowl. I just hate that you even have to talk
to those assholes, let alone work for them."

"I know you do." He hates it worse than I do, and I love him
for that.

"I have some ideas about that; we'll talk about it later. Gotta

go. Love you!" I can hear him shouting something at someone
about basil as his phone hangs up.

A normal person would look at this gift of a quiet evening
alone as decadent relaxation just waiting to happen. You might
think this would be a great time to cozy up to the DVR and
indulge in some serious binge watching, to finally catch up on
Downton Abbey and drool over the houses, but as tempting as
that is, there is something even more tempting.

I press the button on the garage door and watch it open
smoothly, the set of converted antique carriage-house doors,
with their leaded glass windows and beautiful old wood with
iron strapping, now a thoroughly contemporary convenience. I
steer Lola inside to the left, giving wide berth to the old doors
and windows and other salvage items that are stacked carefully
in the middle of the expansive space, big enough for three SUVs
plus storage. The door closes behind me, and I grab my big key
ring out of the glove compartment, letting myself in the back
door and dropping my coat and bag in the roughed-in mudroom.
I breathe in the intoxicating scent of old house and new wood,
make my way carefully through two dark rooms looming with
odd shapes, and finally flip the lights. The place is a complete
disaster. Plaster walls with gaping holes down to the lath, hardwood flooring covered with adhesive from badly applied carpeting, the world's most hideous brass pineapple chandelier
putting out a gloomy yellow light.

It's the most beautiful sight in the world.

I head directly to the bathroom, inching sideways past the
old claw-foot tub that's sitting in the dining room, partially
blocking the entrance of the wide hallway, and find my supplies right where I left them three days ago. Boxes of basket-
weave-pattern white marble tiles with gray accents, sacks of
thinset mix and pale gray grout powder. I grab a nearby bucket,

dump thinset mix into it, and add water with the small hose that I've attached with duct tape to the wall faucet that used to feed the tub. Using a mixing paddle on my power drill, I watch as the mixture throws up a cloud of dust before coming together into a thick paste. I already installed the electric radiant heat floor system last week, and now I can carefully tile over it, thinking of how much someone is going to appreciate getting out of the shower onto a toasty floor on a day like today.

I can feel the stress of the afternoon leave my shoulders. It all disappears here. The Mannings and what that job will be for the next eighteen months. Mac and Murph, doling out minimal praise for the Osborne build, as if any monkey could have brought that job in three weeks early and nearly $15K under budget. Liam, throwing his arm around Oliver Jacobsen's shoulders like they are old friends, blowing smoke up his ass about how he is going to bring the drawings off the page and into a perfect expression of his vision, or some such crap that will ensure that he will get that project, and I'll probably have to do some quickie cheapo job for one of the cheesy flippers that Mac and Murph always seem to have in their back pocket waiting for me. Barbies at every turn mocking me with their perfect bodies and imperfect grasp of the English language.

This is my safe place. Everything else goes fuzzy, and my entire focus is on laying this tile. Getting it perfect. Every piece lined up. For three blissful hours my whole life is this floor, and when I lay the final little trim pieces just inside the doorway, I can feel my heart get bigger. I stand, stretch my back, aching from the meticulous work, and pull off my padded knee guards. I'll come back this weekend to grout once the thinset has cured fully. I take one last look, and then shut down the lights, and head for home.

2

Someone isn't happy with me.

"I know, I know, I'm sorry, I just got caught up at work," I say, on the receiving end of a glare that can only be described as steely. "C'mon, don't be like that." I reach out my hand for a comforting caress.

And get it nipped. Not enough to break skin, but enough to send a message.

"Stupid dog, do you realize you have actually LITERALLY bitten the hand that feeds you?"

Schatzi looks at me with a withering stare, arching her bushy eyebrows haughtily, and then turns her back to me. I stick out my tongue at her back, and go to the kitchen to freshen her water bowl. Damnable creature requires fresh water a zillion times a day. God forbid a fleck of dust is dancing on the surface, or it has gone two degrees beyond cool, I get the laser look of death. Once there was a dead fly in it, and she looked in the bowl, crossed the room, looked me dead in the eye, and squatted and peed on my shoes. I usually call her Shitzi or Nazi. I suppose I'm lucky she deigns to drink tap water. Our bare tolerance of each other is mutual, and affection between us is nil. The haughty little hellbeast was my sole inheritance from my grandmother who passed away two years ago. A cold, exacting woman who raised me in my mother's near-complete absence, Annelyn Stroudt insisted on my calling her Grand-mère, despite the fact that she put the manic in Germanic, ancestry-wise. But apparently when her grandparents schlepped her mother from Berlin to Chicago, they took a year in Paris first, and adopted many things *Française*. So Grand-mère it was.

Grand-mère Annelyn also insisted on dressing for dinner, formal manners in every situation, letterpress stationary, and physical affection saved for the endless string of purebred miniature schnauzers she bought one after the other, and never offered to the granddaughter who also lived under her roof. Her clear disappointment in me must have rubbed off on Schatzi, who, despite having lived with me since Grand-mère died neatly and quietly in her sleep at the respectable age of eighty-nine, has never seen me as anything but a source of food, and a firm hand at the end of the leash. She dotes on Grant, but he sneaks her nibbles when he cooks, and coos to her in flawless French. Sometimes I wonder if the spirit of Grand-mère transferred into the dog upon death, and if the chilly indifference to me is just a manifestation of my grandmother's continued disapproval from beyond the grave.

Schatzi wanders over to her bowl, sniffs it, sneers at me one last time for good measure, shakes her head to ensure her ears are in place, like a society matron checking her coif, and settles down to drink. I jump in a hot shower to get the grit off me. I keep my thick, wavy dark auburn hair just above my shoulders, long enough to pull into a short ponytail or messy bun when I'm working, but short enough to not require too much fussing. I'm twisting it up into a towel turban when I hear joyful yipping.

"Hello, my darling. How are you, sweet girl?" I wander into the living room, where Grant is snuggling the dog, who is submitting to his attentions with clear delight.

Bitch.

Literally.

Grant stops petting the suddenly animated Schatzi to come kiss me, which he does gently on my forehead. "How was your day?" He smiles at me in a way that makes me know he had a good night.

"Long, annoying. You?"

"Same. Probably less annoying than yours. Have you eaten?"

"Not yet, just got home."

"Pasta?"

"Perfect." Grant and I have easy shorthand. I love that we don't have to share every tiny detail of our day first shot out of the gate. We're both busy, we're both under pressure, there are a million pieces of minutia that we've dealt with since last we spoke, and neither of us feels the need to unburden it all. We'll eat, and slowly let the days we've had trickle out, the important bits. My guess is that because we are both only children, both from broken homes with indifferent parenting, we're self-sufficient by nature. He heads to the kitchen, and I follow, perching on a stool across the island from him. He grabs an apron, wraps the ties around his back over his nonexistent tush, and ties it in front on his round little belly. He runs his fingers through his fine sandy hair, and heads for the sink to wash them, almost like a surgeon. Then he pulls the large cutting board from underneath the counter and grabs his eight-inch chef's knife. I love watching him cook. And I'm not the only one.

Grant was both the winner and the fan favorite of season three of *World's Supreme Chef*, handily beating out fifteen other American hopefuls to compete in the international reality-TV competition, and narrowly edging out a win over the French cheftestant. His charming self-deprecating personality made him a darling of the talk show circuit for a few months, and helped garner him an investor partner to help him finally have his own restaurant, which has been packed to the gills since the moment he opened. His place, Nez De Cochon, is right across the street from Stephanie Izard's Girl & the Goat, and they often joke with each other that they both wish the other were less success-ful so that they had a place to send the reservationless walk-in patrons they can never accommodate. He's nearing completion on a second place, a more casual comfort food diner concept, and after being a judge for season six of *WSC*, has been approached by a major network to develop a prime-time cooking show.

The prize package he received, along with the endorsement deals and bestselling cookbook his presence on the show generated, allowed him to purchase this spacious condo in the West Loop, walking distance to his Randolph Street restaurant. It also allowed him to hire MacMurphy to do the design and build of the gut rehab he wanted, which was how we met. We worked closely together on the project, and I was thrilled with how much he relied on me, embraced and accepted my suggestions. He cooked for me. We became friends. Then one night, almost accidentally, lovers. I would have written it off as a one-nighter between friends, but the next morning he made me breakfast and asked if he could take me on a proper date. I figured it would be rude to decline the offer, in light of all the naked the night before, which is also how we ended up in bed the second time. And the third. We quickly became, for lack of a more romantic term, a habit. By the time I finished the apartment, he asked me to move into it, and I couldn't think of a good reason to say no.

Grant is like no one I've ever dated. I always leaned toward big hulking boys with more muscles than brains. Simple boys, not so much emotionally unavailable as emotionally indifferent. I always liked things uncomplicated. I never really needed much more than a strong warm body, the occasional release of straightforward sex. I wasn't really ever very good at romance or being a girlfriend; most of my relationships landed in the nebulous region between friend with benefits and better-than-nothing boyfriend. I liked men who didn't need much from me, ones who let me be in charge. I'd never really been in grown-up love before Grant, and he is the absolute opposite of everyone who preceded him.

Grant is five foot eight to my five foot five, and we weigh the same, 180, allowing for my solid muscular Bavarian build and his soft, chefly poochiness. He's sensitive and tender, a good listener, a thoughtful romantic. No one since Joe had ever made me feel so safe, safe enough to be really open and honest. To share my darkest thoughts, to vent my deepest hurts. And when he proposed last year, he eschewed the traditional ring and instead did it with a stunning pair of diamond stud earrings, two fiery carats each, in a platinum three-prong low-profile setting. The perfect way to spoil a girl who works with her hands and has to wear hardhats regularly.

I fill Grant in on my boring day of bids, the embarrassment of the staff meeting where Murph called me out for signing off on the Rick Bayless restaurant bathrooms without noticing that we installed the women's room door on the men's bathroom. "Apparently our little Anneke can pee in a urinal with no problem, so it didn't occur to her that the other ladies might not have such great aim." This was received with a roomful of laughter, and Liam jumped right in. "Well, she does have bigger balls than you, Murph." It took five minutes before everyone stopped laughing and poking fun, and I sat there smiling and chuckling as if it didn't matter. And then I said that my balls were perfectly delicate and ladylike, but my dick was definitely bigger than Murph's, and the room went totally silent in that way where you can almost hear the needle scratching violently across the record, and he glared at me and curtly told me to get the hell over there and fix it and apologize to Rick for the error. Lucky for me, Rick Bayless is a very kind gent, and pals with Grant, so we laughed about it and he made a delicious torta that he has been experimenting with and we split it and talked about Grant's new place, and he sent me off with a bag of warm churros, so the day was somewhat saved.

Grant shakes his head and mutters about how rude and unnecessary it is to humiliate people, while he slices an onion and chops a bagful of multicolor cherry tomatoes. He drops the veggies in a pan, adds a large sprig of fresh basil from the vase on the counter, smashes a garlic clove, and tosses it in. A hefty glug of olive oil, a sprinkle of red pepper flakes, more salt than you would imagine necessary, a fistful of dried linguine, some water, and the contents of a plastic tub of the gelatinous amber chicken stock that he always brings home from the restaurant. He turns the flame up, gives it a stir, and then reaches into the wine fridge underneath the counter and hands me a bottle of Barolo to open. He begins grating a snowy mound of Parmesan into a bowl, pausing periodically to give the contents of the pan, now at a rolling boil, a quick stir with his tongs. A latch-key kid whose mom worked long hours, he's been cooking for himself since he was eight, and for others since he lied about his age and got an after-school job as a prep cook in a fast-food joint at fourteen. He skipped college in favor of culinary school, and the rest is history.

I pour the inky wine into two glasses, and we clink before taking a deep and satisfying sip. Cheese finished, he stirs the pasta again, and then takes more basil from the vase, picking the leaves carefully and reducing them to a pile of shreds in seconds. Grant has amazing knife skills. It's mesmerizing to watch. He removes the basil sprig and garlic clove from the pan, tossing them in the garbage, stirs again, and pulls one long noodle to taste. Smiling, he pulls the pan from the heat, divides the contents between two shallow white stoneware bowls, and gives each serving a healthy twirl of olive oil, a fistful of cheese, a scattering of basil. He reaches behind him and grabs a half of a crusty baguette off the counter and places it between us.

It's been maybe fifteen minutes. And I have heaven in a bowl. Grant might not be able to pick me up and whisk me to the bedroom, nor do either of us have much energy for that these days anyway. But he wants to know about my thoughts, and he makes me meals full of love, and I always feel so cared for with him. This is as close to home as I've had since Joe died, and it guts me that they never met. I think they would have gotten along famously, and I know that Joe always wanted me to have this, a good man who loves me, a place to live that is safe and stable. Grant and I eat right where we are, ravenously quiet, me sitting on the stool, and him standing behind the stove, pausing only to add more cheese, or drink more wine. As little time as it took to make, it takes less to devour—the perfect thing for a late supper after a long day. I marvel at his ability to do something that on the surface looks so simple, and yet is completely beyond me.

Because for all my massive appetite, I cannot cook to save my life. When Grant came to my old house for the first time, he became almost apoplectic at the contents of my fridge and cupboards. I ate like a deranged college frat boy midfinals. My fridge was full of packages of bologna and Buddig luncheon meats, plastic-wrapped processed cheese slices, and little tubs of pudding. My cabinets held such bounty as cases of chicken-flavored instant ramen noodles, ten kinds of sugary cereals, Kraft Macaroni & Cheese, and cheap canned tuna. My freezer was well stocked with frozen dinners, heavy on the Stouffer's lasagna and bags of chicken tenders. My garbage can was a wasteland of take-out containers and pizza boxes. In my defense, there was also always really good beer and a couple of bottles of decent wine.

My eating habits have done a pretty solid turnaround since we moved in together three years ago. Grant always leaves me something set up for breakfast: a parfait of Greek yogurt and homemade granola with fresh berries, oatmeal that just needs a quick reheat and a drizzle of cinnamon honey butter, baked French toast lingering in a warm oven. He almost always brings me leftovers from the restaurant's family meal for me to take for lunch the next day. I still indulge in greasy takeout when I'm on a job site, as much for the camaraderie with the guys as the food itself; doesn't look good to be noshing on slow-roasted pork shoulder and caramelized root vegetables when everyone else is elbow-deep in a two-pound brick of Ricobene's breaded steak sandwich dripping marinara.

"How are things at the Palmer Square house?" Grant asks, wiping his plate with a chunk of bread.

"Never got there today, the day got sucked up with the endless bids, I had to run all the way out to Park Ridge to put out a fire, and then the bathroom door debacle. But hopefully tomorrow after work I can swing by and do a little something. When I'm there it feels great, and what little I'm able to do is going well. And it's going to be freaking gorgeous."

"Well, there's no doubt of that. How are you feeling about the timing? Another two years?"

I think about what's left to do. It seems endless. When I found the property it was in foreclosure; the previous owner had over-extended himself assuming that the three-flat, which had been converted to apartments, including an illegal one in half of the basement, would generate enough income to be self-supporting. But he overestimated the rents he could charge for spaces that hadn't been updated since the 1970s, and when the housing market crashed, he was so underwater he just abandoned the property completely and declared bankruptcy.

Grant and I thought it would be the perfect first venture for us in the realm of flipping, to restore the place to its original glory and sell it as a spectacular high-end single-family home. Or rather I thought it would be, and Grant was easy to convince. I sold the little house I had gotten from Joe when he died to the people who had been renting it from me, and used half of the profits to buy the Palmer place outright; Grant has been funding the renovations. We got it for a song; it couldn't be torn down due to the historical landmark status of the street and needed so much work no one wanted to touch it. We took it off the bank's hands for literally pennies on the dollar. I've done most of the renovations on my own, bringing in some specialty help for the major projects like upgrading the electricity and plumbing. It's been just over a year, and as of right now, the only room in the house that's completely finished is the kitchen, since that's always the most fun to design and is the only thing Grant really cared about in the project. I may not cook, but I can do a seriously spectacular kitchen design. Grant actually hasn't been to see the place since the final kitchen fixture went in, but he's good about checking the progress verbally.

"I'd like to say two on the outside, but you know how it goes. Verrrry slooooowwwwly."

"But you love it?"

"So much. It's like a gift to get to go there and work." There have been wonderful surprises, original treasures covered up by drywall and paint and carpet and linoleum. For every bad discovery—asbestos in the basement, lead paint throughout, a horror-movie nest of rats in the old coal hopper—there has been a glorious one: marble wainscoting behind drywall in a bathroom, a covered-up fireplace in the living room, gorgeous coffering in the dining room hidden by an industrial drop ceiling.

"What if you did it full-time?" Grant clears our plates and pours us both more wine.

"Leave MacMurphy?"

"Why not? What do you figure we can clear on this flip when you are done?"

"If we stay on budget, and the market stays strong, we should net about 500K, maybe a smidge more if we get lucky."

"That seems like enough to get a second project under way. You hate it where you are. They don't begin to deserve you, and you almost never get the kinds of projects that make it worth putting up with their bullshit. And you love working on that house. Maybe it's time to do it full-time, get it finished, let it take you to the next step? I mean, don't you want to just find wonderful houses like that and restore them and then sell them and stop with all the boring cookie-cutter work for ungrateful clients and shithead bosses?"

My heart flutters. I'd never thought seriously about going out on my own full-time so soon; I just thought it would be fun to do a project here and there. To get a lot of experience under my belt, and then MAYBE in another ten years or so to take the leap. If things were good financially, if the market was conducive. In the meantime, I just figured that working on one personal project at a time, for as long as it took, would be enough to fill that need in me. To have control, to make the decisions, to fully realize a single vision from start to finish. I'm always proud of my work, but when you work for other people, their input takes precedence. The end result is your execution of what they want and need. Hopefully, you're able to convince them to trust you on details here and there, to make them fall in love with your ideas, but at the end of the day the purity is lost. But the thought, the mere mention, of just getting up every day and going over to Palmer Square and working the way I crave? To finish it and then find another project to fall in love with all over again? That makes me all tingly.

"I don't know; that is a huge risk."

"I don't think it is. You're really good at what you do, honey, you know that. You've got all the right instincts, and great taste. You know the market. I just think that life is short, and waiting around for some magical sign that it is time to stop wasting your talent on projects and people so far beneath you is silly. Go big or go home, right? What is the worst thing that could happen?"

"We could lose money on the house and not have any profit to find another project and then I would not have a job to go back to. The whole thing is very risky. Not to mention an expensive proposition for you. You'd have to be the sole bread-maker AND breadwinner."

Grant smiles. He reaches across the counter and traces his fingertip down the length of my nose. "You're worth it. Besides, when the TV thing gets signed this week, the money won't be much of an issue." His idea for the show is a wonderful one. Each episode he would get together with one other chef so that the two of them could cook dinner for a small gathering of chefs, foodies, critics, and other interesting cultural figures who happen to love food. Sort of half cooking show, half salon. The deal would be for a guaranteed full twenty-six-week season, and would pay him handsomely. Even better, he would get to work with his friends Patrick and Alana, whose production company put the deal together, and who would serve as co-executive producers. Grant always said that after the *World's Supreme Chef* experience, he would only do more TV if he was sure about the people he was working with. He's turned down half a dozen offers, everything from *The Next Iron Chef* to recurring judging on various shows. He does a once-a-month lunchtime spot on WGN locally, because they are near to his heart and he loves that Tom Skilling always sneaks in to taste and rave about whatever he's cooking. When Patrick and Alana approached him, he recognized that he could really create a show to be proud of, and that they wanted him to have a tre-mendous amount of creative control, and that was what sealed the deal for him. With the TV show plus the anticipated num-bers for the new restaurant he is about to open, and the second cookbook that comes out this summer, we aren't going to be buy-an-island rich, but the cash flow is going to be really very comfortable. And since neither of us wants kids, it isn't like we

have to sock money away for college educations or to try to create intergenerational wealth. We've both been diligent about
retirement savings, and will obviously continue to be, but the
big bump in disposable income that is imminent does present
some wonderful opportunities.

"Well, let's think about it after, then. You know my motto.
No drinking till the inking!" I carry the chip on my shoulder of
almost every self-made person. On the one hand, you can see
clearly where the financial assistance will help you achieve
what you want faster or more completely. Yet, your very soul
chafes at the idea of accepting, even when offered as generously
and openly and with as much love as Grant offers. Since he is
also self-made, he knows better than to push too hard.

"Okay. But know that I'm more than prepared to support
you in every way. I think you'll be happier, and I like you
happy."

He comes around to my side of the island and gives me a
powerful hug. Grant is a great hugger. I look up at him and he
kisses me softly on the lips. "Dessert?" he asks.

I grin at him. "Absolutely," I say, waiting for the slide of his
hand up my robe or a deeper kiss.

He grins. "Coming up!" And he walks over to the fridge to
fetch something new the pastry chef has been working on.

Oh well. I'm probably too full and tired for bedroom acro-
batics anyway. Grant brings over a plate with what looks like a
chocolate pyramid on it, and hands me a fork, and we have our
cake and eat it.

3

I'm dreaming about getting a facial, Grand-mère standing over me saying that my skin is horrible, that I don't take care of myself, and blowing sulfurous steam at me to open my pores. Then she leans over and scratches at my face with her always impeccably manicured fingers, telling me that I have neglected my exfoliation. I open one eye to find Schatzi pawing at my forehead and breathing foul kibble breath up my nose.

"Seriously, dog? You hateful bitch. I know Grant already walked and fed you." I give her a shove, and she drops lightly off the bed, clicking her claws down the hall in a perfect replica of Grand-mère's kitten-heeled cadence, making me shudder. Two years gone and she still haunts me. Schatzi is only six, so barring some unfortunate accident or unexpected illness, I could have another good eight to ten years of this abuse ahead of me.

I swing my legs out of bed and drop to the floor to stretch. I may be still a few months shy of my thirty-fifth birthday, but my body bears the signs of a life of physical work. My joints take a few minutes to loosen, my neck and back require some coaxing to unclench. My girlfriend Marie tried to get me to do yoga, but I got twisted into some warrior pose and accidentally lost control of a massively loud and horribly smelly fart, the unfortunate result of a La Pasadita carne asada burrito for lunch. Needless to say, I've never had the balls to take another class. I do my own little stretch routine in the morning for a few minutes, and it seems to help limber me up for the day. And if a foul wind escapes me, there is only me and the dog to witness, and frankly, crop-dusting that satanic canine is one of my few deep pleasures. I throw on an ancient pair of jeans, a long-sleeved T-shirt, and a zip-up fleece vest. It's Saturday, my favorite day of the week. I get to spend a whole day at the Palmer house, and then dinner with my best girlfriends, my total me-day.

Saturday is Grant's longest workday. He hits the markets in the morning, plans menus for the coming week, places orders with vendors, and then goes to the restaurant to prep and do a grueling Saturday-night service, usually getting home between one and two in the morning. I try to stay up for him. When he gets home he's usually wired, and we often have a snack and a small glass of bourbon or calvados, which is a very nice way to jump-start our Sundays. If Grant isn't out of town for an event or press thing, rarer and rarer these days, he and I spend Sundays blissfully together, sleeping in, having some sort of brunch adventure, watching shows and movies on Netflix, napping, and having something wonderful for dinner. Since the restaurant is closed Mondays, he often has to get up early on Sunday and fly somewhere for Sunday night and Monday appearances, returning late Monday or early Tuesday to get back to the grind of the restaurant. He's frantically training his executive sous chefs for both restaurants in anticipation of the television work, which will take him away from them even though it will film in Chicago. When we get them, maybe only once a month, Sundays are the days we make up to each other for having jobs that keep us apart and exhausted the rest of the time.

Grant has left me an everything bagel, the crusty seeded roll smeared thickly with herbed cream cheese and covered with a thin shingling of cucumbers and a slice of the white ham La Quercia makes specially for his restaurant. I wrap it in a paper towel, toss Schatzi a treat from the bowl, and head out. The day is Arctic Circle cold, but sunny and bright, a welcome change from the overcast gloom that is typical of January in Chicago. Luckily we have garage parking next door to our building, so I don't have to scrape ice off the car, but it isn't a heated space, so I always give Lola a good eight to ten minutes to really warm up before I make her drive in winter. This gives me a chance to devour the sandwich, naturally dropping a glob of cheese on my huge puffer coat, and sprinkling sesame seeds, sticky bits of onion, caraway, and salt crystals all over myself. In addition to having no cooking skills, my eating skills also lack finesse. Most everything ends up on my not-insignificant boob shelf, or lost off the fork into my lap. Grand-mère sent me to actual etiquette classes when I was seven and again when I was twelve, but while I understood everything intellectually, it never really sank into my bones. As a result, I get giddy if I get to wear anything nice more than once before I spatter it with stains. I've always known that I'm very lucky to have a career that requires grubby dress 99 percent of the time. If I'd wanted to be a lawyer, it would have cost me a fortune in blouses and dry cleaning.

I swing Lola into a parking space in front of Intelligentsia on Milwaukee, and scamper inside to get some fuel.

"Hey, Anneke," Rainn, my favorite barista, says. "The usual?"

"Yes, please." I take a seat at the bar while she efficiently pulls shot after shot of dark espresso. Every Saturday is the same; I get a rich double-shot latte with whole milk to prime my motor, and then two quad-shot iced Americanos with four sugars each to give me bits of pep through the day. And yes, I'm aware that ten shots of espresso in a day seems ridiculous, to say nothing of the eight packets of sugar, but Saturday is my cheat day for caffeine, which I limit to one latte a day during the week, and I believe in full indulgence.

I take my tray of enormous beverages, and head over to the Palmer house. It is so much more fun to work here in daylight, to fully appreciate the high ceilings and oversized windows and architectural details. She is a classic graystone, like a little castle, complete with a turret, the subtly wavy glass in the windows curved to match the curve of the stone. I love doing a full walk-through on Saturday mornings, to visualize the plans, to center my thoughts, to let the building tell me what it needs. I drop my coat and Joe's old leather tool bag on the first floor and put the two iced coffees in the small fridge I've rigged up in the dining room. Then I take my latte and begin my walk-through.

I start at the front foyer, cringing as I always do at the horrid vinyl faux-grass-cloth wallpaper. But the intricate plaster ceiling molding is mostly intact; it will need some repairs, but I should be able to save it. And the original penny tile floor was essentially perfect when I pulled up the industrial carpeting a previous owner had put down; I just needed to strip some old adhesive off and give it a seal. It gleams like new under the protective thick paper I've taped over it to keep it safe and clean. I've been putting off dealing with the wallpaper because I hope that the murals that adorned the walls of the entrance are still there and can be restored.

When I researched the history of the building, I found a lot of newspaper articles on the family who built it, and a couple of them included faded photos of some of the interiors. That was how I knew where to look for the fireplace in the living room.

I love a building that has good history in addition to good bones. The Rabin family emigrated from Russia to Chicago right after the Great Fire, losing the "owitz" from the end of their name, and establishing a profitable family firm of accountants and insurance agents that continues to thrive today. The youngest of their three sons, the only one born here, married the daughter of a wealthy department store family, and they built the house in the up-and-coming Palmer Square neighborhood just before the turn of the century. The mansion was host to grand parties and philanthropic events that pop up in the society pages from 1900 to 1940, when the widow Rabin sold the house to a cousin who used it as a boardinghouse through the late 1950s. The cousin's son took over the building and decided its value was more as a rental property, doing a shoddy conversion to the three upper floors to create apartments, and creating a garden apartment in the half of the basement that used to house the maid's quarters. He sold it in the early 1960s, and nothing is known about it until 1978 when it changed hands again. The new owner did a halfhearted upgrade to some of the systems, and covered everything that could be covered in durable carpet and linoleum. The building passed to his daughter when he died, and she sold it to the guy who lost it to the bank.

It kills me that these rooms that knew generations of family parties, wedding receptions, and holiday celebrations got chopped up into unnatural bedrooms and closets, their details hidden and made generic in the name of commerce. Lucky for me, I had access to the original plans for the house, which had been filed with the city, and was able to gut the walls that had been added over the years, without disrupting the load-bearing originals. I'll give those turn-of-the-century builders their props. This place is like a fortress. Whatever went on with fixtures and finishes, the structure is as solid as the day she was born.

After the Great Fire, the wealthy didn't take any chances with their mansions, so the structure here is steel, not wood, and will support this old girl for another one hundred years at least. The walls are sound; the roof is solid, if in need of new insulation and a fresh coat of tar. Inside, the place may be something of a disaster, but at least the layout is getting back to what it was, if not yet what it will be. I still have massive demo to do in the basement; since that is a gut job, I've been saving it for a time I can take a few weeks' vacation to really handle it right.

In my mind's eye, I can see the place coming together. The

spacious formal double-parlor living room with its restored fireplace surrounded by a carved limestone mantel I rescued from
Liam's Fremont job. The long dining room, anchored by built-in
buffets with glass-door china hutches. The butler's pantry with
its double pocket doors and floor-to-ceiling cabinetry. The new
state-of-the-art kitchen, practically restaurant quality, which
sits upstairs with its shiny appliances all still covered in their
protective blue plastic, waiting for a passionate home cook to
fire it into life.

The bonus rooms I've planned for the basement, waiting to
tell me what they should be. A man-cave? Exercise room? Home
office? Guest suite? Mother-in-law apartment? I'm not pushing
myself to decide quite yet. I may leave them as what Joe always
called a "vanilla box," just framed-out walls and roughed-in
plumbing and electrical, and put it on the market for the buyer
to determine what they need and let me custom finish it to their
specifications.

Despite the gaping holes in walls where the electrician ripped
out the old knob-and-tube wiring that was sitting scarily live
underneath the lath, and the ghastly 1970s bathrooms sprinkled
about, there are things about this house you cannot help but
appreciate. Twelve-foot ceilings with custom crown moldings a
full fourteen inches wide, albeit covered in god-knows-how-many
layers of paint. The windows, which shockingly are in terrific
shape, need a little love and all need the casements stripped and
resealed, but they aren't drafty, and the storm windows appear to
be one of the only places the previous owners didn't cheap out on.
The spacious attic with its built-in closets and cupboards and
shelves, all of them lined in cedar for storing seasonal clothes and
party linens.

I always finish my tour on the second floor, where a pair of
tall, slim French doors open onto a small Juliet balcony. I've
planned this room as an office, imagining it with a beautiful

antique desk, maybe a chaise longue, picturing a creative type, a graphic artist or an illustrator or a writer, someone who would be inspired by the light, by the ability to open these doors and let in fresh air. Unless it's raining or snowing, this is where I finish my coffee, looking out onto Palmer Square Park and clearing my head for the day.

My phone rings just as I'm finishing the grout on the bathroom floor, bemoaning the fact that it has taken me three weeks to get back here to finish. I figured out a long time ago to keep a pencil nearby when I'm doing grubby work like this, so that I don't have to take off my gloves. Caller ID says it's Hedy. I use the eraser end of the pencil to put her on speaker.

"We're going to Caroline's tonight," she says without saying hello.

"We always go to Caroline's." Which we do, despite the fact that she lives in Evanston and the rest of us live in the city.

"I know, but she's making dinner."

"That's how she gets us." Caroline is a very good cook, and I live with a professional chef, so I know whereof I speak.

"And Carl pulled something from the cellar that is older than us."

"Damn them." Carl, Caroline's better half, is a pretty serious wine guy, and when he pulls something from the cellar, you better sit up and take notice.

"I know. They're insidious. I'll fetch you at five thirty."

When Hedy says she will fetch me, what she means is that her driver will come fetch me. Hedy shouldn't drive. As one of the top interior designers in the city, she spends more than half her life in the car, and all of her life on the phone. After six expensive fender benders and four talking-on-her-phone tickets (that she couldn't flirt her way out of, of the ten times she was

actually pulled over), she finally gave up and hired Walter, an
elegant man of indeterminate age, who squires her around in a
massive Lincoln Navigator. And it certainly helps on nights
like this, when you have a friend with really good wine way out
in the burbs. Saves us a fortune in taxis, and no one has to miss
out on the vino to be the designated driver.

I finish the grout, making one final pass over the tiles with a
huge damp sponge. Barely a cup of leftover grout in the bottom
of the bucket, much to my satisfaction. Some people are math
savants, or piano savants; I'm a bucket savant. I can eyeball the
perfect amount of adhesive, grout, Spackle, cement, paint, drywall mud, mortar, anything that either comes in a bucket or gets
mixed in a bucket; I'm usually right on the money. Grant can
measure a precise amount of salt or herbs in his palm, from an
eighth of a teaspoon to a full quarter cup, and yes, I have tested
him. I'm that way with building materials.

My stomach growls, and I wash my hands and grab my
phone. The local Al's Beef delivers, and I'm feeling like I've
earned it. By the time my "Big Al, sweet peppers, dipped" with
a large fries, extra ketchup, extra napkins arrives, I've cleaned
up the grouting supplies. Thank god for the exertion of work,
otherwise, with my appetite, I'd be twice my size. I'm built like
a German peasant, all muscular legs and broad shoulders, wide
hips and big boobs. And while 180 is certainly not an insignifi-
cant weight for a girl who just barely hits five foot five, I'm
solid, not squishy. My doctor tells me that she'd love me closer to
150 to 155 for my build, but I'm healthy as a horse, and my body
does most of what I ask of it without too much trouble. I know
that when I can't do the labor anymore I will have to rethink
my appetite, but for now, youngish and active, I pretty much
eat what I want, and burn it off on the job.

Grant loves that I eat. He says it was the first thing he
noticed about me. I try to take this as a compliment, ignoring

that I might have preferred that he notice my sparkling hazel eyes, or my porcelain skin bespattered with fetching freckles, or my beautiful smile. But I'll take it. I'm frankly glad he noticed me at all. My looks, perhaps one tiny notch above plain, and comfortably in the arena polite people call handsome or attractive or interesting but never beautiful, skipped two generations. I look exactly like my great-grandmother Anneliene.

Both my mom, Anneliese, and Grand-mère Annelyn were stunning beauties, with willow-lithe frames; blond, blue-eyed sirens with quiet voices, light tread, and delicate features. I was a squat little tank of a girl from the day I was born, with a voice like Cathy Moriarty after a bender, thick, wavy dark red hair with cowlicks that tended toward frizz, and a step like a baby elephant. I was enormously disappointing to both of them. My unnamed and unknown-to-me father was, according to Grand-mère, gone from my mother's life and the city before they even knew I was on the way. There was always an implication that he had been in town for business temporarily, eventually finished the job, and likely gone back to a wife and kids, but that sense was never officially confirmed by either Grand-mère or my mother, and frankly, I couldn't care less. My relationship with my mother is proof that blood doesn't make someone family. Her difficult pregnancy and the first year of my life, which kept her tied to the house and off the dating market from the prime ages of twenty to twenty-two, were an offense I was never able to redeem. As soon as I was walking and taking solid food, she put all of her focus into finding a man to take her away from the tragic turn her life had taken.

For my entire childhood, Anneliese jumped from husband to boyfriend to husband, sometimes hers, sometimes other people's, in parts distant from Chicago. Usually warmer climes and occasionally glamorously abroad, and when the husbands or lovers would leave her, or she them, when they would break her spell and go back to their lives or their wives, she would return home for a short time to Grand-mère's care and my company. Long enough to sigh over the state of my hair and clothes, my choice of playmates or lack thereof, my powerful appetite, and the baby fat that never fully melted. Anywhere from six weeks to six months, never more, and she was off on her next romantic adventure, postcards and odd occasional gifts to follow.

I never thought Grand-mère was one for sentimentality, but when she died I found a box in her basement, all of the trinkets my mother had sent me over the years. The Russian nesting dolls and Turkish slippers, the embroidered dress from Greece and the pale pink beret from Paris. The tiny little cowboy boots from Brazil, and half a dozen dolls, each in some sort of traditional garb. The box is in my storage unit; I don't really want the stuff, but somehow can't bring myself to throw it away.

On one of her jaunts at home, when I was thirteen, she met Joe, who had been dispatched when Grand-mère's usual handyman wasn't available to fix the garage door. He was tall, blandly Midwestern handsome, unassuming. He was no match for my mother, who took to him, wooed him, won him, and within a month they were married. A part of me thinks that it was her way of trying to actually give me something that resembled a family life, her sacrifice for me. Or maybe she remembered Grand-mère's unquenchable need for perfection from her when she was a teenager and wanted to protect me the smallest bit. I want to believe she did one thing for me besides the accident of my birth.

The three years they were together were almost normal. We lived in Joe's tidy little house, my mother and I circled each other cautiously, like strangers do, but at least she wasn't mean and dismissive like Grand-mère, just oddly distant. And she required a tremendous amount of rest. I think being beautiful must be exhausting. I spent most of my time hanging out with

Joe in his garage workshop, watching him build furniture while she took long baths and longer naps, and indulged in a daily routine of personal care and improvement that took no fewer than four hours. She slept every day till nearly noon, in the bedroom she kept as cold as a tomb with heavy blackout curtains and a sleep mask for good measure. She would start her day with a long bath, and break her fast with hot water and lemon, a single piece of dry toast, maybe some yogurt. The afternoon was usually devoted to personal upkeep, which was the closest thing she ever had to a job. She gave herself manicures twice a week and pedicures once a week. Weekly facials and deep hair-conditioning treatments. An hour of stretching exercises and calisthenics every day without fail. I always thought it was strange that by the time she finished applying lotions and potions and perfect makeup, it was nearly time for her to meticulously begin reversing the process.

Joe was a contractor by trade, but a master cabinetmaker and furniture designer by nature, and his pieces were stunning, most of them in the Arts and Crafts or Prairie mode, simple functional designs in beautiful woods. He would let me meet him at job sites; I would work on homework in the trailer, and then follow him around and learn about his work. When it became clear that my mother couldn't cook to save her life, or ours, and the constant restaurant meals were going to bankrupt him, he bought a copy of *Joy of Cooking* at a yard sale and, after a long day at work, would put together simple meals for us, or pick up takeout. This was mostly for the two of us; Anneliese, like Grand-mère, was entirely indifferent to food, and would pick at Joe's meals, or skip them entirely in favor of a small salad dressed with lemon or cider vinegar and no oil or salt.

My mom disappeared one Sunday night shortly after my sixteenth birthday. We came home from a long day at his latest project, covered nearly head to toe with dust from my first experience with plaster and lath walls. We had a huge bag of Chinese food to celebrate my new skill, but when we opened the door, the house was dark and quiet and there was a short note on the kitchen counter for Joe that I wasn't allowed to read.

Joe and I simply didn't discuss it at all for three months. We just worked in the garage, and ate a lot of pizza. He brought home pieces of furniture he found in alleys or from job sites and taught me to strip off old paint and do beautiful lustrous stained finishes and limed waxes and the meticulous process known as French polishing. He taught me how to repair wobbly chair legs, to fix wonky drawers. We built a few pieces from scratch, including the Arts and Crafts–style library table I use as a desk to this day. It was strangely some of the best times of my childhood, just Joe and me, school something to get through so I could work with him, learn something new. No tiptoeing around the house or seeing the resignation in my mother's face that I would never become what she wanted or needed. Had it not been for the sadness that lurked beneath the surface of Joe's brave face, it would have been the happiest time of my life. I tried to keep his spirits up, to make silly jokes or ask lots of questions when we were working so that he could focus his energy on explaining things, on being a teacher instead of a left and bereft man.

But when the divorce papers arrived unceremoniously in the mail with a Nevada zip code, we had a heart-to-heart. Did I want to stay? I did. Did he want me to stay? He did. Was I allowed to stay? Nope. Mom's custody request was clear; she reasserted her custodial rights, and I was to stay with Grand-mère till her return. Joe and I knew that there was no way to fight it, no money for lawyers, and even if there were, no law to back us up. Joe held my shoulders tightly and looked deep into my eyes, holding back his tears, and told me that once I was eighteen I could do as I chose, and he would always be there for me.

So Grand-mère took me back. I was resigned. I followed her rules, and tried to keep my hair neat and my clothes unspoiled and my manners as ladylike as I could stand. I worked like a dog to finish high school a year early, and spent as much time with Joe as I could on the weekends. Grand-mère reluctantly offered to send me to college, but only if I lived at home with her, since she thought of college as a hotbed of drinking, drugs, and sex, none of which were appropriate for a young lady of breeding. But she acknowledged that with my looks and manners, marriage prospects were going to be minimal, so some sort of vocation was in order. In her opinion, that should have been some sort of secretarial work or anything in an office where I might meet a man to support me. Joe also offered to send me to college, but could only afford it if I didn't mind living with him, and promised to fix up his basement for me with a separate entrance so that I would have some privacy and independence for the drinking and drugs and sex he didn't want to know about, but figured were unavoidable in college.

You can imagine which option I took. The day I turned eighteen I packed my few belongings and moved back to Joe's little house, where he had created a refuge for me in half of his basement. A small bedroom, a bathroom, and a sitting room with a corner desk. He even took an old Hoosier cabinet and retrofitted it with a small dorm-sized fridge, a microwave, a single-burner hot plate, and a coffeemaker. It was like a mini kitchen, and one of the coolest things I'd ever seen. It's still in my storage unit, waiting for a useful life someday in a future guest suite.

Joe and I lived easily together; separate enough for privacy, but still sharing meals and garage projects with regularity. I finished college in three years, having never really gotten into drugs or drinking, and limiting sex to a series of perfectly normal boring boyfriends and boyfriend facsimiles, acutely aware of how expensive my schooling was for Joe despite my work-study jobs, and not wanting to extend it just for the sake of parties and play. I got a scholarship for grad school and did a master's in architecture in another three years, apprenticing with Joe on vacations and weekends. When I graduated we worked together side by side until he retired, and then I got the job with MacMurphy. Joe died of a heart attack a year later, when I was twenty-five, leaving me his sole heir. I lived in his house until I moved in with Grant, but when I look around this building, I know he approves of why I sold it and what it will become. He would have loved this place, and I hate that he isn't here to see it, to work on it with me. And I suddenly know something else. He'd never approve of how long I've stayed at MacMurphy, of how I let them treat me. He'd have pushed me to go out on my own, just the way Grant is doing. I wish they had met. They have so many of the same tender qualities. The only two men in my life I've ever believed in, who believe in me. Of course, Joe would also have lectured me about how I'd have to tamp down some of my less flattering personality issues before taking that leap. *"There's a difference between honest and asshole, Anneke,"* he said to me once after I'd casually informed one of our clients that their idea for creating a master suite in their dank basement with the low ceilings was simply stupid. *"Everything is in the delivery. It isn't that you're wrong, it's that you give your opinions as if they are gospel, and in a tone that implies that someone else's opinions are wrong, instead of just different from yours."* There is a part of me that knows that one of the major reasons I am hesitant to strike out independently is that knowledge, that I would have to be the face and voice of my own business, that when everything is on my shoulders, I would have to watch everything about how I behave. A large part of me wonders if I would even be capable, if I could carry it all and keep my cool. Joe taught me a lot, but gracefulness wasn't in his wheelhouse, and I was pretty well broken in that arena by the time he even met me.

My mother never came back, not for any length of time. A week here, two weeks there, with longer and longer separations between. She missed my high school and college graduations, neither of which I bothered to attend myself, in her defense. When she came back for Grand-mère's funeral, I hadn't seen her at all in over five years, and hadn't spoken to her for over two. She flew in from Scottsdale, where she lives with her current husband, Alan, a septuagenarian of apparently significant wealth and even more patience; he and my mother have now been married for nearly seven years, a record for her. She stayed just long enough to put the house on the market furnished, transfer the money and bonds into her own accounts, and empty the house of the few bits and pieces of jewelry and the cabinets of any family heirloom trinkets, the Bavarian china my great-grandmother smuggled into the country wrapped in bed linens in a false-bottomed trunk, the good silver. Before it even sank in that my grandmother hadn't specifically left me a single thing, my mother loaded her goodies into Grand-mère's impeccably maintained three-year-old Cadillac sedan, and headed back for Arizona. We had spent approximately seven hours together, five of them at the funeral home. I got Schatzi by default; apparently Alan is allergic. Lucky me. I regret daily that I didn't just drop the dog off at a shelter.

I look around, taking in the glorious bones of this decrepit pile. Grant is right about one thing, we'll clear some serious cash when we're done. But in part because I've called in every favor I've banked with my favorite subs. Nearly every specialist I've brought in has done the work at cost, or even sometimes for beer and pizza. I may be prickly, but I am respected, and a lot of the guys I've worked with over the years in the trades appreciate my style, as long as they aren't on the receiving end. This place is full of overage materials collected from their other jobs, salvage from their clients who didn't want to bother to try to sell the perfectly good stuff that was simply not their style. Conservatively, I've probably saved nearly fifty grand already on the backs of their generosity, and while I know some of that is because they genuinely like me, a lot of it is because they like the work they get from MacMurphy, and they know it keeps them on the top of my preferred list when they show up on their days or nights off to help me put this place back together. If I hang my own shingle? I'll be a very small fish, and on all of their back burners, and for sure I'll be paying full freight on everything. This house will be one big score, but the rest of them will likely have a much narrower profit margin, and I think I need to explain that to Grant before he gets much more flippant about my career path. If he thinks I'm going to be making this kind of money all the time, he's sadly mistaken.

Joe once told me that the reason I was going to be a great homebuilder was that I never really had a home. I assured the big old bear that I absolutely had, he'd given me the best home a girl could ask for, and that was the reason I was going to be great. Because I learned from the best, and got to live with him to boot. It's the only time I ever saw him actually cry. He swore it was the fumes from the stain we were using, but he had that smile he had when he was really pleased about something. And I know that he was right; I am a great homebuilder. But would I be a great independent businesswoman? It was one thing when we worked together; he was yin to my yang, salt to my pepper. Without him by my side, to temper my temper, as it were, I'm awfully doubtful.

I push aside the floor plans to make some space on the six-foot folding table I use for a desk-slash-dining surface, and fetch one of my coffees from the fridge. I put down the plastic bag the food came in for a placemat, and gingerly peel the sodden paper from my sandwich. Most tourists, having done some research on Chicago delicacies, order their Italian beef sandwiches "wet," meaning that a slosh of extra meat gravy is dumped over the beef once it is in the bread. They think it means they are in the know, much as they do when they order a Chicago hot dog and tell the seller to "drag it through the garden." Chicagoans, almost to a person, order their dogs simply with "everything" if they want the classic seven toppings, and their Italian beef "dipped," meaning that the whole sandwich, once assembled, is grasped gently between tongs and completely submerged briefly in the vat of jus. This results in a sandwich that isn't just moist, it's decadently squooshy, in a way that sends rivulets of salty meaty juice down your arm when you eat.

This is the sandwich that necessitated the invention of the Chicago Sandwich Stance, a method of eating with your elbows resting on your dining surface, leaning over to hopefully save shirtfronts and ties from a horrible meaty baptism. Dipped Italian beef sandwiches in Chicago require a full commitment. Once you start, you are all in till the last bit of smushy bread and shred of spicy beef is gone. It requires that beverages have straws and proximity. Because if you try to stop midway, to pop in a French fry, or pick up a cup, the whole thing will disintegrate before your very eyes. You can lean over to sip something as long as you don't let go of your grasp on the sandwich. Fries are saved for dessert.

Most people wouldn't suspect how good iced coffee would be with Italian beef and French fries, but it is genius. My personal genius. Bringing sweet and bitter and cold to the hot, salty umami bomb of the sandwich and the crispy fries—insanely good. You may borrow it if you like. I also like hot coffee with potato chips in the morning. Do not judge me.

I check my watch. I have a good four hours to work before I have to head home to shower for the girls. I pull my ragged legal pad of notes over and look for a small project, something I can complete. I won't be back here for at least a week, maybe longer. The Manning job will start full throttle on Monday, and that will mean long days of meeting with subs, and long nights generating budgets and lists of tasks, and there will be nothing left of me to bring here. I spot, way down on the second page, a small note. *Pantry shelves-lip-chalk.* I had seen a gorgeous pantry online where each shelf had a decorative strip of wood creating an inch-high lip, just high enough to prevent canned goods and other items from accidentally sliding off the shelf when caught with an elbow or moved aside to reach for something in the back. Having had many pantry accidents myself over the years, including dumping over an opened five-pound sack of flour, shattering a bottle of molasses, and upending a large jar of rice, I know the magic of this simple idea. And I've gone it one better. My idea is to paint the strips with chalkboard paint. Everyone and their brother is going full-on Martha in their pantries these days, with matching jars and containers, custom labels and expensive organization systems. This will feed right into that Pinterest-driven passion, allowing the homeowners to organize however they like and label the shelves themselves if they choose. And if they aren't part of the cult of pantry, the matte charcoal will still be a lovely design element.

It takes me less than a half an hour to paint the wood strips. I take an hour to go over my lists, cleaning up some items I've either finished or rethought, and making a new list of the things it makes the most sense to tackle next, and what sort of supplies and materials I will need on hand. By the time I'm done, the strips are dry, and I measure all the shelves in the pantry and use a small Japanese pull saw in my miter box to create the necessary cuts. I'm allergic to butt joints; that sloppy look of two pieces of wood just slapped up next to each other makes my skin crawl. I like a clean cut, a mitered corner, a dovetailed joint. I glue and clamp the pieces to the edges of the shelves one at a time, tacking them in with finishing nails. I'll come back after the glue is set to put a tiny bit of filler in the little nail holes and touch up the paint. But for all intents and purposes, the project is done, with ten minutes to spare. I know it is something of a cop-out; the kitchen is so close to fully complete, this little pantry gilding is really the kind of thing I would usually do at the very end. But for some reason I just couldn't face the idea of starting one of the bigger projects that hang over my head, knowing how little time I will have for this house.

Grant's words from the other night ring in my ears. *"What if you did it full-time?"* I can't even begin to imagine how glorious that would be. But I push it out of my head, take a last look at the work I was able to do today, and know that it will get finished. Eventually.

4

⌣

What's new in the land of nipples?" Caroline asks, putting a forkful of flaky sea bass in her mouth. She's outdone herself tonight; the fish is seared crispy, with a soy-miso-butter sauce, duck-fat-roasted baby potatoes, and green beans with lemon-chive oil. Everything is absolutely delicious. Not to mention the twenty-year-old Riesling Carl left for us, a razor's edge of sweet and acid and the perfect foil for the salt and richness of the food. He's out for the evening at what he calls his "poker night," a BYOB dinner with his best wine-collector pals. They pick a price range out of a hat at each dinner to guide the next. Apparently this is the most challenging annual 7/11 night. As in, wines cannot cost less than seven or more than eleven dollars a bottle. It's Carl's favorite. He can find the most delicious things in that range; you could drink them at the finest restaurants and never know. Plonk is not an option for Carl.

"Must you?" Hedy says, picking up a green bean in her elegant fingers and dropping it neatly in her mouth. Hedy never gets anything on her shirt. It's maddening. I've already had not one, but two potato chunks land in my lap, and my turtleneck sweater is speckled with miso sauce and chive oil. "Do you have to use the clinical term? Can't you just ask her how work is going?"

Marie laughs her throaty chuckle. "It's just a word, Hedy." She turns to Caroline. "All is pretty good in the land of nipples, thank you."

Marie is a tattoo artist who exclusively works with breast

cancer patients. She specializes in faux three-dimensional nipples for reconstruction patients who have lost theirs, giving them small works of art that when seen from the front are indistinguishable from the real thing. The 3-D effect she can get with shading and color is beyond remarkable. I've seen photos of women who have had surgery on just one breast, and you cannot distinguish between the real nipple on one and the tattoo on the other. She also does some work on patients who chose not to have reconstruction, and just want something pretty either masking or highlighting their scars, giving them flowering vines or flocks of tiny birds, rushing water teeming with fish, or a fire-flocked phoenix. But mostly, she does nipples. And she does them better than anyone else. People fly her all over the country to get nipples. She once did a pair for a super-famous movie star, and no one ever says the name Angelina out loud, but we have our suspicions. She can neither confirm nor deny; all those medical privacy laws are in place, damn them. "I did one this week with a faux nipple ring in it."

"I. Am. Eating," Hedy says, waving a potato at the end of her fork at Marie.

"Relax. She isn't tattooing people's labia or sphincters for chrissakes. THAT wouldn't be dinner conversation." Caroline is our resident homemaker and mother hen, and seven years older than the rest of us. She was an incredibly successful Gold Coast Realtor when she met Carl six years ago, twelve years her senior and a venture capitalist. They fell in love, got married, and then two of the tech start-ups he had funded merged and did a very successful IPO and he declared them both retired. They moved out of their condo downtown to a gorgeous Victorian house in Evanston on a corner triple lot with a wraparound porch and an amazing backyard. They travel, do good works, and—what I think is the most impressive—they volunteer time and not just money. They are as likely to be on a Habitat for Humanity work site in gloves and dust masks as they are sitting at the board meeting or dancing at the gala. Caroline discovered that the life suits her; she has time for her gorgeous garden, and a passion for cooking, and she's learning Portuguese. She doesn't miss the cutthroat world of multimillion-dollar real estate in the least. She makes us soup when we're sick, and brings us vases of cut flowers from her garden, sources the perfect presents, plans fun evenings.

"JE-SUS, Caroline, why do you make all this amazing food and then try to ruin my appetite with all your nipple talk?" I love the banter between them. They couldn't be more different, but they've been friends forever. Their dads were colleagues and Caroline babysat Hedy when she was little. According to Caroline, Hedy idolized her. According to Hedy, Caroline was a geeky bookish teenager who couldn't find a better friend than a feisty seven-year-old. But for only-child Hedy, it is clear that Caroline was always the older sister she needed, and for Caroline, the only girl with three older brothers, a little sister wasn't exactly an unwelcome thing either.

I met them at the same time, at a client meeting eight years ago. Caroline was the Realtor, Hedy was the interior designer, I was still relatively new at MacMurphy, and it was the first project I was managing on my own. We worked late, ended up going out for dinner; two bottles of wine later we were best buds. Marie is my oldest and dearest friend, and until I met Grant, the only person who knew my secret heart. We met when we were fourteen, the one summer I went to overnight camp. Joe had gotten a summer job in the North Woods, renovating an old barn to serve as a new mess hall and kitchen, and agreed to also serve as the camp handyman, in no small part so that I could attend for free, and I think in an attempt to get a bit closer with my mom for a cozy summer in the woods. Marie and I were in the same cabin, she was also one of the freebie kids, her fees paid for by some sort of fresh-air-fund program for city kids, and we were both sort of misfits, which bonded us permanently. We didn't live far from each other at home, and although we went to different high schools, we always stayed in close contact, especially since we both remained in Chicago and lived at home for college. I brought Marie to the third girls' dinner I had with Hedy and Caroline, and a perfect square was magically formed. It was like *The Craft*. But without magical hair-color changing. Or the nightmare of high school witchery.

"Nipples are totally allowable. Even men have them." Caroline waves off Hedy's admonition.

"Ooo! I did a man last week, my first one!" Marie is very excited about this. "He cried like a baby. And not because of the emotional psyche part like my women patients sometimes do, he cried because it hurt. The women never mention the pain. Isn't that weird?"

God bless her. Marie went to art school to be a painter, got fascinated with skin as a medium, and started doing all that trompe l'oeil body painting that was so popular in the 1990s after Demi's famous *Vanity Fair* cover. She put herself through school mostly doing that for industrial parties and advertising campaigns, and then got hired to paint fake tattoos on actors for a biker movie that was shooting locally. She met her longtime live-in boyfriend John on the set; he was the consulting tattoo artist. Then seven years ago her stepmom, Leanne, got breast cancer and they couldn't save her nipples. The doctor offered to tattoo new ones for her, and Leanne asked John if he could do it instead. He said he could, but that he thought Marie should do it, since her eye for realism and color and dimensions was so amazing.

Marie spent six months practice-tattooing slabs of smelly pigskin with John training her, and then gave Leanne the nipples she had always wanted. "Jamie Lee Curtis, *Trading Places*. The nipple women want, and men fantasize about." Marie did such a great job that Leanne showed them off to everyone at the hospital and all the women in her support group, and Marie got a call from the surgeon asking if he could refer his patients to her regularly. And a career was launched. Marie specializes in the circa 1983 JLC nipple now. It's her signature. Jamie Lee has no idea how many women are running around with perfect replicas of her perfect nipples.

"ENOUGH." Hedy rolls her eyes dramatically. "Good lord, Anneke, please save us from nipple talk. How are things going with you?"

"Well, let's see. My nipples are a little sore from this new bra I bought last week . . ."

"AAAAAAAAAHHHHHH!" Hedy yells, fingers in her ears. And the four of us collapse in giggles.

So, what is the plan for the big five-year anniversary?" Hedy asks Caroline when we retire from the dining table for tea in the sunroom.

Caroline blushes prettily. "France." She is always a little quiet about the fact that she and Carl are insanely wealthy. Especially since it is mostly his money. She made a very nice living when she was working, the sale of her condo paid for the substantial down payment on their first condo together. But since the IPO they are effectively rolling in dough and she is officially a lady who lunches, albeit with more social conscience than many and less shopping than most. She knows that while none of us are living on the edge of poverty, we are all working-women, and there is still a part of her that hates feeling kept.

"He's buying you France? In this economy? Is that wise?" Hedy says with her serious voice. She does deadpan better than anyone.

"I thought five years was wood?" Marie teases.

"Shut up, you wenches, I want to hear about France." The

one thing Grant and I dream about is someday traveling in Europe together. I've never been out of North America, and only got my passport when Grant took me to Toronto for a food and wine festival a year ago.

"A couple that Carl knows well have a vacation home in Provence, and have offered to let us borrow it." She's hedging, and Hedy smells blood.

"For how long, dearheart?"

Caroline's blush moves from pink to fuchsia. "Five weeks. Next summer."

"HA!" Hedy says.

"Oh, honey, how wonderful! A week for every year. What a terrific trip." Marie claps her hands in genuine delight.

I shake my head. "Caro, you have to stop being apologetic about your wonderful life and fabulous hubby. We are all just really happy for you."

"I know, you are all so amazing, I'm just . . ." She trails off and we know what she is thinking of. She lost some friends when the money went from "comfortable" to "crazypants rich." Some people behaved badly. Some people had expectations of charitable endowments and names on buildings. Mostly it was little things like their more casual friends never seeming to reach for a wallet at dinner anymore. And it put a serious strain on her relationship with one of her brothers, who seemed to think that it was suddenly her responsibility to bankroll his business and put his kids through college, neither of which she was inclined to do, and the rest of her brothers deciding that the care and feeding of their aging parents should all be on her dime, making all future family gatherings strained and awkward. Money creates opportunities for jealousy that can't really be touched by anything else, and we know how much it weighs on her that the simple fact of good fortune is also a source of stress and complications in relationships.

"Fuck the haters if they can't just be happy for your happy, Caroline. Fuck 'em all." Hedy, for all her gibing, is always the first and fiercest defender of Caroline.

Caroline smiles at us, and shakes off her momentary hesitation. "Indeed. Fuck 'em." She raises her teacup and we all drink to her happy.

"Howsh the house?" Hedy slurs, Walter gliding us down Lake Shore Drive back to the city.

"Good. Slow, but good."

"It's going to be beautiful when you're done," Marie says sleepily. We put away a flock of wine.

"Whenever THAT ish," Hedy sneers.

"Grant thinks I should do it full-time."

"Leave MuphMaccy?" Marie asks.

"That's what it would mean. I dunno. There's a lot of moving pieces."

"DO IT!" Hedy says. "Get out of that testosterone cesshpool."

"I think you should at least think about it," Marie says. "You've never loved it there. And they totally don't appreesshiate you."

"And stupidhead Liam is the hair appallrent. Do you want to end up working for that tool?" Hedy hates Liam. In no small part because he once slept with her hairdresser Jessie, and never called after. And the next time he saw Jessie he didn't recognize her. Like, complete blank. Not that she had wanted to actually date him, she was rebounding at the time, but it was still a blow to her ego, and since Hedy had introduced them, that was the end of that. Jessie was a prickly sort. Hedy's hair wasn't the same for months. You don't mess with Hedy's hair.

"No, I don't."

"Damn right you don't. You know that guy is bad news from

the get-go. And he'll only get worse if he ends up your boss. He might even fire you." Marie struggles with Liam's existence. On the one hand, she knows he is a horrible person. On the other hand, he is totally her type, and as much as she finds his personality loathsome, her girl parts don't care, and she's admitted to a sex dream or two starring him.

"I'd quit before I ever would work for him."

"Wouldn't you rather just say a great big Effff Yooou to all of them first, before they passsh you over for promotion and you have to quit like a whiny baby who didn't get her way?" I hate that even drunk Hedy makes a world of sense. Which doesn't mean I'm ready to fully admit it.

"Going out on my own is a huge risk, especially in this uncertain economy. I feel like I should finish this house first, sell it, get some press maybe, make at least a small name for myself before I make the leap."

"That's smart. It makes a lot of sense to really plan it all out, have your ducks in a row." Marie gets my deep need for organization and planning.

"I shtill think you should just go for it. Eshpecially if Grant says to do it."

"I'm mulling."

"Let her mull, Hedy."

"Fine. Mull. Whaddoo I know?" Hedy likes for people to just do what she says. As she says often, she isn't bossy; it's just that her ideas are better than everyone else's.

"Thank you for your permission," I needle her.

"You're welcome," she says in all seriousness, and Marie and I shake our heads and lean back into the deep cushy seats of the car just as the city skyline appears around the bend.

5

A nneke. You'd better get over here." Clark's voice sounds serious. He's finishing up the Park Ridge sunroom, which
should have been done two weeks ago, but we've had a series of
backslides. One of the footings didn't cure properly, so we had to
pull it out and redo it, setting us back a week. Then the custom
windows came in as double-hung instead of casement, and had
to be reordered. I can't imagine what could have gone wrong now.

"On my way. How bad?"

"Bad."

"Who am I pissed at?"

"Not me, I hope."

"Never you, Clark." Clark is one of my best guys, solid as a
rock, gets how I work, and is terrific with the subs and clients
alike. I know for a fact he often steps in to troubleshoot things
before they get to me, which most likely has saved me from
some confrontations that would have bitten me in the butt later.

I jump on the expressway and push Lola's old engine a little
fast. She grumbles a bit, but then gives in, and slowly the odometer creeps up to crisis speed. I pull in behind Clark's truck, and
take the front steps two at a time, despite the protests of my
knees. The door is open.

"Clark?" I call out.

"Back here, boss lady," he yells from the back of the house. I
wend my way through the living room and dining room and
kitchen, out to the new sunroom addition overlooking the
expansive backyard. I feel a cold breeze, and realize that I'm

not looking through crystal-clear floor-to-ceiling windows; I'm looking through empty window casings. Half of the large windows are on the floor of the room, most of them cracked, a couple of them shattered completely.

"What the FUCK happened in here?"

"Best as I can tell, the window guys used some kind of cheap expandable spray insulation between the windows and the casings, which didn't set properly, and didn't nail in the flashings, and in that wind last night, these all just blew in." He is standing next to one of the empty window frames, flicking at the insulation that is supposed to expand and fill all of the cracks between window and house, and it appears to be simply falling to dust at his lightest touch.

"Son of a BITCH."

"Yeah." He looks sheepish. "I'm sorry, Anneke, I should have caught it."

"And yet?"

"Here we are."

"Who did the windows? Jerry?"

"Jerry was over on Fremont with Liam. Murph sent over a couple guys from the Roscoe Village flip."

Figures. "Our guys, or the developer's guys?"

Clark runs a hand over his buzzed-short graying hair. "Not sure, but I didn't recognize them."

"That fucker," I mutter under my breath. I try not to denigrate the bosses in front of other employees, but I just know that this is Murph's cutting corners, and now my anger has nowhere to go. "And when you saw some guys you didn't know doing the already-late window installation, it what? Occurred to you that you should run out and get your nails done? Had more important things to attend to? What exactly is the point of having you manage a project if you don't ACTUALLY MANAGE IT? Where WERE you when the windows went in?" I want so much to not be yelling at Clark, but somehow my fuse isn't long enough to give me any breath to be rational.

Clark's eyes narrow and the color goes from light blue to midnight. "You're right, Anneke, I should have been here. I left the guys doing the windows to go pick up the flooring so that it could settle and acclimate in the space once we were enclosed, hoping to get back a day on the install since we are so behind."

Finally I manage to pry off the lid on my sanity. "I'm sorry, Clark, I know this could have happened to anyone, I get it."

He nods, and his eyes lighten. "No worries. We're all up against it on this one."

"Can we salvage any of this?" I gesture around the room.

"I called in a favor with the window people, they are still feeling the pinch having fucked up the order the first time . . . I may have implied that this was also partially their fault since we had our best window guys waiting with nothing to install on the first go-around, and those guys weren't available when they fixed their first mistake, so they are going to split the cost of the new ones with us, cover freight, and rush it out. We should have them tomorrow."

Now my stomach hurts for having snapped at him. He's a good guy and always has my back, and takes initiative to keep my plate as clear as it can be. "Thanks, Clark, I owe you one. I'm going to call and have a load of plywood sent over so you and I can get this place sealed up for the time being."

"I can do it."

"Nah. If I let you do that I have to go back to the office." And I wink at him. He laughs, and I know we are back to normal.

"Well, if I'm going to let you hide out here, I may need some lunch . . ."

"I'll call for the ply, and then order pizza?"

"Sausage and green peppers and onions." Now he is grinning.

"You know that smells like a foot and an armpit. Having sex. In a fast-food garbage can. In the summer."

He rubs his belly. "I know YOU think that."

"Bastard."

He shrugs, and goes to grab a shovel to start cleaning up the broken glass, and I go to make my calls, and to grab my gloves to do my penance.

You're not laying this off on ME," Murph sputters. "You're the one who hasn't been able to keep this whole project on track."

I'm digging my stubby nails into my palms. I promised myself I was going to at least try not to get myself in trouble at work if I can help it. "I'm not laying it off on you, I'm just saying that I would appreciate it, in future, if you would not send someone else's team to my site without consulting me." I counted to a HUNDRED before I came in here, and I'm swallowing every bit of ire. But after helping Clark clean up the mess, getting plywood covering all the open window holes, and letting Clark take the heat with the client, who has a total crush on him and forgives him for everything, my nerves are fairly frayed. Plus I had to eat pizza with ghastly green peppers on it, which is repeating on me in the worst possible way. I've eaten an entire roll of Tums this afternoon, and I'm still burping up foul wind in my own face.

"I'm pretty sure if you had a handle on the work on your site, I wouldn't have needed to bail you out with labor generously loaned to us by one of our long-standing clients." He squints at me with his piggy little eyes, daring me to take it further. Despite my deep desire to both punch him in the nose AND call him out for being the oily asspimple I know him to be, I'm finding that the searing internal heat of my heartburn is weirdly helping me keep my external cool.

"I take the ultimate responsibility for what happens on my projects, without a doubt. I'm just saying that it would be a help to me to keep me in the loop on such things."

Murph waves me off. "Duly noted." And he turns back to his computer so that I know he is finished with this discussion.

I walked the dog. Left you dinner in the fridge. Try to save these for after. Love you. Grant's note is on the kitchen counter, anchored under a box that is wafting the smell of vanilla tantalizingly. I pop the top. Cannelés. Those crispy-on-the-outside, custardy-on-the-inside little French marvels, caramelized just shy of burnt, flavored with just the merest whisper of rum, one of my favorite treats. Grant told me he was playing with them for the new restaurant, and if he has brought them for me, it must mean he's finally gotten them perfect.

I feel a tug on the hem of my jeans, and glance down to see Schatzi looking annoyed at me, as usual.

"What on earth do you want, Satan's Spawn? Grant walked you, and I know he fed you."

The dog sashays over to her water bowl, turns, and glares at me again.

There is a feather floating like a tiny boat on the surface. I lean down and remove it.

"There."

Her eyes narrow at me even more.

"FINE." Stupid fucking dog. I pick up the bowl, run the cold water in the sink till it is nice and brisk, and refill the bowl. The dog takes three little licks, shakes her ears, and goes over to her perch on the windowsill to give me the cold shoulder. As if this will offend me.

I text Grant to thank him for dinner and the treats, and to tell him that I had a supershitty day and it helps to come home to his cooking if I can't come home to him. He texts me back a simple *XO*, which means he is up under it in the middle of service.

I take a long hot bath with a glass of calvados on the rocks, which finally settles my stomach, and then get into some snuggly pajamas that Caroline bought me last year when we did a girls' weekend and she saw that I was sleeping in a pair of leggings from 1993 and a T-shirt so threadbare it was more like a series of holes held together with a spiderweb of prayers. The containers in the fridge reveal a large tamale filled with spicy pork and cheese, some posole, black beans and rice, perfectly caramelized plantains. Which means it was the line cooks' turn to make family meal. Those boys, a lovely blend of Mexicans, Ecuadoreans, and Dominicans, can cook you fancy fine-dining French all day, but when you let them just make their food? It is a cornucopia of Latin perfection. They'd kill me for eating it all cold, but I don't have the energy to bother to microwave it. I devour it all right out of the plastic DELItainers, washing it down with a Lagunitas IPA, on the couch with a marathon of *Love It or List It* on HGTV. The show is my happy place. Because on my worst day on the job, at least I'm not dealing with a never-ending parade of people who all want an open-concept main floor, more bedrooms and bathrooms, and a finished basement . . . while sitting on a deathtrap of a house filled with asbestos and mold and scary electrical and structural issues. With a budget of four dollars.

I eat all four of the cannelés, savoring how Grant managed to get the outside so crunchy, and the middle so creamy. And I fall asleep to the "David found the perfect new house for you" music, knowing that no matter how little was actually fixed in their old home, and how amazing the new house is, they are probably going to "love it." They almost always love it. What you know has just so much more pull than something new, even if it is tempting and affordable AND in your beloved neighborhood.

When I wake up, the TV is still on, now showing some horrid infomercial. I squint at my phone. It's nearly three. I slide off the couch and head to the bedroom, figuring I was so dead when Grant got home that he didn't want to wake me. Except the bed is still made. Now I'm awake.

I grab my phone off the counter. No texts, no messages. This isn't exactly the first time this has happened; the life of a chef begins after service at eleven or twelve. There are drinks, late meals that range from spectacular to spectacularly greasy. Sometimes a chef from out of town stops by unexpectedly to hang, or a celeb shows up for some coddling. I'm not the clingy type, I don't need someone to account for their every moment and movement. Grant's hours never really bothered me, and the spontaneity associated with the end of the workday and its appeals are not lost on me. When we were first dating, he would text to see if I wanted to come out and meet him, but I never really fit in well with his foodie crowd, so I stopped coming and he stopped asking. But for some reason the fact that it is so much closer to sunrise than sunset and he hasn't even bothered to give me a heads-up? Is really pissing me off. I told him I'd had a shitty day. I could have used a friendly ear, some sympathy, maybe even a comfort quickie.

I shoot him a text. Where R U? Home soon?

I get a drink of cold water; for some reason I always get worse cottonmouth on the couch than in the bed. I brush my teeth, run a hot washcloth over my face, set up the fancy coffeemaker to automatically grind beans and brew our morning cup. I check my phone. No reply.

Sersly, hope you R on ur way!

I take my phone and head for bed. By four o'clock I can't keep my eyes open anymore, and Grant isn't home, nor has he texted me back. Even my anger and hurt can't keep me awake, but the knot in my stomach means my sleep isn't exactly restful or deep. And when the door opens just after five, the noise wakes me like a shot.

"Morning, beautiful," Grant says sheepishly, holding up a paper bag and a beverage holder with two small coffee take-out cups in it. The diminutive size can only mean one thing. He was in Pilsen, and grabbed two tiny cafés sweetened with condensed milk, which also means that the bag must have fresh quince and cheese pastries.

"So it is."

"Didn't mean to wake you."

"Who said I was asleep?" I know it is petulant and horrible to lie and imply I've been up all night worrying like some timid little thing, calling hospitals and police stations.

Grant smiles sheepishly. "The hair gives you away."

I reach a hand up and can feel that there is some definite bedhead happening. "Whatever. Hope you were having fun."

"Look, I'm sorry. We had a killer night, and then the Publican boys came in with the remnants of a private pig roast, and by the time we were ready to go it was almost one and I didn't want to call, I figured you would have crashed by then, so we ended up at Tai's, and then I dropped a couple of the boys home, didn't want them on the bus at that hour." Oy. Tai's Til 4 is never a good idea.

"Did they prevent you from replying to my texts?"

Grant reaches into his pocket, hits the home button on his phone, and his face falls. He turns the black screen to me. "Shit. Phone is dead; I forgot to charge it after service. I had no idea you were texting me. I'm sorry, babe."

Grant is a lot of things, but a liar isn't one of them.

"Well, since you KNEW I had an epically shitty day, if you

weren't going to bother to come home to be with me, it might
have been nice to at least THINK about getting in touch to let
me know you wouldn't be home till dawn."

"Look, I'm sorry. I don't want to fight. Let's just have some
café and a pastry and a couple hours of snuggle sleep before we
have to work, and I'll make it up to you tonight."

"Well, I wouldn't want to put you out."

"What do you want from me, Anneke? I'm sorry. But really,
you're acting like a child. You know my schedule, how things go.
When is the last time you came to the restaurant after work? When
is the last time you came out with my friends and me? It can't all
be about you. And to be honest, I wouldn't have known that yesterday was EPICALLY shitty because ANYTIME I ask you about
work you say it was shitty, and frankly, I'm a little bored."

"Well, I'm so sorry to be BORING," I say snottily, dripping sarcasm, to cover the fact that deep down I sort of suspect that he has a
point, I really never do just head over to the restaurant anymore.
But since I'm human, and the strongest human impulse is to avoid
being discovered to be wrong, I rally. "Maybe if you had even
ASKED me to bid on building the new restaurant we might be
spending more time together." I'd convinced myself that my feelings weren't hurt when he came home eight months ago and
announced that Knauer would be doing his new place. I don't have
any commercial experience, but it would have been nice to be asked.

"That's not fair. The investors hired the designer and the
builder and you know that."

"Did you even ask for me?"

"To be honest? No."

"Well, thanks for that."

"I WANTED TO MAKE SURE YOU HAD TIME FOR
PALMER BECAUSE YOU LOVE IT THERE!" Grant throws
his hands up in frustration, and Schatzi comes clicking down
the hall to see who is annoying her favorite person.

"The consideration is noted." I hate me like this. This? Right here? Is why I never bothered with real relationships. I just don't know how to do them.

Grant sighs, his shoulders sagging. "I'm going to take the dog for a walk for ten minutes and clear my head. When I get back, I'd like us both to have a calmer conversation, can you agree to that?"

"Fine."

Grant heads out and I go back to the bathroom to pee and try to fix the snarled shrubbery on my head. Half of it is mashed flat and the rest is sticking out everywhere, so I can't imagine he could even take me seriously. I stick my head under the cold water in the sink, which wakes me fully, and I can begin to think about rationality. I run a brush through my wet hair and pull it back into a ponytail, brush my teeth, and throw on some jeans and a fleece. I pull on my work boots, coat, throw a hat over my wet head, and put my keys in my pocket. I think for a minute, and then I grab the bag and coffees on my way out.

I catch up to Grant halfway back from his trek around the block. The sky is just lightening, and Schatzi prances proudly by his side. He tilts his head down and looks at me with eyebrows raised, as if to ask if the crazy lady is gone.

"Hi," I say.

"Hi there. Want to walk with us?" He holds out his arm, and I slide my arm through it, gripping his puffy down coat. We don't speak till we get to the park, where we can sit on a bench while Schatzi finds a patch of bare earth under a tree to groom herself, and we each open a cup of fragrant sweet coffee, and begin to munch our pastries.

"I'm sorry I didn't call," Grant says around a mouthful of quince and crumbs, "and I'm sorry it didn't occur to me to check my phone. I knew you had a bad day, and it was shitty of me. I think I probably wanted to avoid you a little bit."

I swallow the last crunchy corner of my own pastry, and brush crumbs off my jacket. "Why? Am I so bad?"

He puts his arm around me and pulls me close. "You're fabulous. You are my favorite person in the world. But you are so independent, so self-sufficient. It kills me how much your job takes out of you emotionally, but I know that the more I push you to quit, the more you shut down about it, so I feel a little stymied. I want you to do something to move your career forward and away from those assholes, but I know you have to do it in your own time and your own way and not feel like I pressured you."

Now I feel like even more of a shitheel. "I love that you want me to be able to do what I want, I really do. It is one of the kindest things anyone has ever offered me. It's like, JOE-worthy. Really." He knows what I mean when I say that, and he squeezes me close.

"I didn't know it hurt your feelings that I didn't ask you to bid on the new place, and you're right, I should have asked you."

"No, you're right, I'm just being an asshole. Those guys are awesome and they're going to make it perfect for you."

"Want to come see it?" he asks expectantly. "You haven't been there in weeks."

"Yeah. I do." I really do. And I can feel my shoulders unclench. "Wanna come to Palmer?"

He smiles. "Of course. Do we have time to do both before you have to go to work?"

"Absolutely. Let's do it."

He stands and offers me his hand, and he pulls me off the bench and into his arms, and a deep, soulful kiss. "I love you, Anneke. More than anything. You know that, right?"

"I do. And I love you." He pulls me tightly against him, and I feel like his embrace is my lifeline. In his arms, all the icky shit just goes away. He knows me. He gets me. He wants me happy. That's all a girl could possibly want or need.

6

There are days and there are days. Mine begins with a six a.m. wakeup call from the Mannings, insisting on a seven o'clock meet at the site. I throw on the cleanest jeans and thermal shirt I can find, and head over. Warren and Susie are there, looking gassy.

"We're disappointed with this," Warren says in his clipped tone, gesturing at the empty lot, overgrown with weeds and scattered with garbage.

"I'm not really sure what you mean?" I say, perplexed. The lot looks exactly the same as when they bought it, with the small addition of some piles of snow and patches of ice.

Susie sighs, as if dealing with a stupid child. "I know we haven't completely finished the design discussions, but the footprint of the plans is set; we're a little curious as to why the foundation has not been started."

Good lord. The obtuseness of these people is gargantuan.

"As I explained when we met in October, we don't dig foundation when the ground is frozen. There are too many complications and risks for future damage. And considering the endless polar vortex this winter, the ground is particularly deeply frozen. So we won't be able to begin digging until late March at the soonest, more likely early April."

"They're doing foundation." Warren points across the street, where a build company I will not name is blithely setting up concrete forms.

"Mr. Manning, I can't speak to other companies' practices.

But I can assure you that the chances you take when you dig and pour in winter, especially a brutally cold winter, are not worth the small gain in timing. Work in winter is a snail's pace at best; workers have to be bundled up and can't move very well, and have to take frequent breaks to warm up. You have to not work at all when there is snow and ice or bitter cold, but you have to pay the workers for their time anyway when there are weather delays. There's the risk of the concrete not setting properly, and cracking when the weather warms up, which would mean a life of leaking and potential flooding in your basement, not to mention structural instability for the house. We want to build you something of the highest quality, and because of that we want to be sure that the most important part of this build, the infrastructure, is done under optimal conditions to prevent future problems. I assure you, we will take these next couple of months to perfect the design, to research and hire the best people for the job at the best prices, and to secure all the permits. A great build is eighty percent planning and twenty percent execution. When the weather is ready for us to get started, we'll have an amazing plan in place and hit the ground running."

"Harrumph," Warren grumbles.

"Hmmm," Susie groans. They both look constipated, and glare at me as if I'm the specific blockage.

I keep smiling. One thing about MacMurphy, the client is always right. Especially the very wealthy ones. "Is there anything else I can do for you both this morning?" I say, maybe a bit more brusquely than I would have if my sleep hadn't been interrupted.

"I think not," Warren says, and escorts Susie back to their long Mercedes sedan.

Good grief. No point in heading back home. I decide just to go to the office. At least at this hour it will be quiet, and I can get some work done.

Hey, Annlucka?" A new Barbie clicks on my door with long acrylic fingernails. Apparently Spinner Barbie got a new gig hocking pharmaceuticals, so she has been replaced with a new one, who is about eleven feet tall with legs up to her ears, and everything she owns is bedazzled in crystals, long rhinestone chandelier earrings dangling in her platinum tresses, a big necklace of enormous sparkers gently lying on her heaving bosom. I call her Disco Ball Barbie. "Mac and Murph want to see you in the conference room."

I look up, stretching my shoulders. I've been eyeball-deep in bids and budgets since I got here at a quarter to eight, and now it's nearly one. I even forgot to stop for lunch, a fact my growling stomach is now quick to remind me. I grab my water bottle, hoping the hydration will stop the audible rumbling, and head over to the glass-walled conference room.

Mac and Murph are inside, and looking grim. The Mannings are with them.

"Hello, Anneke, please take a seat." I walk around the table and take the chair Murph has gestured to, facing the tribunal. As I sit down, I see Liam on the other side of the glass, mugging and waving a finger at me, shaking his head and showing that he knows I'm in some sort of trouble. Which means that Murph must have said something. It irks me to no end that not only have I apparently put my foot in it again, but that the peanut gallery was consulted. I hate when people talk about me behind my back. I'm absolutely the last person to gossip about anyone, ever, and it always feels like such an invasion to be certain that Murph is telling his idiot cousin every bad thing he thinks about me.

"Anneke, the Mannings are a little concerned about having you head up this project. So we thought we should all sit down and go over things, get everyone on the same page," Murph says, clearly pissed off. He hates having to be involved in actual work stuff. Murph likes to show up at eleven, lunch at twelve, flirt with Barbies till three, and then head out. Monday through Thursday. Once-a-month team meetings he attends reluctantly. Actual management is really irritating to him.

"I'm sorry you feel that way," I say directly to Warren and Susie. "I would love to address any concerns you might have."

"You can see the tone to which we were referring," Susie says to Mac, pointing in my direction with an accusatory finger.

"It's like she barely tolerates us," Warren says to Murph.

"Tone?" I'm flabbergasted. "What tone? I'm just trying to ascertain what the difficulties are here so that we can discuss them."

"That's all we want to do," Mac says, ever the reluctant voice of reason. "Just get a handle on the situation." Mac is more hands-on, more present than Murph. But he's also very noncon-frontational, so this must make him really uncomfortable.

Susie nods at Warren. He turns his back on me to face Mac and Murph directly. "The situation is simple. If you want to keep our business, we'd like a different project manager. One who doesn't act like she thinks we're stupid, or insufferable. Someone who doesn't act like she hates working with us."

A red haze falls over my eyes. I've never been anything but respectful with these jackasses. I've been friendly and calm and accommodating. But this? This running to my bosses and tat-tling like spoiled children? Asking to have me removed because I told them that I want to build their stupid house so that it doesn't fall down? This is major bullshit, and my blood pressure soars. My carefully-fought-for bit of restraint that I've been struggling so hard to maintain shatters into a zillion pieces. And before I know it, words are flying out the front of my head.

"Mr. and Mrs. Manning, everyone here at MacMurphy wants

you to be happy with your experience. And you should absolutely work with someone you connect with. I recommend Liam Murphy; he's your kind of ass-kissing suck-up guy. He will tell you what you want to hear, one hundred percent of the time. He will build your monstrous tasteless house and fill it with your cut-rate special-deal fell-off-the-truck fixtures that your buddies pawn off on you. He'll never tell you that you are building something with built-in lack of resale value due to your appallingly bad taste, and that you are doing it at a price nearly twice what the market in that neighborhood will ever bear. He can be the one to ignore your calls in two years when your screening room walls sprout black mold and your ghastly gold-flecked marble backsplash cracks in half as the kitchen settles six inches into your unstable leaky basement. As for your perception that I act like I think you are stupid and insufferable and I hate working with you? Let me assure you. That? Is no act."

I get up, and calmly walk out of the conference room, and back to my office. I can hear a little kerfuffle up the hallway as I gather the few bits and pieces of personal detritus that I have here, and put them in my satchel and fill a small file box with the rest of my stuff. I email my one folder of personal files to myself, and wipe them off the computer. With every minute that goes by, my heart pounding intensifies, my blood boils harder. These bastards have never once been grateful for the work I've done, the money I've made. Never once in years of puff pieces in the local papers and magazines have they ever mentioned me, or any of the other hardworking people on their staff. There has never been a bonus, even in the precrash years when they were raking it in hand over fist. Even the annual Christmas party is chintzy, pizza and beer in the office, and everyone gets the yearly gift-with-logo, the cheap messenger bags and fleeces and travel coffee mugs piling up in desk drawers and only actually used by the most brownnosiest of the employees. So, essentially Liam and anyone on his team.

If they were just cheap, it might have been easy to let it all go, if only they didn't play favorites and weren't so exclusionary. I'm a girl, so I've never once been invited to one of the boys-only sporting events or beers after work. I'm actually a sports fan, thanks to Joe and his devotion to all of the local teams, but have they ever even bothered to ask me? Never. Do the Barbies get to hang out in the skyboxes and studio suites and courtside seats when they are available? You had better believe it. I guess if you want to go to the company outing, you had better be the kind of girl most likely to be sought out in the audience for appearances on the stadium big screens. Well, I'm done. The hell with them. They couldn't even have the decency to have a private discussion with me first, just threw me to the lions? They don't begin to deserve me, and suddenly the supreme rightness of Grant's endless offering to bankroll Palmer and our life together, and the girls' very vocal support, settles in my heart like a balm, and my pulse slows and my breathing gets still. By the time Murph appears red-faced in my doorway, I feel ten feet tall and invincible.

"Anneke, I don't know what the FUCK just got into you, but if you want to have a job here, I suggest you go home now and think about what you want to say to us tomorrow to make us want to keep you."

I look him dead in his beady little eyes and with a deep sense of calm, I unload, pretty as you please with honeyed tones. "You don't have to worry, Murph. I don't want to have a job here. I'm tired of the bullshit kowtowing to entitled crap-buckets like the Mannings. I'm tired of you and Mac never giving me my due or having my back. I'm tired of you feeding all the good stuff to your obsequious cousin Liam and leaving me all the shit. I'm tired of your endless series of talentless legs and boobs and hair extensions that you like wandering around here despite their general incompetence. I'm finished. I'm the best you had and the only one you should have trained to replace you in three years when you want to retire and still draw income. And you've never once done anything to show that you know it. So, since it's clear that you will always take the word of the client over someone who has been a valuable employee for nearly a decade, I am fucking done." I never raise my voice; the smile never leaves my face. I deliver this blow with as much grace as I can muster, throw my bag over my shoulder, grab the small box of my personal effects, and push past him before he can even close his gaping jaw.

I head out of my office, feeling flushed and nervous, but also giddy. Liam is standing next to the front desk, chatting up Pinky Tuscadero Barbie.

"That's a lot of yelling back there, Annamuk." He leers at me. "That time of the month?"

The Barbie giggles.

"Hey, Liam? A word to the wise. That fancy truck? Doesn't mean you don't HAVE a tiny little dick. It just means that you want the WHOLE WORLD to know it."

And with that, I open the door wide, letting the frigid wind blow through, leaving them both gape-jawed in a tornado of papers.

I let Lola warm up a bit while my blood pressure slowly returns to normal. Suddenly starving, I pull out and head over to Half Italian Grocer on Milwaukee, and pick up a sandwich, a bag of chips, one of their decadent cannoli. I eat it all in the car, dripping Italian dressing and cannoli filling on myself, scattering bread crust flakes and chip crumbs all over. I'm flying high. Fuck Mac and Murph and Liam. Fuck the Mannings and their sensitive egos and their money and shitty taste. It's like Hedy said, fuck the haters, fuck 'em all. I hope they start digging tomorrow and spend the rest of their natural lives in their horrible house where the basement floods during every big storm. I'm going to get up tomorrow and go to the Palmer Square house and start something big. Something that's going to take all my concentration, and months of work, and will make all this other noise just a little annoying blip in my past, as I jump headlong into my future.

I'm suddenly filled with heart-swelling enormous love for Grant, for his generosity, for his wanting my happiness enough that he would encourage me to quit this job that never was what I really needed. For understanding me so completely and taking such good care of me. For being so patient and just waiting for me to come to this decision in my own time and my own way. He's going to laugh his ass off when I tell him what I said to the Mannings, to Murph. Grant is a big believer of both grand entrances and dramatic exits. He thinks they make life worth living. At his first job, for a notoriously evil screamy chef, he ended up cutting the tip off his pinky finger when the asshair snuck up behind him to yell at him for something another chef had actually messed up. Grant walked over, seared the bloody finger on the flattop to cauterize the wound, and told the bastard that he would be out of business in three years if he didn't stop selling counterfeit wines, putting half the profits up his nose, and cheating on his wife with the pastry chef. The restaurant closed in two years, concurrent with the chef's divorce and stint in rehab, and the space is where Grant is now building his diner. Karma is a bitch.

I decide that we should celebrate, and head over to Howard's Wine Cellar on Belmont to pick up a bottle of vintage Krug, Grant's favorite bubbly, and a major splurge. I'm feeling amped-up, powerful, irresistible. I swing by Whole Foods and grab some wonderful stinky cheeses, sausages, a baguette, a bunch of grapes, a pint of pistachio gelato, a bar of dark chocolate. We are going to have a little living room picnic, and then I am going to seduce my fiancé.

When I come through the door, laden with goodies, Schatzi raises her head from her perch on the couch, and gives me a look I can only describe as smug. I toss her a treat anyway, and start putting the food away. I've got the champagne bottle in my hand when I hear the noise. Sort of a muffled mumbling coming from the bedroom. My heart stops. I look over at the dog, who has gone back to sleep. Figures. She'd want me to get killed by some meth-addled axe murderer. Then she'd have Grant all to herself. The champagne bottle automatically shifts in my hand, readying itself for a protective blow. I'm so amped it doesn't occur to me to be scared, woe to the thief who entered my home today of all days. Today I am one powerful bitch.

I walk slowly toward the bedroom, where the door is ajar. I push it slightly, quietly, like I've seen done in a million cop shows, and see the bed, still unmade from my quick exit this morning, shocked at how rumpled and destroyed it looks. I can hear the shower going in the bathroom, and breathe a sigh of relief. No wonder the dog didn't care; Grant must have gone to the new restaurant site today and gotten dirty and wanted to come home to clean up before heading to work. Even better. I'll surprise him in the shower. I kick off my shoes, shimmy out of my jeans, pull off my shirt, and discard panties and bra. Then I pick up the bottle of bubbly, rip off the foil and cage, and gently remove the cork with a subtle pop. Naked, I tiptoe over to the bathroom and open the door, stepping inside the steamy room, heading for the large open shower, patting myself on the back for suggesting to Grant he build a decent-sized bench at one end and imagining what we might do to each other thereon.

"Hello, handsome," I say, striking a seductive pose.

"AAAAAAAHHHHHH!!!!" yells Gregg, Grant's new sous chef for the diner, standing under the rain shower I installed, with hot water running over his lanky body and his stagger-ingly impressive erection.

"Shit," says Grant from behind Gregg, dropping the large soapy sponge he's using to wash Gregg's back.

"Fuck," I say as the bottle slips from my grasp, hitting the cushy bathmat I picked out that rests on top of the slate tiles I sourced and installed, and sending an explosion of the five-hundred-dollar champagne straight up into the air and all over me.

Palmer Square: The Next Hot Neighborhood," says the sidebar on the new issue of *Chicago* magazine. It's the first thing that has made me feel good since my life exploded. I flip through the article, sitting in the front seat, reading the kind of neighborhood predictions that make my heart pitter-pat. Describing the area as a developing extension of the hotter-than-hot Logan Square area that it abuts, detailing the new surge of small businesses, restaurants, and coffeehouses that point toward an imminent quantum shift in everything from quality of schools to housing prices. It effectively confirms my belief that I got in on the Palmer house at just the right time, and should be able to find the right client willing to pay what it will be worth when I finish. After what I've been through, and where I'm going, I really needed this bit of validation. It's like the universe saying that all will be what it should be.

I drop the magazine on the seat beside me, turn off the truck, and get out. It's just seven o'clock; Murph and Mac asked me to come in before the office opens to sign my exit paperwork and pick up my final check. I would have preferred to do it all by mail, but they insisted.

I push open the door, and head through the eerily still office to the conference room, the scene of the crime.

"Anneke," Murph says without getting up.

"Murph," I reply as Mac walks over and gives me an awkward hug, which I accept, arms at my sides, wishing he would stop touching me.

"You doing okay?" he asks.

"Just peachy."

"Okay, let's get this organized," Murph says, all business. There are forms to fill out that say that I quit and wasn't fired, so that I can't claim unemployment benefits. A nondisclosure agreement that says I can't talk about any of their clients or their business. A noncompete agreement that says I cannot contact any of their current clients, and cannot accept work from any of their current clients for two years. Some insurance form that says that my projects while I worked for them will all continue to be covered under their policy, and that I am also still covered against liability for any work I oversaw while employed with them. COBRA forms that allow me to get my health insurance for the next year. My final check, including paying me out for nine years' worth of vacation days and sick days never taken. I sign off on a letter that will go out to my current clients and the other employees saying that after a wonderful long run with them I have decided to move on to other opportunities and that MacMurphy wishes me all the best. It's all very businesslike, and relatively painless.

"Hello, everyone. Anneke," Liam says as he walks in the door. So much for painless.

"We wanted you to bring Liam up to speed on all of your in-progress work, since he will be overseeing everything until we find a replacement," Murph says curtly, and then stands. "Good luck, Anneke, we wish you all the best," he says, in a way that indicates that he means the exact opposite, and then he leaves.

Mac gestures for Liam to sit down, and the three of us spend the better part of an hour going over everything I had on my plate. To his credit, Liam is simply focused, listens to everything I say, takes copious notes. When we are finished, I shake Mac's hand and gather up my copies of all of the legal crap.

"Do you know what you'll do?" Mac asks.

"I've got a spec house I've been working on in my spare time for the last year or so; I'm going to work on it full-time."

"That seems good. I hope it works well for you." He nods, and heads out to his office.

"Where's the place?" Liam asks.

"Palmer Square."

"The new hot neighborhood on the horizon?" he says snarkily.

I'm not taking the bait. "Well, only if you believe *Chicago* magazine."

"Urban pioneering, seems smart."

"Just a project I believe in."

"I think it's great." He shrugs. "Plus you are probably the only client you can stand."

I'm not in the mood today. There is too much to do, too much to process; I'm still half-numb and refuse to engage. "I definitely piss me off much less than other people. See you around, Liam."

"Good luck, for what it's worth, I think you'll be fine."

This sudden bit of sincerity catches me off guard, and chips away at my icy exterior a bit. "Thanks. For what it's worth, I'm sorry that my departure is dumping extra work and complications on you."

"Nothing a good ass-kissing, brownnosing suck-up like me can't handle." He grins.

I can't help but chuckle. "You make an excellent point." And with that, I head back out through the office for the last time, relieved to have it over and done with, and try to steel myself to face the part of my day that will be even worse.

Yours or his?" Caroline says, pointing to the lamp on the end table next to the living room couch.

"His," I say, continuing to put DVDs in a plastic tub.

"I got all the hanging clothes into the wardrobe box," says Marie, coming out of the bedroom.

"And I got all the stuff out of the drawers into your suitcases," Hedy says, following close on her heels.

"Thanks, guys." I'm numb, and I'm pissed. It's been the longest week of my life. I holed up at Caroline's in her amazing guest suite, and moped while she plied me with baked goods, homemade ice cream, vats of mashed potatoes, almost all of which I weirdly resented. I frankly hated the fact I even had to stay with her, but I couldn't be in that apartment, even though Grant offered to leave for me to have some time. I spent hours in her deep tub, drinking hot tea laced with bourbon and ginger syrup, emptying and refilling the tub when it cooled, waiting for the tears I knew should come but never did, and all the time wishing she would stop cooking and baking and placating and offering to buy me massages. People break up; I might be sad, but I'm not some broken doll that needs fixing.

"The truck is en route," Caroline says, checking her phone. She has organized this move with the efficiency and precision of a military coup. She bought the tubs and boxes, hired the movers, rallied the troops, all before I could even tell her I'd rather she didn't. "Last time, are you sure about this? You know you can stay with us as long as you like. Carl would love it, and so would I."

"I love you, Caro, but I can't just stay at your place. I have to move forward with my life, and right now, my life, whatever there is left of it, is at that house." I'm moving into the Palmer Square house, since I own it and now it represents my only income opportunity. It's a roof over my head, and I can work round the clock. It won't be luxurious, or even terribly comfortable, but it will be a place to focus my thoughts and energies into something positive. And I'll be able to get away from the smothering constant attention from Caroline.

"I don't think you should make any big decisions right now, you're very fragile." Marie comes over and puts an arm around my shoulders, giving me a firm squeeze, which I can't help but flinch away from. The last thing I need right now is a lot of petting, and Marie's sad little puppy face is just annoying.

"Fuck that, she's the least fragile person we know. Fucking look at her for chrissakes." Hedy makes a face. "She's a rock. And she's going to finish that enormous monolith and sell it for a gazillion bucks and it's going to launch her new business."

"Thank you." Hedy is the only one I don't want to punch right now. "I'll be fine."

"Of course you'll be fine. Better than fine. You'll be great," Marie says, giving me a "you can do it" smile.

I can't stand it, and I can't keep quiet. "Okay, no more cheerleading. Look, guys, this is shitty, but people break up all the time. It sucks, but I'm not dying, I'm just moving. And I appreciate all you are doing for me, but the best thing you can do if you really want to help is just get through today without too much pity, if that is at all possible."

Caroline looks like I hit her. Marie does a weird little spasm, and Hedy gives me a look that says I may have a hall pass, but to watch myself. But she saves me anyway.

"No rest for the weary and no pity for the strong. Let's get back to it, ladies." And blissfully, we go back to packing with minimal discussion. The fact is, I'm far less depressed about losing Grant than I am about having quit my job.

I have just about 150K in savings, the balance of my inheritance from Joe and what little I've been able to sock away over the years. The check I got this morning from Mac and Murph will only last me for basic living expenses for six months or so, and that is on a total shoestring. I have at least 200K worth of work left to do on the house, more if unexpected problems arise, and that is with me doing at least 70 percent of the actual work myself. And now I have no other income. By living in the property while I work I'll obviously save money on housing, but even on a total austerity budget, I'm going to have to get creative about a lot of things. I've been good about saving for retirement, but the idea of tapping into any of that to keep myself afloat is an ulcer waiting to happen. The conundrum is that if I were to take the time to get a job to get some more money coming in, I wouldn't have time to do the work I need the money to fund. Plus it isn't like I have good references available to me; I didn't just burn my bridges, I napalmed them. So for now, all I can do is jump in with both feet and hope for a miracle.

There's a knock on the door, and thankfully, before I have to endure any more pep talks about my suddenly shitty and uncertain future, the movers begin to take what little I own out of the place I thought was my home.

Once everything is loaded into the Palmer house, I head back to the condo alone to pick up Schatzi and leave the keys. Hedy offered to come with me, but I just want to be alone. I pull into a space in front, having already left my garage door opener behind in the apartment. I feel at once leaden and hollow. The hollowness is probably hunger. It's nearly four and the sandwiches and soup Caroline brought with her for our lunch are long gone, and pretending to be grateful for all of their help and platitudes is hungry work.

I unlock the door. Grant is standing in the living room, looking ashen and ashamed.

"I'm sorry, I just, I couldn't let you just . . ." His eyes fill with tears. "God, Anneke, I'm so sorry. Can we please . . . ? Can I . . . ?"

We haven't spoken since the shower incident. Gregg left in a hurry, and I wiped the champagne off of me and got dressed, and Grant had something of a breakdown, blubbering and apologizing and assuring me that the whole thing was a very new development and that he was planning on telling me. I sat there in total shock and listened to him explain that he still loved me, still wanted us to make a life together, and did I think I could explore the idea of an open marriage?

And that is when I got up and walked out and went to Caroline's.

"Grant, I don't really know what there is to say. I feel like a weird cliché in some bad romantic comedy or chick lit book. My fiancé is gay. How terribly unoriginal of me."

"Bi. Not gay."

"Oh, Jesus, Grant, pick a fucking side."

"I can't. Anneke, I meant everything I ever said to you, ever did with you. I meant all of that, I really loved you, love you; it's just confusing. You knew I had some experiences in my past . . ."

"COLLEGE! Culinary school! You were in your twenties, you said, a couple of random drunken fumblings, you said, TEQUILA-FUELED BI-CURIOUS in my youth, you said. Not schtupping the hot young male help while your fiancée is at work. That you never said; I would have remembered."

"That's fair, I deserve that. Seriously, Anneke, it was only the second time anything happened with Gregg. And I know that is two times too many, and I should have been honest with you the minute I felt like I was going to act on my feelings, but I didn't. I'm a shit. I feel awful. But I know that I love you and I still want to be with you, so I want to know if you would go to couples' counseling with me. If we can see if this is salvageable. I promise, I can be strong, I can be strong enough not to sleep with other people."

"Not people, Grant, MEN." I don't know why this distinction matters, except that he is clearly more ashamed by its reality, and I want to hurt him as much as possible right now.

"Right, men. If you won't sleep with other men, neither will I, I swear."

"You know that is really just egregiously stupid, right?"

"Yeah, I know. I just . . ." He throws his hands up and starts crying again. And this makes me even angrier. We were always the best of friends, since the moment we met, so easy together. I still love him. I actually hate to see him so broken. And I hate that I even let myself feel any of this. I hate that he took these years from me, took Joe's house from me, leaving me with no safe place to land now that it has turned to shit. I should have KNOWN that happy ever after is a joke and a lie. If being Anneliese Stroudt's daughter should have taught me anything, it is that you have to rely on yourself, because expecting someone else to provide you a life is a losing battle. I should have known when Joe never ever so much as went on another date for the rest of his life that if you let someone in that deep, they can break you.

"Grant, go fuck yourself. Or Gregg. Or half of Boystown for all I care. But keep your tears and sorries and sadness to yourself. I can't be a comfort to you while you try to figure out who you are and what you want. I just know that what you want clearly isn't really me, and obviously never was. I feel like you stole nearly five years from me, from my life, on purpose. I have to decide how to live with that."

"Where are you moving to?"

"The Palmer house."

"That's ridiculous; it isn't half finished."

"And it won't get finished unless I'm there twenty-four-seven."

"What about work?"

"I quit." His face falls. "That's why I came home early that day."

"Really?"

"Really. Not just quit, but with a grand explosion of fuck you to everyone. Not salvageable."

"Shit."

"Yeah, you said it. So I really don't have a choice, I have to go to Palmer, finish it, and sell it, and figure out what I'm going to do."

"I'm just so, so awfully sorry, Anneke; I'm the worst person in the world."

"Yep. Maybe you and Kim Jong-un can start a club."

He smiles a wan smile, his eyes all puffy, his forehead accordioned with pain and regret.

"I can't believe you quit."

"Someone told me to."

"I'm such a total shit."

"Yep."

"Will you at least let me support you while you finish the house? You wouldn't have left your job if I hadn't told you to, I committed to fund the renovation when you bought the property; please let me fulfill those promises to you."

"No. It's very nice of you, but I can't. I have to figure this out on my own. And frankly, I can't be indebted to you. It'll fuck up dealing with my feelings about you if I also have to be weirdly grateful. I know how much you've spent so far. When I sell it, I'll pay you back for that, with whatever percentage of the profit makes sense based on how much you invested." I hold my hand up so that he can't protest. "That is all."

He looks at me, at my clear determination, and nods. "I don't want profit; you did all the work. If you feel like you need to, I'll accept the return of my investment, but I don't want more than that, okay?"

"Fine." I'd love to just insist on giving him his share of the profits, but to be honest, I'm going to have to clear enough on this project to both find a new place to live and launch a new business. I may be proud, but I'm also practical.

"If you get into a jam, I'm happy to invest more, if you need it; am I allowed to offer that?"

"Yes. You are allowed to offer."

"But a cold day in hell?"

"Something like that."

I walk over to the door and get Schatzi's leash. I whistle for the dog, who comes out of the bedroom where she was napping, and allows me to attach it to her collar. I take the keys out of my pocket and place them on the table next to the door.

"Bye, girl," Grant says, kneeling to snuggle the dog. "If you ever need a dogsitter . . ."

"Thanks. Gotta go." I stand unmoving and receive the hug Grant gives me, unable to lift my arms to hug him back, realizing that it is the second time today I've had a weird and unwelcome good-bye hug foisted upon my person. When he finally pulls away, I think for a moment and then reach up my hands to take out my engagement earrings.

"Please, god, no, Anneke. Don't. They're yours, they were a gift; it'll break my heart if you give them back. If you can't bear to wear them, sell them, use them to help fund the house, whatever you need."

I nod. And Schatzi and I walk out the door.

The inflatable bed blows itself up to a satisfyingly plump rubbery height. Hopefully the acrid chemical smell will dissipate soon. I open the package of new sheets, along with a comforter and a couple of pillows, and make the bed. I've staked out the least destroyed of the third-floor bedrooms, the one that still has a closet in it, next to the only fully working bathroom in the house, and set my stuff up in there. There are gaping holes in the plaster walls, and the window whistles a bit in the wind—I'll have to caulk it tonight before I go to bed or it'll drive me mental. The library table desk Joe and I built is in the corner; the rest of what little furniture I have is all in the garage so that it doesn't get damaged.

When I moved in with Grant I got rid of all of my household stuff: towels, linens, kitchen supplies, my bed. I kept my
personal stuff like books and CDs, the few good pieces of furniture that Joe had either built or invested in, mostly tables and
cabinets, a couple of chests of drawers, but I didn't have that
much stuff. Certainly no basics. Caroline went into her sickeningly perfectly organized basement and gave me some
hand-me-down kitchen stuff left over from her single days.
Some dishes, flatware, a few pots and pans and random uten-
sils, mismatched glasses. The bed and bath things I got at Target, all of it on clearance and none of it matching or my taste.
But my life is purely about functionality right now. Nice sheets
are just not a priority.

I head down the back stairs to the kitchen, where Marie and
Hedy have stocked the fridge with some staples for me, a few
canned goods and boxes in the pantry. I dump some kibble in
Schatzi's bowl, and she reluctantly goes to eat it. When I lean
down to pat her back, the way Grand-mère always did when she
fed her, she literally shrugs me off. Great. I have no job, no
home, no fiancé, and my pet hates me. I'm a country song waiting to happen. I grab a box of Lucky Charms and the gallon of
milk, and head to my folding table. I eat three large bowls
while looking over my massive to-do list, and don't realize until
I taste salt that finally, I'm crying.

8

I pull the plastic protective coating off of the gorgeous eight-burner BlueStar range. After two weeks of pizza, subs, buckets of fried chicken, cheap Chinese, and take-out Thai, I have to face facts. Even mediocre fast food is expensive if you eat it twice a day. I'm going to have to start cooking at home. Lucky for me, the stuff I know how to make is fairly inexpensive. I went to Costco and bought a case of chicken-flavored ramen, a case of classic Kraft blue boxes, a case of canned tuna. A large bag of long-grain rice, since Caroline gifted me a rice cooker last week when she bought a new, bigger one. I'm tempted to believe she bought the new one for the express purpose of giving me the old one, but I'm not going to look a gift horse in the mouth. The poor of every Latin country subsist on rice and beans, and if they can do it, I can do it. I bought large bags of black beans, pinto beans, kidney beans, black-eyed peas. Variety is the spice of life, don't you know. I've never made a bean, but how hard could it be? I assume it's like pasta; you just throw them in boiling water till they get soft.

Since the building has a canning room/root cellar under the stone steps, I figured I'd go all Little House and stock it with hardy stuff that will last till spring. A large bag of onions, one of potatoes, one of apples, and one of carrots. I was tempted to buy cabbages, which I know store well, but realized despite my German heritage, I wouldn't begin to know what to do with them. A case of mixed flavors of canned soups. A big package of gargantuan foot-long hot dogs, which do a good job of adding protein to ramen or mac 'n' cheese. A box of frozen pizzas. Six boxes of spaghetti and six jars of marinara.

I have a huge pantry and a massive seventy-two-inch-wide Marvel fridge/freezer, so I might as well make use of them while I'm here. I'd originally hoped to leave them all pristine, but since this is likely to be my home for the next year or so, I have to give up that fantasy. Costco makes a pretty good rotisserie chicken for $4.99, which should go four meals if rounded out with starches; I picked one up today that should get me through at least two or three days. I'm feeling self-sufficient, almost competent. I also admit to some bags of frozen fries and chicken tenders, and a massive package of Oreos. Apparently they are as addictive as cocaine, and I can't afford cocaine, so it's going to have to be an Oreo buzz for me. I also grabbed a case of beer and an industrial-sized bottle of Maker's Mark.

I rip a leg off the chicken to snack on while I finish putting away my haul. It's salty and greasy, a little dry, but good enough. Goes down easy. I fling the bone into the garbage can, wipe my hand on my pants, and hunker down to figure out my next move. I know deep down I've been putting it off a little bit, futzing around on organization and little tweaking projects and lots of note-taking. But it's clear that I have to pick my next project and commit to it. The basement is the logical place. Right now the ancient boiler is hissing and clanking away and keeping the place alternately hot as a sauna and cold as an icebox the way these old steam radiator systems do. I know that I have to upgrade the building to a forced-air system, I've already laid out the plans for new ductwork, but ultimately I have to get the basement in order first. I can't install new furnaces until the demo is done down there, no point in hooking up a new system and then trying to protect it from insidious plaster dust. That means a total gut job on the basement, followed by pouring the new pad for the mechanicals room, and then running all the ducting to get the system up and running. It's conservatively about a two-month job, depending on what I find during demo.

And yet? There is the tiniest inkling of excitement at the prospect of getting into it. It's the first really major undertaking I've considered since finishing the kitchen, and knowing that I can devote myself to it full-time, while scary, is also the only thing in the last month that is cutting through my general numbness. I've been floating in what feels like a sea of Jell-O. I answer every third call from the girls, just so that they don't show up here for an intervention. I ignore the emails from Grant, who sends brief missives "just to see if you're okay and if you need anything," which alternately make me hate him or myself.

At least Schatzi continues to treat me like my existence is an offense to her delicate sensibilities; it's something of a relief to have one entity in my life that hasn't altered the way they look at me. At the end of the day, while there are other tasks I could start, I'm finally beginning to feel like I need to hit something hard with something heavy. Grant's betrayal, the upending of my life, I've taken it in stride. The way I was raised? Anything that smells the least bit like security also always felt undeserved and impermanent. I'm less sad or sorry for myself than I am feeling enormously stupid for having allowed myself to trust that I could have a normal happy home. There is a weird, unfortunate relief to have had the rug pulled out from under me, to having the truth revealed. Now I can go back to what I know. Self-sufficiency, independence, work.

I grab my sledgehammer, crowbar, and dust mask and head down the back stairs to the basement. This space originally had the servants' quarters in the front half, and the main kitchen in the back. The kitchen was long ago converted to a laundry room and storage, back when they switched the boiler from coal to gas. There's still some evidence of what was there: a small manhole cover in the floor for the old grease trap, the door in the back wall where the milk and ice deliveries used to come in. Since this area is where the new mechanicals are going to go, it makes the most sense to start here. I pull on my mask and grab my hammer, go for the back corner, tapping fairly gently around on the drywall, looking for evidence of electrical wires, plumbing runs, anything that would be dangerous. I know all the HGTV shows love to show homeowners just whaling away at walls, but demo is as much surgery as bludgeoning; you have to know exactly what you are dealing with before you abandon yourself to the destruction impulse.

As I pull the drywall off, I find old plaster beneath, with a layer of plywood. I use the crowbar to wrench the plywood off, old rusted nails giving way with a loud screeching noise, revealing a door. I wondered if the old larder might still be here, and my pulse races; I feel like I'm about to uncover a grand mystery, or secret treasure. I'll probably be all Geraldo, and there won't be anything behind but a brick wall, but still, it's exciting. I turn the handle, which sticks at first, and then gives. The door has swollen in its jamb, and while I know the latch isn't catching, the door doesn't want to budge.

A smart contractor would remove the whole thing. A smart contractor would use a drill and saber saw to cut a small hole in the door to get a peek at what lay behind. But today? I'm not a smart contractor. I'm a girl who wants very much to see if Narnia lies behind this door. So I put my shoulder into it and bust through. Something large and very heavy lands on my head, and the last thing I remember is the copper taste of blood where I have bitten the inside of my lip, and then all is rushing darkness.

I don't know how long I was out, probably only a half a minute or less. I do know that when I come to, my head is throbbing, my lip is blowing up, and my shoulder is aching from where I hit the door with it. The whole doorjamb, door still shut tight within it, is pushed into a small room, the rusted nails that held it in place no match for my Teutonic attentions. And next to me on the floor is a large leather-bound book, a good three inches thick. This must have been what hit me in the head. I turn my head and spit, a thick gob of bloody saliva. My tongue ascertains that I haven't broken through anything, or lost any teeth, just bit down really hard on the inside of my lip, and while eating will be annoying for a week or so, I don't need stitches. Should actually be helpful in the whole keeping-food-costs-down thing. I have a goose egg making itself known on the crown of my head, but no tenderness anywhere else, so I didn't hit my head on the floor when I went down. I'm not nauseated, dizzy, or in any other way feeling odd, so the likelihood of a concussion is minimal. I'll keep an eye on myself tonight, looking for unusual tiredness or other symptoms, but I think I'm probably okay. And kicking myself for not having my hardhat on while doing demo, such a rookie mistake.

Joe would be horribly disappointed in me. I wipe the tears from my hot cheeks, not from the pain, but from frustration and embarrassment. From being so reckless and stupid. I put my head on my knees and give in to the cry, all the while hoping that it's just my situation and not some weird sign of brain damage. Once I remind myself that I'm not the crying girl and I don't have time for brain damage, the tears stop, almost as quickly as they began.

Slowly I get up off the floor, careful not to go too fast, checking myself for wooziness. Once I stand up, I walk over to the fallen doorjamb. I lean over carefully and look inside. As I suspected, it's the old larder. There are hooks on one wall and a couple on the ceiling where meat and game birds would have hung. A low chest that I presume to be an icebox, some simple cabinets, what looks to be either a pie safe or a space to store butter and cheeses or cured meats. The room is small, maybe six feet by eight feet. But it would have been essential to the functioning of the primary kitchen down here. There is also a small door at counter height that I think might be a dumb-waiter, which will be a huge coup if it still has the mechanism in it. Suddenly my little aches and pains assert themselves, and I realize I should go upstairs and get some painkillers in me to keep ahead of it. As I turn to go, the toe of my boot catches the leather book again. I reach down and pick it up; it's unmarked. But the leather is shockingly supple under my hand, and I tuck it under my arm and head upstairs.

I take three Tylenol with a large glass of water, and then grab a small bottle of Coke from the fridge. Joe always kept the eight-ounce glass bottles around; they were a reward for him after a long day of work, icy cold and always tasting so much better than the stuff in the can. Plus the sugar and caffeine will actually help the medicine work faster. I pop it open, and take it to the table, sitting down to examine my attacker. The leather is a worn deep brown, like the sort of leather you would imagine an old fighter pilot jacket would be made of. It's thick, with heavy board covers, and bound with a single, wide leather strap that slides into a loop on the front. It smells of old leather and old paper and a little bit like mildew. I slip the strap out of the loop, and gingerly open the front cover. In elegant rolling script of faded violet ink on the page opposite the marbleized frontispiece, it says:

Gemma Ditmore-Smythe
Journal and Notebook

I feel like I remember this name from one of the newspaper articles about the Rabin family. I drop the book and reach for my folder of research. Flipping through the photocopied pages, I find the piece I'm looking for. A *Chicago Examiner* article with a large picture from September 9, 1907, shows a long, elegant banquet table, full of elaborate trays, roasted meats and game, towering jellies and platters of pastries. At the far end, a short roly-poly woman with a broad smile and in full uniform, with a white bonnet, and white apron over a black dress. The caption says, "*The Rabins' cook Gemma surveys the groaning board before the guests arrive.*" I look closely at the woman. She appears to be maybe forty, which means she was probably only thirty at the time, solidly built like me, but even in an over-one-hundred-year-old photo, and a copy at that, I can sense something of a twinkle in her eye. She's looking at the buffet with pride; she has the air of someone who loves what she does. I put it aside, and turn back to the book. Flipping the pages with one thumb, I can see that it is full of notes and entries, lists, and recipes.

"Well, well, Gemma. Very nice to meet you," I say to the book. My thumb catches and the book falls open to a page near the end.

"*It was very nice to meet you as well.*" The first line jumps out at me, and I drop the page as if it has bitten me. Maybe I have a concussion after all? I lean forward and look back at the page, continuing to read. "*I said to the gentleman, and handed him a small basket of scones for his journey. It was very pleasant to have someone of his stature take the time to come see me in my little hovel and express such a delight with the fare during his visit.*"

I laugh nervously. Not crazy, just the victim of coincidence. "Careful there, Gemma, Schatzi barely acknowledges my existence, and I have no one else to talk to, so you might not want to start a conversation with me!" I turn to another page.

"*Conversation with a new girl is either enormously tedious or exceptionally pleasant.*"

Holy shit. I keep reading.

"*The new housemaid seems sweet enough, if her cleaning is as charming as her chatter, she shall be a most welcome addition to our little family downstairs."*

Whew again. Although, very weird. I decide perhaps I should stop talking to this Gemma book, and maybe eat something. That one chicken leg wasn't exactly substantial, and I've had an emotionally and physically draining morning. I wander into the pantry and grab a can of beef vegetable soup, dump the contents into a bowl, and throw it in the microwave, snapping the other leg off of the chicken and gnawing on it cold while the soup heats up. I can't figure out if today is auspicious or suspicious, but maybe a good lunch will put me right, and I can go downstairs with my head on straight and really get to work. And since I have to admit to the smallest bit of loneliness, maybe this Gemma will keep me company tonight.

9

I'm starting to get a complex. On Monday and Tuesday I went to the Albany Park Workers' Center to pick up a day laborer to help me do demo in the basement. Not only did I not get anyone to agree to come with me, but on both days I had to look at stupid smug Liam filling his garish truck with eager workers. Every time he shrugged and winked at me on his way out of the lot. On Wednesday and Thursday I did what no self-respecting general contractor does, and hit the Home Depot. Where I explained in my broken Spanish what I needed done and what I could afford to pay, over and over, I was denied. On both days I noticed a slight, elegant man in a perfectly wound navy blue turban watching the proceedings. Figuring that he too was in need of some assistance and not getting any, I would smile at him, and he would look at me expectantly, and I would head out alone.

This morning I'm desperate. Not only have I lost two hours of work a day for no reason trying to get help, but the demo is also going painfully slowly. Usually for a job this size I would bring in a four-man crew. Two focused on destruction, two filling large rubber garbage cans with debris and getting it into the huge Dumpster I've rented. This whole week has been a painstakingly slow process of gradually pulling down old plaster on one wall at a time, and then filling and lugging the can, which I can only fill halfway each trip with the heavy old plaster, otherwise I can't lift it up to empty it into the Dumpster. If I don't find some affordable help soon, my whole timeline is going to take a beating. Not to mention my body. I'm used to hard labor, it makes me feel alive, but I'm bumping smack into the limits of my physical abilities, and ending every day with barely enough energy to walk Schatzi around the neighborhood. I collapse every night onto my sad little air mattress, muscles aching in ways that ibuprofen can't touch. And every morning I roll out of bed onto the floor, where my morning stretching isn't just a way to start the day, but necessary if I intend to actually walk upright and get to the bathroom.

I was going to just skip the whole charade today, but I asked Gemma what to do and the journal said, *"Perhaps the fifth time will be the charm."* Of course, Gemma was telling the housemaid Charity why she wasn't discouraged when the fourth honey cake in a row fell in the center and had to be restarted, but her unflappable nature inspires me, and the resignation to simply do what needs to be done seems the best way to tackle my current problems. Gemma didn't have a choice. It was Passover, people were coming to dinner, the Rabins didn't care if the unexpectedly warm and humid April weather was making the flour damp, or the coal stove temperamental. All they wanted was a honey cake, and it was Gemma's job to provide one. Preferably one that didn't sag in the middle like a broken-down horse. I have to build this house and I really can't manage it alone, so I don't have a choice either.

I pull my truck back into Home Depot for one last try. Sometimes on a Friday you can get a guy who doesn't want to take on something that could cut too much into his weekend. It isn't like I need some highly skilled professional; I just need a little bit of muscle. I get out of my truck and head over to where there is a small gaggle of men standing around smoking and drinking coffee out of take-out cups, stamping their feet to keep warm. It oddly looks like an AA meeting has recently let out. I recognize some of the guys from yesterday, mostly by the way they look at me and laugh. I approach a couple of new ones and begin my spiel, but they wave me off. As my one last shot walks away from me, I notice my turbaned friend again standing off to the side, and I give him the nod that says, "A tough week for us both."

He walks over to me. "Are you looking for help with something?" he asks in a shockingly smooth and elegant English accent.

"I am. I have a massive basement demolition project and an insanely small budget, so I'm not having any luck. How about you?"

"I'm here to find some work. Perhaps I might be of assistance with your project?"

I'm shocked. It never occurred to me that he was here looking for a job. I can't help but look him up and down. He is tall, but slim, and doesn't look terribly powerful.

He smiles at me. "I'm stronger than I look. And I work cheap."

I grin back at him. "I'm Anneke. What's your name?"

"Lovely to meet you, Anneke. I'm Jagjeet Singh, my friends call me Jag."

"I can only pay ten dollars an hour." I'm sheepish about this. When I was with MacMurphy I usually paid between twenty and thirty dollars an hour depending on what I needed done. But those carefree budgetary days are over.

"That is fine. I'd be delighted to come work with you today, Anneke."

"Jag? You are a lifesaver."

"I might say the same of you."

"Do you have a car or do you want to ride with me?"

"I have a car, but I'll follow you."

"I'm the old turquoise truck, I'll go slow." I head for my truck, and I think maybe, just maybe, this week is salvageable after all.

Jag, I'm going to make some lunch. Can I make some for you too?"

"Thank you, Anneke, but I've brought my own lunch. If I could trouble you for a microwave, it would be better if I heated it up a bit."

"Come on upstairs."

It's been a good morning. Jag may be skinny, but he is wiry and actually very strong. He made short work of getting all the plaster I'd already pulled off into the Dumpster, and then began working on another wall across from me. He clearly knows what he's doing; he's careful to check for electrical and plumbing runs before starting.

He follows me up the back stairs, and I take him into the kitchen. Schatzi wanders over to check him out, and he drops to one knee, muttering to her in a language I don't recognize.

"That's Schatzi."

"Fräulein," he says, and switches his endearments to what sounds like flawless German. In moments, she is on her back letting him rub her pale gray belly, wiggling in delight. Stupid dog. Last night when I tried to pet her she nipped me. We've been living like roommates that hate each other. She spends most of her time curled up in the front turret window seat, coming to the kitchen to get fed. Our first night I'd set up her plush little dog bed in my bedroom, and in the morning discovered she had dragged it out into the hallway while I was asleep, and there it has stayed. We take a longish walk in the morning; she gets let out at lunch into the yard so she can go to the bathroom, and then another longish walk after dinner. Other than these bits of contact, we don't really spend any time together.

I never minded her indifference when I was living with

Grant, but I'm not going to pretend that it wouldn't be nice to have the littlest bit of warmth from her now that it is just we two in this dilapidated house. Grant may not have wanted to jump my bones every minute, or even every other week, or every other month for that matter, but he was very physically affectionate. We cuddled. We held hands. We kissed. He rubbed my feet and my shoulders, and we slept like spoons. He made up for everything I missed growing up, every scraped knee that didn't get kissed, every mean girl insult that didn't get soothed, every disappointment that I had to comfort myself. I didn't know how starved I would be for contact, and I find myself weirdly jealous of the dog, who is grunting happily under Jag's ministrations.

He finishes playing with the dog, stands and looks around the kitchen, and whistles under his breath.

"Anneke, this is spectacular. Your clients must be very good cooks to want a special kitchen like this. I've never seen one like it. May I ask, who is the architect?"

I grin ear to ear. "I am."

"You're very talented. Is this Poggenpohl?" he says, caressing a cabinet reverently with long fingers, sliding a slim drawer open to reveal the knife rack within, pushing it closed with the slightest touch. I'm impressed. The high-end cabinetry company is simply a cut above, famous for both clean lines and an enormous range of organizational details. When Grant and I did the kitchen at our—I mean HIS—apartment, I turned him on to their stuff, and he was so impressed with both the look and the function that he insisted we use them again when we did this place. It was a huge investment on his part, and I thank god we did the kitchen first, since it will be a great selling feature and I would never have been able to afford it now.

"Yes, it is, you have a good eye. A lot of people don't recognize their stuff."

"You can't mistake their lines or their finishes, or attention to detail. It would be like not recognizing a Rolls-Royce when it drives by you. Your clients have good taste. And are very lucky. This is a kitchen that will make a passionate cook enormously happy."

"No clients. I'm doing it on spec."

"Wow. That is a huge undertaking. And you're doing it all yourself?"

"As it turns out, yes, unfortunately."

"And can I be so bold to ask if you perhaps might need someone more regularly than just the occasional help for a day?"

"I do, but I can't really afford more than what I'm paying you."

"I've been at Home Depot every day for three weeks. You're the first person to hire me. Frankly, you're the first person to speak to me. If perhaps you aren't disappointed with my work, I would be happy to simply come here every day and do good work with you instead of standing in the cold while the other workers call me 'terrorista,'" he says with a wry smile, washing his hands in the kitchen sink, his even, white teeth shining behind his dark beard, which had been lustrous and shiny this morning, and is now matte and pale with plaster dust.

I laugh. "Yeah, I'm fairly sure those guys don't know from Sikh. They see a turban and jump to conclusions."

He turns and looks at me. "And how did you know I was Sikh?"

"Your last name is Singh. The style of your turban. I have a friend who is an interior designer, and her rug guy is Sikh. His last name is Singh too."

"How rare that I don't have to explain."

"You do have to explain why you would want to come work with me for so little money. You're clearly a worldly and educated fellow, not the kind of guy one usually finds hustling for day labor in a parking lot." He doesn't have any of the telltale signs of substance abuse, and I'm hard-pressed to imagine that he isn't qualified to do a range of normal jobs.

He walks over to the microwave and puts a large Tupperware container in it. "Let's see. I was born in India and my family moved to London when I was a boy. My father is in the diplomatic corps. I did a degree in London in industrial engineering, and worked there for a large firm for a few years, and then came here to do a graduate degree at Northwestern. I'm supposed to become a PhD and then either a well-published academic or a wealthy engineer, preferably quickly here where the money can flow and then back in London near my family. But to be honest? What I really love is projects like this. Working with my hands. Building houses."

My heart falls. He's a student. I've worked with them before. They're notoriously eager at first, but then the pressure of school gets to them, or they have to start missing big chunks of time to work on papers or projects.

Then he says the magic words. "So I quit. Actually it was strongly suggested to me that perhaps the rigors of the program weren't a good fit for my skills. So essentially I quit before they kicked me out."

"Ouch."

He laughs. "Yeah. Sort of embarrassing. So now I'm thirty-three, slowly running through my savings, and my student visa now officially has an expiration date. My parents don't know I'm not in school anymore, and my big plans of getting hired by a local construction company dried up quickly, so I'm beginning to despair of shifting my visa from student to work."

"You're overqualified AND underqualified," I say, knowing exactly how a résumé like his would have been received at MacMurphy.

"Exactly." He opens the microwave and retrieves his lunch, now unbelievably fragrant, filling the kitchen with the scent of spices. "I have too much education and experience on the engineering side, and no practical experience beyond helping friends with home improvement projects on the build side. I don't have enough residential architecture design background, and no experience at all with client relations. But because of my education, no one wanted to hire me as a laborer either."

"And you'd really want to work with me for a pittance?"

"I'd look at it as a paid apprenticeship. If I want to really get into this business as a career, I have to get practical hands-on experience. And you certainly look like you could use an extra pair of hands. I'm very good with electrical work, obviously, and plumbing, and of course structural stuff. I've never done detail finish work, but I'm good at simple carpentry, and I'm a quick study. Perhaps a trial period? A week or so to see if it is a good fit?"

I look at his open face, his furrowed brow. I think about the daunting nature of this house and everything that has to be done. I think about Joe, patiently teaching me every aspect of bringing a house to life. He'd like this intelligent, soft-spoken man. Besides, his visa will expire soon, it's not like I'm committing too much, timewise. Maybe a few weeks of some competent help could get me over a hump here, give me more time to come up with a plan, find someone else. And my gut says he is trustworthy. Of course my gut also told me that I should marry Grant, and that I should eat that massive cheesesteak and onion rings for lunch yesterday, so it isn't exactly foolproof, but it's all I have. If nothing else it will get Caroline and Hedy off my back; they've been scared that I'll hire some serial rapist axe murderer who will keep me prisoner here. Caroline and Hedy watch a lot of *Law & Order: SVU* and *Criminal Minds* and such. They think there is a serial rapist axe murderer around every corner.

"A week it is. If it works, we'll figure out something."

He smiles. "Wonderful. I shall not let you down, Miss Anneke."

"Just Anneke is fine, Jag." I go to the fridge and take out the remains of last night's dinner . . . Kraft Macaroni & Cheese with tuna and frozen peas mixed in. I grab a fork and eat it cold out of the container. This used to be one of my favorites, salty orange pasta, sweet little pops of peas, little meaty chunks of tuna. But three years with Grant has clearly had an effect on my palate. The noodles are gummy, not al dente, and the tuna is overly fishy. Grant got me turned on to good Spanish tuna packed in olive oil; this cheap Costco stuff in the water tastes vaguely like cat food. But I can't think about that right now; it's fuel and it's in the budget.

We pass a lovely half an hour eating and resting, and getting to know each other a little bit, and then head back downstairs to keep working. By the end of the day I already know that I don't need a week, I really want Jag to keep working with me. He's smart and funny, but also a strong worker. Good company, but not overly chatty or inquisitive. I fall easily into teacher mode, channeling the way Joe would casually chat about what he was doing and why while he worked. Jag asks good questions, but not so many of them that it slows us down, and by the end of the day we've accomplished more together than I was able to do on my own in the past four days combined.

"Thank you, it was a great day," I say, handing him a wad of bills for his work. He receives it, doesn't count it, and puts it right in his pocket. Very classy.

"I had a very good time, and look forward to seeing you again tomorrow."

I'm shocked. "You know tomorrow is Saturday."

"Are you planning on working tomorrow?" he asks.

"Yes," I admit. I caved in and said yes to dinner plans with the girls, despite the fact that I really don't want to see them, but want to get a good workday in before.

"Then I will be here. Shall we say eight?"

"Sounds great. Thanks for all your work today."

He bows to me very formally, and then leaves.

I head upstairs to my bathroom, where the sad little trickle of water the shower provides does little to alleviate the stress in my shoulders. But it is enough to get me clean, which is more important, since after a full day I am covered in a gritty layer of dirt and smell more than a little bit ripe.

I get dressed, and head downstairs to figure out what to do for dinner. Lunch was deeply unsatisfying, and I'm already getting pretty sick of my rotation of processed-food salt-bombs. Dinnertime is always when I'm most angry with Grant. I haven't figured out if I'm more pissed off that he ruined my taste buds with all his deliciousness and fabulous ingredients, or that his wandering wiener means that he won't ever cook for me again. All I know is that until I met him, I ate the same stuff I'm eating now without a problem, and now that he's gone, none of it tastes right or makes me happy.

I spot Gemma's journal on the counter and flip it open. It lands on a page, and I look at the entry.

"When nothing else seems to suffice to tempt her to eat, I know that it is time to make rice soubise."

Hmm. I wonder who isn't eating? I keep going.

"She's a picky little thing, especially when she's pouting and feeling sorry for herself, and often says she hates everything I have available to her in the kitchen."

Certainly sounds like a girl after my own heart.

"But the moment the onions begin to melt into the butter, it softens her heart and she changes her mind."

I wonder. I have butter. I have onions. I have rice. I look down the page to the recipe. It looks simple enough, a sort of casserole of onions and rice with cream and cheese. How hard could that be? I even have a brick of cheese that will probably work. The only thing I don't have is cream, but there is a convenience store that Schatzi and I pass on our walks; they would have some. Suddenly I'm feeling motivated. I get up and pull on my boots and coat, and call for Schatzi, who is carefully grooming herself in the corner. I pull her leash off the door handle and attach it. In fifteen minutes we are back home with a pint of heavy cream.

I look over the recipe again. It sounds very simple. You boil some rice in water like pasta, I can do that. You cook some onions in butter, stir in the rice, pop it in the oven. Add some cream and grated cheese and mix it up. And voila! A real dinner.

I pull out a couple of the pots Caroline gave me, and begin to get everything laid out. Grant always yammered on about mise en place, that habit of getting all your stuff together before you start cooking so you can be organized. It seems to make sense, and appeals to the part of me that likes to make lists and check things off of them.

I manage to chop a pile of onions without cutting myself, but with a lot of tears. At one point I walk over to the huge freezer and stick my head in it for some relief, while Schatzi looks at me like I'm an idiot. Which isn't unusual. Or even, come to think of it, wrong. But I get them sliced and chopped, albeit unevenly, and put them in the large pot with some butter. I get some water boiling in the other pot and put in some rice. I cook it for a few minutes, drain it, and add it to the onions, stirring them all together. Then I put the lid on the pot and put it in the oven, and set my phone with an alarm for thirty-five minutes. The kitchen smells amazing. Nothing quite like onions cooked in butter to make the heart happy. While it cooks, I grab a beer, and grate some Swiss cheese into a pile. When my phone buzzes, I pull the pot out of the oven and put it back on the stovetop, stirring in the cream and cheese, and sprinkling in some salt and pepper.

I grab a bowl and fill it with the richly scented mixture. I stand right there at the counter, and gingerly take a spoonful. It's amazing. Rich and creamy and oniony. The rice is nicely cooked, not mushy. And even though some of my badly cut onions make for some awkward eating moments, as the strings slide out of the spoon and attach themselves to my chin, the flavor is spectacular. Simple and comforting, and utterly delicious. The bitter beer cuts through it and is the perfect thing. I finish the bowl and dish up another. I'm halfway through dialing Grant's number to tell him of my kitchen triumph when I remember where I am and why I'm even experimenting with cooking at all, and hang up.

"I'd give you some, you horrible dog, except onions would make you sick, and while I love the idea of your discomfort, I wouldn't want to have to clean up after you," I say cheerfully to Schatzi, who has wandered over to see what smells so good.

I eat half the pot, and put the rest in the fridge for lunch tomorrow, feeling absolutely swelled up with pride.

"Thanks, Gemma, I really needed that," I say to the book, glancing down at the bottom of the recipe.

"*You're welcome*," it says, startling me again with how much it seems to feel like Gemma is speaking to me directly. "*I said to my poor girl, knowing that she doesn't mean to be difficult. She gave me a big hug and then ran back upstairs to join her family for dessert. I worry about her sometimes, but I think I believe in my heart she will be okay.*"

"I hope so, Gemma, I really hope so."

10

The buzzer rings just as I'm slipping my shoes on. I check my watch, it's only six thirty and Hedy isn't supposed to pick me up till seven, but maybe she's early. Being up on the third floor with no intercom system is a huge pain in the ass. I have to run from the back bedroom down the long hallway to the front bedroom and wrench open the window to yell down like a fishwife to see who is at the door.

I make the trek, open the window, and get slammed in the face with a flurry of snow for my trouble. I lean over and see the top of a head covered in a hot pink hat with a pompom on top.

"Hello?" I shout down against the wind, using my hand to push the snow off of the windowsill in hopes that it will stop blowing in at me.

A face turns up to look at me; she looks like some little girl. It can't possibly be Girl Scout Cookie season yet, but if this industrious kid is getting a jump on things, I'm going to order a dozen boxes to support her. Plus I could use a thin mint or forty.

"Hi, are you Anneke?" the girl yells up at me.

This stops me cold. Who the hell is this kid, and who sent her? "Stay there."

I grab my purse and head downstairs, wondering exactly what's going on. I take a deep breath and open the door. In person, the little girl turns out to be not so little. She's probably at least in high school, and has a good four inches on me. I look up at her peaches-and-cream complexion, pinkened in the cold, wide blue eyes fringed with barely there blond lashes, golden bangs held down over her forehead by the ridiculous pink hat, which up close turns out to have pale pink polka dots in addition to the fuzzy pompom on top. She is grinning at me like a crazy person, making twin dimples in her cheeks. She is staggeringly beautiful, in that natural and unfussy way that is impossible to achieve for mere mortals. I can't see a lick of makeup on her, and yet she is flawless.

"Anneke? I'm Emily!" she says, smiling wider, if such a thing is possible, with so much excitement in her voice that I'm afraid she might pass out. She sees the blank look on my face. "Emily Walsh!"

"Okay. Do I know you?"

"I'm Emily WALSH," she enunciates.

Now I think she might be lightly damaged in some way.

"That's lovely, I'm sure. What can I do for you?"

She shivers fetchingly, Cupid's bow lips starting to turn the littlest bit purple in the cold. "Can I come in?"

I consider for a moment. She's tall, but the skinny jeans show that there's nothing to her; she might have four inches on me, but I have at least sixty pounds on her. I can take her. And I'm pretty sure her lurid orange puffer coat doesn't conceal any deadly weapons. "Sure." I step aside and let her come in.

She follows me through the vestibule and into the front parlor. Schatzi comes clicking down the stairs to see what is going on.

"Oh, hel-LO, you pretty thing! Who is a cute doggie? Who?" Emily kneels down.

"She doesn't really like people," I warn, just as Schatzi walks right up to this colt of a girl and LEAPS INTO HER ARMS, snuggling under her chin, biting her ponytail. Perfect.

"Oh, you like me, don't you, you precious darling." Emily cuddles the dog and stands up in one fluid motion. "What's her name?"

"Schatzi," I say, stunned.

"Schatzi, you are a pretty girl, yes you are." Emily is clearly light on the whole brain-cell thing, since apparently her purpose in coming here is eluding her now that she has met the damn dog.

"So, Emily Walsh, why are you here?"

She puts the dog down. "Well, I graduated a semester early, and figured I would take some time off before I start grad school in the fall, so I thought I'd do kind of a cross-country adventure, and I've never been to Chicago, and even though everyone thought I was insane to come here in the winter, one of the girls from my sorority lives here now and said I could come stay at her place, and I thought it would be good for you and me to spend some time together and hang out for a while, and Chicago is so awesome, even in the winter, and it gave me a chance to buy some cool winter duds for the first time, my dad called it an epic shopportunity, and I'll need all this stuff anyway when I get to Boston in the fall." This comes out in one breathy expanse of a sentence, eyebrows raised at me in all sorts of expectation of my delight.

"I see. Well, that is a tremendous amount of information."

She looks at me and then smiles even wider, her dimples threatening to become black holes of happy. And she throws her arms around me, hugging me so tight I can barely breathe. "I'm SO HAPPY TO FINALLY MEET YOU!"

My instinct kicks in and both of my hands reach up and break her embrace, pushing her forcefully away from me.

"EMILY. WHO. THE. FUCK. ARE. YOU?"

Her face falls for a second, and then the smile returns. "Emily WALSH, silly. I'm your sister!"

"The fuck you are."

"No, I am, I'm Emily Walsh!"

"You seem very clear on that. But I have no idea who you are, Emily Walsh, and I sure as hell don't have a sister."

"Well, stepsister, technically, Andrew Walsh is my dad." She laughs as if I have said the silliest possible thing.

"Who is that?"

Now she looks confused. "You're Anneke Stroudt."

Good lord, this kid is down a quart in the brain-cell department. "Yes. And before you say it again, you are Emily Walsh, daughter of Andrew. But that doesn't mean anything to me."

"Your mom is Anneliese. She was married to my dad."

Oh. God. "Oh. Well. Yes, she is, but we aren't really in touch. Sorry. Never heard of you or your dad."

She looks confused. "She never mentioned us?"

"Not ever."

Now she looks crestfallen. "Oh. GOD! You must think I'm an insane person!"

"Pretty much."

She shakes her head. And reaches her hand out. "Hi. I'm Emily. I'm your former stepsister. And not insane, but very embarrassed."

I look at her hand, but somehow I can't bring myself to shake it.

"Well, Emily, this has been deeply weird, but I have someone picking me up for dinner in about ten minutes, so whatever it is you want, I need you to spit it out, if you can manage that."

"Oh, yeah, right, well, um, since you don't know who I am it is going to be weirder, but your mom was married to my dad for like five years when I was little after my mom died, and she was just amazing and such a good mom to me, and my dad loved her so much and then one day she was just gone and it totally broke my dad, but I just have always missed her and I was always so sad you never came to Florida to visit us, because my real mom always promised me a sister someday but when she thought she was pregnant it turned out to be the cancer, and anyway, I just thought since I have this free time I could come and meet you, because family is really important to me, I'm going to be a family therapist someday, and it's never too late to have a sister!"

I hold my hand up. "I'm going to stop you right there, and not just because you are sucking all of the available oxygen out of the room. I'm sorry my mom did a runner on you and your dad, it's just what she does, not your fault. I'm sure there are enough former stepkids floating around to start a Facebook group or something. But I have neither time nor inclination to help any of the broken birds she's left in her wake figure their shit out. If you have stuff you want to deal with, I get that, but it doesn't include me. Anneliese is in Scottsdale. Maybe you have a sorority sister there who can put you up if you want to go deal with her."

She tilts her head at me and furrows her brow, her cornflower blue eyes filled with empathy. "She really hurt you too, huh?"

"Yeah. Whatever." I check my watch. "Time to go, Emily Walsh, I've got plans. Sorry I couldn't help you."

"I'm sorry, I know this is a lot, it isn't at all how I expected this to go. You need time to get your head around it, I mean, you didn't even know I existed and here I am and I'm just saying Emily Walsh at you over and over like some freak show! You go have a great time tonight, and I'll come back, maybe like, Thursday? Give you a couple of days to just process, and maybe conceptualize me or whatever. Do you like coffee? We could go for coffee. Maybe we can take Schatzi for a walk and we can just talk, okay? So like, maybe three-ish on Thursday? Bye, Schatzi! See you Thursday." She starts to come at me for another hug but steps back. I'm stuck like lead to where I am standing.

"Um, no, really, I, um . . ." I cannot formulate words.

"Okay, then, no hugging yet, I get it, it's cool." She reaches out and squeezes my shoulder. "I'll see you Thursday." And she

leans down and pets Schatzi. "See you Thursday, sweetheart."
And then she pulls on a pair of knitted mittens that honest to
god have little mice eating cheese embroidered on them, and
fairly skips out the front door and is gone.

I take a deep breath and reach for my phone.

"I'm almost there," Hedy says when she answers.

"I'm thinking I might not be up for it tonight." Snippets of
things that Emily said in her barrage of information are subtly
registering in my addled brain one by one. "*She was such a good
mom to me. I'm your sister! We were so sad you never came to
visit.*" Each one a delayed punch in the gut.

"Nonsense. You have to eat. And you have to get out of that
house sometimes. Be there in five." And then she hangs up on me.

I've never been good at getting out of things. I'm a bad liar,
my tongue gets tied up, and whatever fib I've practiced invariably is the wrong one. I once told Caroline I was coming down
with a cold in order to avoid a ladies' luncheon with some guest
speaker I didn't care about, and she showed up that afternoon
with soup. At the Palmer Square house, where she figured I
was when I wasn't AT HOME IN BED. She said she didn't care
and that I hadn't missed anything, the speaker was boring, but
I know she was hurt that I both blew her off and lied to her.

Hedy says you always have to pull the diarrhea card. "Something I ate" is something we all relate to, and no one wants to
be near it. Which is great, except you can't use that with Hedy
because she knows you're faking. Marie, ever the Pollyanna,
says that you should just suck it up and go to things because
invariably you'll have a great time in spite of yourself. Which
I'm sure Marie does. I only even said yes to tonight because I've
been really blowing them all off, and I knew if I didn't agree to
this one, they'd just plan some sort of tedious intervention or
something.

"*I'm your sister! I'll come back Thursday!*" Good grief. That overgrown cheerleader can come back Thursday all she wants. I won't be here. I got a call from one of the stonemasons I used to work with on MacMurphy projects who is doing a job in the Gold Coast, and it has some amazing marble that they want ripped out, and he knew I'd want the salvage. I have to pay him and his guys, which wasn't exactly in the budget, but the stone is spectacular and if we can remove it without damaging it, it will make for some wonderful details around this place.

The buzzer makes me jump, it is shrill and insanely loud, and I make a mental note to find a new one sooner rather than later.

Hedy whisks herself into the house in a swirl of snow. She's wearing the most spectacular floor-length black leather coat, fitted at the top with a set of diagonal buttons that almost look military, and then swooping to her ankles. I love that coat. It's lined in mink. It's the tiniest bit like *The Matrix* meets Chanel. But I can't pull off a look like that; I'm too squat, it would make me look like a leather club chair. She kisses me on the cheek.

"Get your coat, lady, we're meeting the girls at Sumi Robata." I must have blanched or looked panicked, because she quickly adds, "My treat. Just signed a massive new client. We're celebrating."

Sumi is one of our favorite restaurants, a traditional Japanese robata grill place with just insanely delicious food. All small plates, which we love. We just sit and keep ordering until we want to burst. The food is clean and simple but gorgeous. And worth every penny. When one has pennies to spare. But there is a difference between a good value and not expensive. As Grant used to say, the French Laundry is a good value, but you might have to hock a lung to afford it. I never used to think twice about Sumi, where by the time you order a zillion dishes and a few beers to wash it down you might be out a hundred dollars or more per person. But that is more than my current weekly food budget these days.

I grab my coat, and we head out.

"So, what is it?"

"What is what?"

"Whatever you've got happening in your life that has given you this deer-in-headlights look and made you try to blow us off. You're really bad at that, by the way, you know that right?"

"I know. I'm just tired."

"Bullshit."

"And stressed."

"Better."

"And apparently I have a sister."

"Come again?"

"Just before you came. Some little picketytwick of a girl showed up at my doorstep looking for a family reunion. Some discarded stepdaughter Anneliese left behind a decade ago who wants to bond with me."

Hedy is silent and contemplative. "Well, if she's a step, she can't be looking for a kidney or bone marrow or anything."

"She can be looking for whatever she wants, she won't find it here."

"How'd she even track you down?"

"I'm listed."

Hedy shakes her head and clucks. "Have I taught you nothing, dearheart?" She reaches over and pats my hand. "Unlist yourself tomorrow. Who knows what other victims of your mother are out in the world who might find you?" She is smirking as if she has said something clever.

Her condescension is really annoying. I love Hedy, but her tone is always authoritative, and at the moment, it grates on me.

Walter drops us off at the corner of Wells and Huron and we

head inside, greeted warmly by Gene, the chef, as we pass by the open kitchen and toward the table in the back where Caroline and Marie are waving at us.

We order a round of a Japanese chocolate stout, a perfect beer for the food, and the first set of dishes.

"Little Anneke has a long-lost sister," Hedy says, after we clink our beer glasses.

I shoot her a look. I'd told her about Emily in something of self-defense, but I didn't really want to talk about it. She shrugs.

"What is she talking about?" Marie asks.

I take a deep draught of my beer, and tell them about Emily and our little encounter.

"So she just wants to get to know you?" Caroline asks.

"I guess."

"But you don't want to?" Marie pipes in.

"Why would I want to?"

"Why wouldn't you?" Marie asks gently. "I mean, you said you hoped when your mom married Joe they would have a baby. That you could have a little sister or brother."

"I was thirteen. I also wanted to marry Adam Ant, and grow up to be an archeologist so I could meet Indiana Jones."

"Okay, but what is so awful about her?" Caroline asks. She gets that blood family can be complicated, so I know she'll understand.

"She's maybe twenty-one. She's perky and pretty and full of life. Frankly she's like a fucking Labrador puppy. She did everything but lick my face and pee on the floor. She may say she wants a sister, but seriously, this has got to be about Anneliese. She said my mom was a good mom to her, and I bet she was. This girl freakishly LOOKS like my mother, all blond and blue-eyed and willowy. She's gorgeous. I'm sure my mother petted her and doted on her and dressed her up like a little doll. Whatever. I don't have time or inclination to babysit some innocent who thinks that if she befriends me she'll get her perfect mommy back."

None of them say anything.

"What?" Great. Judgment time.

The waiter comes by and places a hot stone in the middle of the table, and a plate of thinly sliced marinated New York strip, and Hedy immediately lays two slices of beef on the rock, where they sizzle and release a heady aroma.

"It just seems to me that maybe it might be worth just meeting with her once and getting a better sense of her before you dismiss the idea outright," Caroline says.

"I'm sure she was just full of nervous energy; maybe if you see her again she'll be calmer, and better able to articulate why exactly she is seeking you out," Marie adds.

"You can always decide not to see her again if she turns out to be a basket case." Hedy pulls the two pieces of meat off, placing one on my plate and one on hers, and two more pieces on the rock.

I stab the meat with my chopsticks and bring it up to my chin, promptly dropping it into my lap. Hedy chuckles under her breath as I fetch the morsel from my pants and pop it in my mouth with my fingers. A little linty but still delicious.

"Why bother?" I say around the mouthful of tender beef. "What do I need it for? I mean, maybe if we were the same age or something, or if she were moving here permanently and wanted a connection in the city, MAYBE. But this is a Millennial on a gap year. She's maybe here for a couple of weeks. She's moving to Boston to be a family therapist! To solve the problems of the world's sorority girls!"

"Maybe she is. Or maybe she isn't. What does it hurt to find out?" Marie pulls her own piece of beef off the stone and places it delicately into her mouth.

"Exactly. Give her a couple of hours and see what she's really about." Caroline pulls the last piece of beef off the rock just as the waiter arrives with a plate of pot stickers connected with a lacy web of crunchy yumminess.

"Because what else have I got to do?"

Hedy narrows her eyes at me. "Because what have you got to LOSE."

"My time. My energy. It isn't at quite the premium pricing it once was, but it isn't without value. I have enough going on right now, placating some bored little rich girl isn't top on my list." I know I'm being petulant, but for some reason I just can't help it.

"You'll do what feels best in the moment. And it all just happened, so maybe we should just talk about something else and let you process." Marie, who knows me better than anyone, can tell when I've hit my limit, and as annoyed as I am at her siding with Caroline and Hedy, I am still grateful for the save.

"How are things going at the house?" Caroline asks, acquiescing to the shift in topic.

"Good. I've got some help for the moment, so that is making things go much easier."

"You finally convinced someone to come work with you? Magic!" Hedy says.

"Yeah, no kidding. Anyway, he's very cool, actually has a degree in industrial engineering, hard worker, really nice guy. And willing to work for what I can afford, which is even more amazing."

"So what's wrong with him? Ex-con? Substance abuse? On the lam?" Marie jokes.

"He's not a citizen. Visa expiring."

"I suppose that's better than no visa at all," Caroline says. When she and Carl moved to the burbs, she thought she would have to get a new cleaning lady, and hated to lose Blanca. But Blanca was afraid to ride the Metra that far; there had been rumors of immigration doing roundups at some of the suburban train stations. So Caroline decided there must be a reason to have her newfound financial wherewithal and immediately bought Blanca a Prius and hired an immigration attorney. Blanca now has social security, an IRA, and a green card, and Caroline's house is spotless.

"True. And he is just a laborer, so I'll keep him as long as I can, and deal with the rest as it comes."

"Very Zen of you," Hedy says.

"Namaste, bitches." I raise my beer to the girls, delighted that for now at least, everything can just have a semblance of our regular banter.

"So guess what famous musician slash actor John just did a tattoo for? One hint . . . he's in my five!" Marie says excitedly.

And thankfully the focus turns away from me and onto Marie's crush's new ink, and Hedy's new big client, and Caroline's new recipe for lamb stew, and plate after plate of yummy nibbles, and for an hour or so, I can almost feel normal.

11

I wake up feeling extra achy and uncomfortable and discover that my air mattress has deflated in the night, leaving me in a pile of linens and crumpled rubber on the hard floor. I fill it back up, but can hear a small hissing noise that indicates I have a leak somewhere. But after fifteen minutes examining it, duct tape at the ready, I can't find it, and give up. Perhaps I shouldn't have bought the off-brand one that was on clearance. I'll have to bite the bullet and get a new one.

When Schatzi and I get back from her morning walk, a bitter wind having kept it very perfunctory, I find a deliveryman on the stoop.

"Anne, um, Anne . . ." he struggles, looking at the slip in his hand.

Sigh. "Anneke. That's me." Family tradition, every firstborn daughter given an unpronounceable gift. When I was six, I begged Grand-mère to just call me Anne, and it was made very clear to me to never make that particular request again. But by the time I got to high school, I kind of liked it. And when I met Marie at camp, one of the first things she told me was how much she loved my name. "*It's exotic and mysterious and romantic*," she sighed. She said my name like it was a little poem or prayer or a delicious sweet. She made me love it, and I've never tried to be anything or anyone else since.

He looks relieved. "Sign here." He points. I sign. He hands over a large box, covered in brown paper.

Inside, I put the box on my table, and rip open the paper. It is a lovely plant display, the kind I like best, full of greenery and succulents and mosses, and interesting shapes, planted in a deep pottery saucer. I've never been one for girly bouquet flowers, foofy colors and dead in three days in a vase swamp of stinky slime, but an arrangement like this, one that can survive if you water and feed it, with cool plants that I love, this is right in my sweet spot.

I pull out the card.

Thinking of you. Call if you need anything. Grant

It's the first time he's tried to contact me in a couple of weeks, and I wonder why now, and why with such a grand gesture.

I don't have to wonder long.

"How are you doing?" Hedy asks when I answer my phone.

"Fine. How are you?"

"Well, fine, but you know, I know today must be hard. How about I come take you to brunch?" She sounds very concerned.

"Nah, I've got stuff here, I'll just grab something and get to work. Jag can't come today, he has some sort of meeting, but I have plenty to do."

"Well, that's good, keep yourself busy today. What about tonight? I'll pick something up and bring it? We can stay in and eat too much and drink a really good bottle of wine?"

"Sure, sounds like fun." It actually sounds tedious, but I haven't seen her since Sumi almost two weeks ago, and even though we've spoken a couple of times, it's been a little stilted. When I got back from the salvage project last Thursday, there was a note from Emily that she was sorry she missed me, and that she would stop back by another time. She actually signed her name with the tail of the *Y* ending in a little heart. It had a small lavender card attached with her cell phone and email and Facebook and Twitter and Pinterest and Instagram information all printed in a sassy navy blue font, with a spray of cherry blossoms on the back. I sort of hope I'm dead before this generation is fully in charge of the world.

"Good. That's a plan. I'll see you around seven. Leave it all to me. And, Anneke?" She pauses. "Happy Valentine's Day, honey." And then she hangs up.

Crap.

I'd completely forgotten. Frankly I've barely left the house except to walk Schatzi since we had dinner. I've needed very few supplies, the work has been all consuming, and the weather has been horrific. One thing about the insulation of staying hunkered down, you avoid the onslaught of marketing for whatever holiday is coming up. My heart sinks. I may be a tough broad, I may not be a princessey kind of girl, I may occasionally even be something of a tomboy. But I love Valentine's Day. Or I did.

I always had pretty good Valentine's luck. Usually I had some sort of boyfriend or at least a guy I was seeing casually, and even if they weren't my soul mates, they were sweet boys who gave me chocolates and teddy bears and roses and cards and made me feel good. After Grant and I got together, he would always have me dress up and come sit at a little table in the kitchen at his restaurant, and somehow manage to make me feel cosseted and special and cared for, even while he was expediting a hundred covers of romantic fare for strangers. He would send me one-bite courses of whimsical yummy, and tiny wine pairings, and slip me love notes, and when the evening was over, we'd go home and have some sort of decadent dessert creation and there would be gifts and funny cards, and a bubble bath with champagne for two, and tender and satisfying love-making.

You can see how I might not suspect he was secretly pining for Channing Tatum. We didn't have a lot of sex, but we didn't have NO sex, and the sex we had was pretty good, as far as I was concerned. He was very interested in my pleasure, often more interested than in his own, and he was spectacular at oral sex. Apparently this is not uncommon among chefs, which makes a lot of sense when one thinks about it. So even though we had slowed down the intimate end of our relationship exponentially, it certainly wasn't some big red flag. I've never been the "have to have it right now" kind of girl anyway. I like sex fine, but if I'm to be honest, I didn't really miss it horribly on the occasions I was between partners, and have never had any that made me insane or obsessive the way people talk about. I certainly haven't missed it at all in the last few weeks.

But romance? Romance I miss. Little gestures, words of endearment, touches. I can do without passion, but I've gotten used to affection, to feeling cared for and loved. And before I know it, I'm crying again. Which really pisses me off, because romance or no romance, I'm not a wallower. All this crying bullshit is annoying the bejesus out of me. I'm an up-by-my-bootstraps, dust-myself-off, get-back-to-business broad. I wipe my cheeks, and add it to the ever-expanding list of shit I'm angry with Grant for, and head for the kitchen.

I'm starving, and I need comfort, and when I see the left-over boiled potatoes in the fridge from last night, I know just what to make. The only thing Grand-mère ever made me that felt the littlest bit like love. Grand-mère didn't really cook much. She was fastidious about her appearance, was a perfect trim size 6 from the time she was twenty till she died. She assembled salads, we always had lots of vegetables in the house "for snacking," fresh fruit. Tubs of cottage cheese. Melba toast. She would poach chicken breasts or fish. Small omelettes. I never really minded. Mealtimes were an exercise in frustration, trying to have perfect manners, to gently pat the corners of my mouth with the linen napkins, to use my knife and fork in the perfect Continental way, the fork in my left hand, and knife in my right. The stilted conversation. Meals couldn't be over soon enough, so I could get out of the stiff "good clothes" and back into jeans or sweats, to retreat to my room for homework or music or phone calls with friends. I always had a reasonably generous allowance, god forbid our public face showed anything less than being comfortably well-off, and there were plenty of convenience stores and fast-food joints close to home and school. Grand-mère never minded when friends' mothers wanted me to stay for dinner. Lord knows I was always able to amply fill my endless hunger, and by proxy, my equally ample pants.

But every once in a great while, the pull of her heritage would hit her, and Grand-mère would cook something real. I could never figure out what it was that triggered her, but I would come home from school to a glorious aroma. An *Apfelstrudel*, with paper-thin pastry wrapped around chunks of apples and nuts and raisins. The thick smoked pork chops called Kasseler ribs, braised in apple cider and served with caraway-laced sauerkraut. A rich baked dish with sausages, duck, and white beans. And hoppel poppel. A traditional German recipe handed down from her mother. I haven't even thought of it in years. But when my mom left, it was the only thing I could think to do for Joe, who was confused and heartbroken, and it was my best way to try to get something in him that didn't come in a cardboard container. I never got to learn at her knee the way many granddaughters learn to cook; she never shared the few recipes that were part of my ancestry. But hoppel poppel is fly by the seat of your pants, it doesn't need a recipe; it's a mess, just like me. It's just what the soul needs.

I grab an onion, and chop half of it. I cut up the cold cooked potatoes into chunks. I pull one of my giant hot dogs out, and cut it into thick coins. Grand-mère used ham, but Joe loved it with hot dogs, and I do too. Plus I don't have ham. I whisk six eggs in a bowl, and put some butter on to melt. The onions and potatoes go in, and while they are cooking, I grate a pile of Swiss cheese, nicking my knuckle, but catching myself before I bleed into my breakfast. By the time I get a Band-Aid on it, the onions have begun to burn a little, but I don't care. I dump in the hot dogs and hear them sizzle, turning down the heat so that I don't continue to char the onions. When the hot dogs are spitting and getting a little browned, I add the eggs and stir up the whole mess like a scramble. When the eggs are pretty much set, I sprinkle the cheese over the top and take it off the heat, letting the cheese melt while I pop three slices of bread in the toaster. When the toast is done, I butter it, and eat the whole mess at the counter, using the crispy buttered toast to scoop chunks of egg, potato, and hot dog into my mouth, strings of cheese hanging down my chin. Even with the burnt onions, and having overcooked the eggs to rubbery bits, it is exactly what I need.

Schatzi bumps my calf with her head, and I drop a piece of hot dog on the floor for her. She snarfs it up, and briefly rests a paw on my foot in thanks. I lean down to rub her head, and she gives my fingers a quick lick, and then, in case I should forget my place, she nips me sharply, then walks away. I send a small thought of thanks to Grand-mère for this one bit of happy memory, and then drink orange juice right out of the container to remind her it doesn't make up for the rest of it. I leave the dishes dirty on the counter, and head for the basement, where I can demolish something.

What's all this?" I ask, when I open the door to find Hedy, Caroline, and Marie all on my doorstep.

"GIRLS' NIGHT!" they say in unison.

"I've got the booze," Hedy says, holding up a carrier with three bottles of champagne.

"I've got the food!" Caroline is carrying a large insulated bag in each hand.

"I've got the entertainment!" Marie pipes in, holding up her DVD of *Heathers*.

"You guys are too much. You should be with your boys tonight." Poor Carl and John, left Valentine's bachelors because Grant decided he was heteroflexible.

"Carl is watching an entire season of some zombie show in surround sound and eating pizza with a twenty-five-year-old. Barolo, that is." She grins wickedly. "It's the best gift I could give him."

"John is at the shop; you'd be amazed how many couples come in for Valentine's tattoos."

"And I was going to be here anyway!" Hedy says, clearly pleased with her little plan.

"You guys are the best." I plaster a fake smile on my face. This is the last thing in the world I wanted. Hedy by herself with a bottle of wine and some takeout? Not my first choice, but manageable. I could distract her with the house, ask for her help on some design choices, keep the focus away from the shitty stuff. But now it's either going to be all "let's cheer up poor little Anneke and her sad, sad life" or some kind of tough-love "we're worried about you" lecture on how to fix myself. I'm not interested in either.

"And we're starving and cold, let us in already!" Caroline says, and I step aside to welcome my rescue party, feeling very much like a castaway who would really, deep down, rather just stay on the island in peace and not be rescued at all.

I totally forgot you didn't have a TV," Marie says, as I point to my laptop as our possible movie viewer.

"The one at the apartment was Grant's. I don't watch that much, and I can do pretty much everything on my computer or iPad. Can't run any of the media cabling yet, not till all the new walls go in."

"The place doesn't really look any different to me, what on earth are you and that boy doing here all day, hmmm?" Hedy

met Jag day before yesterday when she was in the neighborhood for a client meeting and stopped by to bring me coffee. I
was at Home Depot, so thankfully I missed the drop-in, but she
gave my coffee to Jag and did a little bonding in my absence.
She thinks he is very cute.

"Infrastructure. We're gutting the basement. And stop
twinkling at me like that, I'm not in the market."

"Well, back on the horse might not be the worst thing."
Marie smiles at us.

"Leave the poor girl alone, and give her some more bubbles." Caroline gestures at my empty juice glass. "And remind
me to bring flutes next time."

"Sorry, Martha, I haven't been doing much entertaining."
This comes out snippier than I mean it.

She looks sheepish. "Sorry. Carl has ruined me. I'm all team
'right glass for the right wine' these days."

"Well, we're all team 'any vessel that gets it to my face' ourselves," Hedy ribs her.

"Anyway, maybe we should skip the movie," Marie says.

"Yeah, much as I'm in the mood for a flick where the guys
mostly end up shot and blown up, without a couch or chairs . . ."
I wave around my empty space.

"Or a proper television," Caroline says, starting to clear the
table. She brought over insanely spectacular lasagna, a zillion layers
of paper-thin homemade pasta with a thick meaty ragù, creamy
ricotta, and traditional béchamel. It must have weighed ten pounds,
and even after the four of us attacked it like sharks hitting chum,
there is still most of it left. I watch Caroline deftly portion it into
large servings in the disposable containers she naturally brought
with her, and put one in my fridge and the rest in my freezer.

Hedy drops the empty salad bowl in the sink while Marie
stacks the dishes and snags the last piece of garlic-herb focaccia
off the plate.

"Thanks, you guys, this was awesome," I say, loading the Miele dishwasher with the detritus, always weirdly delighted at the magic silverware rack on top, each piece of flatware nestled in its own little slot. I'm determined to be outwardly grateful; I know in my heart that they mean well and they love me, and it isn't their fault that their efforts are more annoying than comforting. I'm realizing these days how much my work and having Grant insulated me from too much together time with other people. Marie is right about one thing: I'm not a social animal. We all spoke on the phone maybe once a week, and got together for a girls' night maybe once a month. Occasionally Grant and I would do a double date with one of them, or go to a party. But now that I'm all "Poor Anneke," at least one of them calls me practically every day, and they never call to just chat; it always includes some offer to get together—to be precise, to "take you out." For brunch or breakfast or lunch or coffee or dinner or a movie. And they are all really emphasizing the "take you out" part, reinforcing that they know I am broke and can't afford to do much of anything, and making sure I know when they offer to get together that they are also offering to pay, which just pisses me off more. It's like I'm not even their equal anymore, just some charity case. I miss when things were easy and we talked about television and our men and houses and jobs. When Hedy's latest conquest or Caroline's latest philanthropic effort was forefront of the more serious conversations we had.

"Well, it's not over yet," says Caroline, reaching into one of her bags and pulling out a square cake box.

"CHOCOLATE," Marie says with the reverence of a true acolyte. Marie is the biggest chocoholic any of us has ever met. She has chocolate stashed everywhere. When you go to her house, it doesn't matter if you are looking for a pen or a spatula or your keys or a tampon, you're likely to run into a candy bar first.

"Well, what else would it be?" Hedy reaches for the box and

opens it, carefully lifting out a nearly black single-layer cake, dusted prettily with confectioners' sugar. She turns to Caroline. "Did you put a freaking doily on this before you did the sugar?" She says the word *doily* like it tastes bad.

Caroline blushes prettily to the roots of her perfect ash-blond bob. "Yes. I did."

"Wow. You have doilies. My grandmother loved those things," Marie says wistfully. "She had a whole drawer of them, every size, shape, white ones and some silver ones too."

"Grand-mère loved them. When she had her turn to host her bridge games, she would put everything on them, little tea sandwiches, cookies and pastries, plates of candies."

"See, Hedy, you heathen, doilies are perfectly acceptable."

"Um, did you notice we both mentioned our GRAND-MOTHERS?" I poke her in the ribs with as much jollity as I can muster. Fake it till you make it.

"Yeah, Caro, just because you're SO MUCH older than us, doesn't mean you have to act OLD," Marie says, putting the last plate in the dishwasher.

"HA!" says Hedy, pulling out clean plates and forks.

Caroline calmly reaches into the freezer for the tub of pistachio gelato she also brought with her. "You can tease me all you like, look at the cake."

Three heads turn to look at her masterpiece. And it becomes immediately apparent that the lacy pattern of snowy sugar on the dark moist cake is actually just the thing. It looks beautiful. And celebratory. And perfect.

"Point taken," I say.

"Can we please eat it?" says Marie.

"Yeah, Nipple Girl hasn't had chocolate since the ride over," Hedy scoffs.

"One little square!" Marie says. "I barely had time for lunch today."

Caroline shakes her head and begins to cut large wedges of the cake, while Hedy scoops generous spoonfuls of gelato next to them. We retreat back to the table, where we sit in stupefied silence for the five minutes it takes to wolf down the dessert. The cake is moist and deeply chocolaty, and grown-up, not too sweet, with chunks of chocolate dotted throughout. The gelato is soft and creamy and studded with crunchy slivers of pistachio.

"Holy crap, Caroline, that is amazing," Hedy says, using one manicured finger to pick up the last couple of crumbs.

"So, so good." Marie sighs contentedly.

"Really yummy, the whole meal, thank you so much," I say.

"My pleasure. So how are you doing, really?" she asks, reveling in her maternal role.

Here it comes. "Really? I'm gonna need more cake for that."

"Way ahead of you." Hedy is already halfway to the kitchen, bringing the whole platter back with her and cutting the rest of the cake into four equal pieces, and passing them around.

"Thank god," Marie says, as if she had been worried she wouldn't get seconds.

I take a bite, and my heart smiles. It actually makes me calm, and I figure I'd better give them what they want and need or these bitches will never leave. "I'm okay. It's still kind of surreal. But what can I do? I'm just plugging along, focused on the house, getting through the days." I feel like one of those athlete interviews after they've lost the game. *They were tough competitors. We have to try harder. We did a lot of good things, but it just wasn't enough this time, we'll do better next time.*

"That seems good," Caroline says.

"Especially if this Jag is as yummy as Hedy tells us," Marie adds.

"He is an employee, nothing more."

"Well, it could be more," Hedy pokes. "After all, you're here alone all day, getting sweaty. And you said yourself that you really like him. He's smart, cultured, educated, sophisticated, and he's got that total Mr. Darcy accent on him. Plus the whole swarthy handsome thing. Seriously, Anneke, even if it is just a transitional fling, I say go for it."

"Look, I don't disagree that Jag has his charms. If I met him at a party, I'd probably go for it. But he works for me."

"If you met him at a party? Since when do you go to parties?" Marie asks. "You're the most antisocial person we know."

"Very funny. I'm just saying that there is no way I'm even entertaining the idea. NOT that he has shown the least bit of interest in me romantically."

"Maybe he's gay," Hedy says, absentmindedly, the toss-away phrase we've all always used when some attractive man didn't demonstrate lust.

"HEDY," Marie says in a hiss.

Hedy realizes what she's said and blushes deeply. "Aw, shit, Annie, I'm sorry, I didn't . . ."

I'm stunned, but then I laugh. What else can I do?

"What about Jag, aside from his adorableness, professionally he's good? Useful?" Marie asks, coming in for the rescue yet again, having demolished her second piece of cake in record time.

This actually makes me smile for real. "Professionally? He's terrific, actually, supersmart, really good at the stuff we are doing now, and I think he'll learn the rest fairly handily. He's meticulous, which you know I love. And he fixed the front porch light and the doorbell, which the other electrician couldn't figure out to save his life. I just hope that he sticks with me for the duration, because to be honest, I don't know how I can do it without him."

"And there's the aforementioned adorableness," says Hedy, eating the last of the gelato out of the tub and licking the spoon lasciviously. "He's tall and wiry, with caramel skin and a dark shiny beard with perfect white teeth, and amazing hazel eyes. I want him to tie me up in his turban."

"Okay, that is a little disrespectful," Marie says.

"Hedy, you can feel free to date him if you like, but I'm not going there." Hedy never lacks for male companionship, but she isn't much for anything long term. Caroline wants nothing more than to find her the guy that will make her settle down.

She sighs. "Fine. What about going somewhere else, then?"

"Dating? Are you serious?" The last thing on my mind.

"People do, you know," Marie says. "John has a new guy at the shop who is very nice."

"One of the guys in Carl's wine group just got divorced," Caroline pipes in.

"STOP. Ladies, you know I adore you, and I appreciate your concern, but I'm doing okay. I seem to be shifting back and forth between anger and acceptance on the Grant front. Most days I want to kill him, and some days I want to call him and see how he is holding up."

"That bastard, you cannot be concerned about how HE is doing, he lied to you, he cheated on you, with a BOY no less; he upended your whole LIFE." Hedy is very black-and-white. If someone is good to you, she is his biggest fan. If he hurts you, she wants him drawn and quartered. Like a good girlfriend should.

"Look, I don't forgive him for what he did, but as pissed off as I am, I still care about him. I still love him, if I'm going to be honest. I hate what he did to me, to us, but I also don't want him to be in horrible pain, and I know that he must be."

"As well he should," Marie says. "The more pain the better."

"He sent me that today." I gesture to the counter.

"It's beautiful. That was nice of him," Caroline says.

"It's manipulative and shitty," Hedy says. "A reminder that he blew up their happy home and now she is alone in this dilapidated hovel on Valentine's Day."

"Where she is eating delicious food and drinking great champagne and having a good time with her best girls," I remind them, and myself. Even if I'm in a bad place and their efforts to support me are irritating, they are my girls, and I'm lucky to have them. I just hope that we can get back to normal soon.

"Point taken." Marie raises her glass.

"Did you call Emily yet?" Hedy asks after draining her glass and reaching for the bottle.

"Not yet."

"Are you going to?" Marie asks, gesturing for Hedy to top her off as well.

"Not sure." And I'm not. I have just enough Grand-mère training in my bones to know that simple courtesy says I need to at least call her and acknowledge that I know she came by, but the idea of getting together with her just gives me a stabbing pain between my eyes.

"Do you think you know why you might not want to? I mean besides the surface stuff?" Caroline asks.

I take a deep breath. "Nothing earth-shattering. I don't know what her agenda is, and maybe she doesn't really have one, but I also don't know that I have the bandwidth to even find out."

I see the three of them make eye contact, and I can almost hear the conversation they had when planning this little shindig. *It's Valentine's, don't push her too hard, don't get too serious, bring things up gently but back off if she gets prickly.* I just know that it happened, and it pokes at the deepest, ugliest part of me. I hate knowing they talk about me, plot about my life, judge how I'm dealing with things. I swallow my desire to tell them all to just back the fuck off.

"Besides," I say through slightly clenched teeth, "I'd hate to have to break up our little coven. We're perfect just the four of us, and we don't need a fifth wheel, especially one half our age with boobs that defy gravity." They all nod and make another round of eye contact, clearly silently agreeing to let it go for now, and I feel my shoulders relax the tiniest bit.

"Truer words," Hedy says.

"I like being the baby of the family," says Marie, six months younger than me.

"Here's to us." Caroline clinks.

"Here's to what's next." Hedy reaches her glass over to me.

"I'll drink to that." I clink around the circle, and drain my glass, wishing like mad that I knew what I was actually drinking to.

12

From Gemma's Journal:

Sometimes things are very unexpected. Last spring when Mr. Rabin's elder brother arrived unannounced from New York, we thought he was just coming for a short visit. And then, the bigger shock. It seems that he and Martha the housekeeper have taken quite a fancy to each other, and he has proposed. I thought for certain they both would be thrown from the house in disgrace, but today there is joy. The Missus came downstairs to tell me that there would be a wedding celebration to plan. There will be a ceremony in the judge's chambers for the families, and then a reception here at the house for family and friends. The Missus made me promise to do the party as a buffet, which I can set up beforehand, and has asked me to inquire with a local agency for servers so that all of the staff can attend the celebration, which is the deepest kindness of her heart to include us all.

I love reading Gemma's journal. It's the little gift I give to myself at the end of a long day, just allowing myself a page or two a night, doling it out to myself like an expensive box of chocolates you want to make last a long time. It always seems to have a message of hope, or an answer for a question, or a bit of a pep talk. I've even begun to use it as something of an oracle. Asking it a question and then letting the book fall open where it may, dropping my finger on the page and reading my answer. And it works. Like, every single time.

Yesterday I asked it what to do about my bed. I'm on my third air mattress; they keep deflating in the night from some mysterious leaks that develop and I can't find. And even though they're cheap, they're not disposable; I can't continue to go through them every couple of weeks. So I turned to Gemma and asked her what's to be done about my bed, and flopped the journal open and let my finger fall.

There is no point in wasting money on the poorest quality of things, you will outspend yourself in the future replacing them, and suffer from their shoddiness in the meantime.

I shit you not.

Of course, she was giving a lesson to her new scullery maid about why it's important to invest in very good pots and pans and knives, and to keep them impeccably maintained, but the sentiment is no less true. For what I have spent so far on my deflating inflatables, I could have already gotten a cheapish mattress and box spring set. So I bit the bullet and bought a real bed, since I do have to finally admit to myself that I'm not just camping out here temporarily, not here in my house, not here in my life. I'm on my own and wherever I am, I'm going to need a bed. Caroline told me about an online company that has all the top name brands for about 70 percent off, so I ordered a midlevel Serta for what it would have cost me to buy a cheapo no-name in a local store, and it's being delivered tomorrow. Maybe in a real bed I'll get restful sleep. I'm a little worried about falling out of it, though.

I'd gotten so used to Grant on my right, and I'm something of a sleep migrator, so as I would wiggle over in my slumber, his warm presence would be my sleep speed bump. He called it encroachment. I told him I just loved him so much I wanted to be close to him. Which was true, but also probably more because I tend to run slightly cold and Grant ran slightly hot, so I was seeking his warmth to borrow. But without him there, I seem to just keep going, and I often wake up in the middle of the night, teetering precariously, one millimeter from dumping myself off the right side. I may need to install a safety rail, or push the bed right up against the wall.

For now, I just have to get through one more night with what is essentially a half-blown-up pool float.

Today Jag and I are having a tutorial on bathrooms, starting with the first-floor bathroom and powder room. It will be a welcome change from being stuck in the freezing basement. We've finished the gutting, opened the place up to the stone foundation and the dirt. The stone and masonry work down there is truly beautiful. English and Irish stonemasons hand chiseled the stones to fit flush together with only the barest minimum of mortar. The brickwork, classic Chicago Common Brick with beautiful decorative work at the corners, is in impeccable shape. Jag assessed the space and asked if I might consider leaving it exposed.

"Your space here seems to be dry, you have only the minimum of spall and efflorescence. This stone is a good three feet thick and the brick is four courses; you won't need insulation for warmth. And the work is so very lovely. We can clean it, remove any loose mortar by hand and tuck-point, wash it with a lime solution, and then do a linseed oil seal on it to keep the dust down and bring out the color in the stone and bricks." Then he got sheepish; it was the most he had ever said all at once since we began working together. And obviously he was having a vision.

"I like that, go on. What else would you do down here?"

His whole face lit up. "Well, I think this basement could be a space to really honor the more industrial end of the age. I know you are keeping so many of the original details upstairs, so why not strip away the coverings and let the building artistry shine here? Those steel beams are works of art, with those wonderful big square beveled baseplates and huge rivets. You could leave the beams and walls exposed, really give it a cool industrial vibe, but not contemporary industrial, not like a loft with all that horrible painted metal ductwork, but more early nineteen hundreds industrial?" Then he smiles a wicked smile. "You know, like the robber baron who built this mansion didn't care enough about the help to give them real walls or floors."

This makes me laugh. "I LOVE it. Jag, you are a genius. It's practically Steampunk." I could already see it, and the space began to come to life a little bit in my mind. "We could put the bathroom over here, get a big soaker tub for this nook." I walked over and pointed out a six-foot-by-four-foot niche, stone foundation to four feet high and brick above, suddenly screaming out for a large deep bathtub with a slate surround, like a grotto pool.

"Exactly! And then the open shower right over here . . ." And we were off. We spent the better part of two hours designing a gorgeous basement bathroom, with a large guest bedroom suite, making the basement a luxurious spa-like getaway as opposed to making your company feel like they are garrisoned. Once we have a chance to flesh out Jag's ideas, we head upstairs for a coffee break.

"I have to say, Anneke, this project is the most exciting thing I've ever been involved with. Thank you for letting me work with you."

"The pleasure is all mine. You're definitely bringing much added value. Have you talked to your folks about the school thing yet?"

He shakes his head. "It's hard, you know? They have given

me so much, and they want what's best for me. They will tell me that all they want is for me to be happy, and deep down they mean that; it isn't like they would disown me or anything. But I know it will be a huge disappointment. That's why I'm trying to figure out my visa problem. If I could stay here, finish out this project, get a job in the industry, then I could present the news to them from a place of strength."

"And your dad, he's a diplomat, couldn't he pull some strings for you?"

"He's a stickler about stuff like that. When we first got a sense of the whole diplomatic corps stuff, he always told us that as far as he was concerned, there was no such thing as diplomatic immunity, and if we ever got into trouble, we would have to deal with the consequences like anyone else. I'd never ask him to help me with something like this. I'm a grown man, I can't have my daddy bailing me out."

"I get that. You have to stand on your own, make your own way."

"Exactly. I just want to introduce them to the life I want in a way that makes them believe that my future is secure. Especially because I've fallen so in love with Chicago that I know I want to make it my permanent home, I don't want to go back to England. And I especially don't want to go back a failed student with no job, slinking home with my tail between my legs to start all over."

Every time Jag reminds me that his time here could be limited, my stomach turns over. I just can't imagine being here without him. In such a short time, he's become a friend, a good friend even, and a hard worker and inspiring partner. It feels a little like working with Joe in a strange way, even though I'm taking on the teacher role; Jag has the same calming energy, meticulous attention to detail, and easygoing manner. I love working with him, and personal affinity aside, I'm not sure at all what I will do if he does leave. Every sub I've called since I left MacMurphy, all the guys who used to show up at the drop of a hat to help me out, they are insanely busy; not one has been able to fit me into his schedule. If Jag leaves, I'm monumentally screwed.

"What's going on with trying to get the different visa?" He has a friend who encouraged him to apply for a six-month tourist visa to replace the soon-to-be-defunct student visa.

"Waiting to hear back. The primary concern is that they know how long I've been here and that I am here on a student visa, and they may question my reasons for staying if I have no work and no school. But maybe it will go through; I should know something soon."

"Well, I'm keeping my fingers crossed! I really don't want to have to finish this beast without you."

"Thanks, Anneke, that means the world to me. We'll just keep hoping. And working. Aren't we on upstairs bathroom duty today?"

"Absolutely."

"I'll go pick up the tub from the glazer, and grab the stuff on the list from the Home Depot and be back in about an hour and a half or so."

We need a break from the cold and filthy downstairs, and frankly, I need access to a better bathroom than the one upstairs. Now that the flooring tile is grouted, we can reinstall the freshly reglazed claw-foot tub and the new toilet, put in the vanity cabinet and sink; by the end of today it should be functioning, and we might even get to the powder room demo if we work clean and fast.

First I have to take Schatzi on her morning walk. I hate the morning walk. At night, dog people respect solitude. The evening walk is about two things: getting your dog tired enough to sleep and hopefully not wake you at some ungodly hour, and getting your dog to poop. It isn't big socializing time, especially in the cold. But daytime walks? Then everyone in the neighborhood wants to meet and let the dogs cavort and make chitchat. I'm terrible at chitchat. And Schatzi is terrible at cavorting these days. The neighborhood is full of dogs, and it should be a way to meet people and make friends. But so far, no such luck. In the few weeks we've been in residence, Schatzi has kicked dirt in the eye of a Chihuahua, resulting in a squealing of eardrum-perforating shrillness. She nipped the fingers of a very nice young woman walking her terrier mix when she tried to pet her. She growled at a Yorkie so menacingly the dog had immediate violently explosive diarrhea. All over my leg. It was like some invisible hand just squeezed her in the middle and hot liquid poop shot out of her with such velocity that despite being only like eight inches tall, she hit me from ankle to over the knee. I'm still grateful she wasn't a bigger dog.

Schatzi was never mean to other dogs, or owners for that matter, when we were in the West Loop. She had her neighborhood pals, Otto the black Lab, who always tried to give her gifts of mangy tennis balls, Lucy, the sweet old arthritic collie who would nuzzle Schatzi like a doting grandmother, and her best buddy, Klaus, a giant schnauzer, the perfect replica of Schatzi herself, just supersized. They would romp around and then put their square bearded heads together and have what appeared to be very serious conversations about things. Jimmy, Klaus's dad, would always lean over and ask, "Do you think they're planning to invade Poland?" which never failed to make me laugh. And thinking of that makes me sad. I haven't thought much about what she has gone through, but I realize these past couple of years must have been hard. First she lost her person, and got uprooted out of the only home she had known since she was eight weeks old. Then she came to know Grant, whom she loved, and got comfortable in the condo and that neighborhood, made new friends. And now, with no warning, upended again, in a drafty dusty place, with no Grant and his little nibbles and bits, no Otto, no Lucy, no Klaus.

I realize I know very much how she must be feeling.

I spot Gemma's journal in the kitchen. Might as well.

"Gemma? What can I do for poor Schatzi to make her a little bit happy?" I reach over, stand the large book on its spine, and let it open. Closing my eyes tightly, I point my index finger, make a couple of dramatic circles over the page, and drop my hand.

I have few skills beyond what I can do in this kitchen, but what I can do in this kitchen can make you happy, can comfort your sorrow.

Apparently Gemma thinks I need to cook for Schatzi. I scan the next paragraph to see whom she is cooking for and what she is making.

Poor Mr. Rabin. The Missus has taken the children to visit their grandparents in Ohio for the week, but work keeps him so busy he cannot join them till the weekend. He is a man who is only fully alive when his beautiful wife and their lively children are near him. The only thing I can do is try to cheer him with his favorite things, nursery food mostly, soft-boiled eggs with buttered toast soldiers and crispy bacon. Sausages baked in sweet beans. Shepherd's pie. Cookies and cakes. Bread and butter pudding with candied ginger. The food seems to soothe him, and he often takes it in the kitchen with me and the other staff, letting us share a growler of beer or bringing up a bottle of wine from the cellar to pour. His twinkle comes back a bit, admonishing us all to not tell Missus of his adventures belowstairs.

Hmmm. Maybe that's it. Maybe I really should try to cook something special for her. Maybe that's why she loved Grant so much. I grab her leash and we do a quick walk around the block. It's still insanely cold, so she isn't interested in anything more than a quick pee, a ladylike dump, and a fast return to the house.

I head back to the kitchen to assess the fridge. Gemma mentioned soft-boiled eggs and bacon and buttered toast soldiers. I've got some eggs, which I know Schatzi can eat, and there is still a half a packet of bacon. Well, eggs and bacon sound good to me; I only had a bowl of cereal before Jag got here, and I'm a breakfast-all-day kind of girl, and I bet the dog will like it too. I'm almost giddy when I get them out of the fridge. And then I stop. I've never made a soft-boiled egg in my life. I've eaten a zillion, Grand-mère was good at them, as was Grant. And I do love dunking little strips of buttery toast in the gooey liquid center. But I've never even tried to make one. I flip through the journal till I find it.

Soft-Boiled Eggs. Bring a small pot of water to a roiling boil. Drop in three fresh eggs. Cook for precisely three and a half minutes, and remove to a towel, dry the eggs, and place in the egg carrier.

That seems simple enough. Despite not having the egg carrier, I think I can manage it. I put some water on to boil. I put a skillet on high heat. Take six strips of bacon out of the package and lay them in the skillet. The sizzle is intoxicating. Nothing in the world smells as good as bacon; I defy you to disagree. The water comes to a boil in minutes, this BlueStar range can crank up to 24,000 BTUs; it never ceases to amaze me how quickly I can get pasta made here. I drop in the eggs, and turn back to the bacon and flip it over. It is spitting grease all over the stove, and when I turn it my arms get speckled with peppery little stings. I remember that Grant always made it in the oven, but I don't know how, and Joe always did it on the stovetop. Of course, when Joe did it, it was always a mess; I'd forgotten that part. The bacon is almost done when I remember I was supposed to cook the eggs for three and a half minutes. I have no idea how long they've been in there. One minute? Two? I figure two, and check my watch. The acrid smell of burning hits my nose, and I look over to see that my bacon is scorching, and quickly pull the pan off the heat. I drop the now-mahogany brittle slices on the waiting paper towels. Just shy of black. Crap. By the time I turn back to the eggs, my watch says it has been almost two minutes, so I quickly get them out of the water and onto a kitchen towel. I let them sit while I make a couple of slices of toast, butter them, and sit down to open an egg. But there is no gooey runny inside, just a powdery hard-boiled yolk, with a thin film of green around the edge. Figuring Schatzi won't care, I cut it up, break up a couple of strips of bacon, and dump them in her bowl with a half cup of kibble.

Schatzi wanders over and sniffs at the bowl. She looks up at me quizzically.

"Go on, girl. A special treat." I pause. "Because I love you."

The dog turns back to the bowl, and gingerly takes a piece of egg out. Then she makes a happy grunting noise and tucks in, wolfing it down like I didn't feed her last night. Within minutes, the bowl is empty, licked clean, and Schatzi is grooming herself contentedly.

"You're welcome." I reach down and scratch between her silky ears, and she whips her head around and bites my hand, not hard enough to draw blood, but hard enough to leave marks. Then she heads out of the kitchen.

I fucking hate that dog.

I look back at my own meal of burnt bacon and rubbery

eggs and now-cold toast with the butter congealing, and take a breath. Goddammit, I should be able to cook a freaking egg. I dump the mess in the garbage and start over.

I put the water back on to boil and get a couple more eggs out of the fridge, a few more slices of bacon. I put the bacon in the pan over low heat in hopes of having better control. When the water comes to a boil I drop the eggs in carefully and set my watch for three and a half minutes. I turn back to the bacon, which is actually cooking well and not making nearly as much of a greasy mess all over. My watch says I have a minute and a half left, so I put a couple more slices of bread in the toaster. The bacon is looking perfect, and I take it out of the pan and put it on the paper towels. My watch beeps and I gently remove the eggs from the water. The toast dings and I grab it and butter it generously.

I sit back down and say a little prayer. And slice the top of the egg off. The white is set, and the yolk is a puddle of liquid gold. I dunk a piece of toast in the egg, and my eyes roll back in my head. So yummy. I pick up a piece of bacon, and it's just how I like it, fairly crispy with the fat well rendered, but still with a little bit of chew. I wolf it all down; it may be the single most delicious breakfast I've ever eaten. And I don't know why, but I start to laugh. Really laugh. Belly laugh with tears running down my face, in a way I haven't laughed since I can't remember when.

I'm just drying off the skillet when the doorbell rings. Since Jag replaced it, it now peals a series of musical pings, very old fashioned, and no longer reminiscent of an air-raid siren. I almost look forward to it.

"Hello there!" I throw open the door expecting Jag with his arms full of materials, and instead am greeted with the only sight that could immediately put a damper on my decent morning.

"Hi, Anneke! I was in the neighborhood and thought maybe we'd have that walk or something before you head to work, if it's not a terrible time for you. Hello, Schatzi girl! How is my sweet pup?" Emily scoops the dog up in her arms, and begins to waltz her around the porch, laughing and murmuring to her that she is the most beautiful of all the doggies. The dog, who not fifteen minutes ago savaged me for deigning to cook her a custom special breakfast, is now nuzzling this unwelcome stranger, and reaches her head up and licks Emily's cheeks with the tenderness of any mother cleaning a dirty child. Of course.

"Hey, Emily, um, sorry I haven't called . . . um . . ."

"Oh, goodness, you must be busy as anything, no worries at all, it's why I figured I'd swing by, you know, try to catch you before you head out for work."

"I work here, actually." Why the hell did I say THAT?

Her eyes widen. "How cool is that! I feel terrible; I actually don't really know what you do. But whatever it is, I bet it's awesome to just be able to work from home. Especially a home as beautiful as this one, they just don't make them like this anymore." She looks around reverently. "It's one of the reasons I'm so excited to move to Boston; I can finally see some serious architecture. I've been wandering all over Chicago just marveling at the buildings, and last week I went to the Frank Lloyd Wright Home and Studio in Oak Park and that was just, I mean, LIFE CHANGING!"

She puts the dog down, and before I know what is happening, she has come right on in, and is taking off her coat. Today's hat is powder blue with some sort of yarn Mohawk in various shades of green, and earflaps, and the mittens are purple with yellow sunflowers. Apparently her winter-gear "shopportunity" was not just epic, but may have happened while high. She looks around for a place to put them, but I haven't done the front closet yet, and don't have a coatrack, so when she doesn't find a logical place, she stuffs the hat and mittens in the pocket of her coat, and drapes the bulky thing over her arm.

"Come on in," I mutter, taking the bundle of outerwear from her and dumping it over the back of the one chair in the living room.

"I know it's a horribly rude thing, but would you mind awfully maybe taking me on a tour of your house; it is just one of the most gorgeous things I've ever seen!"

Well, for whatever faults she clearly has, at least she has an eye for a nice building. Might as well get this over with; if I can spend a little time touring her around the house, then I can hopefully get rid of her for good.

"Sure. Follow me, and just be really careful and try not to touch anything."

She grins at me as if I've handed her a Wonka Golden Ticket, and claps her hands excitedly. "Hooray!"

Hoo-freaking-ray.

Apparently the building is magical. As soon as I started taking Emily around and showing her the house, explaining what it was and what I am trying to do, she shut the hell up. She oohed and aahed appropriately, asked a couple of questions, but essentially we did a tour and I talked and she listened, Schatzi clicking along at her heels. We finish up in the kitchen, and feeling magnanimous, I offer to make some tea.

"Anneke, this place, it's amazing. I have to ask, how are you ever going to leave it when you're done? I mean it's so YOU, not that I know you even a little bit, but I feel like I kind of do just seeing what you are doing here and how you think about every detail and it will just be perfect, how on earth will you be able to give it up?"

And she's back. I offer her a cookie from the glass jar on the counter, in hopes that if she puts food in her face this noise will stop coming out of it.

"If I don't sell it I will be bankrupt and unable to eat, and I'm pretty sure the new owners aren't going to see me as a feature they want to keep."

"Do you always live in your projects?"

"This is a first."

"Well, I can see why you would, even just for a little bit of time, I would totally want to live here, to be in this place, I suppose even if I knew it couldn't be my forever home I could always have the memories of having lived here for a while, and I'd probably have done the same thing."

"That's a nice way to look at it." I'm wondering exactly how I'm going to extricate this gangly child from the house.

"Hello!" Jag's voice floats up the stairs. Hallelujah!

"Up here," I call out, and I can hear his tread on the steps. Schatzi leaves her perch under Emily's chair to go greet him. He enters the kitchen, removing his coat and dropping it over the folding chair at the worktable.

"I'm sorry, I didn't know you had company." He crosses over and extends his hand. "Jagjeet Singh. Everyone calls me Jag."

"Hi, Jag! I'm Emily Walsh. Everyone just calls me Emily."

"Lovely to meet you, Emily." They both look at me, waiting for me to fill in the obvious blanks. I swear to god, these days I cannot stand people.

"Jag is working with me on the house. Emily is visiting Chicago." I'm not really sure how else to describe her, but clearly she has some ideas.

"I'm Anneke's long-lost never-known stepsister from Florida. Her mom was married to my dad, and I dropped in on her head like the house in *The Wizard of Oz* all excited to meet her and she never even heard of me! But I'm in town for a little bit, and I always say that family is about the best thing you can ever have in your life, so I'm just pestering her and imposing on her time while I'm here so we can get to know each other."

I love how I'm suddenly the Wicked Witch of the East in this little florid scenario she's just painted. Although, if someone dropped a house on me I wouldn't have to listen to her voice anymore, so it does have some merit as an idea.

"I see." Jag turns to me, probably registering the pained look on my face, and then nods. "Well, then I should leave you sisters to each other. Anneke, I will be downstairs in the powder room doing the demo. Emily, nice to have met you." And giving Schatzi a quick pet, he heads out of the kitchen.

Et tu, Jag?

"I'm sorry, you must want to get to work. What are you doing today?"

Whew. "Yeah, I should. We are working on the first-floor bathrooms."

"What are you going to do in there?"

"Nothing fancy. Install the tub and toilet and vanity in the full bath, which is almost done, then demo in the powder room. We have to rip out the plaster and replace it with tile backer board, tile the walls and the floor, install a new toilet and a small sink, hang a mirror, do some lighting."

"All for two little rooms. How long will that take?"

"Three days or so, depending."

"Cool." She pauses. "Do you think, I mean not today, but maybe another time I might come watch? I mean, I'm really interested in all of this, I watch HGTV like NONSTOP, and I'm always doing little DIY projects with furniture and stuff and I think it would be amazing to just see how some of this happens live and in person. You know, if I wouldn't be in your way or anything. I could even help, if you wanted, I'm good at painting for sure, I repaint my room wherever I am at least once a year when I get bored and need a change, but I could even just be the garbage girl or coffee fetcher . . ."

"Yeah, maybe," I say, just to get her to shut the hell up. Except now her whole face lights up and I realize that I have just opened Pandora's freaking box. "But not today. I'll, um, let you know if we're doing something worth seeing." Not.

"You're so awesome, Anneke."

"Thanks. But I really should . . ."

"Oh god, yeah, I'm totally leaving, I promise, just one more thing, do you like really get completely immersed in the work all day? Where disruptions like really mess with your flow and stuff?"

"Pretty much." Maybe this will keep her from more drop-ins.

"I figured. So I'm wondering, if you ever wanted me to come over and walk Schatzi, or take her to the dog park or something, like be her doggie day care person, I would totally love to do that. If it would be helpful, you know, so you didn't have to worry about her or stop work when she wants to go out or needs her exercise or whatever."

"That's very nice of you." Which it is, even if it is the last thing I would ever agree to. Schatzi can go all day without a potty break, and the fact that she likes Emily so much means that by saying no I both prevent ADHD Emily from being in my airspace AND deprive the undeserving dog of loving companionship, which I think is a win-win.

"COOL!" she says as if I have said yes, and now I have to rack my brain to see if she has tricked me into something. "Okay, well, I'll maybe come by tomorrow afternoon to play with her, around two or so, that will be awesome, and if you don't want to be bothered, you can just leave the door unlocked or something and I can just pop in and grab her quiet as a mouse. Thanks again, Anneke, have a good workday, I'll see you later!" And she pops out of her chair, and picks up the dog. "I'm going to be your dog walker, pretty girl, what do you think about that?"

"NO."

She stops twirling with the dog, who glares at me with the fury of a thousand suns.

"Emily. The dog is fine. It was a nice offer, but I have to decline. And I have to get to work."

Her face falls like I just took her ice cream cone away from her.

"Oh. Well, if you change your mind . . ."

"Yeah. I'll let you know."

I follow her downstairs, and she gets back into her festive winter garb.

"Thanks again, Anneke, I'll talk to you soon. And really, the house"—she gestures around—"it's just, EVERYTHING." The look on her face is killing me, and I can feel myself soften the tiniest bit.

"Thanks, Emily, it means a lot to me that you appreciate it." I know I should probably let her walk the hateful dog. Or that I should tell her that later this week we are going to do a cool conversion of an antique sideboard into a bathroom vanity for the second floor. But I can't make the words come. I can't give her what she wants or needs from me.

"Cool. Good luck with the bathrooms." And she leaves.

My main feeling is one of relief to have her gone, but there is the smallest little part of me that feels shitty about how I treated her. Which pisses me off. Why should I feel bad for this unwanted interloper who keeps foisting herself on me? Why on earth should I care what she feels or thinks, when two weeks ago I didn't even know she fucking existed?

Which does make me think. She did know about me. My mother might not have mentioned her little mini-me of a step-daughter on the rare occasions we would have spoken during her time as Mrs. Walsh, but clearly she said something about me to

Emily. Something that wasn't so awful since it made Emily wonder why I never visited, made her want to seek me out. And despite myself, I'm very curious about what exactly my mother might have said about me, how she described me, what characteristics she attributed to me. Was there even the smallest bit of pride on her part?

Doesn't matter. Can't matter. I do not have time to get embroiled in this kind of familial bullshit. The only good thing about not having family is that you don't have to put up with family crap. I look at Caroline and her siblings; who needs that kind of hassle? I've safely removed my mother from my life. And I realize that all she knows about me right now is my email address. I had to get a new cell phone when I left MacMurphy; the old one and its number belonged to them. I didn't exactly send out an I've Moved card when I left Grant's and came here. Of course, Emily found me, since the landline here is in my name, but that would require someone caring to look me up, which Anneliese never has. I certainly haven't missed her.

I can't help but wonder what sort of fictional daughter she created in my name that would make Emily so hell-bent on weaseling into my life. I already have a dozen reasons to be annoyed at that girl; the very idea that she has me even pondering my mother in the most superficial way is just one more.

I head into the front room and catch Schatzi perched on the windowsill, staring out the window like a war bride waiting for her soldier to come home. When she turns to look at me her gaze is downright soulful, and from her mouth dangles a single sunflower-adorned mitten.

13

From Gemma's Journal:

Cooking is both an art, and a craft. Anyone with time and inclination can become a good cook. To be a great cook, one must have deeper passions.

"Anneke? I've brought leftovers from my potluck dinner last night, can I offer you lunch?"

The smells wafting from the containers Jag has brought make this a very easy decision.

"Yes, please! What are we having?"

"Tandoori chicken, rice and lentil pilaf, samosas."

"Yum. Lucky me." The past two weeks have been a sad backslide in my tentative new relationship with cooking. It started with my attempt to make a baked sweet potato. For whatever reason, I just wanted a simple baked sweet potato. With butter and a little cinnamon. And Gemma keeps saying that you can smell when things are done, which Grant always said too, so I didn't set the timer. Some people can smell when things are done. You know what I can smell? The smell of a baked sweet potato that has exploded inside a very high-end oven, and burnt into unsalvageable superglue all over the interior. You know what that smells like? It smells like two and a half hours on your knees with your torso in an oven, huffing oven-cleaner fumes till you hallucinate the dancing-hippo scene from *Fantasia* as reimagined by Lady Gaga. This triumph was followed by two days of

ramen with cut-up hot dogs in it, which was a level of sodium
that turned my fingers and toes into plump little sausages. Then
when I got my courage back up to try to cook something again,
the unfortunate discovery that the pork chops in the clearance
bin at the little convenience market should probably not hang
around for three days before you cook them. Remember the
exploding Yorkie? I think I may have shat one out. Want to know
why I invest in Toto toilets and no other brand? Three words:
Double. Cyclone. Flushing. Essentially, they sort of automatically
clean the bowl while they flush. The stupid old toilet that was the
vessel of my unfortunate post–pork chop buttpocalypse? Needed
cleaning after every event. I'm so excited to have the new Toto
installed downstairs. Not that I have plans to poison myself
again, but one never knows.

You would think two days of essentially living in the bathroom with cramps doubling me over, my poor little pink star-
fish ravaged by liquid colon acid and subpar toilet paper, would
have taught me a lesson, but nope. I went back to the kitchen as
soon as I was feeling better to whip up such classics as "Not
Enough Ketchup in the World Meatloaf" and "Brick Chicken:
Not Cooked Under a Brick, Cooked to the Consistency of a
Brick." I tried to make Caroline's famous mashed potatoes, she
sent me the recipe generously, but I didn't have a ricer, or even
know what one is for that matter, so I just attacked them with
the hand mixer and made something so gummy and gluey I
was tempted to save it for spackling. Apparently my early successes were not an indication of being any sort of natural cook.

The past three days I've just made microwaved frozen meals
for dinner, followed by enormous bowls of popcorn. Whatever
else I suck at in the kitchen, which is turning out to be pretty
much everything, I make spectacular popcorn. Especially on
this stove. I do it over the simmer burner, which makes it all
pop up huge and fluffy and never burns. The same cannot be

said of my one attempt at salmon. Let's just say that charred salmon jerky does not a lovely supper make.

I let Jag serve me a plate, and tuck into the weirdly vivid magenta-tinged chicken, still tender and moist despite being reheated. The rice pilaf is studded with whole spices and sweet strings of fried onions and nuts and nuggets of dried apricot, and the thin crisp pastry of the samosa hides a spicy mix of potatoes and peas. It is the best thing I've eaten in forever, and I wolf it down. Jag laughs at me, and my lack of manners.

"Did you cook this?" I say around a huge mouthful of rice, at least the rice that didn't fall off my fork into my lap.

"I made the chicken, my friends made the rice and the samosas."

"Please thank them for me."

"I shall. I shall."

We eat our plates in contented silence. It's been a good productive couple of days; we finished the first-floor bathroom, and it is a full realization of the design I had in my head. The Carrara marble wainscoting I'd discovered under the drywall cleaned up like a dream, brilliant white shot through with subtle gray veins. The basket-weave-pattern marble tile on the floor is a classic pattern, and Jag was a very quick study in fixture installation. In addition to the Toto toilet I picked out, one with simple traditional lines, I got their matching pedestal sink. I had the original claw-foot tub reglazed, and we put it in with a vintage nickel-plated floor-mounted faucet and handheld showerhead I found at a salvage yard.

The small square shower I wanted to install in the corner had been troubling me. I wanted the bathroom to have a separate shower, I personally hate taking showers in a bathtub, and we had the room to include it, but all of the surrounds I saw just felt clunky and didn't match the clean, open feel of the elegant space. Then Jag suggested we use a pair of old greenhouse doors I had in the garage, tall with weathered iron strips holding nine-inch squares of wavy old glass. The two were big enough to create a comfortable square; we firm mounted one door and left the other to swing open and serve as the shower access. When we got it in, it was clear that it was the perfect choice, mostly glass, the shower floats in the corner, and the dark squares look terrific against the pattern on the floor. More than ever I'm grateful for Jag and his ideas, his assistance, and especially for his very pleasant company in these very long days of hard work.

"There is something we need to discuss," he says, looking down at his plate.

Uh-oh. I feel the proverbial rug begin to shift under my feet. "Sure, Jag, what is it?"

"Um, this is very bad timing, I know, but it's about my visa. The six-month visa was denied."

Suddenly this delicious meal turns to lead in my stomach.

"I'm so sorry. What did they say?"

"No real info, something about it being in conflict with my existing visa. The good news is that means that school hasn't sent any info to anyone that I'm no longer enrolled, so my current visa is still okay. But the bad news is that it makes me ineligible for the tourist visa, and now that I've been denied that once, apparently it makes it unlikely that I would get one again unless I go home for a few months and then come back."

"Crap."

"Indeed."

"What about just staying illegally? Good lord, people do it all the time. You're not a criminal, just stay and if you get caught, you can just say you didn't know your visa was up or something."

"I can't take that risk. If I got caught? It would be horrible for my dad. He has an impeccable reputation, and takes his good name very seriously. As much as I love it here and want Chicago to be my home, I would never stay and risk any sort of public humiliation for him. The tabloids in Britain are horrific

and relentless; you've seen the lawsuits and scandals. The minute they get a whiff of anything, they'll attack. And while you
and I know what's real, things over there are xenophobic enough
these days; no one needs another guy in a turban on the cover of
a paper doing something that can be blown up from illegal to
insidious."

"Never thought about it that way."

"It's just too complicated."

"Can I ask? You keep saying how much you want Chicago to
be your home, why is that? I mean, I know why I love it here,
but I'm always interested in what it is about the city that gets
under people's skin."

"I find it magical. The people have been wonderful. I've
found a surprisingly rich Sikh cultural community that has
welcomed me despite the fact that I am somewhat modern in
how I practice my faith. I've built a wonderful circle of friends
that I feel deeply close to. I actually love the extremes of the
weather, and I don't have to tell you that there is no better city
in the world for food, or art, or theater. I love the sports teams,
even as they break my heart. As someone who has fallen in love
with architecture and buildings, it is so beautiful here. And
considering how I want to make my living, I love that it can be
done here in a way that is both affordable and manageable."

It touches my heart to hear him express everything that I
adore about my hometown. "I hear you. There is no other place
in the world like it."

"I'm trying to figure something out, I still have a little time
before the student one runs out, provided Northwestern doesn't
send in the paperwork, so no need to panic yet, but I didn't want
it to be a surprise in case you wanted to try to find someone else."

"No."

"Well, I mean . . ."

"No. Stop talking. You aren't leaving. I'm not doing this

without you. I will figure it out, I'll get you a work visa or something." I cannot let this injustice happen. I will not let this wonderful man be ripped away from the city he loves, or the work we still have to do together.

The smile is both sweet and sheepish, perfect white teeth shining in his dark beard. "That is much appreciated. I'm very hopeful we will figure something out together."

"Don't you worry, I'll fix it."

I can't fix it."

"What do you mean?" Marie says. We're having a quick lunch at Manny's. I needed a massive matzo-ball fix, and Marie has a weird affinity for their chocolate pudding.

"I mean I can't fix it. I don't actually have a business, not an incorporated established business; I can't get him a work visa. And I can't afford the legal stuff involved in becoming an incorporated established business, and even if I could, I don't have time to get it all squared away before his current visa runs out."

It's been a long week of exploring options and talking to friends of friends, and trying to figure out how to make good on my promise to Jag.

"He'll understand," Marie says soothingly.

"Of course he will. That isn't the point. I can't lose him."

"You'll find another helper."

"You don't get it. He isn't a helper. He can do the electrical stuff I'm not fully comfortable with, the plumbing."

"You do plumbing."

"No, I do installation of plumbing *fixtures*. I take the existing pipes that come out of the wall or floor and attach things to them, toilets and tubs and sinks and faucets. But getting the pipes from the water supply line to the floor or wall? Not. Qualified. Not to mention the structural engineering stuff and the heavy lifting, and he has amazing ideas about design to boot. Seriously, Marie, I can't lose him."

"Can I say something without you getting mad?"

"Of course."

"Do you think you want to fight so hard for Jag because you feel badly that you didn't fight harder for Grant?"

"What does that mean?"

"I dunno. I mean you loved Grant, and you were together and great for a long time, and yes, he cheated, but he wanted to work on it, he wanted to go to therapy, to try, and you didn't try at all, so I wonder if any part of this is about that?"

"Marie, he cheated on me. Twice. With a MAN. What exactly did you expect me to do? Buy a rainbow flag and ignore it?"

"You said you wouldn't get mad."

"That's before I knew you were going to psychobabble analyze me and accuse me of some sort of weird projection just because I didn't want to try to save my relationship with my gay ex-fiancé, and I do want to help a kind, talented man who is making my life possible stay in the country to do the work he wants to do."

"Bi."

"Excuse me?"

"Grant said he is bi. Not gay. And yes, if he were gay, I would say that marriage would be a bad idea, but he's bi, and if he's bi then he can equally be madly in love with you as he could with a boy. Besides, why is it so different for him to have to resist the temptation to cheat than it is for you?"

"I cannot BELIEVE we are even having this conversation."

"Look, I'm not saying you should still be with Grant. I'm not. I get the hurt and betrayal, I do. But I know that people come back from infidelity if they love each other; it's possible, I've done it."

"John?"

"Once. Five years ago. He was at a tattoo convention in Vegas, got hammered, hooked up with an old flame from when he worked there. Came home and confessed, cried, we went to therapy, dealt with some of his commitment crap, got over it."

"Why didn't you say? Why would you go through all of that alone?"

"Because it was none of your business. And before you say it, I know that this is none of mine. But I do want you to recognize that Jag isn't going to be deported to some horrible third-world country to work in a factory under some oppressive regime. He'll have to go back to London to live with his ambassador father and get a fabulous high-paying job at an industrial design firm. Perhaps you not fighting for him would be something of a blessing, at least for him."

I look at her. And then I start to laugh. "He'll make so much more money."

"Yep."

"Marie, you know that Grant and I, that just couldn't . . ."

"I know. I do. I just hate where you are, I loved Grant, I loved you together, and I hate all of this for you."

"Thanks. I hate it too."

"You heard from Emily at all?"

"Not since she popped by to tour the house, thank god."

Marie is silent.

"Okay, fine, spit it out."

"You should call her. See her again. I think it would be good for you."

"And why, exactly, is that?"

"Take this the right way, and know that I love you."

"No good conversation ever starts with that sentence."

"You are running the risk of becoming a complete asshole."

"Well, how could I take THAT wrong?"

"Hear me out. You aren't accountable to ANYONE right now. You have no job, so no bosses or clients to answer to. You have no family. You've got the three of us, but you have no problem pushing us away or ignoring our advice when we give it. And that is IT.

You just have you, and I know that you don't mind, that you are a lone wolf and all of that, and perfectly fine on your own, except you can fall into just being all id like an enormous four-year-old. Do only what you want when you want, and it isn't healthy. If you aren't careful you will get so set in your ways that it will be impossible to let anyone else in, to let their opinions matter. Maybe that is why I'm worried you didn't fight for what you had with Grant. Because I liked seeing you happy with a partner in your life and I don't want to see you never connected to someone like that again."

"And what, pray tell, is so amazing about being connected to someone like that again? Why on earth would I be focused on that, of all things? Not everyone is cut out for that whole paired-up thing. I tried it; I gave it a good old shot and look what happened. I'll tell you a secret; I don't know that I ever WANT to have that again. Alone isn't the same as lonely, Marie."

"I never met anyone with a healthy relationship history who thinks so."

"So let me get this straight, playing big sister to Emily is going to, what, exactly? Remind me to get out there and get a boyfriend?"

"Remind you to care about someone else besides yourself."

"Maybe you need to be reminded to care more about yourself than about me. I'm not a fixer-upper, Marie. And I like myself just fine, even if you think I'm broken."

Her eyes shine with unreleased tears. "I love you, honey, and I don't think you're broken, I just think you've maybe lost your way a bit."

"Well, when I'm interested in your opinion about that, I'll be sure to let you know." I get up and grab my stuff and stomp out, leaving her there at the table, and I'm halfway home with a knot in my chest of equal parts hurt and anger before I realize that on top of having essentially the first real fight of my life with my best friend, I also stiffed her on the check for lunch.

14

I take advantage of the decent weather to walk to Lula instead of driving. It's still cold, but the sun is out and the wind is pretty calm. I need to get out of the house, out from under the dark cloud I've been living with. Even after a long mea culpa phone call with Marie, I still feel shitty. I know she forgives me, but I also know that I'm going to quickly run out of Get Out of Jail Free cards with my girlfriends. I don't know how to get across to them how uncomfortable this whole situation makes me. How much I feel like "less than" when I am with them. None of them are under the pressures that I am, not financially, not emotionally; they just don't get it, and it makes me feel like they don't get me. At all. Which scares the bejesus out of me, because Marie is right about one thing: They are pretty much all I have. If I lose them, I'm in even deeper shit than I am right now.

Which is the only possible reason that I even agreed to this lunch.

I get to Lula and am told that my party is already here, and the waitress leads me to the back room.

Emily gets up and comes to greet me, and I suffer the hug she clearly can't help giving me. "I'm so glad you called, and I just love this place, it is the cutest!"

"Well, um, I figured you must be pretty close to leaving soon, so I thought we should get together one more time." She had implied that she would be in town for a little while, so it seemed a safe bet to suck it up and take her to lunch. Do a good deed, make Marie and the girls happy, and get them off my back for a bit.

"I thought maybe I'd stay longer. You know, if you were up for that."

Great. "Up for it in what way?"

"In the way of spending some time together. Hanging out. Getting to know each other."

I take a breath. "Emily, I don't know if I'm really—"

The waiter interrupts us, and I order coffee, and she orders hot chocolate, and I order a plate of the pastries for us to share.

"Just hear me out, okay? I know you don't want me here, I totally get it, and it doesn't even bother me that you don't want me here. But I want to be here. Maybe the fact that once upon a time your mom was married to my dad and I called her Mom for a little while isn't much of a bond. But it's all I have. And I need it. I need family. I don't really have any, just my dad. He is awesome, but not enough. I know you think I'm some annoying kid and a complete flake and you're probably right. At least I own it. I'm not going to apologize for being me. And I'm not going to apologize for wanting to know you. When I was little, you were this combination mythological creature, imaginary friend, possible superhero. And you were imminent. Mom always talked about 'having both her girls together,' and I believed her and waited for it and believed that you and I would meet and be best friends and playmates and soul sisters and happy ever after." Her blue eyes are steelier than I remember them being. "I want you to be real. You don't have to love me, or think of me as a sister or whatever, but maybe you could just talk to me. Tell me who you are. Tell me why the mom I remember wasn't the mom you had. Tell me why you find the idea of me so horrible. Help me make you a real person, and reconcile the fantasies of my childhood."

"Why?"

"Because I need it."

"Why do you need it so badly?"

"Because I just do." This is beginning to sound fishy.

"Bullshit. Why do you need this? Sounds like you have plenty of girlfriends, every sorority girl I ever met talks about having just so many sisters; why do you need me to be another one?"

She blushes behind her blond bangs. "Because I lied."

"About what?"

"About you."

"To who?"

"Harvard."

"You lied to Harvard about me."

"Yeah."

"In what way?"

"In the way of who you are and what you are to me."

"What exactly does that mean?"

She looks me dead in the eye. "Do you have any idea how hard it is to get into a graduate psychology program right out of undergrad? At an Ivy League school?"

"Nope."

"It's damn near impossible. And I'm a white girl with a privileged background from Miami. I'm a dime a dozen. I needed an edge. You were my edge."

"In what way?"

"In my essay, in my interviews, I made you up. The step-sister who became like a real sister. The story of a blended and created family torn apart and then reunited. I told everyone that when your mom left she ripped me from your arms, and it took us years to find each other again, and then when we did, we bonded tighter than if we had been related by blood. When you want to do family therapy, having some strong family background reads really well. The girl whose dad was so fucked up by the death of his first love and the abandonment of his second that he never really stopped being the sad guy? That is boring as FUCK. I needed an edge, and I just gave voice to some of my youthful fantasies and it goddamned worked. It worked really freaking well. I got into HARVARD."

My, my. "Well, that's good, right?"

"It's a lie."

"Maybe you should see if you can switch to their creative writing program."

"That's not funny, this is all I ever wanted. But I did it totally wrong and I can't get out from under it."

"It's just a grad school essay."

"And the interviews. And the group entry sessions with the other students. And the orientation meetings with my future classmates."

I start to laugh. "I'm like that football player's dead girlfriend."

"It's not funny. I went too far. I made up too much. My acceptance, apparently, wasn't unanimous, but was pushed through by a professor who wants to work with me, to mentor me. He thinks that my experiences will make for a wonderful dissertation."

"So all this about needing family and connection is just bullshit. You fucked yourself at school and you need me to be real so that you don't get caught."

She looks down at her mug of hot chocolate. "Yeah. Pretty much."

I think about this. "You know what? That? Actually makes me like you more. Fuck it. What do you want to know?"

She looks up with a furrowed brow. "Really?"

I shrug. "Why the hell not? *Sis.*"

She grins. And we start over.

No way!" Emily says, taking a bite of the banana cream pie we decided to share. "He was in your shower with a GUY? That is so like right out of a movie or a book or something."

"Yeah. A really stupid predictable one." We've been at Lula for over three hours. I've officially shared pretty much my entire life with her, and to her credit, she's a good listener when she's eating. She'll probably actually make a decent therapist, in spite of the whole false pretenses thing. She knows about my horrible childhood and Grand-mère and Joe. She knows about Grant, and my job, and the house, and everything I'm up against, and how my best girlfriends are all up my ass about living my life completely wrong. And I weirdly feel sort of better having unburdened a bit.

"Wow. That is rough. And your besties, they're just not really supporting your choices at all?"

"They mean well. They want what's best for me. They thought Grant was good for me, balanced me out."

"Are they right?"

I think about that. "In a lot of ways. Marie isn't completely wrong; I'm a solo artist in a lot of ways. I've never minded the alone thing. Grant forced me out of my comfort zones. He pushed me, he made me feel safe, he loved me, warts and all. It felt like he really got me. But he still called me out on my bullshit."

"Do you miss him?"

"I do. The bastard. He was my best friend. My girls are awesome, but even they don't know all of me. He knew all of me."

"Did you ever cheat?"

"On Grant? Never."

"On anyone."

"Once. A college boyfriend. There was a TA in one of my classes, really hot in that bookish way. I was struggling a bit with the papers, he was helping me . . . I think it was a combination of proximity and the fact that he thought I was smart and capable; it just sort of happened." I hadn't thought about him in a very long time.

"How many times?"

"Three. And then the semester was over and he graduated and I spent the summer working with Joe and I ended up dumping the boyfriend anyway."

"But like, did you love him?"

"No."

"Did you love the boyfriend?"

"Sort of. In that college love sort of way."

"But you loved him. Did you feel bad about the cheating?"

"Very. Horribly guilty."

"Did the cheating mean anything, I mean anything real?"

"No, not in the least, it was just a weird thing that happened."

She sits, silent, and waits for me.

"It's not the same."

"Of course not."

"IT'S NOT THE SAME. I was nineteen. And I wasn't engaged to be married."

"It's not the same, but it is similar. I mean, you said Grant was working long hours with this guy, training him to run the new restaurant . . . You can see where the situations aren't completely unrelated."

Holy crap. She may be a liar, and she may be annoying as hell, but this kid isn't entirely off track. If I think back to how the whole thing happened for me, and imagine the place Grant was in, I hate to admit that I can see how it could have happened. Why it might have happened. What it might have meant, or not.

"Doesn't matter."

"Probably not." She nods. "Because you know who you are."

"I do."

"And you know what you need."

"Exactly."

"So that is your answer, isn't it? If you know who you are and what you need, the rest is just details."

My eyes snap open at eight thirty. After the epic lunch and emotional purging, I needed a serious nap. But as I lay in bed, I couldn't help replaying my conversations with Emily and Marie over and over in my head. Wondering if Marie was right, if I should have tried harder to save my relationship with Grant. If I should try less hard to keep Jag. Wondering if Emily was implying the same thing, telling me that only I know who I am and what I need. Wondering if I'm losing my mind even considering that this twenty-one-year-old pathological crazy person might have any sort of actual insight. I finally fell asleep and into the kind of fitful dreams one only has during a nap that goes too deep, and woke to find myself a half centimeter from falling off Grant's side of the bed. Or what used to be Grant's side of the bed. I wonder if I could be as forgiving as Marie, if I could get past the betrayal enough to honor everything that was good.

Then I remember the sight of Grant and Gregg in the shower. God bless Marie, I'm truly glad that she and John worked it out, because I adore him and I love them together, but it just isn't the same. Maybe it is terrible of me to think that if Grant had cheated with a girl, I might have been able to forgive him, maybe that is very small minded and intolerant, but I can't help it; it just feels different.

I throw on my robe over my pajamas, and head downstairs. I put on a pot of coffee, and get a bowl of Cinnamon Toast Crunch, which they should really call Cinnamon Toast Crack the way I go through it. I wolf down one bowl and pour another. Schatzi comes downstairs and I dump some kibble in her bowl. I should go get dressed so I can walk her, but for some reason I pick up Gemma's journal.

Tomorrow is the day. I've worked all week to make sure that everything is prepared, we all have. The house sparkles, and smells glorious, full of roses and gardenias. The silver sparkles at the ready, and the larder is filled to bursting with cold roasts and a grand turkey. I couldn't be happier for Martha. It was unexpected, this love, but she didn't shy away from it, she didn't resign herself to what she thought she'd have to settle for, she didn't back down from her heart. She fought for herself. For her love. And now she gets to have the life she truly deserves, truly wants, and really, could any of us hope for more?

I stop the spoon halfway to my mouth.

Because as usual, Gemma has hit the nail right on the head.

15

A nother beer?" I ask Jag.

"Please, allow me." He stands up from the table and takes both of our bottles, dropping them into the recycling bin and grabbing two more from the fridge, deftly popping the caps and returning to the table. We've been making endless lists: what needs to be done and in what order, supplies that need to be ordered and delivered and supplies that can be shopped for in person.

"Thanks," I say, taking a long pull on my beer, and stretching my neck back and forth. "Long one today, but good."

He nods. "I feel like every day is something new. This house is a master class all on its own." Schatzi clicks over and jumps lightly into his lap as if her little legs have springs in them. He allows her to get settled into a dog-shaped loaf, and then begins to stroke her silvery fur and massage her silky ears. She is practically purring, and looking at me with smug satisfaction. Whatever.

"Big plans tonight?" I ask.

"Just meeting up with some friends for dinner."

"Where?"

"My friend Balbir is hosting tonight."

"You all cook a lot together, you and your pals I mean."

"In our community, coming together for home-cooked food and conversation is very much how we connect with people."

"It's nice. I mean, it sounds nice."

"You should come."

I can feel myself blush, wondering if he thinks I was angling
for an invite. Which, in my current state, is the last thing I
want or need. I'm having a hard enough time avoiding my own
friends, let alone having to meet and engage with someone
else's. "Thanks, maybe another time. I've got a date with a very
hot shower, a very greasy pizza, and an early bed."

"Perhaps another time? I know my friends would love to
meet you, they've heard so many good things."

"Are you lying about me to your friends?" I'm joking, but
something about it feels weirdly forced.

"Not in the least. I've just told them the absolute truth, that
you are a skilled homebuilder who found a beautiful house in
need of saving, and that you quit your job and gave up your
home to focus all of your time and energy on it and launch your
new independent business, and you were kind enough to take
on an untested and inexperienced apprentice whom you have
been meticulously training in your art."

I start to laugh, and then I can't stop. I'm laughing with
tears streaming down my cheeks, making dolphin noises. Jag
looks at me as if I've got three heads. And one of them is purple.
And speaking Swahili. While high on shrooms.

"I'm sorry," I say, wiping my damp cheeks. "It's just so . . .
WRONG." I hiccup.

"What do you mean?"

"I'm a skilled homebuilder, all right, who quit her job
because she was probably about to be fired, in a manner that
ensures she will never get a decent reference or be employable
by anyone else, hence the need to be self-employed. Who is living in her only future source of income because she caught her
ex-fiancé having sex with another man in the apartment they
shared, but was in his name. I took you in because every other
day laborer in the greater Chicagoland area had turned me
down and I was in desperate need of help from any reasonably

able-bodied person to try to have one thing in my life not be spectacularly fucked up. Finding you is the one good thing and shining light in the enormous disaster that is my life."

Jag takes a thoughtful sip of his beer. "Well, thank you, I suppose."

"No, Jag, thank YOU. It is sweet of you to have thought such nice things about me, and to have described me like that to your friends. It's been a while since anyone looked at me through a kindness filter instead of a pity filter."

"You feel like your friends pity you?"

"I do. A short time ago I had a good job, a gorgeous apartment, plenty of money for the life I was living, and a loving partner and best friend who I was going to marry. I had three amazing girlfriends who I could have fun with, and this beautiful old place to putter around in. Now I'm just a sad sack, living alone in a construction site with a dog who detests me, no money, no job, and a very uncertain future."

"I don't see that person you describe. I see a strong, capable woman, who is facing a difficult situation head-on."

"Thank you for that."

He tilts his head. "You caught him with another man?"

I nod, and then decide to go with the moment. I tell Jag all about the day I quit and caught Grant. I've finally got just enough backbone to tell it in a funny way, describing myself as a snarky tornado whirring through the MacMurphy offices like an evil dervish, spewing insults in my wake. Really playing up my saucy little naked prance into the bathroom. I may have embellished to have Gregg shrieking like a girl when I announced my presence, and running out of the apartment wet and naked with an armload of clothes. Pretty soon, Jag is laughing almost as hard as I am, and shaking his head at the ridiculousness of it all.

When we both catch our breath, he shakes his head. "That is a lot, Anneke, I had no idea. It must still be very painful for you."

"What can I do? I mean, I miss him, which sucks. I'd never been that close to a man before, that trusting. I really let all my defenses down. Whatever issues we had, and clearly we had many more than I was aware of, it wasn't like we were unhappy. I really loved him, as much as I've ever loved anyone, or even felt capable of loving anyone, so while the betrayal is horrible and gut-wrenching, the missing him is worse."

"Did you think about trying to make it work?"

"I did. I do. I know if I called him tomorrow he would want to. But I don't know. I don't trust myself or my feelings anymore; that's the nut of it. I trusted how I felt about him, about us, about the life we were building together. And he broke that trust, and in a way broke me. I'd been fine up until I met him, just assuming I would never get married or be serious about someone, and that was comfortable. Then he made me imagine a different kind of life. And then he shattered it. So now, I don't really know who I am. A big part of me is back to believing that marriage is not for someone like me, partnership is not for someone like me, and that I should be okay with that. But then I miss him, and wonder if I really am that girl anymore. I think about calling him to say that we can try again, but then I think that it is just the loneliness and fear talking, and if I go back, I'm just a weak and stupid person who is trying to make pieces fit that will never fit. And I wonder if a big part of my being conflicted is also because of my very precarious financial situation, which scares me even more, because I have fought my whole life to not turn into my mother, who only ever saw men as a means to financial security."

"Maybe it's too soon to know. Maybe the fact that you are still conflicted means that you don't yet know what your new reality is going to be, and you just have to let it come to you in its own time. There is a saying in my culture, 'I seldom end up where I wanted to go, but almost always end up where I need to be.'"

"You don't think I'd be an idiot to go back to him?"

"I think you'd be an idiot to close yourself off from any life experience that has the potential to bring you happiness, or let you know yourself better. I think if your heart contains enough forgiveness and hope to return to someone who betrayed you, because you believe that after some hard work your life will be fuller with him, then that is a beautiful thing. And if you know yourself well enough to know that you could never give so much of yourself to someone who was able to hurt you that deeply, and that you would rather be a strong woman standing on her own by choice and design, then there is no shame in choosing that life."

"Do you want it? The whole marriage and kids thing?"

"Very much. But it's complicated."

"The cultural thing?"

"I very much would like to find the right woman, settle down, have a family. But while I've never been particularly drawn to Indian women romantically, I am very drawn to them in a spiritual way, and while I have loved women of many different races in my past, none of them ever felt like the right permanent match. And yes, it was often the cultural differences that parted us."

"Well, maybe you just haven't met the right Indian woman yet."

"Or the right non-Indian woman."

"That too."

"I believe when I meet her, whoever she is, I'll know, and so will she. And so will you, for that matter, however it is supposed to work itself out."

"You're a very wise man, Jagjeet Singh."

"It's the turban. Makes us all look like gurus and genies."

"If I rub your belly, do I get a wish?"

"If you rub my belly, you might get a surprise. Genies aren't priests, you know."

It's the first time he's ever been remotely flirtatious with me, and it makes me laugh.

"I'll be careful, then; I know how all of this can affect a man." I make a dramatic sweeping gesture down my body as if I am Jessica Rabbit, making note of my torn and filthy baggy jeans, my tattered oversized fleece, and my hair, which is probably looking like an auburn version of Einstein's famous do.

We laugh, and it feels good to have shared with him, to let him in a little bit and to know that he doesn't think less of me.

"Well, irresistible as you are, I should go home and take care of all of this"—he mimics my movement—"before dinner. Sure I can't get you to come? You'll be most welcome, and if you don't want to dispel the myth I've created around you, your secrets will be safe with me."

I'm briefly tempted to say yes, but the word catches in my throat. The best I can do is ask for a rain check, which Jag accepts, but only after I promise to come with him in a few nights when there is another potluck dinner planned. "I'll bring stuff here and teach you a dish and it can be from both of us. I'm dying to really cook in this kitchen."

"Okay. Deal."

Jag gives me a hug, and for the very first time since my life blew up, I'm able to actually hug someone back. Because his embrace is filled with friendship and respect, and not one ounce of pity or charity. It is the hug of someone who is thinking, "That sucks for you, but you're bigger and better than that." The hug of someone who thinks you're just fine. And I had no idea how much I needed it until right now.

Jack. It's Anneke. Long time no talk."

"Oh, um, hey, Anneke, how are you doing?" Jack is a masonry guy I worked with a ton when I was at MacMurphy, and was the one that taught me how to deal with the stonework in the basement.

"I'm great. Wondering if I can bribe you for a little more work over here at the Palmer house?" Jack is usually good for some free labor in exchange for food. His wife has slowly gone from healthy eater, to vegetarian, to gluten-free vegan, and the mere mention of a Giordano's stuffed sausage and pepperoni pizza is often all it takes. "I need to do limestone sills for the basement windows."

There is an awkward pause. "Um, Anneke, I can't."

"I didn't even mention a date, are you just swamped? Usually this weather means you are really slow. I could sweeten the deal with a little under-the-table cash."

"No, it isn't the timing, it's just, I can't take the chance."

"C'mon, she'll never know. I'll have mouthwash on hand, even an extra toothbrush if you want. I can even give you a carrot for the road."

He laughs. "It isn't Sherrie I'm worried about; she knows I eat stuff when I'm out, as long as I don't bring it home I'm cool. It's, um . . . Anneke, if I tell you something in confidence, you have to swear to me that you won't go off the handle and that it doesn't ever come back on me."

"Okay, now you've got me worried."

"Murph has you blacklisted."

"Blacklisted?"

"He's told every sub and laborer that if any of them ever do so much as help you hang a picture, they will never work for him again, and he won't give them a reference." That enormous butthole.

"No wonder everyone's been dodging me."

"Look, kiddo, you know we all are rooting for you, and that house is going to be amazing. And when you are a big-shot developer, we all hope you'll remember us fondly. I, for one, since we're off the record, would love nothing more than to tell Brian Murphy to stick it right up his arse. But I got three kids to get through college, and all that organic gluten-free crap Sherrie is making us all eat is damned expensive. I just can't lose that big a chunk of my business, much as I'd rather help you for free than work for him."

"It's okay, Jack, I get it. No worries. And thanks for being honest with me; I was starting to get a complex. Now I can stop calling everyone and making them uncomfortable."

"Yeah, I ran into a few people last week and they were all talking about how shitty the whole thing is. Is it true you told them to go fuck themselves in front of an asshole client?"

"Yeah, I did."

"That is the best thing I've ever heard. I wish there was video."

"Oh yeah, that would be great PR for my new business! Me losing my shit and telling clients I think they are stupid and devoid of taste."

"Well, sure, if you put it that way. Look, I'll tell you what, I got a guy out in McHenry; he's good and things are quiet out there, and he usually doesn't work downtown, so no MacMurphy conflict. You'd have to pay him in money and not food, but I can put a word in. Maybe he'd be willing to drive down, make you a good deal?"

"Thanks, Jack, I'd really appreciate that."

"I'll check with him and email you his info if he says yes. Stay tuned."

Fucking Murph. I thought everything was cool after I signed the paperwork, but clearly he holds a grudge. Makes me wish I'd punched him physically instead of just verbally. I'm going to have to go back to my budget and make some new adjustments, since now I know I can't count on any of my guys to lend a hand for love or money. And, which is worse, I now have to think about a future in which I do what I do while finding a completely new set of tradesmen who are as good as the ones I've just lost. This is a serious setback, since my hope had been to sell this place, maybe do three or four quick two-month flips to build something of a portfolio and keep cash moving, and working with the guys I know and trust was a big part of that plan.

I plug my phone in to charge, and flip open Gemma's journal, which is sitting on my desk.

I can't be responsible for anyone but myself. My successes, my failures, they rest with me. And if I can get through my days shouldering that truth, that is enough.

Isn't that the truth, Gemma? Isn't that just the damnable truth?

16

I get out of the shower with butterflies in my stomach. You'd think I was going on a first date or something. I suppose in a way, it is, even if it isn't a romantic thing, it is the first time I'm socializing with Jag outside of the house. It does feel like he has become a true friend in such a short time, I genuinely trust him and feel safe in his presence. So when he insisted that I keep my word and come tonight to his friend's house for potluck, I couldn't really say no, despite every fiber of my being wanting to avoid the gathering like the plague. However, when Gemma tells me, *"Every now and again it is essential for the well-being of your soul to do something for some-one who cares for you to show them that their joy is important to you, however directly it may be in conflict with your own. Set aside your petty objections and simply embrace the challenge, whatever it may be, and try to find pleasure in the act of selflessness, if not the thing itself,"* I take heed. After all, Jag is in many ways saving my bacon on this job; going to dinner and meeting some of his crew isn't exactly the worst punishment in the world.

We spent a lovely couple of hours this afternoon in the kitchen, and he taught me his grandmother's recipe for biryani, which I'll never be able to replicate, but look forward to eating tonight. He's picking me up, which is probably part of why it feels so much like a date. In my past life I'd have just blithely Ubered my way to and fro, so that I could drink if I wanted, and not worry about parking, but those easy days are over; if I don't drive somewhere, I'm on the bus or the train. I think Jag figured if he offered to pick me up, I couldn't wriggle out at the last minute, which means that he is really starting to know me, since a big part of me definitely wants to beg off.

I'm wearing my one good pair of dark "dressy" jeans, a black cowl-neck sweater, and my black motorcycle boots. A cool, wide silver chain-mail bracelet Hedy gave me for my birthday a couple of years ago. My hair is sort of behaving itself, so that is something. I do my usual minimal makeup routine of blush, mascara, and lip gloss, and I'm girded for battle.

"You look very nice," Jag says when I open the door. "Although I sort of miss the 'grout in hair' thing you usually are sporting."

"Very funny." I hand him the casserole dish containing our biryani, and lock up the house behind me.

On the way to his friend Nageena's house we chat about the people I'm going to meet. Nageena is a teaching fellow at DePaul in the history department; they met when Jag first got to town, at the Punjabi Cultural Society at a lecture. Their friend Balbir, who hosted the last event, is still in the graduate program that Jag dropped out of. Balbir's roommate, Chuck, is a CPA, and his girlfriend, Sarah, does freelance marketing and social media stuff for nonprofits. A friend of Nageena's named Geeta, who is a pediatric oncology resident at Lurie Children's Hospital, and her boyfriend, Ben, who is an ob-gyn and neonatal surgeon at Prentice.

"It's a shame all your friends are so dumb and unaccomplished," I tease him.

"Yeah, because all of your pals are such slackers."

"True enough. But I think I may not be smart enough to hang out with your peeps."

"You're fine. Besides, every one of the people there will someday be in the market for a house or a renovation. Think of it as a networking event."

"You make an excellent point."

Nageena's apartment in Uptown is lovely and bright. The building looks to be about 1915, classic redbrick six-flat, with two units per floor. High ceilings, good space, some of the original built-ins and stained glass, and it smells of cooking onions and spices. Nageena herself is a beautiful curvy woman, with skin the color of a perfect cappuccino, deep brown eyes, and a generous smile. She is wearing a beautiful swingy dress in deep magenta, and a stack of gold bangles make a joyous clatter. Her long black hair is positively gleaming it is so thick and shiny, and she's wearing it pulled back off her face with a bright teal scarf; intricate gold dangling earrings with tiny pink stones float just above her shoulders. She welcomes me with a hug, and she smells of sandalwood and cinnamon.

"So delighted you could join us, Anneke." She relieves Jag of the casserole dish, and accepts a kiss on each cheek from him, looking up at him from beneath the fringe of long lashes that frame her sparkling eyes.

"Biryani," he says.

Nageena closes her eyes, lifts the dish to her nose, and inhales deeply. "Heaven. Thank you. I'll pop it in the oven to keep warm, get Anneke a drink. Everyone is in the living room."

Jag helps me out of my coat, which he hangs on the hall rack with the others, and we head down the hall toward the happy buzz of people having a lively conversation.

Wait a hot minute, lady," Sarah says, accepting a piece of pistachio cake from Nageena. "Your ex-fiancé was Grant MATHESON? From *World's Supreme Chef*??? We LOVED him!"

"Yep. That's the one."

"Oh, man, that guy can freaking cook," Ben says. "One of my patients gave me a gift card for his place; we had a ridiculous meal. The pork belly haunts my dreams."

"Seriously," says Geeta, popping a dried fig into her mouth. "One of the top five meals of our lives."

"He can definitely cook," I say.

"How are you not the size of a house after living with him?" Balbir asks.

"BALBIR!" Nageena slaps his arm. "Please excuse him, you are starting to see why he's still single."

"And what is your excuse?" he pokes back at her.

"I'm waiting for perfection that matches my own, of course." She smiles her beautiful smile, and I absolutely believe her. She isn't the kind of girl who makes you wonder why she doesn't have someone, you just know that the kind of guy who is good enough for her is rare, and she projects the kind of strength that says she is perfectly happy to wait till he shows up. As opposed to me, who apparently projects the kind of aloofness that says I don't believe for one minute that there is such a thing as the guy for me, and I don't expect anyone to show up.

"Really, though, it must have been kind of cool to have a chef at home to cook for you." Chuck takes a sip of hot sweet tea that Nageena has served in delicate etched glass cups.

"It was pretty awesome. And Balbir isn't wrong, I'm lucky my job is so physical or I'd be twice this size!"

"We totally voted for him for fan favorite," Sarah says. "I mean, when he won that challenge with the free trip for two to Hong Kong, and gave it to his teammate so she could take her husband to meet her grandmother? I totally cried."

"Us too!" Geeta says. "How about when the German chef accidentally left her marinating pork shoulder on the counter overnight, and he just jumped in and helped her make those sausages, and then she won the challenge! And he was HAPPY for her. Real class."

"It's true," Ben says. "We called in about a dozen times to vote for him after that one."

"Well, thank you for that, that extra twenty grand paid for our powder room!" For some reason this happy crew just makes me feel at ease, and I've had a better evening than I can remember. They are warm and funny; Nageena and Jag flanked me at the table and were sure to fill me in on inside jokes when they came up. We have talked about movies and television and Chicago. The food is all really spectacular, with the exception of Balbir's saag paneer, which was soupy and underseasoned and a little bit slimy, but he accepted everyone's good-natured ribbing about his cooking skills. He seems to be comfortable being the socially awkward oaf of the gang, and while they all tease him, it is apparent that it comes from love.

"Perhaps we could talk about something besides how much we all like Anneke's ex, no?" Nageena says pointedly.

"It's okay," I say. "He's everything you guys saw on TV. He is a genuinely nice guy, and a really spectacular chef." They're reminding me of the reasons Grant was the first person I ever could even consider spending my life with, and despite myself, I can't help but be proud of him.

"Are you guys still friends?" Geeta asks.

"We're taking a break for now. But I still care for him a lot, and hope that someday we can be friends again." Which slips out, and I realize as I say it that it smacks of the truth.

"Well, if he really is that nice a guy, why'd you dump him?"

"BALBIR!!!!" they all say at once.

I can't help but laugh. "We had some fundamental issues that I just couldn't get past." This seems the easiest thing to say. After all, Grant is a public figure, and his sexual-identity midlife crisis is nobody's business.

"That is enough out of you, mister, help me clear, and the rest of you head to the living room." Nageena shoos us out of the dining room, and picks Balbir up by his ear to help her. I turn to try to help, but Jag shakes his head to indicate that this is the way things go.

"Her kitchen is tiny, and she hates a lot of people in there. Don't even try."

I'm full of delicious and new-to-me flavors, good wine, and the warmth of good fellowship. Back in Nageena's comfortable living room, the conversation turns away from Grant and onto easier topics. Jag pours me more sweet tea, and I settle into the couch.

"Jag tells us that the home you are working on is going to be just amazing, Anneke. Did you always want to do what you do?" Chuck asks.

"Pretty much. My stepdad was a general contractor and master carpenter, and I started learning from him when I was about thirteen. He made me fall in love with building things, with fixing things, and especially with saving old homes. Can't imagine doing anything else, really."

"That is just so cool," Geeta says. "Ben here can do a C-section in seventy-four seconds, but ask him to replace a toilet handle, and you end up with a flooded bathroom."

"ONE TIME!" Ben says, mock offended.

"Ha!" says Sarah, pointing her thumb at Chuck. "This one tried to assemble an IKEA dresser for our closet, and hammered the pegs right through the fronts of all the drawers."

"I just can't control my own strength," Chuck says, making exaggerated body-builder moves to show off nonexistent biceps. I think I could definitely take him in an arm-wrestling match. With my left hand. Using my pinky.

Balbir and Nageena come back out to join us, with a fresh pot of tea and a plate of cookies.

"Good job, everyone. Another fabulous meal. Mostly," Nageena says, patting Balbir on the arm in a placating fashion.

"It was amazing," I say. "I seriously don't know how you all do it."

"What are you talking about? Your biryani was perfect," Geeta says.

"My biryani was Jag's biryani, I mostly chopped things and washed dishes. I'm just learning how to cook, and everything I do is totally hit-or-miss."

"Is that because Grant just automatically did all the cooking?" Sarah asks.

"Partially, I suppose. Cooking wasn't a big thing in my house growing up. I was mostly raised by my grandmother, and she really considered food to just be fuel, and she was always concerned about her figure, so there wasn't a lot going on there. And then with my stepdad, he was a steak and potatoes or takeout kind of guy."

"What about your mother?" Nageena asks.

"She was mostly absent, and when she was present her hair and makeup took way too much time and effort to leave time or energy for cooking."

"So you lived with your stepdad even without her?" Balbir asks.

"Sort of. We all lived together for almost three years, which is actually the longest continuous stretch I ever lived with her. When she left I had to go back to my grandmother for a couple of years, but then I lived with him during college and grad school, and we worked together for a couple of years."

"I'm sorry about your mother, that must have been very hard," Nageena says.

I shrug. "I was so little when she left the first time that I didn't know I was supposed to miss her, I guess. It was just normal. She'd come home every now and then for a time, but never for long. I never really learned to rely on her, she was sort of helpless anyway, so I just kind of accepted her presence when she was there, and went back to my normal routine when she left."

"What about now?" Sarah asks. "I know a couple of people who had hard relationships with their folks growing up, but now that everyone is an adult, they can sort of relate to one another in a different way."

"We don't speak. I saw her for a few days a couple of years ago when my grandmother died, but nothing since. It's not some melodramatic tragedy, I'm fine. She should never have been a mother, and since I don't want kids of my own, I sort of get that.

And I do just fine without her." But this feels a little like a lie. Emily's arrival has me questioning her maternal instincts. After all, while Emily wasn't enough to make Anneliese stay, she continues to tell me that she was loving and doting and a real mother to her. She took care of her when she was sick, kissed boo-boos, soothed nightmares. None of which she ever did for me. So I have to face the fact that perhaps it wasn't that my mother didn't have mothering in her, I just wasn't the right kid.

"Good for you," Balbir says. Everyone turns to him, waiting for him to follow it up with something inappropriate or accidentally offensive, but nothing else comes out. And when we all realize that we were pausing conversation for the same reason, it makes us chuckle, and then giggle, and pretty soon the room is filled with laughter and kindness and I feel utterly, completely, at home.

Thank you, they're all wonderful," I say, as Jag pulls up in front of the house. "I had a really good time."

"I'm glad you came. They all loved you."

"It was just the thing I needed, even if I tried to pretend I didn't need it, so I really appreciate your making me come."

"I think sometimes the best thing about making new friends as an adult is that there is a little bit of a clean slate, no baggage. When they meet you, all they see is who you are in that moment, no memories of a younger you to cloud things. No knowledge of your history to hold against you, as it were."

"I think you're right. It was just easy to be with them, get to know them, not feel like they were basing their opinions of me on anything other than what was in front of them."

"I'm sorry if there was too much discussion about Grant."

"It didn't bother me. The fact is, I've been thinking of him quite a lot lately. Everything that has happened, Emily showing up, the house, cooking. It was sort of nice to be with people who think of him fondly. The girls are so angry with him for what he did; when I'm with them I feed off of that. But tonight I was reminded of the guy who really was my best friend, and my partner, and my love, and it felt nice to think of that Grant for a while, instead of the guy in the shower with the other guy."

"Do you think you might be rethinking your connection to him?"

"Maybe. There's a part of me that wants to try to be friends again, but that part is also scared that if I do reconnect then I might be weak and fall back into the relationship, and I don't know what to think or feel about that."

"That's a lot. But maybe you should just follow your instincts and see what happens."

"Maybe. Maybe I should just call him and see if instead of ending up where I wanted to go, I end up where I need to be?"

"Exactly. Do you want me to walk the dog with you?"

"You're sweet, it's late. I'm just going to let her out in the backyard; I'll walk her longer in the morning."

"Okay, then. Will you come again sometime?"

"You bet. See you Monday?"

"Of course. And, Anneke?"

"Yeah?"

"You are everything you ought to be. Other people's opinions can't alter that reality. Don't forget that."

I climb into bed, thinking about the night, about Jag and his wonderful friends, about Grant and all that was good between us. About who I am and who I want to be. About the life I have and the life I could have. I grab the journal.

"What do you think, Gemma?"

"Where there is the greatest risk lies the greatest reward. No fantastical thing was ever achieved by aiming for mediocrity. Safe is easy. Extraordinary requires a little bit of danger."

I reach for my phone.

17

From Gemma's Journal:

When Martha and her husband enter the dining room, I burst quite into tears and laughter at once. She looked so beautiful in her lace dress, and he was dashing in tails, and they both simply glowed. I feel quite certain that they are very much in love, and I'm so thrilled for them, for the life they are beginning together. It's never what I wanted for myself, I saw my mother suffer under my father's thumb and couldn't wait to apprentice myself when I was fourteen to get out of the house. I like the control of the kitchen, and to keep my own counsel, and I've never missed having a man in my life. But I appreciate it for those who do, and I can see that Martha's life has gotten infinitely better since she fell in love, despite the bumps in the road, and I know that this marriage is a good thing for them both, and that makes me giddy with delight. I borrow the light of their joy and it warms me.

My fancy dress rustles, and I glance at all the upturned faces, most of them looking as if they are trying really hard to appear happy.

At the foot of the stairs, Jag is waiting for me. "Are you quite certain, Anneke?"

"I've never been more sure of anything."

"It's a very big deal. And not too late to back out. I have my car out front if you want to make a run for it."

"Well, when you figure out what's important, what's irreplaceable, it doesn't seem so big. It just seems right. It seems like ending up where you are supposed to be."

He nods his head, smiles warmly, and offers me his arm. He escorts me to the window, and we stand in front of John, who nods at us.

"Dearly beloved. We are gathered here today to witness the joining of Anneke Stroudt and Jagjeet Singh in holy matrimony . . ."

What?

When you find a really good contractor that is awesome and talented and fun AND in your budget? You don't let him go. Full stop.

After John, newly ordained on the Interwebs, declares us husband and wife and my new hubby kisses me softly, his beard tickling my chin, we all repair to the dining room. Caroline has laid out a beautiful spread, which is a combination of some of my favorite things that she has cooked, and traditional Sikh wedding dishes provided by Jag's friends. There is a whole roasted beef tenderloin, sliced up with beautiful brioche rolls for those who want to make sandwiches, crispy brussels sprouts, potato gratin, and tomato pudding from Gemma's journal. The savory pudding was one of the dishes from Martha's wedding, which gave me the idea for this insanity to begin with, so it seemed appropriate. I actually think Gemma would strongly approve of this whole thing. And she certainly would have appreciated the exoticism of the wonderful Indian vegetarian dishes, lentils, fried pakoras, and a spicy chickpea stew.

From what I can tell, Gemma was thrilled anytime she could get introduced to a completely new cuisine, whether it was the Polish stonemason introducing her to pierogi and borscht, or the Chinese laundress bringing her tender dumplings, or the German butcher sharing his recipe for sauerbraten. She loved to experiment in the kitchen, and the Rabins encouraged her, gifting her cookbooks and letting her surprise them with new delicacies. Her favorite was *With a Saucepan Over the Sea: Quaint and Delicious Recipes from the Kitchens of Foreign Countries*, a book of recipes from around the world that Gemma seemed to refer to frequently, enjoying most when she could alter one of the recipes to better fit the palate of the Rabins. Mrs. Rabin taught her all of the traditional Jewish dishes they needed for holiday celebrations, and was, by Gemma's account, a superlative cook in her own right.

Off to the side of the buffet is a lovely dessert table, swagged with white linen and topped with a small wedding cake, surrounded by dishes of fried dough balls soaked in rosewater syrup and decorated with pistachios and rose petals, and other Indian sweets.

Jag's friends are all very sweet, very gracious, and obviously very confused. Jag and I decided that the only way to handle the need for secrecy attached to a green card wedding was to be sure that we are the only two people who know that it isn't real. His greatest fear is that we'll get exposed and open his dad up to shame and scandal. His philosophy is that there is no such thing as a secret between three people, so the idea of telling three people on my end, and half a dozen or so on his end . . . it made him panic. It took me the better part of a week to convince him that it was a good idea to begin with. I called him the night of Nageena's party with my brilliant solution, and at first he dismissed it out of hand. But after a few days of pleading my case, he softened to the idea. I explained that the whole Grant thing had really finally crystallized for me, and that I've come to the conclusion that I am just not built for love ever after and all of that. My work is everything to me now, and needs to be for the foreseeable future, and I want him to continue to work with me for as long as he wants. I told him that I trusted him and felt safe with him, and that I deeply care about him as a friend, that if I were the kind of person to even think about marriage, he is the kind of guy that I would want to marry. When I told him that in many ways the marriage would be as big a help to me as to him, saving me from dealing with my friends and their expectations, letting my life find its balance again, he relented.

We've spent the last month convincing everyone around us that we have just fallen crazy madly in love and decided to go for it. I feel badly about that part, because I adore his friends and hate to mar our new connection with lies. I can tell that they are looking at me skeptically, wary of my motivations, so I do my best to look at Jag with heated love in my eyes.

The girls are another story. They think I have completely lost the plot.

"You have GOT to be kidding me," Hedy fumed at me when I told them. "I thought he wasn't your type?"

"I changed my mind."

"Is this because I said I was afraid you'd stay alone forever?" Marie asked.

"Of course not."

"He's wonderful, darling, of course he is, but this is just so fast . . ." Caroline said.

"We discussed it at length and realized that there is no good reason to postpone the inevitable, when you feel something in your gut that you know is right, you just do it."

"Very convenient for him, about to be deported," Hedy snarked.

"He wasn't about to be deported; he had offers from a different school if he wanted to retain his student visa, and his former firm offered him a job in their Chicago office and would have taken care of the visa issue." Both of these were true; Jag was determined to stay in Chicago and had explored every possible solution, but neither of the available options would have allowed him to spend the time and energy working with me that we both wanted and needed.

"Then why not take one of those and wait?" Marie asked. "You have to see how suspect it is, all of this falling in love right when his visa issues were coming up."

Marie was the one I most needed to convince if this was going to work at all. "I told you. It was how upset I was at the idea of losing him that made me realize I had feelings for him!" This is the story we've concocted. That we both had ignored our fondness because we were working together, but that when it seemed he might actually have to leave, not just Chicago and the job, but me, we had to face what was in our hearts.

"And you are sure that your feelings for him aren't just some misplaced guilt that you couldn't do more for him in other ways? Or simple loneliness?" Marie was a dog with a bone, and I think that she really suspects this whole thing is a farce. Which, of course, it is, and deep down I really wish I could tell her the truth, even more than the other girls. But I can't ask her to keep that secret, to give her that burden, and I can't betray Jag's trust that we wouldn't tell a soul. This is the ultimate test for an unnatural liar like me, but I don't have a choice.

"I promise you. And I thank you. Because you warning me about the future I faced made me have to really look into my heart, and when I did I realized that all this time I spent with Jag I had been pushing my feelings away because I didn't want to get hurt again. When I decided to be honest and brave the way you told me to be, I had to admit that I really wanted him in my life in a romantic way and the whole thing just fell into place!" Marie's eyes softened, because at her core she just wants me happy, and she's a sucker for a good romantic story, and I knew that I had her. Which made me feel even shittier. But I needed to seal the deal. "I know it seems fast, but I promise you, this is exactly what my heart most wants, you guys, and I really just want you to be happy for me."

Which is true. Marrying Jag is about the smartest thing I could do. I keep my partner, keep plugging away at the house, get the girls all off my back on dating and romance and my being alone. For someone who has given up on the very idea of a real marriage ever being in her future, a fake marriage that gets me what I need professionally? It's kind of genius, actually.

Emily is the only one who wholeheartedly approves.

"It's so ROMANTIC!" she gushed when I told her. "Like a fairy tale!" She did grow up like two hundred miles from Disney World. But she was immediately, unequivocally in favor of the marriage, so there are apparently some benefits to having a twenty-one-year-old around. She and I are slowly figuring out what exactly we can do to help get her out of her Harvard jam, and I agreed reluctantly to let her be Schatzi's dog walker, as long as she promised not to ask a lot of me. I'm only finding her tedious and annoying about 75 percent of the time, but it is really nice not to have to deal with the dog, so she gets some points for that.

"You are just the most beautiful bride, Anneke! Thank you so much for including me," Emily says. She's wearing about a half a yard of flowy fabric on her leggy frame, a bare swipe of mascara and a dab of lip gloss, and her blond hair twisted up in a messy bun. She looks like a supermodel. Who just had sex. With Taye Diggs. On a unicorn.

"Wouldn't have done it without you." I'm feeling weirdly giddy and magnanimous.

The whole wedding got pulled together in less than ten days; we wanted to be sure to get married well before the information about Jag's dropping out of school became part of his

official record. This way our story is that he dropped out
BECAUSE we fell in love and got married and want to renovate
the house, not that we got married because he dropped out of
school.

We sit together and play our parts, accepting the toasts, the
good-natured ribbing about the speed of our courtship, and the
speculations about whether there would be a tiny little Singh
arriving soon. We kiss when people clink their glasses, Jag's lips
shockingly soft on mine, his beard scented with something that
smells like lime and spice. We drink delicious champagne from
Carl's ample cellar. In general, it is a wonderful wedding. I'm
enjoying myself immensely. It isn't anything like the wedding
Grant and I had been planning, but in many ways, it feels more
real. Personal and meaningful. The wedding Grant and I
talked about was to get all of his chef pals to create an insane
meal; the ceremony was almost incidental.

"Time to cut the cake, newlyweds." Caroline ushers us over
to the sweet little two-tier cake, round and covered in white
fondant with what appear to be traditional henna tattoo pat-
terns drawn on it in pale gold. We take the mother-of-pearl-
handled knife, apparently the one Caroline and Carl used at
their wedding, and, his hand on mine, cut a small slice. We feed
each other a generous bite, marveling at the tender almond
cake with the poached apricots and white chocolate mousse,
light-as-air buttercream scented with vanilla and orange blossom water.

I'm taking a second bite when the front door flies open.

"Stop! Don't! Please!" An out-of-breath Grant runs into the
room, wild-eyed and sweating.

Everything stops.

John and Carl jump into action, quickly heading for Grant's
side, and ushering him forcefully into Carl's study.

Crap.

"I'm so sorry. I'll be right back," I whisper to Jag, and Caroline rushes to cut slices of cake for the bewildered guests, while Hedy and Marie go into "nothing to see here" distraction mode, and Emily stands in the middle of the room, jaw hanging open.

I open the door to the study, and enter quickly, shutting it behind me. Grant is receiving a tumbler of scotch from Carl's desk stash, muttering about being too late.

"Guys, can you excuse us for a moment, please?" I say to them.

"We're right outside the door," John says.

"Thank you." John and Carl slip out, and I turn to face Grant. "What on earth are you doing here?"

"I ran into Naomi," he snaps at me.

"Shit." Naomi is the owner of Tipsycakes and a friend of Grant's. She makes the most amazing cakes, so Caroline must have ordered the wedding cake from her.

"Yeah. Shit indeed. She asked if I was going to the wedding and that she hadn't realized you and I had broken up but that she hoped we were still friends, and did I know anything about the groom since the cake was exotic to honor his heritage and I stood there like an ASSHOLE trying to figure out how it was even possible that you might be getting MARRIED. TODAY."

"And so you thought you'd do what exactly, your best Dustin Hoffman impersonation? Come flying in to save me?"

"I don't know. Naomi said she delivered the cake here and the wedding was today and I just got in the car and came. I assume I'm too late?"

"Yes. Very much so. Globally. And it is horrid of you to be here, Grant, just so wrong and inappropriate."

"I know I hurt you, and I'm so sorry, but this? Marrying some guy you can only have known for, like, ten minutes?! You aren't your mother."

"Fuck you, Grant. Fuck you, and fuck your grand gesture,

and your righteous indignation, and fuck you having any opinion at all about me and my life, and particularly my MOTHER. You have no right to be here, to be anywhere near me. We are done. Go home, Grant."

"I love you, Anneke, that gives me the right to care."

"Perhaps you should have thought of that before you banged that boy in our bed."

"I deserve that, I do. But seriously? Married?"

The door opens, and Jag enters, tall and handsome with concern in his eyes. "You're Grant? Anneke's ex-fiancé?" he asks.

Grant is speechless, so he just nods.

Jag walks over to him and extends a hand. "My name is Jag, I'm Anneke's husband. Very nice to meet you." My husband. That sounds so weird. I'm tempted to giggle, but it would be very déclassé.

Grant shakes the hand that is offered him, jaw hanging open.

"Now, I can certainly understand that you must be very upset, having lost this exquisite woman such a relatively short time ago, but I think you of all people will understand that the heart wants what it wants, and to deny it is tantamount to a slow death." Grant nods, his mouth slowly closing. Jag continues, in a tone that one would use to soothe a child mid-tantrum or a slavering dog. "Grant, I appreciate how hurt you must be to no longer have her in your life, but I know just from your being here that you still must love her. And if you love her, you must love her enough to want her happiness, and I want to assure you that I am completely devoted to that. You don't have to worry about her anymore, she is loved and protected." Grant looks down at his shoes, clearly beginning to register the wild inappropriateness of what he has done. "I do have to ask you to leave, my friend, because this is a celebration and you are upsetting my beautiful bride, who deserves only joy on our magical day. Will you do us both that great favor and go home so that we can continue our party?"

His tone is so smooth that Grant just keeps nodding. "I'm, I'm so, I'm sorry, I shouldn't have . . ."

"I know, it is a shock for you and you reacted from your gut without thinking. I am quite certain I would have done the same in your position. It is a shock to us as well, but what is right is right, and if you know it, then time is irrelevant. Now you can see that all is well and Anneke is happy, and you have nothing to worry about." Jag gently guides Grant toward the door.

"Yes, of course, I . . ." Grant's eyes are filled with tears. He turns to me. "I truly do wish you nothing but happiness, Anneke, forever and ever."

Which I will have, if he will just leave. "You too, Grant."

"Very good. Let's go quietly now." And Jag takes him out of the study and on a straight, purposeful line to the front door and they exit together. I'm shaking and my heart is racing. I'm furious for Grant coming here, and yet, it felt so strangely good to see him be so demonstrative about me, about his feelings for me. Jag returns in a few minutes, and brings me a fresh glass of champagne.

"Are you alright?" he asks.

"Yes, are you? Your friends must think I'm a complete disaster."

"Please. We're used to arranged marriages, and secret elopements to escape arranged marriages, and all sorts of dramatic nonsense. This is nothing! I think it adds to the reality."

"Yeah, nothing says we're a real couple like my ex trying to stop our wedding!"

"Exactly. Let's go back to our party and pretend it didn't happen."

"Let's."

"And, Anneke?"

"Yes, Jag?"

"I hope your next wedding is as beautiful as this one, and to someone who really will make you happy forever."

Next wedding. Bless his heart. Never going to happen.

"Yours too." And we toast, and kiss, a deep genuine platonic kiss of friendship and understanding, and go back to the festivities.

18

From Gemma's Journal:

I never like the calm before the storm, but the storm itself thrills me. Literally and figuratively. I don't cotton to the anticipation of things. I like to know what's what, straight out in front of me, so I can deal with it, so I can make preparations, so I can see the end. But once the drops begin to fall, then I can relax. If it's life, sending difficulties, I prefer for it to just arrive in all its glory and make itself known to me. If it's God sending the fury of wind and water, I love to sit with my tea, watching the sky flash, hearing the deluge. In both cases I most love what comes after, what gets washed away, and what gets revealed. It is always a kind of small miracle.

Strangely enough, being married to Jag isn't that much different from living with Grant, cuddling and occasional nookie aside. We had a long discussion about how to handle the appearance of our new life together. We fixed up the bedroom next to mine, since actually sleeping together isn't on the agenda, but we have been sharing the upstairs bathroom, trying to keep downstairs as new as possible and only using it sporadically. Since Jag's bed is actually a sleeper sofa, when he closes it up in the mornings his room looks more like a small den, so on the off chance someone is in the house and comes all the way upstairs, it still looks like we only have one bedroom. In general, we've begun doing all the things that married people do. We grocery shop together, and at least three nights a week we take turns cooking with the other serving as helper or dishwasher. He's teaching me some of his traditional dishes, and when I read something wonderful from Gemma's journal, I copy it out and we cook from that. I haven't told him about the journal, it still feels private and magical and just for me, so I assume he thinks I'm coming up with these recipes by looking online or borrowing from Caroline.

In lieu of a "honeymoon" we've spent our postnuptial time really hitting the basement hard. We jackhammered up the old concrete in trenches where necessary to run the new plumbing lines and roughed-in the bathrooms and the laundry room, poured new concrete over them, and finished designing the space on paper together. Working with Jag is constantly inspiring, our aesthetic is very compatible, and while he completely defers to me for final decisions, he's very free with his ideas and they are invariably good ones.

We've decided to turn the former root cellar into a wine cellar, and have expanded the guest suite to include a sitting room and small walk-in closet. We've also decided on a media room, and bonus room with three-piece bathroom that can either be an office, second guest room, or exercise room. Laundry and storage. Mechanicals room. We debated long and hard about the possibility of keeping the elevator I had originally planned, but it's such a huge expense, we've decided to create a series of appropriately sized stacked closets all the way up that will accommodate an elevator shaft should the future owner decide to install one. For now, they'll just serve as extra storage on each floor.

The stone and brick walls only took four days to tuck-point and limewash, and they look amazing. Jack made good, sent me a step-by-step email for us to follow, and his friend is working on the limestone sills for me at a really good price. He came downtown to make templates and is having them fabricated, and he will install them for us. The stone foundation and brick walls cleaned up beautifully, and the architectural interest they have added to this space makes it very special. We were able to get all the new interior stud walls in; laminate hardwood flooring went down in most of the rooms, carpet in the media room and bonus room. We laid the electric radiant flooring pads in the bathrooms so they are ready for tiling, and we did thick cotton insulation and special drywall in the wine cellar, and now we're getting ready to start doing finishing touches.

Jag's training kicked right in, and he was able to make a good time and action plan for our work, and it looks like we should be able to get the basement completely finished in about another month or so if we don't hit any snags. Another seven to eight months to finish the upper floors, and if all goes well, a quick sale and we can figure out what's next. We have to live together for two years to get Jag a ten-year green card, but at least for now, since he entered the country legally and we had a public wedding and reception, they didn't question our paperwork and we only had to apply for a change of visa status. I also filed the papers to put the Palmer house in both our names, since joint property ownership is considered a mark of a bona fide marriage, and we'll file our taxes jointly. Jag has requested that I no longer pay him for his time, and instead I just pay the bills here, and I'll give him a share of the profit on the house when we sell it. He was able to sublet his apartment in Andersonville for a small profit, so he has a little cash flow from that, and he still has this semester's tuition in his account, so he's participating in paying for utilities and food and such. He's trying not to tap into the tuition money, knowing it's his only nest egg, but he doesn't want to take money from me now that I married him to keep him in the country.

We also have a rock-solid prenup, protecting us both for the eventuality of our divorce, which Jag insisted on paying for as my wedding present, in addition to all the visa paperwork stuff. But I don't really think we need it. I just trust him completely, and ever since we got married, I feel calmer and more me than I've felt since I got here. Things feel like they are a little bit on solid ground again, and I do have to admit, I like having him living with me. While I don't yet have the kind of friendship with him that I had with Grant—I doubt I will ever let anyone in that deep again—we are completely easy and fun together, we laugh a lot, and enjoy the company. There is something very comforting about just knowing he is here. And in a weird way, at this point in my life, it feels like he is the only thing I can rely on, personally and professionally. He is the only person who really gets me, the me I am at this place in my life. And with all of the guys I used to be able to count on for work avoiding me like the plague to cover their asses, Jag is the one keeping this project moving ahead.

The funniest thing about Jag moving into the big house with me has been Schatzi. As much as she was bonding with him before, ever since he moved in she seems to hate him. She has always hated me, so I'm used to the fact that it doesn't matter to her in the least that I'm making a concerted effort to talk to her and give her treats; she maintains a chilly distance. But Jag? She was his pal before, but not anymore. She's nipped him a few times, destroyed three shoes, from different pairs, of course, and shat on his floor. Twice. He's taking it in stride. I keep telling him that it's just that she's leery. The last man I lived with she loved, and has since lost. She's just protecting her broken heart. He's good-natured about it, but I sense that his patience, while impressive, is not inexhaustible.

Emily, on the other hand, continues to have a passionate love affair with this dog that defies all logic. She has been pretty respectful of our time, very good about popping in quietly to take the dog for a long walk and some park time, and returning her without too much imposition on Jag and me. My guess is that she thinks she is giving the newlyweds some space, but whatever the reason, it's fine by me. Her leaving date seems to be something of a moving target. I have let her come observe a few times, she does seem genuinely interested in the process of building a house like this, and Jag is amazing with her, patient and kind and sweet. I love hearing him talk her through what he is doing, especially since when he takes her on, I don't have to. I know I agreed to get to know her because of her ridiculous, and I think overblown, Harvard issue, but with everything going on, I haven't really had any energy to focus on her.

The girls seem to be reluctantly accepting my new marital status, and have stopped calling to check on my mental health every day. As annoying as it was before, now I do sort of miss those calls. I wish that I had felt like I could have been honest with them about the true nature of my marriage, but Jag was so concerned, and deep down I knew they'd have worked even harder to talk me out of it, and I'd still be sad little Anneke in their eyes. Not that crazy little Anneke is much better. The problem with lying, when you aren't a natural, is that you have to create all these walls to protect your lie. Classic "be careful what you wish for" situation. I wanted them to get off my back, to stop worrying about my love life, to stop treating me like damaged goods. I wanted to take the public pressure off of myself to be anything other than what I want to be: a girl focused on her work, moving toward professional goals with determination, and not giving a thought to social or romantic relationships. I've succeeded a little too well. As much as I miss them, I'm also leery of spending too much time with them, because now I really can't slip on the whole green card thing; I don't think they would ever forgive me. When I think about the next two years, keeping up the façade, keeping the secret safe, and trying to keep my girlfriends as well, it gives me butterflies in my stomach. I wonder if we'll all survive, if we'll ever get back to being friends the way we used to be.

There's a big storm headed our way, the first real rainstorm of the season, and it promises to be a doozy. Early April showers in Chicago are always a little dangerous, and while everyone is claiming April Fools' on this one, since today is the first, these storms are actually no joke. There's still enough snow and ice pack on the ground after this particularly brutal winter, and that will double the water volume when the rains come and melt it. And then, without fail, the brief warmth will return to subzero temps and turn all that runoff into slicks of ice that won't melt fully till much later in the month, if not early May.

Knowing that it's going to be miserable out for the next couple of days at least, Jag thought he'd pick us up plenty of supplies, both building and food, so that we can hunker down and work and hang out. I'm taking advantage of his absence to take a bath in the new first-floor tub. As much as we've avoided making the new bathroom our primary bathroom space, continuing to use the upstairs bathroom for most everything, I can't help indulging in the tub. I've missed the big soaker we had at Grant's, especially after these long hard days of physical labor. The trickly water in the upstairs shower barely gets me clean, let alone truly refreshed. But this old claw-foot is just the ticket. It is a full six feet long and twenty inches deep, and I fill it with steaming water and lower my aching body into it. The water nearly covers my shoulders, and as I sink down, I can feel my muscles give in to the heat. The old cast iron holds the warmth, and I realize I haven't taken a proper bath since I left Caroline's. Grand-mère was a proponent of a proper bath. She took a bath every evening before bed; cool in the summer and scalding hot in winter, scented with some strange aromatic oil, sort of a combination of tarragon and rose. It smelled like floral fish stew.

I like my baths pure and simple. Hot water, scented like hot water. In a tub with no bells and no whistles. I don't want jets shooting at me. I don't want little tickly bubbles flying up my butt. I don't want it to change colors or squirt me with aroma-therapy. I've installed enough ridiculous over-the-top tubs in my day to know that people don't really use them, not the way they think they will. The clients who talk about how much they love their bath? They have basic bathtubs that are scaled appropriately to them, fill quickly and drain easily, keep the water hot a long time, and are easy to clean. The rest of it is just rarely really used. I love an old refurbished tub like this one, especially in a period bathroom, but the new soaking tubs, par-ticularly some of the heavy acrylic ones, are lovely too. Jag and I have been talking a little bit about the future master bath, joking about making the whole master suite "our dream." He's put me in charge of the tub. My husband? Is a shower guy.

As comfortable as it feels to be living with Jag, it still feels very weird to use the word *husband*. Grant's dig about my mother hit closer to home than I like to admit. I never really associated marriage with love or need or longing. It represented friendly companionship at best and a weird combination of res-cue from boredom mixed with financial security at worst. In my darker moments in the past few months I've wondered more than once why I wasn't more broken by what Grant did to me. If I said yes to him with my whole heart to begin with. Our dating was brief, and mostly focused on his cooking for me while dealing with issues related to the apartment, and sponta-neous sexcapades. And then it was finished and I just moved in. We lived together easily and then he asked and I said yes. But I never dreamed of it; it seems like it was just a path I was on. A perfectly pleasant path. Hedy once said that the worst sex she ever had was with a guy she slept with because in the moment she couldn't think of a good reason not to. Which, apparently, is the single BEST reason not to. I'm beginning to think it isn't impossible that I said yes to Grant, to the whole thing, from moving in to the engagement, for that simple reason. At least with Jag I feel specific and proactive and in charge of my own destiny.

"Hellloooo? Wife?"

And he's home.

"I'm in the tub," I yell. I hear footsteps down the hallway that stop outside the bathroom door.

"Very good, you relax. I'll put everything away. I picked us up some lunch for when you're finished." His smooth British tone is muffled by the heavy wood door that separates us.

"Thank you. I'll be out shortly."

"Take your time."

I let my body submerge completely under the water, feeling the heat sink through my thick hair to my scalp, the pressure of it on my cheeks, the pleasurable weight on my closed eyelids. Just my pursed lips break the surface, and I focus on breathing very slowly, keeping myself under, little bubbles escaping from my ears as they fill with water. Keeping the noise in my head blissfully muted and far away.

Today I think it is important that you learn how to roast a chicken," Jag says when I meet him in the kitchen. We spent the afternoon mired in paperwork, finishing the basement bathroom design and getting the tub, toilet, tiles, and other fixtures ordered. About an hour ago the skies opened, and the deluge shows no signs of slowing.

"Really."

"Yes, really. Those dried-out greasy salt licks you keep bringing home are not roasted chickens."

"They are doing a masterful job of imitating roasted chickens."

"No, actually, they aren't. And you should know better."

"I know, but roasted chicken is hard. It's every chef's test for a newbie."

"Roasted chicken isn't hard."

"Okay, GOOD roasted chicken is hard."

"No, darling, it isn't. Come." He reaches out a hand to me and I take it easily, and he pulls me around the side of the kitchen island. "Anneke, this is a chicken. Chicken, this is Anneke."

I shake the chicken's drumstick formally. "Hello, chicken."

"Very nice. Now, you want to relax your bird." He reaches for the olive oil and pours a generous amount in his palm, and begins to massage the chicken all over.

"Shall I get the chicken a cocktail? A Xanax?"

"Very funny. Now you season inside and out." He deftly sprinkles a mix of kosher salt and ground pepper into the cavity, and all over the outside. "Onto the rack with you, bird." He places the chicken, glistening and seasoned, onto a V-shaped rack in a small roasting pan.

"Don't you have to tie it up?" Grant always trussed his birds.

"Nope."

"Don't you have to put things up its bum? Lemons or something?" Grant always put lemon slices and shallots and fresh herbs in the chicken.

"Nope."

"Huh. Now what?"

"Four-hundred-degree oven till you smell it." He opens the door to the oven and pops the pan in.

"Smell it?"

"When it stops smelling like cooking chicken and starts smelling like roasted chicken, it's done."

"I'll let your nose be the guide. Otherwise we might have burnt chicken." I'm remembering the sweet potato incident.

"So you say. But I bet you'll know. Potatoes?"

"Sure."

He takes two large russets out of the basket on the counter, washes them, rubs the outside with a tiny bit of oil, and goes over to the oven, putting the now clean and shiny potatoes right on the rack next to the chicken.

"Hey, don't you have to poke those so they don't explode?"

He looks at me like I'm insane. "No. They won't explode." Little does he know, but if he explodes potatoes, he gets to clean the aftermath.

"Wrap them in foil?" Joe always wrapped his in foil.

"I like a crispy skin, do you?"

"Yes."

"No foil." He grins at me. "We'll steam some broccoli when the chicken is resting."

I smile back at him. "You know, I was engaged to a fine-dining Michelin-starred chef, and you've just taught me more about cooking than he ever did."

"That's why you married me and not him."

"Well, that and the whole cheating on me with a guy thing."

"That too. You keep a nose on that chicken, I'm going to get a little more work done on the electrical plot for upstairs." He reaches over and squeezes my shoulder, and once he's out of the room, I grab my phone and look up roasted chicken times, and it appears that forty minutes to an hour and fifteen is the range depending on the size of the bird. I set my alarm for forty minutes from now. Jag might trust my nose, but I'm not taking chances.

I told you your nose would know," Jag says, licking his fingers. "Didn't I?"

I put down the drumstick bone I've gnawed clean. "You did." And he was right. Despite my backup alarm system, there really was a moment when the chicken just smelled *done*.

He looks all puffed up and proud of himself, and we sit in companionable silence as we devour the crisp-skinned juicy bird and the potatoes, crunchy on the outside and fluffy within, stuffed with butter and sour cream and sprinkled with chives. And steamed broccoli. Which is as good as steamed broccoli can possibly be, being steamed broccoli and all. But I put a fancy Gaggenau in-counter steamer in the island, so it makes getting your veggies done a dream, and even I recognize the need for some fiber and greenness in one's diet.

We clean up the few dishes, and Jag refills my wineglass.

"Who taught you to cook?" I ask him. "Take this the right way, but I would have thought it wouldn't be on the list of parent-approved activities." Jag's discussions of his folks have been sort of textbook cultural-and-generational-divide stuff. Old world versus new and all that.

"No, it wasn't. But we had a wonderful cook in London, and I would sneak down to the kitchen and watch her. She was chatty, so she couldn't help but tell me what she was doing and why. And my grandmother, Mum's mum, she lived with us for a while and taught me the old family dishes."

"That sounds nice."

"It was. I'm surprised Grant never taught you how to cook."

"In his defense, I never asked him. Cooking was his greatest expression of love and I let him express it. Plus he wasn't terribly patient; the few times I tried to help him he just got annoyed."

"You're not bad, you know. You just need practice."

"Thank you, husband."

"You're welcome, wife."

"Now for some unpleasantness." I hate to bring it up; things are so cozy right now. The storm is still raging outside, but these thick stone walls keep it a distant thrumming and rumbling, the lightning brightening the rooms in flashes of blue.

"Uh-oh."

"I think we have to tell your parents that we got married. In this day and age, social media being what it is, it will be better if they hear it from you."

"I know. I've been . . ."

"Putting it off."

"Avoiding it."

"Because you can't tell them the truth."

"It would be a dishonor. It's going to be bad enough."

"That you married outside the faith? The race?"

He smiles. "That I married without them. They're traditional, but not archaic. I've dated all kinds of girls; as long as they're smart and kind, my folks are happy enough. But they'll be hurt that it was a secret, worried that it was so fast."

"Can't really blame them on that. My mother would completely approve."

"Until she finds out I'm not rich."

"Yeah. Best not tell her."

"If I have to, you have to. Anneke, I know she isn't what you want, what you deserved to have, but she is the only family you have in the world."

"I have Emily. Isn't that really enough family for one girl?" I say with more than a touch of sarcasm.

"So you do," he says pointedly, ignoring the implication in my tone. "But as you keep pointing out, she isn't real. Your mother, for better or worse, is your last known living blood relation. Don't you want to be connected at all?"

"Honestly, not really."

He tilts his head at me.

"Maybe a little."

One arched eyebrow raises dramatically.

"FINE. I'll tell her. Eventually."

"And I'll tell my folks next week when they get home. I don't want to disrupt their annual trip to India with this news."

"When you do, I will."

We shake hands on our pact, both of us struggling with our own shit of how to handle this unexpected wrinkle. Perhaps there were a few little details we didn't really think through before we got the marriage license.

"Should I go check the basement for water? It's really coming down out there," Jag asks, folding the dish towel neatly, peering out the back window at the sheets of water that are pouring down outside.

"You don't have to. This place has had a dry basement for over one hundred years, and this certainly isn't the worst storm we've ever had."

"Well, that's good, then. I'm going to see if I can finish up those plans from this afternoon."

I take my glass of wine and head up to the second-floor balcony to watch the rain, and try not to think about calling my mother. Wondering if Gemma would consider this the storm, or the calm before.

19

From Gemma's Journal:

We should have known it was coming. Life had been too easy, too smooth. There had been too much happiness. In this life, there is too much uncertainty, and if you let your guard down, you'll be caught unawares by sorrow. Our poor girl Charity has died of the influenza, sending the house into chaos. Mr. and Mrs. Rabin have whisked away with the children to Ohio to wait out the illness in fresher air and safer climes. The rest of us are quarantined in the house, maintaining busy disinfecting every inch of the place, and keeping a watchful eye on each other for the slightest hint of disease. In the meantime, I'm trying to find a new housemaid to replace what we've lost, but I'm having problems reconciling myself to letting someone new into the house, into my heart. Charity was but fifteen, rosy cheeked and dear to us all. Close as I might have gotten to a daughter of my own. I am bereft, and know not how to manage my temperament.

I'm stretching on the floor in my pajamas when there is a light knock on the door.

"Anneke? Are you awake?" Jag is whispering right outside. I haul my carcass off the floor and go to open the door for him. He looks crushed.

"What is it? Are you okay?" There is a sudden knot in my stomach.

"We have a problem." He gestures to my boots, and I slip them on. Then he takes my hand and leads me to the stairs. My mind is spinning. Did we have a break-in? Last night had been so cozy, so easy. We'd stayed up late together, watching old movies on the small television Jag has in his room, laughing and drinking calvados, and listening to the storm outside. Jag made a tubful of popcorn, which he sprinkled with nutritional yeast and dried herbs, which sounds gross, but is actually nutty and delicious and sort of like Parmesan. We laughed and he practiced what he was going to tell his parents, and we didn't go to bed till well after two. It was, without a doubt, the best night I've had in months.

We wend our way downstairs, heading through the house, which has an odd blue light at this time of day, before we turn any lights on, when the skies outside are gloomy. We head through the living room, open the door, and go down the front stairs to the basement. Jag leads the way, never letting go of my hand. At the bottom landing, he stops, and turns. As his turban moves out of the way, I can see into the basement. It's dark. And it's moving.

"Jag?"

"Oh, Anneke." His voice sounds devastated.

I peer into the gloom and see that the movement has shine. Water. Everywhere. It is lapping the third stair, which means there is at least a foot and a half of it down here. And since we haven't installed any of the doors, if there is a foot and a half of water here at the foot of the stairs, there is a foot and a half of water everywhere. The base of every wall is getting waterlogged, all the flooring we just finished installing will be unsalvageable, the insulation is wicking the water right up inside the walls. Everything will be ruined, the radiant heat pads, tens of thousands of dollars in damage. And then the smell hits me.

Not just water.

Sewage.

Jag catches me as my knees buckle, and we sink together onto the landing, like a tiny little life raft on a sea of horrible.

We head upstairs to make a plan. At this stage, the best thing we can do for the project is to be smart and calm and efficient. An extra hour or two isn't going to make a bit of difference in the end; if we don't pay attention or get reactionary or start running around like headless chickens, we could actually make things worse. But I do realize that an extra set of hands would be useful. I know I should call the girls, but I feel like I don't have the right to ask them for help, as much of a problem child as I've been these past few months. My old anger at Murph rears its ugly head, since all of the guys I used to be able to call to help me can't take my calls anymore, and at this moment all I really want to do is hit Brian Murphy as hard as I can. In the balls. With my car.

Reluctantly I pick up the phone.

"Good morning! Wasn't that storm amazing? It was almost like a hurricane." Emily is perky at all hours of the day apparently.

"Yeah, it was bad and now we have a major flood in the basement."

"OH NO! You just were finishing it up and it was looking so beautiful! I'm so sorry, that is just terrible, is everything just completely horribly ruined or will you be able to save some stuff?"

"EMILY. Please. I hate to ask, but could you come over soon and take Schatzi for her morning walk? Jag and I have to figure out what we are going to do, and then get moving, and I just don't have time. So if it wouldn't be a bother . . ."

"Bother? Of course it isn't a bother, I'm on my way. Did you want me to bring you guys some coffee?"

I start to refuse, and then cave. "Yeah, actually, that would be great, thank you."

"Hang tight, I'll be there very soon!"

I shudder. Having Miss Sassy Pants on-site for all of this mess may just shred my last frayed nerve, but we are in crisis mode, and that means putting everything else aside.

"Emily is on her way; she'll take care of the dog today while we get this in hand."

"Good thinking. I've reserved the pumps, so if we make a list of everything else we will need, I can run out and grab it all."

We sit down and begin to detail everything we know we will need to manage this unexpected project. By the time we have made a specific plan and gotten the list ready, Emily rings the bell.

"Hey, guys," she says, handing off a tray with large coffees, and a bag that turns out to contain several varieties of doughnuts and Danish. "Thought you might also need some quick energy."

"Thank you, Emily, that is very kind," Jag says, taking a coffee and a glazed long john. "Anneke, I'll take the truck and be back soon." I toss him the keys, and he heads for the garage.

"Can I see?" Emily asks as I take a deep draught of my coffee, a perfect latte with plenty of sugar, which means that Emily has been paying close attention.

"If you want." I gesture to the stairs. "Just breathe through your mouth." I look into the bag and spot a classic chocolate doughnut that wants very much to be in my face.

I'm snarfing down the last bite, and I'm eyeing a raspberry and cheese Danish when Emily returns. Her usually creamy paleness has a hint of green and there are tears swimming in her baby blues.

"Oh, ANNEKE," she says, and throws her arms around me tightly. "I'm just SO SORRY."

I wriggle a bit, uncomfortable in her grasp, but she refuses to release me; after a few seconds, I let go and receive the embrace and the emotion that it contains, and give myself over to her Ivory soap smell, and her still-damp hair, and her genuine sense of my loss, and eventually, I hug her back.

It takes us all day to pump the sludgy ick out of the basement, working quietly in the dark with our miners' flashlights strapped to our hardhats, since we had to shut down the main electricity. The water was below the level of the electrical outlets, but we didn't want to take any chances. Jag rented a gas-fueled generator and industrial pumps, getting the last two available, and picked up a stack of disposable hazmat-style suits, masks, and tall waders. Emily, to her enormous credit, returned from walking the dog in a new outfit of grubby leggings and Hunter boots, hair in pigtails under a bandanna, and before I even knew what was happening, she had pulled on her own suit, grabbed one of the extra hardhats off the worktable upstairs, and was downstairs with us.

Emily sticks with me, and Jag works at the opposite end of the basement, pumping the water and sludge out. At one point Emily leaves to walk the dog again, and when she returns she calls us upstairs, where she has sacks of cheeseburgers laid out for a quick lunch. We scarf them down in less than ten minutes, and return to the horror downstairs; the three of us hunker down and get it out, over twelve disgusting hours all told, banishing it like the unwanted unwelcome invader it is.

I ordered a huge Dumpster for tomorrow, when we'll have to pull up all the flooring, remove all the soggy drywall and other damaged materials, so that we can begin to dry it out and make a plan. By the time we're done, we are all filthy, pruny, utterly defeated. The combination of sewage and damp rotting leaves is a smell I'm not sure will ever leave my nose. And there is a part of me that wants to just walk away from this house and never look back. Or blow it up and collect the insurance and move to Costa Rica.

"Emily . . ." I start, but can't keep going.

"I know. No problem."

"It was above and beyond."

"Not for family," she says.

"Do you want to clean up here? I could lend you some clothes if you want to shower before you go."

"That would be good," she says, looking down at her outfit. Despite the hazmat suits, we are terrifically grimy. "I think if you have a garbage bag, I might just dump these entirely." I gesture to the box of industrial black bags on the table, and head upstairs to find her something to change into. I get her some yoga pants and a fleece, and a towel. Jag is already in the shower upstairs, singing "Yellow Submarine" of all things, and for the first time all day, I manage a smile.

"Here, why don't you shower down here." I hand Emily the clothes and towel, and motion to the bathroom.

"Okay. Thanks. And, Anneke?"

"Yeah?"

"Thank you for letting me help today. I know I was probably the last person you wanted to call, but I'm really glad you did."

I think about this for a minute. "You were, but I'm really glad I did too."

She nods at me, and heads into the bathroom. When I get back upstairs, Jag is out of the bathroom and in his room, and I strip off my clothes and get into the shower. I soap myself thoroughly five times, and wash my hair three. And then I just stand under the hot water, feeling it stream through the thickness of my hair, dividing into a dozen even-smaller trickles, over my body in rivulets. It doesn't really soothe me, but slowly I can feel more human warmth come to the clamminess of my skin.

When I get into my clothes and come downstairs, Jag has a large pot simmering on the stove, and Emily is standing at the island eating, the towel twisted into a turban on her head; my yoga pants, tight and a little long on me, are baggy on her coltish legs and hitting her midcalf, my fleece enveloping her lithe frame. She looks like a little girl, for all her height, and I feel a weird sense of protectiveness toward her, which I assume is a combination of ravenous hunger and emotional raggedness.

"Come eat something before you fall over." Jag takes a bowl and ladles up a fragrant slosh of some kind of stew.

"Whaddizit?"

"Leftovers. I pretty much just chucked the contents of the fridge in a pot with a bunch of chicken stock, and filled in with both rice and pasta."

I take a spoonful. I couldn't begin to tell you what it tastes like specifically, just that it is hot and filling, pleasantly salty and savory.

"Thank you."

"It's really good," Emily says, holding out her empty bowl for a refill.

The three of us devour the entire contents of the pot, and for dessert we eat the rest of the morning's slightly stale doughnuts with glasses of bourbon.

All three of us decide to take Schatzi on her evening walk, in need of the brisk and clean air. Emily walks ahead with the dog, and Jag puts his arm around me. Grant and I could never walk like this; we were too close to the same height, my wide hips kept nearly knocking him over. But Jag is tall and slim, and we fit together pretty well.

"Are you okay? I mean, as okay as can be expected?" he asks.

"Not remotely."

He squeezes my shoulder and kisses my temple. "We'll fix it. Together. It's all going to be okay."

I nod, and watch Emily skip ahead with the dog, and wish like hell that I could believe him.

In the light of day, with the electricity back on, the place is even worse than I remembered.

"Far as I can tell, last fall's early big snow trapped all the fallen leaves on the roof, and then when we got that deep freeze right after, it just became a huge ice block full of crap, and every time it snowed and got cold all winter it got bigger. When the rain the other night gave us a complete melt, all the leaves that were up there clogged the drainpipes, which are directly connected to the sewer lines for the house. When the old clay sewer line got all that extra stuff, it must have had a little crack somewhere that burst when it got so overloaded," Jag says.

"A perfect storm. A perfect shitstorm."

"To be sure."

"So we have to dig. The whole thing." When we did the demo in the basement, we'd only trenched the old concrete pad where we needed to for new plumbing runs. Now that we have a faulty sewer line and a water problem, we'll most likely have to pull up the whole pad, run drain tile and install two sump pumps and a backup pump against future flooding, create an ejector pit for the water, replace or repair the sewer pump, and figure out a new drain spout system for the building. Conservatively, if you add in the lost materials that we have to throw away, this has been about a thirty-thousand-dollar snafu.

"I don't really see a way around it, no, although I would potentially like to talk to someone who has handled this sort of thing before, since I'm going strictly on what I've read in texts." Jag is in total professional mode today, with an actual clipboard in his hands, taking detailed notes so that he can make a plan of attack for us to fix this setback.

"Crap."

"Literally and figuratively," he says, so seriously that I can't help but laugh. And then he joins me. Pretty soon, punchy from lack of sleep and way too much adrenaline, the two of us are in stitches. Jag is laughing silently, shaking, with tears running down his cheeks, glistening like dewdrops in his dark beard. I'm making what can only be described as squeaker-toy noises, and Schatzi, ever the delicate flower, is standing at the top of the stairs barking her fool head off at the racket. Apparently we're disturbing her nap.

When we finally get hold of ourselves, I leave Jag to finish the notes and go to take the rented pumping equipment back to Home Depot so that we don't get hit with another full day of charges. Jag loads it up into Lola for me, and I head out. The day is actually lovely. The rains have completely melted the ice and snowpack that made everything dingy and sad, and the sun is shining. It's maybe only in the midforties, but in Chicago in early April? That feels almost balmy. We've had months of subzero windchill, and this soft humid air reminds me that spring is actually going to come eventually.

I pull into the lot off Clybourn, and grab a large orange pallet on wheels. After a couple of the guys who are hanging around give me a hand, I'm able to wheel the two pumps inside and get my deposit back. I'm heading toward the car, when I hear something that makes my stomach knot up and the hair on the back of my neck come to attention.

"Having a little water problem, Annamuk?"

Fucking Liam.

I turn, and there he is in all his smug douchey glory. Smirking at me.

"Hello, Liam."

"Hello, you. How bad?"

"It's fine."

He raises one eyebrow. "Two pumps doesn't sound fine."
Damn. Hadn't spotted him inside, but clearly he saw me.

"It's fine now."

"Sump pump fail?"

"No sump."

"Ouch. How deep?"

I think about lying and blowing it off, but I'm too tired to be deceptive. "About a foot and a half."

"Finished or unfinished?"

"Flooring and drywall."

"That sucks."

"Thanks, Sherlock. You've got a finger on the pulse."

"Well, us tiny-dick boys compensate with spectacular levels of perception and deduction." He is still smirking at me, and I'd like to slap his stupid face.

"You get the Manning foundation in yet?" At least I can dig too.

He runs a hand through his hair. "Oh yes. Weeks ago." His face says it all, and my spine feels a little straighter.

"And did you get water?"

"A little." HA! "But nothing major, and it told us where the problems are, so we'll be able to get it fixed before we build out." Damn.

"Well, I should get back to it."

"Me too. See you around, Annamuk."

"Not if I see you first." And I turn on my heel and head for the car, feeling like I held my own fairly well. I get in and turn the key.

Chhhhhh gggggggeee chhhhhhh gggggggeeeee chhhhhh gggg-geeeee.

No.

Chhhhhh gggggggeee chhhhhhh gggggggeeeee chhhhhh gggg-geeeee.

NO!

Chhhhhh gggggggee chhhhhhh gggggggeeeee chhhhhh gggg-geeeee.

This can't be happening. Lola can't die on me now.

Chhhhhh gggggggee chhhhhhh gggggggeeeee chhhhhh gggg-geeeee.

Fuck. FUCKFUCKFUCKFUCK. I slam the steering wheel. And then I feel it, the thing I hate more than anything. The tears. My very eyeballs are betraying me again.

"Stupid fucking car stupid rain stupid Grant stupid house stupid Liam," I mutter, as the unwelcome emotions erupt. I believe I am actually projectile-crying, tears squirting directly out the front of my face like a cartoon. I'm slamming my fists on the steering wheel and muttering and sobbing.

And then there is a knock on the window.

"Need a jump?" Liam asks.

I can't tell him to go fuck himself with his tiny little dick, because I'm crying so hard I can't form words. I can feel a line of snot drop out of my nose, and the knowledge that of all people LIAM is the one to see me in this state makes me so angry that I cry even harder.

And then the door opens, and Liam somehow lifts the enormous soggy bulk of me out of the cab, and I'm enveloped in his arms, and my face is buried in his chest, which smells of sawdust, and his hand is cradling my head, fingers dug into my hair and massaging my scalp, and his stupid voice with his stupid accent is in my ear saying, "Hush, lass, hush now." Which makes me cry even more.

How about a hot dog?" Liam asks me once my fit is reduced to the occasional hiccup. The front of his shirt has a huge wet spot, not to mention several iridescent snail trails from my snot. He doesn't seem to care in the least. Of course, a guy like Liam probably makes girls cry all the time, so he would be used to it.

I can do nothing but nod. I'm wrung out. I feel like all my bones have dissolved. He reaches into Lola and pulls out the keys, and closes the door. He walks me over to his garish truck, and deposits me inside, reaching over my lap to turn on the seat warmer.

"You like them plain with just pickle, yes?"

I nod again, wondering how and why he remembers how I like my hot dogs.

"Sit tight and warm up, you're shivering." And he leaves, heading back for the store entrance, where a permanent hot dog kiosk is set up. Every fiber of me wants to jump out and leave, just run away, but my car doesn't work, and it's too far to walk. Plus the seat warmer is making my butt pleasantly hot. In a couple of minutes Liam returns, handing me two hot dogs and a can of Coke.

"Thank you," I squeak, with a small hitch still in my voice.

"You're welcome."

Suddenly starving, I wolf down both hot dogs, and guzzle the Coke, as if the cure for what ails me is in that sweet fizzy elixir. Then an enormous, loud, rumbling belch erupts from me before I can stop it.

"Nice one," Liam says without irony, and lets one of his own rip.

I'm clearly in an alternate universe. There is no way that in my actual world I would be having some sort of bonding belch contest with Liam Murphy. No. Way.

"How bad is it really?" he asks around a mouthful of hot dog, a smear of mustard in the corner of his mouth.

I take a very deep breath. It's none of his flipping business, hot dog or no hot dog. "Why would you think it's bad?"

"Because you are probably the single strongest, most capable person I've ever met, and you just had a total meltdown. I was there when you came to work the day after your stepdad's funeral. I was there when that idiot accidentally shot you through the hand with a nail gun, stapling you to a stud wall, and you calmly whipped the hammer out of your belt, got the nail out, and without batting an eyelash or dropping a tear told him to get the rest of the wall together while you went for a tetanus shot. You're a seriously tough cookie, Miss Anneke, so if you're this upset, upset enough to let my distasteful hateful personage come anywhere near you, let alone comfort you? Things must be bad. How bad are they?"

I look over at him and see something shocking. He actually cares. He isn't looking for material to rib me with; he isn't trying to gloat. His brow is furrowed and his eyes are kind, and my defenses are down.

"It's bad. The flood wasn't just water, it was sewage, and probably put us tens of thousands in the hole, and there was maybe only ten grand in the contingency budget. Also put us at least eight weeks behind."

"Well, the money is a lot, but I just read in the *Trib* that Grant's new place is going to be the hottest ticket in the West Loop when it opens, and I know the other place is packed to the gills every night, and he just signed up to do some television show? Does he care that much about upping the budget?"

"Grant and I split up."

"Oh, shit. I'm sorry, I didn't know. When did that happen?"

"Um, the day I quit."

"Was that part of your plan? Tell us to fuck off, tell Grant to fuck off, head out into the sunset?"

"No, actually. Grant was the one who thought I should quit, focus on the house full-time. I just hadn't anticipated coming home and finding him in the shower with someone else."

"That wanker. Who was she?"

"He. Sous chef."

Liam's jaw drops open. "He?"

Oops. Didn't mean to let that slip out. "Don't even. It feels like a million years ago. I'm beyond caring. And I'd really appreciate if you forget that I said that. But I'm also on my own to fund this project, so while I'm delighted that he's having such success, it doesn't mean shit to me or my budget."

"That sucks, Anneke. Really."

"Yes. Yes it does."

When he finishes his hot dog, he drives us around to my car, and fortunately, one jump does the trick. I thank him, and drive the truck across the parking lot to the Pep Boys and replace the battery, another unexpected expense. Banner day for me. I head back out of the parking lot, and point her toward home, or what's left of it.

20

Liam's helping you? When did that happen?" Marie asks, stealing one of my fries. We're at the Athenian Room eating gyros salads, you know, because if you put salty crispy gyros meat on a SALAD, it is healthy for you. And I can't resist their vinegary seasoned Greek fries.

"Liam isn't helping me, he's just coming over to take a look at the basement and consult a little bit on the new post-flood situation. Jag wanted a second opinion of someone who really knows working in Chicago and dealing with Chicago weather, and before he came to MacMurphy Liam worked for a restoration company that specialized in this sort of stuff. I actually have never dealt with fixing a wet basement, just done brand-new ones or renovated dry ones, and everyone else would charge me, so . . ."

"I think it's nice that you reached out to him."

"I didn't. He called to check up on me and my hands were full and Jag answered and before I got to the phone they had already made a plan for him to come over. Trust me, I wouldn't have done it."

"Why did he do that? I thought you left it at, 'Fuck you, Little Dick.'"

"Yeah, um, I ran into him at Home Depot the other day and we chatted a bit." I haven't fessed up to any of the girls about my parking lot meltdown and Liam's kindness. Or my newfound ability to cry all the time. Or Gemma's journal. Or the actual magnitude of how big a financial hit this flood will turn out to be. Turns out I'm not so bad at this whole lying thing after all. Especially lying by omission, which is now becoming something of a specialty.

"Does Jag know about your history with him?"

"No. Never thought to tell him before, and now I don't want to be the shitty person that tries to poison the well. Jag will meet Liam and make his own decisions."

"How terribly grown-up of you."

"Thank you."

"You're going to tell him anyway."

"Probably. But I'm going to try very hard not to; we'll see if I'm successful. On the one hand, it would be really annoying if they hit it off and became pals. But then again, I hate to admit that Liam might be a good connection for Jag, especially if he decides he wants to go work for a real firm sometime."

"You'll have a real firm when this is over, and Jag will be your partner in business and in life." The message is a little pointed, but I ignore that part.

"I'll be lucky if I have a pot to piss in when this is all over. My current goal is to clear enough to find a real place for us to live and maybe, just maybe, enough to start another small project. We have to be prepared for the very real possibility that both of us are going to need to find regular jobs when we are done, so if I can get him connected to the community, I have to do that."

"How is married life?"

"It's lovely." I try to put on a wide grin, as if Jag and I are working hard all day and making wild passionate love all night.

"Really?" She looks at me with deep concern in her face.

Sigh. "Really, honey, it's great. Easy and comfortable and fun. I feel like this is exactly where I'm supposed to be and with the person I am supposed to be with. This whole flood has bonded us even closer." All of which, technically, is true. I'm slowly learning that the key to deception is to try to phrase things so that they contain as much truth as possible.

"As long as you're happy, you know that's all I want, right?"

"I know."

"Okay, then." Part of me knows that this lunch is something of a test shot, that she will report back to Caroline and Hedy that I seem good, maybe the beginning of us getting somewhat back to normal. I wish I even knew what normal was.

"We're going to need more fries." She looks down at my now-empty plate, and licks her fingers with a wicked grin as I wave the waitress over. Because if Liam is coming over to my house, and I can't have a single honest conversation with my oldest and dearest friend, more fries are the bare minimum of what I'm going to need.

On my way home, my phone rings.

"Miss Stroudt? Jeff Steinfeld." From Steinfeld Diamonds. I took my engagement earrings in to Caroline's diamond guy, to get a sense of what I might sell them for. I know Grant had them insured for about a hundred thousand dollars, so I'm hoping if I can get at least seventy thousand or so it will offset the new setback at the house and give me more of a cushion against potential future disasters. I'm of two minds about them. On the one hand, since my mom emptied Grand-mère's jewelry box, they are pretty much the only piece of real jewelry I own, other than Joe's old watch that I wear every day, and the little gold oval locket with my initials in diamond chips that he bought me when I graduated from college. So I hate to give them up. But they are also a reminder of where I was and where I am, what my life was supposed to be and what it has become. In a perfect world, I'd keep them and wear them as a sign of my inner power and ability to rise above. But at the end of the day, if I have to give them up to make this house happen, I won't mourn their loss for too long.

"Jeff, thanks for getting back to me so quickly."

"My pleasure. And these are lovely stones, I'd be delighted to buy them, if you like. I can do ten thousand."

"I'm sorry, did you just say ten thousand? They're insured for ten times that! I know my former fiancé spent about that on them, did he get ripped off? Is the quality bad?"

"No, of course not, they're quite spectacular, and I'd be surprised if he had spent less. But Miss Stroudt, they are insured for replacement value at retail prices. I'm a wholesaler. I have to buy at wholesale prices."

My stomach ties itself into a knot. My backup plan, my nest egg, my "break glass in case of emergency" turns out to be nearly nothing. He seems to understand my shocked silence.

"You can always try to sell them yourself, perhaps on eBay? I could maybe go up to twelve thousand, because of your connection to Mrs. Randolph, but I get the sense that you need more than what I will ever be able to do for you."

"Yes, that's, well, that's it in a nutshell I suppose."

"For what it's worth, Miss Stroudt, they are very special, and you'll get much more enjoyment from them than you will ever get commerce out of them. I hope you will decide to keep them and wear them in good health."

Yeah. All unemployed, effectively homeless women should rock four carats when they can.

When I get back to the house, I hear voices and laughing. Crap. Liam must have come early. I drop my stuff in the dining room, and head to the living room, where Jag and I set up his couch and other furniture in a sort of den-cum-office. And in the living room is a sight that makes my blood run cold. Liam and Emily are sitting on the couch together, both canted sideways with one knee on the seat and one arm resting on the back of the couch. Schatzi, that ungrateful, unfaithful little bitch, is lying akimbo on Liam's lap, letting him rub her belly, and squirming in delight. She barely looks up when I come in the room. Jag is in the chair, and the three of them are laughing at god knows what, looking cozy as can be.

"Hello, everyone."

"Hello. How was your lunch?" Jag asks.

"Lovely, thank you, Marie sends her love. Hey, Emily."

"Hey! Just came by to walk the pooch, but she appears to be in love, and refuses to leave." Emily blushes when she says this, sneaking a peek at Liam from under her bangs, and my stomach turns over. I face him, and he is smirking.

"Hi, Liam, thanks for, um, coming over."

"Of course. That's a helluva mess you have down there." Schatzi absentmindedly licks Liam's knee.

"Yep. That's kind of an understatement."

"I have to say, I'm a little shocked you didn't check it during the storm, since you're living here and all. You're usually such a stickler for being overprotective and conservative."

My face flushes, and I can feel the heat rising in my chest.

"I thought we should, and suggested it, but in Anneke's defense, it has always been a dry basement for over one hundred years, and that wasn't exactly the storm of the century." Seriously, Jag?

"Wow, were you still here working that late? You've got a good one here, Annamuk, that puts in those kind of hours."

Jag laughs. "Not working, I live here."

Liam raises one dark eyebrow. "Really?"

Oh crap. "Well, of course!" Emily says brightly. "Where else would he live but with his wife?"

"Wife?" Liam turns to me.

"Of course, silly! They're married."

The look on smug Liam's face is fairly priceless. His square jaw literally flops open. "Married?"

"Yes," Jag says, "for over a month now."

"Wow. I, um, hadn't heard about that." Liam is looking at me like I'm a crazy person. Hah. He has no idea.

"Yes, well, it surprised us too. But when it's right, it's right." My standard answer. No one could possibly argue, and it doesn't have me professing love and passion all over the place. I walk over and lean down to kiss Jag, and stand behind him, my hand on his shoulder, his hand easily reaching up to clasp mine warmly.

"Sometimes you just know," Jag says.

"Isn't it the most romantic thing you've ever heard?" Emily says. "It's just amazing when the right people are just tossed together so they can find each other." She is fairly radiating hearts and flowers.

"Well, then, um, congratulations to you both. I'm sure you'll be very happy." Liam's tone says that he's actually sure we'll be divorced by summer, but he's kind enough to gloss over it and get back to the task at hand. "Anyway, as I was saying to, um, your *husband and sister* before you arrived, you are definitely going to have to replace the sewer line and reroute the downspouts. You'll want drain tile around the perimeter, and two sumps with one backup system. I recommend that you don't replace that wood flooring or carpet down there, but maybe do polished concrete or tile, just in case of future water; you won't lose flooring again. If you have to do carpet, do the carpet-tile squares, easier to replace and clean in an emergency. And for sure do closed-cell spray-foam insulation instead of the cotton batt, think about using metal studs, and upgrade to the moisture-resistant drywall. A little overkill, but the last thing you want is to get calls the rest of your life from the new owner."

Shit. It's pretty much what I thought it would be, but it sucks to hear Liam confirm it.

"Very much what Anneke and I were thinking, but it's nice to have the validation," Jag says, nodding.

"My pleasure."

"That is so amazing that you just know how to fix that mess so quickly," Emily says.

"Just what I do," Liam says. "Speaking of which, I'm doing a similar install in a couple of days at one of our projects. It isn't far from here; if you want to come by and watch, see how it's done, you're most welcome." He turns to me. "You, on the other hand . . ."

"I know better than to show up at one of your projects."

He nods, glad that he doesn't have to say more.

"I'd really love to come, if that's okay with you, Anneke," Jag says.

"Of course." I swallow my irritation. "It would be a good idea for you to see it. Thanks, Liam, I appreciate it."

"I think it would be awesome to see something like that, do you think it would be okay if I came along as well?" Emily says breathlessly.

Liam grins. "Of course, lass, the more the merrier. But I warn you, these guys have never seen such a lovely thing as you on a job site." He pauses, then turns to me. "No offense, Anneke."

"None taken." After all, I always took great pains to just be one of the guys, why would it hurt my feelings to have him simply acknowledge the truth? Except that it does, a little, deep down where I'd prefer not to think about it.

"If you'll excuse me," Jag says, rising from the chair, "I'm going to head down and close everything up. Liam, thank you again, your input is much appreciated; I'll confirm with you about the site visit."

"Me too! I'm very excited about it." Schatzi makes a grumbling noise. "I should really get this dog out. C'mon, girl, with me," Emily announces as she rises from the couch, and Schatzi gives Liam one more lick on the hand and then drops lightly to the floor, lets Emily attach the leash.

"Will you still be here when I get back, Liam?" Good lord.

"Probably not, lass, have to get back to work."

Her whole face falls. "Well, it was very nice to meet you, and I'll look forward to seeing you in a few days!"

"Very nice to have met you, lovely Emily." She blushes again.

Liam watches her walk out the door. Then he turns to me. "Rebound much?"

"Pretty sure my personal life is none of your business."

"You're right. I just, um, well, I like him."

"So, what? You're worried he settled? Could have done better? Maybe you could have grabbed a couple sets of tits from the office and double-dated."

"So bitter, little Annamuk. I wish you and your husband nothing but a lifetime of joy and attractive children." He raises his hands in surrender, stands and pulls on his coat. "Good luck with everything."

"Thanks." Deep breath. "And thank you for coming over, Liam, I do really appreciate your take on things. I'm sure Jag seeing your install will also be very helpful."

"Anytime. You need help, just give me a call. Better yet, have your little sister there give me a call." He grins.

I shudder. "First off, she's not my sister. Second, that child is half your age and twice your intelligence."

He holds his hands up again in surrender. "Easy, mama bear. I'm not going to defile your cub. I just think it is fascinating that in one day I've met your husband AND your sister, the existence of both complete news to me. You're quite the enigma, Anneke, a puzzle inside of a riddle."

"What can I say, Liam? A woman needs some mystery."

"Aye. A girl who can surprise you? No man can ask for more than that." He winks, and heads for the door. "Talk to you soon, Anneke."

God, I certainly hope not.

o what is Liam's deal?" Emily asks when she returns with
Schatzi, who is running around the place clearly also looking for her new crush. Apparently his pheromones work specifically on the dim and the canine.

"What do you mean?" I ask, knowing exactly what she
means.

"I mean, he works where you used to work, right?"

"Yep. Sure does."

"That must have been awesome." She looks dreamily at me,
as if the very idea of being so lucky to be in his presence for any
length of time would have been an enormous gift.

"Really wasn't."

"He seems to know what he is doing," she says.

"He is a very competent builder."

"But?"

"But not a very nice man."

Her face falls. "I thought he was your friend?"

"Liam Murphy is the friend of no woman." I don't know a
simpler way to express it.

"Oh." She seems to take my meaning, and looks like I've
just ripped the head off of her favorite doll.

"Well, girls, we seem to have a plan," Jag says, returning
from the hellhole. "Liam was certainly very helpful. I'm glad
he agreed to come over. I think the best plan is to wait till I've
had a chance to observe what he is doing at his project so that I
really know the scope of what we're facing."

"At least we know where we have to start," I say.

"Can I keep helping?" Emily asks. "I'd really like to. It was
so awesome to get to see some of it come together before, and
now that you have to start over, after this whole mess, I just
would really like to help if you would let me."

"Oh, um, thanks, Emily, but, um . . ." Not a chance.

"Let us talk about it?" Jag says. "It's a lovely offer, we just need to figure out our specifics. We'll let you know tomorrow if we think it would be possible. We have to deal with some potential insurance issues and things before we say yes." I snap my head to look at him, but stay mute. I can explain to him later why having her helping is a nonstarter.

"Cool! Okay, then, um, I'll see you guys tomorrow."

We watch her ponytail swish out the door, and I turn to Jag. "No."

"We should talk about it."

"N.O. She'll make me nuts."

"Maybe, but we have a lot of stuff to do down there now that doesn't require skilled labor, and she's free."

"That doesn't seem like a good enough reason."

"Except that it could speed up our recovery timing by at least twenty-five percent."

"Crap."

"Exactly."

"I still need to think about it."

"Of course. I just want you to be realistic about what we're facing and that at the moment, we can't really afford to look a gift horse in the mouth." He smiles. "Even if she is something of a flibbertigibbet."

"Did you just use 'flibbertigibbet'? Out loud?"

"I did, lovely wife. And so she is. But she has a strong back, as we've discovered, and can do basic work without complaining, so I have to vote to let her help as much as she's inclined while she's here. Think of it this way, you're helping her out like you promised, and getting free grunt work in exchange. Seems fair."

I hate to admit it, but it does.

21

From Gemma's Journal:

Sometimes you cannot plan. Things go awry. The weather turns and the delivery doesn't come, or the family decides to go out. At the end of the day, the difference between being a cook and just cooking is your ability to assess your resources, and make something out of nothing. Any fool can follow a recipe and end up with something edible. But until you can open the larder and see a dish come together in your head, till you have an innate sense of what flavors are good friends, you are just cooking. You cannot call yourself a true cook.

The house is eerily quiet. Jag and Emily are over at Liam's job site for the day observing his sump pump install, and Schatzi is spending the day at the vet for her annual checkup. I'm here on my own, with nothing to do, and it makes me edgy and nervous. We've done all the demo downstairs, I reluctantly agreed to let Emily help, and even more reluctantly admitted that she was a tremendous and uncomplaining asset. There are huge fans set up to help dry the space out, and until it's fully dry we can't get started on anything else down there. There are a couple of smaller projects I suppose I could work on upstairs, but my heart isn't in it today. For some reason it makes me very uncomfortable to know that Jag and Emily are spending a whole day with Liam. The stories he could tell them, the picture he could paint. They both see me the way I want to be seen, someone strong and competent, someone who has it together. They both know about Grant and my blowup at work and they still care about me and respect me. I don't want to believe that any of that could change, but the idea of Liam Goddamned Murphy spending the next eight hours regaling them with embellished tales of Annamuk and her quick temper and her inappropriate interactions with clients and vendors . . . It puts a knot right in the center of my stomach.

No. I'm not going to let that arrogant ass pick at the little bit of solidity I've scratched out for myself. Jag is awesome, Emily is annoying but useful, and despite this setback, the house is going to be wonderful and saleable. My future is not some uncertain fog. I won't let it be, and I won't let Liam's sudden and irritating reappearance in my life shake me.

Instead, I decide that today will be about me. I call and make a long-overdue appointment to get my hair cut this afternoon, since it's officially hit the length where it gets as wide as it is long, and I lose all the curl in favor of pure frizz. I walk down to the Cozy Corner and have a huge breakfast of chorizo chilaquiles with a side of pancakes. The weather is still cold, but sunny, and it feels good to walk, so I take the long way home, and then head over to the park. I'm sitting on a bench just enjoying the breeze when my phone rings.

"Hi. You have a minute?" And my newfound calm evaporates.

"Hello, Grant. Yes, I suppose I do."

"Look, I feel bad having to make this call, but I need to talk to you about my investment in the house."

"What about it?"

"I've had an offer on my share."

"What do you mean you've had an offer?"

"I got a call, someone interested in buying out my share of the investment in the property."

"You've got to be fucking kidding me. How did someone even know to make you an offer?"

"Not sure. The offer came in through my lawyer, but it appears to be genuine. And normally I'd just let it go, but, um, there is some stuff going on for me financially at the moment . . ."

"What kind of stuff? According to your ample publicity you are on the verge of taking over the world."

"Don't believe everything you read. One of the investors in the new place dropped out. They offered me a chance to buy in and take over his share, which would give me a much bigger piece of the place, as well as future sites if the concept goes national. But I don't have enough liquid right now to make the first payment happen."

"What about the TV show? I thought that was the funny money?"

"It is, or it will be, but we've pushed it forward. Patrick and Alana were concerned about how many conflicts I have with the new place, they want to be sure that we launch strong, and the network is giving us a shot at a fall season instead of a summer replacement show, so it makes sense to move it, but I was counting on that money a little too much and I'm just a bit over-extended. So I thought maybe you could buy me out. Straight deal, no profit or interest or anything."

Crap. Crappity crap crap CRAP. "Grant, I just don't have it, you know that."

He sighs. "I know, but do you think you could get it? Borrow from Caroline or Hedy maybe?"

"ABSOLUTELY NOT." There is no way in hell I'd ever take money from my friends, and he knows it.

"I don't know what to do, Anneke, I just don't. It isn't like I want to let someone else buy my share, but my financial adviser says that there is no way I should let this opportunity go by, it could completely secure my future. And the trust I set up on the apartment to keep it separate from my business stuff so that if I ever went bankrupt no one could go after it means that I can't take out a second mortgage on it either."

My heart is racing. "It isn't that I want you to miss out on this chance, Grant, I get it, I just don't have the money, not till the place is sold. How long do you have to make the decision?"

"I can probably ask them to give me a couple of months."

"Would you do that? Get me some time to figure out how to maybe pull it together?"

"Of course. Yes. I'll do that."

"Then I will try to figure out if there is some way to pay you back. Just get me as much time as you can."

"Okay. For what it's worth, Anneke, I'm really sorry, it was the last phone call I ever wanted to make."

"I know, Grant. I appreciate your giving me a shot and not just selling your share without discussing it with me."

"I'd never do that. How is, um, married life?"

"It's really good, thank you for asking."

"Good. I'm happy for you, Anneke. So, you'll call me soon?"

"Within two months, I promise."

"Okay, then. Talk soon."

I get up from the bench and head back toward the house, stopping briefly at the garbage can to throw up my breakfast.

When my phone rings I'm thoroughly unprepared to hear Liam's voice on the other end of the line.

"I want to talk to you about this project."

Great. "Yes?"

"It's really special. That house, I get why you're there, why you're doing this."

"Thank you."

"I had a chance to talk to Jag when he was at my project, he filled me in on how things have been going. And I think you should let me come in on it."

"In what way?"

"As a partner."

"Hold on, I have to check the weather."

"The weather?"

"I have to see if hell has frozen over."

"Very funny. Hear me out. You guys are doing great work, but the two of you? It's going to take forever, and every month it isn't sold you're losing money. I know this basement has got to be setting you back probably even more than you anticipated, timewise, moneywise. I'm not an idiot, Anneke. And it's going to really suck and hurt your potential upside if you have to cut tons of corners to come in at what you can afford. You have what looks to be a hundred-thousand-dollar kitchen in there, all sparkly and pretty with that insanely gorgeous Poggenpohl cabinetry. You can't start installing shitty tubs and cheap faucets and discount tile all over the place and expect to get the buyer you want and need; they'll wonder if you cut corners on infrastructure, they'll underbid, you'll panic, you'll take less than you need, less than it is worth. You need this place to be spectacular, and to sell fast. The neighborhood is hot, but it isn't Lincoln Park. You're looking to be a pioneer at the top end of the market; people need to covet this place."

"I can't afford to bring in another partner, Liam. Even if I thought it was a good idea, which I don't. Jag and I are going to need to clear enough to find a new place to live, and I'm going to need to launch a new business. How on earth could I afford to cut you in as well?" Plus the whole Grant problem; if I can't figure out a way to buy him out in the next two months he could legally sell his share of the house to someone else, and while it wouldn't be a big enough share to have any control over execution, it would be big enough to both have an opinion about sale price, and require profit sharing, which for the moment I had written off on Grant's insistence, and any dollar given up on the sale is one less dollar I will have to invest in my future security.

"From where I sit, you can't afford not to at least consider it. I have about a hundred grand liquid now that I could invest, will have access to another fifty or so in the next six months. And some sweat equity to offer. Nights and weekends, some vacation time. You know as well as I do that if you spend a little more on some of the finishes and fixtures, you have the best shot at upping the final sale price. But we'll do it straight up. Whatever the gross dollar amount turns out to be, that can be how we figure my percentage on the back end, and I don't need credit or pay for the physical work."

Shit. I hate to even admit that I'm tempted. His cash infusion would certainly save the project in a lot of ways, maybe even allow me to hand some cash back to Grant to push off the prospective buyer. And while losing a chunk of the profit to Liam would be awful, I also know he's maddeningly right about getting it done sooner and better and getting a potentially bigger sale. And since the threat of losing a chunk of profit to Grant's mystery buyer is a possibility, I'm having to actually think about the devil I know. I doubt we'd increase the ultimate number by enough to totally cover his percentage, but there is also the part of me who just wants to do the project right, and cutting back on things the way Liam has pointed out I will have to do? Will break my heart.

"Anneke? You there?"

"Yeah, um, I'm just . . ."

"Hey, just promise me you'll think about it. I think it's a potentially good investment for me, and it's the kind of project I like to work on. You dumped Manning on me for the next year, letting me do something real in my off time is kind of the least you could do for me."

"I promise I will think about it. And I have to talk to Jag, obviously." I haven't talked to Jag about the Grant situation; I don't want to dump that on him.

I can hear the smirk in his voice. "Obviously."

J ag is out for the evening with his gang; I was invited but didn't feel up for it. I get the sense that Jag is fairly relieved that I don't insinuate myself overmuch in his outside life. He says everyone completely understands how exhausted I am after working, that I also have my own friends to manage. I wonder sometimes if they all are beginning to suspect the true reason behind our quickie nuptials, and if that is why they don't push him harder or wonder more about me. I try to go every fourth or fifth time, just to make sure they see my face now and again, and it's always lovely and fun, but never achieves the ease and comfort of that first party, because of course now there is a big lie to maintain. Regardless, I've got a quiet night in for myself, which is a welcome bit of respite. So I'm looking to Gemma for inspiration. For dinner and beyond.

Liam's offer is haunting me almost as much as Grant's bombshell. I can see every bit of logic in it; I can see all of the upside. Then my hackles go up at the idea of working with him, so closely, for so long, and my stomach turns. Yes, perhaps he has, in this very recent past, shown himself to be the tiniest bit less douchetastic than usual. But he can't keep it up forever. And once I say yes, if I say yes, I'm locked in to the bitter end. He can claim that he'll just be a worker bee and investor, but this place is my heart; I don't want to have discussions about design, I don't want to have to argue about why the place doesn't need some overgrown frat-house man-cave or ridiculous expensive organizational system in the stupid garage. I don't want anyone to have that control or power over the project, or me for that matter.

Then again, if I don't figure out a way to get Grant at least some of the money I owe him, he might have no choice but to get it elsewhere. I know how he is about his future; for someone in such a risky business, he has always been very careful about making sure he has financial stability for his present and his future. His folks were "spend it when you have it" kind of people; they declared bankruptcy twice before he finished high school. I get why he is so determined to make this deal for himself. I can't imagine who on earth could be offering him money for a share of my house, but at the end of the day, whoever it is has created a real problem for me, and I have to explore every option. Even if that option is Liam Murphy.

It feels like adding insult to injury, since reluctantly I have agreed to let Emily work on the house with us. Jag wore me down, and yesterday we told her that she could help. She was so excited that she literally jumped up and down and clapped her hands and squealed and generally made me regret saying yes within thirty seconds.

I look back down at Gemma's soft round handwriting. I suppose the question I have to ask myself is if it is important to me to be a true cook or not. I know I have to be able to feed myself, literally, with all that means. Am I willing to put in the time, to do the hard part, to feed myself well? Can I make the sacrifice with this house to make something out of nothing, and use the resources at my disposal to end up with a masterpiece, or do I let my pride win out? Or is my pride trying to protect me from making a bad decision that seems like an easy fix?

Maybe I need to start with the smaller problem. What to have for dinner. I walk over to the fridge and check out my options. There is a cooked chunk of lamb left over from the butterflied leg Jag grilled last night. Some leftover steamed broccoli florets. The lamb was marinated in a Provençal mixture of Dijon mustard, lemon, herbes de Provence. I could just reheat the lamb and broccoli and be done with it, but suddenly I remember a dish I had once at a Greek diner with Joe. It was their special of the night, a chicken and broccoli pasta dish, with a warm vinaigrette-style dressing. I think the flavors are similar; I wonder if I could do it with lamb instead of chicken?

I get a pot of water on to boil, and grab a box of penne pasta out of the pantry. Red wine vinegar, olive oil. I cut the lamb into chunks, and chop the broccoli fairly fine. There is half an onion in the fridge, the layers just beginning to separate and dry out; I might as well use it, so I chop it into smallish bits. I put a large pan on, remembering that Grant always did two things with pasta. One, he made the sauce in a pan large enough to add the noodles to, so that they could cook together for a little while, instead of my habit of just dumping the noodles in a bowl and dropping sauce on top. Two, he always saved some of the cooking water from the noodles and added it to the sauce when it was all coming together.

I heat some olive oil in the pan, and add the onions. When they are a little bit golden, I toss in the lamb chunks and hear them sizzle. It smells pretty good. I toss them around so that they start to get browned, noticing that they are leaving some crusty bits stuck in the pan. Grant always said those bits are where all the flavor is, and Gemma called it the fond, and joked that she was fond of it. Both of them always added some sort of liquid to the pan—usually wine—and scraped the bits up. I look around and see the vinegar. Vinegar is just old wine, right? I open the bottle and pour a generous glug into the pan, using my spoon to scrape at the crusty stuff until it melts into the vinegar, giving me a pungent facial in the process and making me have a massive sneezing fit. I lower the heat and add the broccoli, and drop the penne into the now-boiling water. I taste the stuff in the pan, and add some salt and pepper. I taste again. It's fine, but a little flat. I head back to the pantry and get the herbes de Provence, figuring if they were in the marinade, they should work for this too. I put a generous pinch in the pan and taste again. Better. Still a little vinegary, so I add more oil, since I've learned from Gemma that when you make vinaigrette, the easiest fix is usually either more vinegar if it's oily, more oil if it's too sharp, and more salt if it's too boring. I taste again and it is pretty good. I taste the pasta, and it's about done, so I take a coffee mug and scoop out some of the water, and then drain the pasta and dump it into my pan. Worried that all this starch will affect the sauce, I think about Grand-mère making her famous German potato salad and how she always added vinegar when the potatoes were still hot so that they sucked up some flavor. So I sprinkle some of the vinegar on the pasta, and some more oil for good measure. Grant always said you have to season at every step, so I add salt and pepper, and then begin to mix the noodles into the rest of the stuff. I taste it. It's pretty good, but missing something. I go back to the fridge and see a chunk of Parmesan, and figure it's pasta, so that will work. I grate a bunch over the top. Then I spot the pasta water and dump it in too, figuring maybe it will help the cheese melt and mix into the pan better. Much to my delight it does, and I taste one more time.

It's really good.

I turn off the heat and taste it again.

It's fucking delicious.

I stand at the counter and eat the whole mess, right out of the pan, with a cold beer, tossing Schatzi a piece of lamb now and again. And pretty soon I'm looking at an empty pan, and Schatzi is licking her chops and begging for more.

I can cook.

And if I can do that, maybe, just maybe, it's possible I can do anything.

22

I check myself one more time in the mirror. My hair is reasonably tamed; my makeup is subtle but there. I'm wearing my favorite sweater, a gift from Caroline, pale bluish celadon, in a soft thin knit that drapes beautifully, minimizes the bulk of my bosom, but shows off my decent clavicle. I have on dark jeans, not that it will matter. And I took a half a Xanax, a gift from Hedy, who keeps a stash around for emergencies. I've never been so nervous.

"You ready, Anneke?" Jag says, appearing in my doorway.

"Ready as I'll ever be. You?"

"Same. Shall we?" He offers his arm to me, and escorts me down the hall to his room, where he has his computer set up on a folding table, with two chairs in front of it.

"Do you want to talk to them alone first?" I ask.

"Probably. But not *alone* alone; don't leave, just stand over there where you won't be in the line of the camera."

I walk over to where he has pointed, and he logs on to the computer. I can't really see from where I'm standing, but suddenly there is some movement on the screen and I hear a lilting voice with a subtle Indian accent.

"Hello, my son, you look very well!" Jag's mom says.

"HELLO, YOUNG MAN!" Jag's dad's voice comes blasting out of the computer.

"Dad, you don't have to shout, just speak normally, the microphone will pick it up," Jag says in a tone that indicates it is not the first time he has said this.

"Stop yelling, Bahal, your voice doesn't have to try to reach America on its own."

"Stop scolding me, Bahula, I'm just excited to TALK TO OUR SON!"

They sound sweet and affectionate, which is a relief. I know that their marriage was arranged, but according to Jag, it is a happy and loving one.

"Amma, Appa! Hello? Remember me?"

"Yes, of course, my little peanut, we do indeed," Jag's mom says, and I remember to use that against him later.

"I have some important news for you, and I hope that you will not be overly shocked and will be happy."

"This sounds OMINOUS, my boy," Jag's dad says.

"Not at all, it is very good news in fact." I see him take a deep breath, and steel himself as if expecting a blow to come through the computer screen. "I have met a wonderful woman, and we have fallen madly in love . . ."

"I KNEW IT WAS SO!!!" Jag's dad explodes at full voice.

"It's true, he said so when you requested that we both be here at once."

"It's okay that she isn't Sikh, my boy, if you are in love, THAT IS THE ONLY IMPORTANCE," Jag's dad says. "We aren't your grandparents; we trust your judgment, and ultimately your compatibility is the ONLY THING THAT MATTERS."

"True, so true!" his mom pipes in. "Plus the mixed-race babies are so beautiful! I shall have the most adorable grandchildren."

Jag shakes his head. "No, she isn't Sikh, you have guessed that correctly, but that isn't the shocking part of the news." He looks over at me and I nod. "We got married."

There is a deafening silence from the computer, and for a moment I wonder if the connection got dropped.

"And what is the name of our new daughter-in-law?" Jag's dad says in a chilly voice. "Stop sniffling, Bahula, here . . ." I can only imagine that Jag's mother is now weeping and has been handed a handkerchief.

"Her name is Anneke, Appa, and she is the most wonderful, kind, beautiful, intelligent, special woman I have ever known, and you are going to love her as much as I do, I promise." He says this in a way that even I believe it, and my heart swells the teeniest bit. "We're so sorry it was sudden, we just got caught up and excited, and it all fell into place very quickly."

"We're sure she's lovely, son, we just are very, um, SURPRISED, YES."

"Am I going to be a grandmother very soon?" his mother says with a hitch in her voice.

"Goodness no! It isn't like that, we have no plans for children anytime soon, I swear!"

"WELL WHY NOT?" his dad shouts. "We're not getting younger, and neither are you! Some grandchildren would be nice while we are still physically able to pick them up."

If it weren't my life, it would be hilarious.

"Where is she?" his mom asks.

"Right here . . ." Jag gestures for me to come over. I feel like a dead girl walking. I sidle over to the table and take my place in the chair next to Jag.

"Hello, Mr. and Mrs. Singh. I'm very pleased to make your acquaintance." The couple in the computer look resigned. Jag is the spitting image of his dad, whose beard is shot with gray, with the same elegant features. His mom is a petite woman in a beautiful turquoise sari, with her dark hair in a thick plait over her shoulder.

"HELLO, DAUGHTER," Jag's father says. "I hope you understand our shock is not to be mistaken for being unwelcoming."

"Of course, Mr. Singh, I completely understand, it was something of a shock to us as well. But your son is an amazing man, and I feel so blessed to have met him."

"You will call us Amma and Appa, please." Jag's mom manages a smile.

This touches my heart in a very unexpected way. My mom always made me call her Anneliese; she thought Mommy or Mom made her feel frumpy and old. I can feel my chest get tight, and tears prick hot in my eyes. "Thank you, Mrs., um, Amma."

"Of course."

"You don't mind my saying, this lovely woman deserved more than to be CARTED DOWN TO THE COURTHOUSE to be married by some minor city official, my son," Jag's dad says.

"Of course, Appa, I wouldn't have dreamed of it. We got married in the home of one of Anneke's dear friends, and another performed the ceremony."

"YOU WILL SEND US PICTURES!" he explodes again, and I almost laugh. I love these people already. I almost forget that they aren't really my forever in-laws.

"Yes, of course we will." Jag smiles and squeezes my hand.

"And you'll come here for a proper reception," Jag's mother says.

Jag's mouth drops open and he begins to sputter. "Um, well, um, we . . ."

"YOU ARE OUR ONLY SON AND WE WILL CELEBRATE YOUR MARRIAGE PROPERLY!"

"We'll talk about it, Appa, I promise, it's very generous of you, but we are very busy here, as you can imagine, and . . ."

"Oh, we know it will have to be summer, when you are done with classes for the year, little peanut, not to worry. I will need time to plan, the cousins will need to make travel arrangements, we'll take care of everything." Jag's mother grins, clearly already making plans in her head.

"Leave it to your mother, Jagjeet, IT WILL ALL BE FINE. Anneke, we are happy that you make our son so happy, and look forward to MEETING YOU IN PERSON."

"Thank you, Mr., um, Appa."

"We will talk again soon, son, SEND THOSE PICTURES."
And just like that the screen goes black and they are gone.

Jag looks at me, stricken. "I couldn't tell them about school."

"Thank god, if they knew you weren't in classes we'd have
to go get married again in London this weekend!"

"I'll talk them out of it, I promise."

"That doesn't sound easy, from what little I've just witnessed."

"I'm sorry, did you *want* to go to London for a three-day
wedding with eight hundred guests?"

Oy. "No, little peanut, I certainly don't."

And we both burst into semi-relieved laughter, and hold
each other tight, as it begins to sink in that it may be possible
we actually bit off a little more than we can chew on this one.

I sit down at my desk with all my notes, and Jag's, spread out
before me. My laptop is open to the master spreadsheet for the
house. No matter how I move things around, no matter how I
tweak things to account for reductions in pricing on finishes and
fixtures, even just taking everything down one notch, not to cheap,
but to more affordable, the numbers don't jibe. Jag is out celebrating the birthday of some Sikh guru, and I'm home trying like the
dickens to figure out what to do. And then I look at the email again.

*Anneke- Not trying to pressure you, but I need to make a deci-
sion about my investment pretty soon. I don't want to keep the money
liquid, so if you aren't going to let me come in on your project, I need
to hand it off to my financial planner to invest somewhere else. Did
you get a chance to speak to Jag about it? Let me know, Liam.*

I haven't said a word to Jag, not about Liam's offer or Grant's
ultimatum. Or anyone else. I just can't bring myself to face the
fact that all of this is happening, just when I was starting to
feel like maybe everything was going to be okay. Marrying Jag

felt so right from the moment I thought of it. Help keep him here in the country and working with me. Get the girls off my back and move things more toward normal with them. Not have to think about anything but work. The numbers added up. The columns balanced. The best possible two-year plan. Focus on finishing this house, use the profit to find a new place to live, and another project. Flip a few small places for a year or so to get the nest egg back up. Get Jag his ten-year green card, and then get divorced. And then maybe I could think about dating again, MAYBE. Everything was perfectly clear.

But now, it's starting to seem murkier. Grant's lack of family connection was equal to my own, so it just never occurred to me that my in-laws weren't fictional people who lived in faraway places, but instead were real people, loving people who would want to know me and celebrate my joining their family. It never occurred to me that not only would my marriage get the girls off my back about dating and my sad little life, but it would also create an even bigger distance between us, as I deal with not being able to be truthful with them, and they give me space to enjoy my newlywed life. I hate that now that the shit is hitting the fan AGAIN, I'm not in a position to lean on anyone. Jag is dealing with his own issues, figuring out how to get around to telling his folks about dropping out of school. Dealing with his own deception with his best friends. I don't want to dump anything on him, especially because I don't want him to offer his savings to me. He is going to need that money in a couple of years when we get divorced; it is essential to me that he not invest it in this project.

The worst thing is that Emily is the only one who seems to instinctively know that something is off with me. Damn that girl, she is horrifically intuitive. She keeps asking if I'm okay, offering to be a confidante, telling me that it's what sisters are for. I keep telling her that I'm not her sister, and if she wants me to continue to play along with this little Harvard farce she's cre-

ated for herself, she'd better not poke too hard or too deep. I'll
share the stories of my childhood, so different from hers. I'll listen to the fiction she created about the years we supposedly were
together as sisters, and how Facebook brought us back together.
This required that I let her help me actually join Facebook and
set up a profile. She was very excited, explaining that the minute you join, all these people you've forgotten from your past
suddenly find you and start friending you. I've been on for nearly
three weeks and so far the only friend requests I've gotten are
from Middle Eastern men who think I'm "pritty and wold be
good frend to me" and a girl that went to grammar school with
me, whom I don't remember at all, but who posts every twelve
seconds with an update of what her kids are doing. I keep telling
Emily that nothing is wrong, but she raises her eyebrows at me
and shrugs, and tells me that when I'm ready, she will want to
listen. I can't wait till she leaves for Boston.

I've been putting it off all night. Jag is out again, a habit
that now seems to be at least three nights a week. I don't
begrudge him the time, and lord knows I don't mind the quiet.
I took a long soak in a hot tub, curled up with the latest Amy
Hatvany book, now wrinkled and damp from my wet hands. I
made myself a simple but substantial dinner of about a half a
pound of pasta tossed with butter and Parmesan and a lot of
ground black pepper and a last-minute squirt of lemon juice.
Jag had picked up the first asparagus of the season over the
weekend, and steamed a couple of bunches of it, dressing it
with olive oil and lemon, and keeping it chilled in the fridge; I
made a fair dent in it. I ate a squidillion Oreos while watching
a marathon of *Fixer Upper* reruns on my iPad. I took Schatzi for
a long walk. I asked Gemma for some magic wisdom, and she
said, "*Don't borrow trouble. Focus on the task at hand, and quiet
the fear of the unknown with hard work. Deal with the actual
problem when it arises and not before.*" But here and now, with

three fingers of bourbon and two ice cubes swirling in the glass beside me, it is all becoming very clear.

The problem has arisen. It's here, today, not tomorrow.

We're just never going to make it.

I was momentarily tempted to let Jag's parents throw us some huge wedding in London, since according to him we'd make a ton of money in gifts. But his folks were so sweet, and we couldn't do that to them under false pretenses. It's bad enough that they sent us a complete service for twelve of both elegant bone china and the most beautiful sterling silver. We could entertain for the queen with this stuff. Apparently the china was their wedding china, and the sterling belonged to his maternal grandparents. It arrived in three huge wooden crates a couple of weeks after we told them about the wedding. We repacked it all in its protective gear and put it in my storage unit for safekeeping. But at least that can stay with Jag once we split up; money we couldn't possibly accept, no matter how tempting.

I take a deep draught of the bourbon, letting it warm my insides. Despite my huge meal, I'm still hungry. Or at least I'm feeling compelled to fill this hole in me with something.

"Let's go get a treat, girl," I say to Schatzi, who is sleeping on the floor by my feet. "Mama needs to eat her feelings."

I get up and head downstairs, the dog close on my heels. I rummage through the pantry and fridge, not sure what I'm looking for, other than something to tamp down the pit in my stomach. Then I spot it. The Hint of Lime Tostitos chips. Perfect. I reach into the jar on the counter and pull out a piece of the dried-chicken-jerky dog treats that Schatzi can usually gnaw on for the better part of an hour, and she takes it gently in her mouth and tilts her head at me. "Yup, back upstairs." And I with my bag of salt and sour and crunch, and she with her rock-hard strip of poultry, head back upstairs to see if the paperwork has magically improved in our brief absence.

I'm halfway through the bag when I give up. My brain can't find the solution tonight. Tomorrow I'll sit down with Jag and we'll have to make a plan. A real plan. I'm not anticipating a fun day.

I eat one more chip, and then close the bag, leaving it on the desk. I go to the bathroom to brush my teeth for good measure, knowing that I'll be tempted to open the bag and keep eating unless I'm minty fresh and flossed. I change into my pajamas, and crawl onto my bed, reaching for Gemma's journal on the TV tray I'm currently using as a nightstand.

"There's a distinct difference between a true evil and a necessary evil. Once you learn to recognize that difference, it makes difficult decisions somewhat easier. Not enjoyable, but manageable."

Damn you, Gemma. I'm starting to think that your being right all the time is not only annoying, it's actually actively making my life unpleasant.

I toss the book back onto the TV tray with a little too much force, and the whole thing collapses. My alarm clock ends up in a puddle created by the open water bottle I had there, and quickly shorts out. The lightbulb in the small lamp I use for reading shatters, leaving the base firmly screwed into the lamp socket, which I have neither the time nor inclination to fix.

"GODDAMMIT!" I yell at the universe, quickly salvaging Gemma's journal from the mess, and using the hem of my pajama top to wipe off the water that did get splattered on the leather cover. Thankfully the pages didn't get wet. As I walk over to put the journal safely on the desk, I manage to step squarely on a shard of glass from the broken bulb.

"Fuck EVERYTHING AND EVERYONE." I hobble over to the bathroom, where it takes me the better part of ten agonizing minutes to dig the thin piece of glass out of the arch of my foot, bleeding like a stuck pig, while trying not to break it into little bits inside of my foot. I manage eventually to get it out in one piece, and wash the little hole I've now made in my foot with the tweezers with a splash of the witch hazel Jag keeps under the sink for his slightly oily skin, which stings like a mother.

A splooge of Neosporin and a Band-Aid, and three Advil and I'm sort of patched up. But it hurts like a bitch.

"Why can't one thing just go right, dog, huh?" I say to Schatzi, who has been sitting watching this whole procedure with strange focus. "Was I some terrible horrible person in my last life? Is your former owner down in hell devising new punishments for me for having been such a huge disappointment to her during her life? Is the God I don't believe in making His presence known as one big 'screw you'?"

I swear the dog shrugs at me before heading down the hall. When Jag moved in, she dragged her little bed all the way to the other end of the floor, so that she can snub us both.

I hobble back to the bedroom and get into bed. "I hate my life," I say to the darkness. And then sheer exhaustion kicks in and I sleep. For at least two hours.

"ANNEKE!" Jag's scream wakes me with a start, and Schatzi skitters down the hallway at full speed, barking at a volume just slightly louder than a Led Zeppelin concert. The room is suddenly flooded with light, blinding me.

"Jesus Christ! Are you okay?" He rushes to my bed, eyes wide.

"Um, yeah," I mumble. "What the hell?"

"The blood! There's blood all down the hallway and I . . ."

I lean over and look on the floor. There is a distinct trail of blood drops leading from my bedside out the door, and I presume right down the hallway.

"Oops. Cut my foot, didn't realize I'd left such a mess."

"You scared the ever-loving CRAP out of me."

"Well, now we're even!" He looks a little sheepish. Schatzi glares at him, and then heads back down to her end of the hallway.

"I'm so sorry, I didn't mean . . . What the heck happened in here anyway?" In addition to not cleaning up the blood, I didn't clean up the mess on the floor next to the bed either.

"I had a small fight with my nightstand."

"Clearly. Are you okay?"

"Yeah. Just cut my foot on the glass."

"Okay, then. Sorry for scaring you."

"Ditto. How was your night?"

I could swear he looks even more sheepish. "Good. Yours?"

"Annoying. I've run all the numbers. We're not going to make it without help."

"That is the conclusion I've been coming to as well."

"How would you feel about Liam coming in as a partner?" This may be the single most nauseating sentence I've ever uttered, but at the end of the day Gemma is wise. Liam isn't a true evil, and in our current situation, he looks more and more like a necessary one. "He has some money he wants to invest, and sweat equity as well. He'd just want a cut based on the cash infusion, not the work hours."

Jag listens thoughtfully and nods. "I think that is your choice to make, entirely. But if it helps us finish this project, I think it's certainly worth considering."

"We'll talk about it more tomorrow, then." I was really hoping he'd talk me out of it.

"Indeed." He leans over and kisses my forehead. "Good night, sweet wife. I'm glad you're not hacked to bits."

"Good night, dear husband. I'm reasonably glad of that myself." Mostly.

23

From Gemma's Journal:

The Rabins have a new addition to the household. Mr. and Mrs. Rabin were taking a stroll in the park and were adopted by a young pup. The beast, once we deloused him, and cut the mats out of his fur, turned out to be a handsome fellow of about a year, some sort of terrier we believe, and a complete disaster, much to the amusement of Mr. Rabin, and the distress of the Missus, not to mention the new house-keeper. The dog isn't remotely housebroken, and seems only to love to relieve himself on the Persian rugs. He is good for the house, having already proved himself a decent ratter, and an excellent watchdog, barking his fool head off at any stranger who comes near the house. We're all looking for-ward to a time that his positive attributes outweigh the con-stant cleaning and shoe replacement.

So far, I haven't killed Liam. This is my mantra every morning when I face myself in the mirror. I swallowed my enormous pride without choking on it, and accepted Liam's offer, and drew up the paperwork. I reluctantly accepted his money, and even more reluctantly, his help. He took a full week off from work to help us do the big prep on the basement 2.0 projects, and even though he originally said that he could come the occasional evening or weekend, he's been here pretty much every night from six to ten, and every weekend day since we brought him on. He works fast and clean, and even I have to admit that he's pulling my bacon out of the fire. And, which is worse, he is BONDING with Jag. And Jag seems to enjoy it. Since Jag needs the apprentice hours, and since I still find Liam to be just shy of loathsome, I let the two of them pick projects to work on together and I tend to do something else. They did the drain-tile dig and installed the sump pump system, while I started demo on the first-level dining room. They worked on the three separate concrete pours it took to replace the full pad in the basement, and I spent a week up on a scaffold installing coffering and crown molding on the dining room ceiling.

The concrete downstairs is currently curing, so no work can happen down there for a few days, and we're waiting for the delivery of a matched pair of built-in china hutches that will be installed at either end of the dining room. Originally I'd thought we'd do them custom, but Liam found the perfect set at a salvage place in Virginia; they're the same period as the house, completely intact, and while they were a bit pricy, it was still ultimately cheaper than building new ones and trying to match the style. They're gorgeous, with glass-door hutches on top, and plenty of drawer and cabinet space below. By mirroring them on either end of the long formal dining room, we're not only maximizing storage in the room, but we're also restoring the original design.

One of the previous owners pulled similar units out and probably sold them, but the pictures from my research show them intact, and ever since I saw the design—an unusual one for the time, when most rooms would only have one—I've been in love with the idea. They are on a truck at the moment, but apparently there are many deliveries between the East Coast and us, so we aren't likely to see them for at least another couple of weeks, which puts the dining room on hold. When they arrive we will install them, fix any drawer or door issues, and line all the shelves with leather and the drawers and cabinets with silver felt. These are tricks I got from Joe. Leather on shelves where you are storing good china and crystal and the like both provides a nonskid surface, and means that if something topples over it is cushioned against breakage. Cabinets and drawers are most likely to contain the good silver, and by lining everything, including the backs and tops of doors and drawers in silver felt, it keeps things from getting scratched and helps minimize tarnishing. They are the kinds of touches that seem minor, and a potential waste of money, but homeowners unfailingly tell me that these are the kinds of things they most love about their homes when I finish them.

I hate having to stop a project in the middle, especially when it is starting to look so great. The ceiling coffering and crown molding came out beautifully, and I'm dying to see the room with the hutches installed. But if this job teaches you anything, it is patience, and being willing and able to change things up on a dime. So today we are working on the master bathroom. Jag and I have moved our bedrooms downstairs to the second floor, where the bathroom is even worse than the one upstairs, but there is a huge amount of work to be done on the upper level.

We're turning the whole third floor into a wonderful master suite. A huge bedroom, with a nook for watching television, and a built-in deep, circular window seat in the turret section, perfect for curling up with a book. His and hers walk-in closets. A small laundry room. A bonus room with its own small three-piece en suite bathroom, which could be a nursery, caretaker's bedroom, or office. And a massive bathroom that incorporates a small separate room for the toilet, his and hers vanities on opposite walls, his with a large trough sink, hers with a smaller sink and a place to sit down and apply makeup. A large freestanding soaker tub, and a two-person walk-in shower. The bathroom is bigger than most people's bedrooms, but we have a lot of space to fill, and anyone who can afford this house will want a retreat. I've always envisioned this

third-floor space as a spa-like sanctuary. Sort of the presidential
hotel suite you would imagine getting to celebrate your lottery
win. On your honeymoon. In Paris. With George Clooney.

Jag and Liam did the minimal necessary demo on the bathroom space last week, and installed the tile backer board for the
floor and shower, and two coats of RedGard sealant in the
shower area, an extra step that ensures that once the place is
tiled, you don't ever run the risk of water or mold, even if the
grout cracks. So today we start tiling. In the shower we're going
with supersized tiles, twelve inches by twenty-four inches, in
matte charcoal gray soapstone. Instead of the expected offset
brick pattern, we're planning to stack them right on top of each
other. They're cut with very clean knife-edges, so they butt
right up against each other, and the dark grout we're using will
disappear and the walls will look like smooth panels of stone.

The floor of the shower is getting the same stone, but in a
small two-inch-by-three-inch herringbone pattern. Liam came
up with the idea to do one of the new line drains against the
built-in teak bench seat where it will be almost undetectable,
instead of the usual round center drain, which I agree will look
pretty cool. The shower will have no door, just a six-inch step-
down from the main bathroom area, and two mounted panels
of frosted glass on the sides. It isn't dissimilar in style to the
shower I installed at Grant's, which annoys me to no end, considering what I witnessed in that shower, but it's a terrific
design and I refuse to let Grant's damp infidelity make me
abandon a good idea. We're doing his and hers showerheads,
with both wall-mounted and handheld fixtures, and six body
jets each, plus a rain showerhead in the center. The bathroom
floor will be the same size tiles as the shower walls, but in a
white marble shot with gray veins, which will be a very striking contrast to the dark shower. It is a huge amount of work, all
of it painstaking and meticulous, and my knees and back are

already tensing in anticipation of the deep ache that they'll be enjoying for the coming days.

I was almost looking forward to it, a few quiet days with Jag, just hanging out and tiling, but then the hammer dropped. Jag and I got invited to a weekend away with Chuck and Sarah; Chuck's folks have a place in Lake Geneva that they are borrowing. I declined, claiming both the dog and work as an excuse, but encouraged Jag to go, not realizing that it would coincide with both the tiling project, and the three-day Memorial Day weekend. Emily has decamped to meet her dad for the long weekend in Maine, where one of his business partners has a house they visit every year to start their summer. Which leaves me here for the next seventy-two hours. Alone. With Liam. And, which is worse, I have nothing else to escape to. Caroline and Carl are doing a Habitat for Humanity project in New Orleans until Saturday, Hedy is in the Hamptons with a client, Marie and John got a B and B for a romantic weekend in New Buffalo.

Schatzi and I take our morning walk; it's a beautiful end-of-May day, with sweet breezes made sweeter by the sudden appearance of white apple blossoms and the first early lilacs of the season, and you can feel the magic that will be June teasing you. At least Caroline is excited that the farmers' markets have started, and will be coming down on Sunday to take me to the Logan Square market for lunch, which is the only bit of respite I'll have for the whole weekend. She is a little snobby about the Evanston market, it being probably the best one in the area and walking distance from her house, but she acknowledges that Logan Square does a great job, and I haven't seen her or the girls much at all since the wedding.

It feels so good to be out and moving that our walk goes a little long; by the time we get home I'm ravenous. Last night I read about a dish Gemma made for the staff for breakfast, which sounded really good despite its horrible name. Toad-in-the-hole. Seriously, British people, who names your foods? Spotted dick? Bubble and squeak? Bangers and mash? It's off-putting. But the recipe itself, sort of a baked pancake with sausages embedded in it, sounded really good. I have a package of sausages in the fridge, and the rest is just pantry ingredients and eggs, and the most complicated part is searing the sausages. I've got the pan in the oven and Schatzi settled down to a bowl of kibble, when I hear the front door open.

"Something smells good," Liam says, dropping his leather tool bag on the floor, and walking over to the coffeepot to pour himself a mug. He grabs the half-and-half out of the fridge and lightens his coffee to nearly white, and then adds a hefty four teaspoons from the sugar bowl.

"You do realize that your coffee is more like hot melted coffee ice cream, right?"

"I do. And it's delicious. And you're just jealous that I can drink this all day and never add an inch to my girlish figure," he says while slapping his flat abs proudly, winking at me.

"*Girlish* would be the operative term, considering the coffee."

"I'm secure enough in my masculinity to take my coffee yummy."

The alarm on my phone goes off, and I pull the casserole out of the oven. It is puffed and golden and the sausages are spitting and the whole thing smells delicious.

"Perfect! I haven't had breakfast yet." Liam goes over to the cabinet and gets two plates, grabbing a pair of forks out of the jar on the counter. I hate his presumption, not to mention the easy way he operates in my kitchen, not so at home, but it's going to be a long weekend and I promised myself I would be Zen-like in my demeanor.

I dish us both up a large square that contains two sausages each. Liam goes to the pantry and gets the maple syrup, which he pours with a heavy hand over his plate. He offers it to me, and I decline. The dish is pretty good. Sort of like a Yorkshire pudding with meat in it. The sausages are a little bit spicy, and the pancake part might be the tiniest bit overcooked, it is just shy of rubbery, but overall a good breakfast. Liam wolfs it down, and quickly dishes himself up a second generous portion.

"Where did you learn to make toad-in-the-hole, lass?"

"You know this stuff?"

"It's the food of my childhood. And not half bad at that. But I don't know many people here who know how to make it. Makes me crave a bit of brown sauce."

"I found it in an old cookbook, seemed interesting."

"Well done." He stuffs another huge bite in his maw. "So, I think we do the tiling today, grout tomorrow, finish work Monday?"

"That's what I was thinking as well." I'm feeling strangely awkward around him, and I realize that while I've known Liam for the better part of a decade, I don't really know him. I've never really spent any significant time with him, and the time we have spent together has been full of barbs and insults and thinly veiled distaste for each other's company. He joined MacMurphy just three months after me, and from the day he arrived he teased me mercilessly. I was also the only female he has apparently never hit on. Not that I wanted his attention, but at a certain point when you've seen the man flirt with every pair of boobs from seventeen to seventy that crosses his path, it does make you feel like a troll.

That, added to the fact that he quickly started edging me out of the best jobs and the coolest clients, would have been bad enough. But he also had that immediate boys'-club in with Mac and Murph, going to all the sporting events, golf outings, and out to the bars after work. Murph's boat in the summer and up to Mac's weekend place at the Dunes, the kind of quality social time that helps your career, the kind of invitations that never came my way. Every chance he got he rubbed it in, throwing it in my face. It's true that recent events have been surprising, his kindness, his openness. But just because a dog doesn't bite you every time you pet it doesn't mean it isn't still a biter. I like having Jag for a buffer, and I'm starting to wish I had decided to just go away with him, despite the awkwardness it would have created to have to share a room and a bed, to play at being in love twenty-four hours a day.

Here's what I do know. It's going to be a very long weekend.

These. Are. AMAZING," Caroline says around a mouthful of apple cider zeppole. We're at the Logan Square Farmers Market, and have eaten our way around the square. We started with a couple of meat tacos from Cherubs, simply seasoned small cubes of beef on soft steamed corn tortillas, with a garnish of onion, cilantro and lime. A perfect amuse-bouche. Then we shared an insane grilled cheese sandwich, buttery and crispy and filled with gooey, perfectly melted Wisconsin Butterkäse cheese. A pork empanada from Pecking Order, with their homemade banana ketchup. A porchetta sandwich from Publican Quality Meats. Schatzi got her little bits and pieces, plus a huge organic dog biscuit from a local bakery. She's thankfully interacted quite beautifully with three French bulldogs, two Boston terriers, a corgi and six children in the "shorter than my waist" age range. We are in hipsterville, so there are nothing but small dogs and sassy toddlers about.

As I always do, we finish with a bag of the fried-to-order zeppole, odd little fritterlike doughnuts with apple cider in the batter, tossed with cinnamon sugar, while I try almost successfully to ignore that this was one of Grant and my summer Sunday traditions. I may have let that man make me leave my home and quit my job and put me into a death spiral of shit, but I refuse to let him keep me from sugar-encrusted hot fried dough.

"I'm so full," I say, reaching for another little bit of crispy delicious.

"I could burst, but I can't stop eating them," Caroline says. We take our iced teas, acquired at New Wave Coffee, and our bags of produce, and find spots at one of the picnic tables to sit and digest a bit. Schatzi seems perfectly happy to curl up under the table, giving her a bit of a break from the sensory overload of other dogs and children and crowds. Caroline has three fabric tote bags bursting with treasures.

Late May is a riot of tiny things. Fiddlehead fern tips, tiny shoots and microgreens, baby lettuces. Pencil-thin asparagus. Ramps are everywhere, those wild leeks that everyone goes nuts for, and Caroline must have bought six bunches. She has a pickling project she's very excited about. Teeny tiny baby beets in three colors, marble-sized turnips, spring onions. Poor Carl is in for a week of twee baby vegetables. She found some racks of spring lamb, fresh goat cheese, several kinds of sausages. Fresh fava beans, so tender they won't need peeling, peppery arugula for salads. Some wild-looking shoots that turned out to be garlic scapes, which made Caroline all excited to make homemade ravioli, which apparently she is going to stuff with a mixture of favas, the goat cheese, and these garlic thingies, in a butter sauce with the morels she just spent a fortune on.

I've been somewhat more judicious, sticking with carrots and bags of baby spinach, spring onions. Some rhubarb, since Gemma has a recipe for rhubarb jelly that sounds weirdly interesting. A bunch of radishes, since Jag mentioned an affinity for them served with cold butter and salt. I even bought a lump of fresh butter for him.

Caroline takes a deep draught of her tea, sensibly dosed with lemon and a single Splenda packet. "So, on a scale from one to ten. How is it?"

I sip my own tea, less sensibly doctored with a healthy squeeze of simple syrup. "The house? Coming along. We've probably made up nearly a week of the time we lost, and so far, no new disasters."

"I don't worry about your work much, lovey. I'm talking about your marriage, and the new partner."

"You're sweet to worry. I'm doing pretty well. Jag is easy to live with, and we are enjoying the whole newlywed thing. He's really saved me."

"You're ridiculous, you're not the 'damsel in distress seeking prince on a white horse' type."

"I know that," I say, trying to look dreamy and in love. "But it's nice to have someone WANT to save you. To have someone to lean on, and get through it all with."

"It was just so fast, and you were so sad and angry . . . We all just want you to be happy, and it makes us nervous. We worry for you." Clearly she and the girls have still been chatting about me, which makes me more than a little uncomfortable. I know I shouldn't have expected them not to have opinions, but I really had hoped that getting married would at least mitigate their need to weigh in overmuch.

"Well stop. I never had a mother before, I'm certainly not looking for one now," I say, perhaps a little more harshly than I intend. I immediately regret it, Caroline's face stays impassive, but her eyes show that I've hurt her feelings. "I'm sorry, Caroline, I didn't mean . . ."

"No." She stops me. "You're absolutely right, I have no right, not my place."

"It isn't that I'm ungrateful for your care and concern, I just, I'm in a place of trying to keep an even keel, and I can't think about anything that isn't related to getting through my days, to getting the house done, to moving me bit by tiny bit toward something that looks like a future. Jag is the only part of all of this that is in the least bit enjoyable, and he is my safe place and my sanity. Does that make sense?"

She smiles, a little wanly, but still warm. "It does. Of course it does. And I'm glad for you both, truly. Subject closed."

"Thank you."

"And your Irishman?"

"I'm glad for the break today, frankly. He's been fine, mostly. He's still himself, so the banter is more than a little annoying. There are a lot of references to the late nights and stupid clubs, he doesn't say outright that he's in a different bed every night, but the implication is there. He seems to be spending a lot of time at places that cater to overgrown frat boys, not that it should surprise me. But then on the flip side, he'll go off on these rants about the clients at MacMurphy and the goings-on over there, in a way that seems like he is sort of trying to make me feel good for leaving."

"That is nice of him."

"It is. I'm a little leery of his motives and sincerity."

"Maybe he's trying to make an effort because of being business partners?"

"True, and I hope that's it. And he and Jag are getting along brilliantly, so that is good. I'm sure I'm just oversensitive; it's been a long couple of days of close quarters without Jag around for a buffer."

"Why didn't you go with him? His friends are so lovely, and it would have been a nice break."

"Just couldn't do it. Emily is out of town, and I couldn't take the dog, Chuck is allergic. And with Liam having the long weekend off and wanting to put in so many hours? I hate to say it, but we really do need his help, and I couldn't afford to turn down such a productive weekend. And I'm a big believer that even after you get married you should still maintain your independent friendships."

Caroline laughs. "Aren't you just the expert!"

"Yes I am! I've been married almost two months, you know." I check my watch; we've been gone over an hour and a half. "I should get back to it, before Liam installs a stripper pole in the master bedroom." We toss our empty iced-tea cups in the bin behind the table, and relinquish our places to a grateful couple wrangling two small children and a large mutt. I walk Caroline to her car, thanking her for lunch, and then Schatzi and I head back to the house.

"We're back!" I yell when I get to the kitchen, unhooking Schatzi's leash and beginning to put my small bag of treasures away.

"And how was the market?" Liam comes into the kitchen, gives Schatzi a rub.

"Good. Here . . ." I toss him a porchetta sandwich, still warm.

"Ooo, yummies. Very kind of you." He unwraps the sandwich and begins to wolf it down.

"You're welcome."

He's finished with his lunch in no longer than it takes me to get all the stuff put away and get my hands washed, and we immediately head back upstairs to the bathroom to keep working. We started the grouting this morning, and got the shower mostly finished before I had to leave. In my absence, Liam has finished the grouting in the shower and installed the built-in bench as well. Now we have to tackle the bathroom floor, which is a vast expanse that seems even bigger now that we have to deal with it. The good part about big tiles is that large spaces get filled quicker. The bad part is that you have to be absolutely meticulous when you lay them, because even the tiniest spacing differential becomes glaring. And grouting, while you would think it would be easier, since there are fewer grout lines, is still a bitch, trying to keep the face of the tiles as clean as possible. Armed with the grout and buckets of water and huge sponges, we strap on our kneepads and start at opposite corners.

"You know, I would have worked on this if you had wanted to go with your husband for a weekend."

"Thank you, Liam, that's kind, but between the work, and the dog, just not good timing."

"For newlyweds, you guys seem to spend a lot of time apart." He says this like it's a casual observation, but my stomach knots immediately. These close quarters are dangerous; it's really important that Liam not question my marriage.

"Well, you wouldn't know this with your bimbo-of-the-week club, but in actual mature adult relationships, you don't need to be attached at the hip twenty-four hours a day."

"No need to get defensive, little Annamuk, just hope all is rosy here in the land of wedded bliss. After all, we have to finish this house together; that's going to be uncomfortable if the two of you are on the rocks."

"Ha!" I say, probably a little loudly. "We couldn't be LESS on the rocks. I feel bad for you, Liam, you clearly have never met anyone who touched your heart in any kind of profound way. Jag came into my life when I was at my lowest, and looked at me like I was a queen. He didn't think I was an idiot for quitting a stable job to focus on my dreams, and he didn't care that I was living in this place to make that happen. He is the smartest, handsomest, kindest, most amazing man I've ever known, and I thank my lucky stars every day that we found each other. I hope that someday you understand love like this, Liam, I really do." This pours out of me in a manic gush, my voice pitching higher and higher, the words moving faster and faster. I want to stop but I can't. "Jag has given up everything for me. He gave up school so we can work on this house; he's committed to staying in the US to live, leaving his family four thousand miles away. He is a prince among men."

"Easy there, kiddo, you don't have to hard-sell me, I like the guy. I just was saying it seems that he spends a lot of nights out with his friends without you, and it is a little weird to me that this is your first holiday weekend since you got married, and you're here and he's off for a play weekend with pals."

"Lucky for me, you don't have to understand it." Now I'm getting snippy, and I hate the tone in my voice. And he's totally right; I'm overdefending. When I told Jag to go for his weekend away, all I was thinking was that he could probably use a break from me, and the house, and some quality relaxing time with his friends. It never occurred to me that it might look like some sort of red flag to the outside world, and now I'm worried that Jag's friends may be giving him a hard time as well.

"True enough. At any rate, I wasn't trying to start anything, I was just saying, for future reference, if you ever want to take a weekend off with your *insanely amazing prince of a husband*"—his emphasis oozes insincerity—"I'd be happy to work here in your absence. I'd even watch the pooch. She loves me." Ugh. Even when he's making a very generous and kind offer, it comes off sleazy.

"Well, I appreciate the offer, but I can't help but worry that you'd host some sort of weekend orgy in my house."

"We can't all meet our dream person in the parking lot of Home Depot, dear Anneke."

"And you're unlikely to meet her while doing shots at Rockit Bar, just so you know."

"Probably true." He stands up. "Looking good in here, what do you think?" I stand up and survey the room, immediately grateful for the change of subject. There is something about getting grout in that just gives you that sense of what it is going to be, weirdly even more than getting the tiles down.

"I think it looks fantastic." It really does. Liam pulled in a favor and got all the stone and marble tiles from a contact at a huge discount, saving me from using the less posh porcelain I had been contemplating.

"Okay then, let's knock this out!" He gets back down on his knees, and I can't help but notice the strong lines of his back and shoulders, the round tush. Why on earth does that personality have to live in such an attractive package? I wish he were a troll. Or a nice guy. It would make things so much easier.

"Let's do it." And thankfully, at least for now, we can stop talking, and just do the work.

We finish up on Monday, and after I wash the grime from my hands and arms, Liam hands me a beer.

"That bathroom is fucking gorgeous," he says, taking a swig out of his own bottle. "I love the contrast between the dark shower and the light floor."

"Thank you. And thank you for working your magic with the stone guy; it looks a million times better with the real deal than it would have with the regular tiles."

He winks. "Stone girl."

I laugh. "Should have known. Well, keep working that pretty-boy magic, if it gets us discounts like that."

He flutters his eyelashes and places a hand delicately on his chest, as if a blushing girl. "Do you think I'm pretty? Really?"

I swat at him, my hand connecting with the insane solidity of his shoulder. "Whatever. I'm just glad for you to use whatever you have at your disposal for the benefit of the house."

He makes a mock-horrified face. "You would have me basely prostitute myself for the sake of your little project!"

I can't help but giggle. The hard work of the whole weekend, the awkwardness of yesterday, it all goes away in the glow of a job finished, and done well. "Yep. You are officially my bitch, and I intend to turn you out." I snap in the air.

His jaw snaps shut. "Did you just seriously call me a bitch and threaten to 'turn me out' with a snap, lass? Seriously? How much HBO late-night pseudo-documentaries are you watching, Pimpzilla?"

His calling me Pimpzilla makes me literally snort beer out my nose.

"Well, now that is classy." He hands me a handkerchief. A real one. Linen. From his back pocket. I stare at it, beer, and likely snot, dripping from my nose. "It's clean, you suspicious girl. Wipe your nose."

I clean myself up and go to give him back the handkerchief. He raises one eyebrow, looking at the small piece of damp cloth warily. "No, keep it. Really. I insist."

"I don't have Ebola, you ass."

"And how would I know that for sure? You could be handing me the plague right there. Or rickets or something." Which cracks us both up all over again.

When we stop laughing, there is something of a sheepish silence. I think we both realized all at once that for the first time since we've met, we've just behaved something like friends.

"Well, I should go. Your beloved will be home any moment, and I'm sure you'll want to clean yourself up and greet him properly." He looks me up and down. "You know, reignite your love after your weekend apart." Oh, he is maddening.

"Don't really need to," I quip, calmly as I can. "He likes me dirty."

"Can't argue with him there," Liam says without the slightest hint of irony or mocking, and this makes me blush despite myself. "Enjoy your homecoming. I can't come tomorrow night, but I'll be here Wednesday."

"Hot date?" I ask, intending to be casual and flip, but it comes out weirdly snippy.

"Don't I always?" He smirks. And then he walks around the

kitchen island and kisses my temple. "Good night, little Anna-muk."

And then he is gone.

Schatzi looks at me with her head tilted to the left.

"I have no idea, dog. Don't even ask." And I pick up the phone to order a huge pizza to sate what appears to be a new hunger.

It was great, but everyone missed you," Jag says, reaching for a slice of pizza the size of Montana. Dante's is one of the only delivery places in Chicago that cuts pie slices instead of the traditional squares. Since their pizzas are literally twenty inches across, each piece is about as big as your head. I'm a one-handed fold girl, but Jag likes to use the two-handed flat method.

I pick a large piece of meatball off my slice, and relish the spiciness. "I'll come next time for sure."

"How was Liam?"

"Fine. We got a lot done. When we're done eating I'll show you the progress."

"You're okay with him being here?"

I think about this. "Not really. I hate that we had to accept his money, his time. But he's very skilled, and he is right that his being here and partnering with us will get the job done faster and better, and get us a bigger sale. So it's annoying, but I know it's worth it in the long run."

"Like marrying me."

I look at him, seeing something a little sad in his eyes. "You are worth it in the long and short and every possible run, and never ever annoying."

He smiles. "Thank you for that."

"Anytime." The doorbell rings just as I've taken a huge bite of pizza. Jag looks at me and I shrug. He motions for me to stay and eat and heads down to see who is at the door, Schatzi close at his heels. In a few seconds I hear happy dog barking and a high-pitched barrage of indecipherable chatter, with heavy footsteps clomping up the stairs, which can only mean one thing.

"ANNEKE!" Emily grabs me around the shoulders from behind, effectively Heimliching me and sending my large bite of pizza shooting straight out the front of my face, and into the sink.

"Oops," she says, covering her mouth as she smiles.

"Three points," Jag says, laughing.

"Hi, Emily. How was Maine?"

"It was really good, the weather was perfect, and the black-flies weren't too bad and I totally ate like my WEIGHT in lobster every day, and we sea kayaked and did some antiquing, and I brought presents!" This all comes out in one breath, and makes me laugh.

She reaches down and unzips her duffel bag, rummaging around. She pulls out a beautiful old hammer, the handle clearly hand-carved and worn smooth with years of use, the iron head still bearing the marks of the blacksmith. It is one of the loveliest things anyone has ever given me, and the pizza sticks in my throat and tears prickle my eyes. I shake it off, and look up at her.

"Thank you, Emily, it's just the perfect thing, and very sweet of you."

"You're welcome! I just saw it and thought of you and the guy said it was like from the late seventeen hundreds or something, and anyway, I just figured you'd kill me if I brought you lobster soap or something."

"You didn't have to bring me anything, but this is really special and I will treasure it."

Clearly very pleased with herself, she smiles so wide I think her head is going to snap in half. She leans down and rummages some more and comes back up with a stuffed lobster chew toy that she tosses to Schatzi, and a small package for Jag.

"You shouldn't have, Emily," he says, unwrapping a small flat leather box that opens to reveal antique drafting tools. "How wonderful. Thank you so much." He leans over and kisses her cheek, and she blushes fetchingly.

"I'm glad you guys like them." She wriggles out of her jean jacket, which she tosses over the back of a chair, and reaches over and snags a slice of pizza. "And I'm glad that I got them so I can use them to butter you up."

Uh-oh. "Butter us up for what, pray tell."

She looks down at her hands. "Um, I was wondering if maybe I could stay here for a little while."

Crap. "What happened to your sorority sister?"

"When I went there tonight she seemed surprised to see me, I guess she thought I wasn't really coming back, and she said that she's just loved having me, but it is making things complicated with her boyfriend, who was, um, there when I got back, if you know what I mean, so I just came here and thought maybe you'd let me crash here to give her some space for a bit."

Ten. Nine. Eight. Seven. Six . . .

"Of course, Emily, you're most welcome," Jag says, looking at me over her head with his eyes wide open, encouraging me to do the right thing.

Sigh. "Yes. No problem. I've got a blow-up mattress upstairs . . ."

"You guys are the best! Seriously, love you. Really appreciate it. Why don't I just use the pullout couch in the den?"

And with that one sentence, Jag and I suddenly realize what we've agreed to, and our jaws drop open in unison.

I t's probably only for a couple of nights," Jag says in the dark from his side of the bed. We're both lying as far to opposite sides of my queen-sized mattress as possible. Jag in full paja-mas, and me in leggings and a T-shirt. We both have our own blanket and sheets, and I've wrapped myself up in mine like a burrito.

"Well, that will be restful."

He snickers. "We can just think of it as good research for the green card interviews."

"Oh, yeah, terrific. I can tell them what tune you fart in your sleep."

"And I can tell them how loud you snore."

This makes me giggle. "Seriously, what are we going to do?"

"We're going to be grown-ups. We're going to share this bed and get some sleep."

"Right. Grown-ups. Good night, Jag."

Ppppprrrrrrruuuutttttt.

"SERIOUSLY!"

He laughs. "Excuse me, wife."

"HOLY CRAP. What the hell did you EAT this weekend?"

"Lots of dal."

"Jesus. Are you trying to kill me? That smells like a dead wombat. In Death Valley. Covered in Camembert."

"You wanted to know the tune, I thought I'd oblige." He's still laughing, and the whole bed is shaking.

"It's on now, husband, when the pizza kicks in, you are in TROUBLE! I might blow you right out of this bed."

"Based on what I've heard through the wall in the mornings, I don't doubt it."

And both of us laugh till we stop, and then, eventually, sleep.

24

Today Jag and Emily are working on refinishing the floors in the living room and dining room on the main level. We were lucky when he sanded them this week to remove the old yellowed finish to discover that they haven't been redone more than once in the building's history. You can really only sand down a hardwood floor twice after it's been installed before you start to see nailheads, and I was really worried that we'd take off the finish and find that we would need to rip up and replace all the flooring. But for once the renovation gods were smiling on us and the horrible finish came up easily, and now that we've cleaned them three times with adhesive cloths to make sure there isn't a speck of sawdust or dirt anywhere, the floors are all prepped for staining. The three of us went round and round on the color; Liam likes a light floor to contrast with the rich deeper chestnut brown of the woodwork, Jag likes a dark floor for its elegance and visual impact. I'm always Goldilocks, wanting it right in the middle, close to the color of the woodwork to create a seamless look, but one tone lighter to ensure that they don't show every bit of dirt and dust that gets tracked in, the way very light or very dark floors do. The boys deferred to me, as they always do, knowing that while I love and appreciate their input, I do have a bigger vision.

Jag and Emily are working carefully from the back of the first floor toward the front staircase to make sure they don't stain us all into a corner, and Schatzi is corralled on the second floor in the kitchen to make sure we don't end up with doggie paw prints in the fresh stain. It's been four days. As far as we can tell, Emily has no plans to leave. I want to broach it with her, but Jag has convinced me to let it alone. As it turns out, a little gassiness aside, we are actually pretty compatible sleepers. He crashes almost instantaneously, falling deeply asleep on his back like a dead guy, and never moves till morning, like flipping a switch. So the fact that I'm a flippity-flopping side sleeper, who always needs the cool side of the pillow and does what Grant used to call the floppy salmon dance all night long, doesn't disturb him in the least. So even though it is still a little weird, it isn't horrible.

I'm up on the third floor in the larger of the two walk-in closets, fully indulging what little girly side I actually have. I finished the smaller closet, the "his" closet across the hall, yesterday. Lots of narrow shelves for sweaters, plenty of deep drawers for jeans and T-shirts, pullout pants racks, built-in organizers for ties and belts and hats. A window seat for putting on socks and shoes, with storage underneath. One wall has sliding paneled doors that reveal a cedar-lined hanging space for suits and sportcoats, and one has floor-to-ceiling generously sized shoe cubbies, large enough for a size 12 EEE width to put his shoes in side by side. I learned from having to totally rip out a wall of shoe cubbies for a previous client that men's "standard" shoe storage is notoriously undersized, and that guys who like nice shoes like to keep shoe trees in them, so they don't want to store them on their sides as if nestled in a shoebox. Ever since, I have a custom template that I use to make sure that the boys get shoe storage as thoughtful as the ladies'.

But for all the nice details in a man closet, there is nothing more fun than doing a built-in girl closet, especially one as generous as this. Since this whole level had originally been the family bedrooms, it had three rooms in graduated sizes. We've kept the larger front bedroom as the master bedroom. On the original plans it was actually a large bedroom and a small attached sitting area, with a smaller bedroom on the other side, creating a three-room suite. This would have been so that as the couple got older, or if either was ill, one of them could move to the separated bedroom with a shared sitting room between them. When the place was converted to apartments, this whole space was opened up to create a large L-shaped living room. We've decided to leave the footprint as is, but turn it back into a bedroom suite, making the original smaller bedroom area into a space for watching TV, and the former sitting room a cozy place to read or sit and chat. The two other bedrooms would have been the children's rooms, one smaller than the other, and it's these two we're converting to the master closets.

The space I'm working in today is my former bedroom, a generous twelve by twelve feet, and I've designed it to work almost like a tiny boutique, so a woman can feel like she's shopping every time she goes to get dressed. Over the years I've done everything from small organization units in condo closets with sliding doors, to one massive one-thousand-square-foot duplex closet for a pampered socialite that included a wall of climate-controlled storage for her substantial fur collection, and no lie, a CIA-level fingerprint lock on the door. The only thing that was ever more fun was doing a panic room for a paranoid woman who had recently lost her husband. She wanted to be sure that if someone broke into her Gold Coast brownstone she could survive in comfort for at least a week. We referred to her as the Preppy Prepper, giving her a large panic room with en suite bathroom, which included a mini kitchen stocked with canned caviar and smoked oysters and splits of vintage champagne, completely upholstered in a huge-scale blowsy floral chintz.

This room is a good size, big enough for me to create an island in the middle that combines very shallow drawers for organizing jewelry and scarves and other accessories toward the top, and open cubbies of varying sizes for handbags around the bottom. The window wall gets a built-in window seat on top of tall cubbies for boots. I found a great shoe system at IKEA that I love to incorporate in closets like this, essentially a slide-out drawer of shoe trees on sticks. You can fit sixteen pairs of even the tallest heels in a space about three feet by a foot and a half. Most built-in closets do these skinny little shelves that take up a huge amount of wall space and don't store that many shoes. By using these drawers, I can fit four times the number of shoes in the same wall space, and the drawers are flush with the other shelves and drawers in the closet. I do these deep drawers all the way around underneath the hanging and shelving sections, and then one small area of more traditional angled shoe shelving for the footwear that gets the most use or are the special pairs someone would want to show off most. A tall section of shallow shelves designed to hold only one or two folded sweaters per section, all lined in cedar. Four pullout valet bars around the room so a girl can plan a long weekend of outfits, or debate between options for a special night out. All of the clothes live behind glass-front doors that are done with special UV protective glass, the kind of glass they use to frame artwork, so that a girl can see her stuff but it isn't getting dusty or damaged by light. A built-in wall safe behind a hidden magnetic-catch panel. Since the floor in here was structurally sound but water damaged in a way that wouldn't work for re-staining, I painted it in large squares, pale dove gray offset with a slightly darker tone, and all of the woodwork was stained to match the original wood of the house. And my favorite part, an oversized chandelier dripping with crystals that we scored from Liam's Fremont project. It used to be a dining room fixture, and is the kind of over-the-top touch that embraces the joy of the nonpractical side of a closet like this.

While Jag has been working with Emily all week on the

floors, keeping her out of my hair for both of our sakes, I've been pre-building drawer and shelving units so that the closets come together more like a kitchen, installing section by section, leveling and tweaking fit, attaching one piece to the one next to it, installing filler strips where necessary. When everything is in, I'll be able to come back and put in the doors. The island, which is essentially like a four-sided piece of furniture, will go in last so that I have plenty of room to work. In the meantime, I've got thick paper covering and protecting the floor. The units get screwed into each other and I've done a row of cleats around the room, that way if someday someone decides that this room needs to be a bedroom again, the closet system can come out in its sections to be repurposed. We're using standard closet organization systems in the rest of the house, but it was important that these two closets got the really custom treatment.

"How about I give you a hand in here?" Liam's voice behind me shocks me right out of my skin, and I give a yelp.

"Jesus, you oaf, you scared the shit out of me."

He grins sheepishly. "Sorry. I have a strangely light tread for an oaf. My mum always threatened to bell me like a cat."

"Smart woman."

"Yes, she was." There is something in his face that falls a bit, but he recovers quickly. "You've been busy up here this week, I see; that looks amazing over there." He gestures across the hall to the other closet. "Jag and the bairn seem to be all squared away downstairs, so I've been banished up here to help you, if you'll have me."

I almost wish Jag had sent Emily upstairs instead. "Come on in and I'll show you the plan."

I've got the layout for the closet install taped up to one of the windows; each piece is numbered, so it should go in pretty smoothly. I walk Liam through the plan, and we decide to start with the wall to the south of the window wall, since that wall and the one opposite the windows create an unbroken L, which requires a little trickiness in the corner, where I've designed a wedge-shaped unit of open shelving. The other wall is all hanging storage and shoe drawers, and we'll wait till all of this is in before we link the two with the window seat unit, and then we'll install the chandelier before we bring in the island.

"It's like you're planning an invasion of Kamchatka." He gestures at my color-coded, numbered, three-dimensional printouts.

"Ha! I loved that game when I was a kid." Risk was one of Joe's favorites, and we used to play sometimes after dinner.

"Me too. Shall we begin?"

We grab the first piece and bring it into the room, using shims underneath to get it level, and screwing it into the cleat on the wall. While we're working, it becomes clear that Liam is in a chatty mood today.

"I have to hand it to you, little Annamuk, this is not what I would have expected."

"Why is that?"

"It's so, um, romantic."

"And you don't think I'm romantic?"

"I think you're refreshingly unsentimental. It's what makes you a great builder."

"I don't think I follow."

He pauses for a moment. "I think that your eye always goes to what will make a home function smoothly, what will make the people who live there comfortable. That is different than the romance aspect. Romantic people get focused on things like brand names and labels that evoke a certain feel for them, or focused on elements that may or may not work well for their space. Old-world crown molding in a modern loft space, commercial kitchen appliances for a family that doesn't cook, the kinds of touches that actually make a space feel awkward or just off. Your places are always fully kitted out, with amazing attention to detail, and always designed with the actual usage and client in mind."

"So why is this different?"

"I don't know. Don't get me wrong, it's amazing, and still super-functional, but the chandelier? The painted floor? Very girly."

"And I'm not a girl?"

Liam looks me dead in my eyes. "No, my darling. You are not now and have never been a girl. You are a woman. Every inch."

His gold-flecked green eyes hold my gaze when he says this, and for the first time since the day I caught Grant soaping up his sous chef, my girl parts remind me that I am indeed a woman. One who cannot remember the last time a man looked at her with anything remotely indicating that he noticed.

"Thank you, I think?"

"It was intended as a compliment."

"So you think we should change the design in here? Make it less sentimental?" I'm flushed and flustered and very much wanting to get back to work.

"Nah. I like it. It's like a lovely little surprise. I like that you surprise me now and again."

I can feel myself blushing deeper. "Glad I can keep you amused."

"Oh, you do at that, lass, you certainly do."

No wonder this man gets so many women. Despite the fact that my intense distaste for Liam has recently converted to reluctant tolerance, even occasional appreciation, my biology apparently could give a flying fart about anything other than the span of his shoulders. The stupid accent even works; he says nice things to me, and all of a sudden it's all damp pants and sweaty palms.

Which is why when we go to grab the next section, it slips right out of my now-slick hands, and when I grab wildly to stop it from careening right into the wall, my wrist torques uncomfortably. "Ow, damn!"

Liam quickly shifts his grip to take the full weight of the piece and sets it down gently.

"Show me," he says.

"It's nothing, it's fine." But he takes my hand anyway, holding it firmly and moving each finger gently. This does nothing to stop my heart, and parts southerly, from quickening.

"Seems okay. Not sprained?"

"Don't think so."

"Good. But what say you let me be the big lunk I am and do the heavy lifting, and you focus on finesse." He doesn't say this like it's a question, and I don't argue. I move aside and let him lift the piece alone, watching his arm muscles flex underneath his thermal shirt. He brings the piece into the room and we shim it up, clamp it to the piece we already installed. He screws it into the cleat while I predrill holes to attach it to the first piece and then proceed to grab the wrong length screw, watching as the one I pick goes clean through both pieces, leaving a good half inch pointing out the other side, into the shelf space.

"Damn it." Liam turns around to see what I've done, and since we're working on the same three-foot-wide piece, when he does, he ends up standing right behind me, so close that I can feel the heat of his body along the full length of my back, his breath tickling the nape of my neck. "Oops. A little miscalculation there, lass." He reaches his arm around me, resting his forearm on my shoulder, drill in hand, and deftly removes the screw. "Try this one." He hands me the proper screw, from a small leather pouch on his belt.

I take the new one from him and it goes in smoothly. I'll have to use a little wood filler on the other side, but not a big deal; it won't be noticeable in the end. I'm not sure what is wrong with me today. We get that wall finished without further incident, but then, when we start the next one, I bring in a piece upside down, requiring we uninstall and reinstall it.

Then, while doing the drawer slides for the shoe drawers, I put the first three I install in backward before Liam catches me.

"You're not quite yourself today, eh? I think I know what's distracting you."

"You do?!" This raises alarms. If he knew that I was all thumbs today because he is being funny and charming and unintentionally sexy, I will simply die of mortification.

"You've got a lovely evening planned with your hubby, and can't wait to stop work."

I'm totally puzzled. "And what makes you think that?"

"I saw the fridge when I grabbed a bottle of water on my way up. Looks like the makings of quite the dinner."

I'd read about a very delicious dinner Gemma made for Mr. and Mrs. Rabin for their 45th anniversary, the last menu fully outlined in her journal before it just stops. Steak Diane, all the rage at the time in the posh hotels, steamed asparagus with hollandaise sauce, classic potatoes Dauphinois, a chocolate souf-flé. It sounded like fun, and nothing beyond my capabilities, although the soufflé worries me a bit. Today would have been the Rabins' 115th wedding anniversary. Seemed fitting to give the menu a try. Not that I'm going to tell Liam that.

"Yep, going all out."

"Lucky man, Jag. Tell you what, you love-struck thing, let me finish in here. I've got your meticulous plan, and frankly, you're getting in your own way a bit. You go start your dinner prep, take an afternoon off for a change."

I begin to protest, and then realize that he's given me the perfect way to get out of this room where his horrible testosterone is getting all over me.

"Thanks, Liam. I appreciate it." I leave him to the work, and head downstairs. I snap on Schatzi's leash, and we head down the front stairs.

"Taking the dog out for a bit," I yell down the hall to Jag.

"Want me to do it?" Emily yells out.

"Nope, I got it, could use the air, thanks."

"Have a nice walk!" Jag yells back, muffled behind the mask he's wearing to protect himself from the fumes.

The fresh spring air is a little brisk today, but it feels good to get out and clear my head. Schatzi and I take a quick walk around the park, and then head back. I pull the recipes I've copied from Gemma's journal.

A special private anniversary dinner. The party is Saturday, with all the children and grandchildren and friends coming to celebrate, but for tonight, it is just the two of them, and I wanted to do something very special. I spent a day with my friend Marcel who works at the Drake, learning how to make Steak Diane, the popular restaurant dish that Mrs. Rabin fell in love with on their last trip to New York. Instead of the dining room, I've set a table in the small sitting room upstairs, in the turret where they can see the park while they eat, abloom with spring, lush and green.

Once Schatzi is back in the kitchen, safely behind the dog gate, I go to the bedroom. I'm still weirdly hopped-up and on edge from my day with Liam. I'm hoping a shower will help clear my head a bit. I slip out of my work clothes and into my robe, grab my towel, and go to the bathroom. When the water is hot, I get into the shower, not a much better trickle than the one upstairs, and certainly not the luxury of the downstairs bath, but still, the water feels good. I soap myself, feeling the sweat and grit wash away, and luxuriating a bit in the slick motion of my hands over my skin. Before I even realize what I'm doing, I've got one hand braced against the wall, my forehead pressed against the cool tile, my other hand feverishly working, until I find a quick explosive release. A small "oh" escapes my lips, and then an embarrassed giggle. I can't even believe I've just indulged myself, especially with three other people in the house. I feel sort of wicked, and a little sheepish, but altogether better.

Sated, and feeling at once clean and dirty, I dry off, twist my hair into a bun, and put my robe back on. I go to my room and get dressed, pulling on jeans and a black V-neck T-shirt. I head to the kitchen and begin to prep dinner. I invested in a fifteen-dollar handheld mandoline, knowing that my knife skills would never be good enough to get the potatoes thin and uniform. I shockingly manage to slice them all without opening an artery, and briefly cook them in a mix of cream and half-and-half, with a pinch of nutmeg, a sprig of thyme. I've got a buttered dish at the ready, which I've dutifully rubbed with the cut side of a half clove of garlic, but I'm suspicious of this maneuver; I can't imagine it will really impart much flavor. When the potato slices are pliable but still not cooked, I transfer them to the dish, discarding the sprig of thyme, and add enough of the cooking liquid to barely cover them. I pop it in the preheated oven, wondering how that soupy mess of potato and cream will come together into a sliceable dish.

I follow Gemma's recipe for hollandaise sauce to the letter, and it comes together beautifully. I put it in the warming drawer, which will hold it at the perfect temperature until I need it. Grant loved warming drawers, and there are two in this kitchen, one beneath each wall oven. Like the stove, the ovens and drawers are all BlueStar, top of the line and gorgeous. In addition to simply being the best equipment for serious cooks, their products come in pretty much the whole Pantone rainbow, so while we kept the range a charcoal gray to blend with the cabinets, we did the wall ovens in a deep poppy orange. Since they are on opposite walls, it creates little splashes of color that really save the kitchen from being too monochromatic.

Grant hated side-by-side or up-and-down wall ovens. They are either too high or too low, or you are elbowing your partner in the eye while you are basting the Thanksgiving turkey and they're baking the rolls. We installed ours on opposite sides of the kitchen at counter height, with the warming drawers below. One gas oven, for roasting, next to the range, the other electric, for baking.

My preparations go smoothly, and soon I've got the meat seared, ready to be reheated in the sauce last minute, the asparagus in the steamer, the soufflé in its dish, buttered and lined in ground almonds. I'm just putting the soufflé in the fridge to hang out till I bake it off while we eat dinner, when Jag comes into the kitchen. I toss him a bottle of water, which he drains in one go.

"Smells good in here, what are you cooking?" he says, wiping his brow.

"That is the potatoes Dauphinois in the oven. You do not want to know how much cream is in them."

"Yum. Are the girls coming over?"

"Nope, just for you."

His face falls. "Oh, Anneke, did we?"

I'm an idiot. I never checked with him to see if he had plans tonight. "No, we didn't. You going out?"

"I was supposed to, but I can try to . . ."

"Don't even think of it! I'll have a feast here with Emily, and you can have leftovers for lunch tomorrow."

"You've gone to such trouble . . ."

"Really, I was just in the mood to cook, don't worry about it. Go!"

"You're sure?"

"If you don't, I'll be horribly angry with you."

He comes around and kisses my cheek. "Best wife a guy

could want." And he heads off to his room to get ready for his night out.

"Bye, Anneke, I'll see you later." Emily pokes her head into the kitchen. "Mmmm. Smells good!"

"Where are you off to?"

"Meeting Georgia for a movie night. Have fun!"

I look around the mess I've made of the kitchen. I'm more disappointed that I won't have a witness to what I think will be the single best meal I've ever made, the one I'm going to be proudest of, than I am about Jag and Emily both going out.

"Looks like just you and me, pup. Hope you like steak Diane."

"I actually love steak Diane," Liam says behind me, making me jump half out of my skin.

"LIAM! Seriously, you have to announce your presence when you enter a room or I'm going to have a fucking heart attack."

"Sorry. I'll get that bell coordinated. I'm done upstairs if you want to come inspect."

I follow him past the bathroom where we both laugh at the sound of Jag singing a Beatles tune in the shower. He actually has a pretty good voice, and the joy in the way he is warbling makes me believe that he does in fact want to hold my hand. Liam and I head upstairs.

"Ta-da," he says, pushing the door open, to reveal the closet of any girl's dreams. He has installed not only the closet components, but the glass doors as well; the island is in place, and the chandelier sparkles overhead.

"Oh, Liam, thank you. It's perfect!" I say, and without thinking, I throw my arms around him in a jubilant hug.

"You're welcome. Smells quite tasty down there; how is the big dinner coming?"

"Little dinner, just me and the pup, I totally forgot that Jag had a previous engagement."

Liam's face goes dark. "Something he couldn't switch? In light of the anniversary, all your effort . . ."

"It isn't our anniversary, if you want to know the truth, it's the anniversary of the original owners of the house, actually, my own weird thing. And he did offer to change his plans, I insisted he keep them. The cooking is as much for me as anyone else, I'm teaching myself. So not a big deal."

"Well, if you don't mind putting up with me a while longer, I'm ravenous, and my evening is wide open."

Ha, like I'm going to let Liam stay here and have some delicious sexy dinner with me.

"Sure, there's plenty if you really want to stay." I could kill my mouth right now. I blame Grand-mère's stupid etiquette training; I might want Liam to go home and leave me to my dinner, but there isn't a single polite reason to decline his offer.

"Lovely. I will trouble you for a towel, if you have one, tidy myself up a bit."

"Of course."

I fetch him a towel, and he heads downstairs to the first-floor bath, while I go to finish the dinner. Jag spins through on his way out to say good night, and is gone in a flash, beard oiled and shiny, smelling of cologne. I'm just flaming the cognac for the steak sauce when an unexpected voice behind me says, "*Opa!*"

Which is how I singed off my left eyebrow.

More?" I ask Liam, pushing the soufflé dish toward him. "Don't mind if I do, Cyclops." He winks at me.

"You ASS. If you hadn't scared the SHIT out of me and distracted me, I wouldn't have leaned over the stupid pan."

"I'm kidding. It's not terrible."

He's lying. It's terrible. I went to the bathroom after to find that my left eyebrow was weirdly curly, and when I ran my finger over it, the whole thing crumbled and smeared black ash across my forehead. Now my eyebrow is just a bit of stubble over my eye, and I look strangely surprised. And the kitchen smells like chocolate and burnt hair.

"So much for my eyebrow modeling career." I can't help but laugh.

"It'll grow back, sweet. My sister once plucked hers completely out altogether, and they came back."

"Older or younger sister?"

"That one? Younger. Youngest, actually."

"Of how many?"

"Sisters? Six."

"And brothers?"

His face gets serious. "Was one."

"Was? I'm so sorry."

"Thanks. He and Mum were coming home from his basketball game, hit by a drunk driver."

"Oh, Liam, that's horrible. I'm just so, so sorry."

He shrugs. "It is what it is. I still have the girls, plenty of mothering I can tell you, most of it unpleasant, almost all of it unnecessary, and yet not unwelcome."

"And your dad?"

"Pissed off to the pub when I was four and never came back. It's why we moved here; my mum's brother, Murph's dad, had made it big enough to bring us all over, sponsor us for citizenship. We lived with him and his family for three years before we could get our own place, that's why Murph is so good to me. He's more like an older brother than a cousin; we shared a room."

I'm totally gobsmacked. And more than a little sheepish. "Wow." And also, apparently a brilliant conversationalist.

He smiles. "Wow indeed. So that is me sad little tale of woe, what's your'n?" he says, exaggerating his accent.

"Not as bad, but in some ways worse, I suppose." I give him the brief: mom, Grand-mère, Joe. "I wish I'd had siblings, someone to know me, go through it with me, or help me get through it. I have a mom, but I feel like an orphan; when Joe died it was the last person I felt was mine. Then it was just my once-a-month obliga-tory awkward dinners with my grandmother for a dose of disap-pointment until she died two years ago. You're lucky to have family." I don't talk about that with people. Not the girls, not Jag, not Grant, not even Joe when he was alive. It is my secret sorrow.

"What about Emily?"

"She's not really my sister, you know. My mom was married to her dad for a few years; I never even met her till a couple of months ago."

"I dunno, she seems like a sister to me. And if you never had any before, probably a nice thing to have one show up. I'm grateful for the girls, and Murph and his gang, every day. I'm sorry you don't have more family, Anneke. You should have had. But Jag's family sounds good, and Emily is sweet and clearly devoted, and you can always have a flock of little ones if you'll start before your eggs dry up completely."

And, he's back. "My eggs are fine, Mr. Murphy, thank you very much. Jag and I would prefer to do our family planning on our own time, and hopefully when we aren't living in a natural disaster."

"Suit yourself, I just think you'd rather have them, you know, with all their limbs and wits and such."

"You're quite the smartass, you know that?"

"Aye. That I do. Better, I say, than being a dumbass. You know us tiny-little-dick boys. Always compensating." He gets up and clears the dishes, and we wash and dry in near silence. I'm tempted to tell him about Jag and me. I think he would understand, being a naturalized citizen himself, and I know he likes Jag. I feel like maybe he actually likes me too. But I also know I have to think about it more, and talk to Jag about it first. Maybe about Emily as well. If she is going to be staying here for much longer, both of them here all the time, it would make life so much easier to just let them in on it. If for no other reason, it will allow us to go back to our own bedrooms. I'll wait up and if he doesn't come home too late we can see if it's a good idea.

When the last plate is loaded in the dishwasher and the final pot dried, Liam folds his dish towel and places it neatly on the counter.

"Thanks for a spectacular dinner, Anneke. I thoroughly enjoyed it." He turns to me and kisses me gently on the cheek. "See you in a couple of days."

The kiss, which was the barest whisper of lips on my cheek, nevertheless leaves a heat that doesn't go away, even after I hear the front door close behind him.

Wife." Jag greets Schatzi and me as we return from our walk.

"Husband! How was your evening?"

"Quite good, thank you. And yours? How did the dinner turn out?"

"Shockingly delicious. You'll have the tastiest lunch imaginable tomorrow."

"I'll look forward to that."

We head inside. "Jag, can we chat about something?"

"Of course, let me change and check my email quickly? I'll meet you in the kitchen; we can have a tea."

"I'll put the kettle on."

I head to the kitchen and toss Schatzi a treat. I get the teapot and fill it with water, setting out two mugs and some of the PG Tips teabags that Jag loves so much. I rehearse in my head the arguments for letting Liam and Emily into our confidence. Not having to be on edge around them. Not having to play slumber party every night. The ruse is one thing to keep up with all of our friends, but Liam is spending huge chunks of time with us, and will be for the better part of the next five to six months. Emily is living here, and even though I assume she'll have to head out to get ready for school in about a month, that is still a lot to manage. It all sounds good in my head. The water is just starting to boil when Jag comes into the kitchen, looking surprisingly ashen for someone with such a rich complexion.

"I have something to talk to you about too," Jag says. "But ladies first . . ."

"Nonsense, you look like you've seen a ghost."

"Worse. Email from my parents."

Oh no. I know it is the fear of every person who lives far away from their loved ones that something bad will happen and they won't be close by to help. "Are they okay?"

"Yes. Fine."

"Thank god, I thought something bad happened to them."

"Not to them, to us."

"What happened to us?" I wonder if somehow they found out.

"They are coming to visit."

And suddenly, telling or not telling Liam and Emily that we aren't really a couple is the tiniest, most minute problem that could ever be imagined.

25

From Gemma's Journal:

Bread is the staff of life. If you can take water, yeast, salt and flour and make it into bread, you will never starve. And if you find some skill with it, a loaf and a lump of sweet butter, maybe a jar of preserves, that is a feast worthy of any king. You can be a very good cook without serious skills in pastry arts, as long as you can throw together a simple biscuit or cake to end a meal sweetly. There are quality goods in cans and jars available for sale or trade with neighbors, so if you don't need to stock a cellar for survival, you don't necessarily need to learn to can or preserve. But you cannot be a good cook if you cannot put forth a decent loaf of bread. Sometimes, when the stomach is tender, bread is all one can manage to eat, and sometimes, when the heart is, it is all one can manage to cook.

Gemma says I have to learn to bake bread. And so, I'm learning to bake bread. She has provided a simple recipe for the family's favorite yeast rolls, the ones she bakes almost every day. They are served essentially every night with dinner, regardless of what the dinner is. She says she alters the shape of the rolls; sometimes they are a single puffy round, sometimes three pressed together in a muffin tin, sometimes shingled squares layered together. She makes them in twists and figure eights. The only night she doesn't make the yeast rolls is Friday, when she makes three large challah breads, braided sweet egg bread that the family uses for Sabbath dinner, toasted for breakfast and for luncheon sandwiches when they return from Saturday-morning services. But Saturday night they return to the yeast rolls, sometimes garnished with sesame seeds or poppy seeds, or rolled with minced onions for a special treat for Mr. Rabin, who loves them despite his wife's teasing objections that onions are bad for his digestion and worse for his breath.

It is funny reading about how Gemma learns to incorporate the traditional Jewish foods into her cooking, noting that the family is religious enough to attend services regularly and keep the holidays, but that they do not keep kosher, and in fact, that Mr. Rabin in particular takes enormous delight in Gemma's glazed hams, bacon buns, and braised pork shanks, and Mrs. Rabin would live exclusively on delicate shellfishes if allowed. I think about my own upbringing, which was entirely devoid of religion, despite our technically Jewish background. I never thought much of it, but there are moments now that I wish I'd had that cultural touchstone, if not the faith aspect. I realize that I'm actually learning more about my own history through Gemma's journal than Grand-mère ever gave me growing up, and I add it to the list of things that she denied me. I can't cook, I have no religion, I have no family, no talent for relationships, clearly. But at least, maybe, I can learn this bread thing.

The rolls seem simple enough. Not quite the *"water, yeast, salt* and *flour"* that she speaks of in the journal, but not horribly complicated. I had to look up how to clarify butter, and had to do it twice when I took a quick pee break during the first batch and returned to find black bits floating in the bottom and a horrid smell in the kitchen. But the second batch went smoothly, and the dough itself was pretty easy; you make it the night before and it rises in the fridge, or the *"coolest part of the larder,"* overnight, and then you roll it out and let it rise again.

Lucky for me, there is no kneading or punching down or any such nonsense, which is probably the only reason I even thought to try. Well, that and my in-laws are coming.

Not tonight, thank goodness; we've convinced them that the best time to come will be Thanksgiving. We told them it's because we're planning on taking the whole holiday weekend off, so we'll have time to show them Chicago and have a good visit. They presumed it would be an easy time for Jag to have a short break from his studies. Regardless, it gives us five months to prepare, most importantly to get the house in better shape to hopefully impress them, so that when we tell them about Jag dropping out of school to work as a builder, they will be able to really see the quality of the work he wants to do, the potential serious and lucrative career he could have even without the doctorate they wanted for him.

We've already gotten the girls to agree to come to a Thanksgiving potluck, knowing that some buffering will be necessary. When we get closer we'll add whichever of Jag's friends are Thanksgiving orphans. In light of everything, I haven't broached the Liam thing with Jag; he's very much feeling the pressure of the reality of what we've done and what it means for him and his family, and I don't want to put anything else on his plate. Except maybe a delicious roll or two.

By the time Liam shows up, I have the rolls formed and nestled on their baking trays. The recipe makes a lot of rolls, and they have to rise somewhere cool, so I moved all the folding chairs to the room I refer to as the Kitchen Library. It is right off the food pantry, and was originally a small maid's room. Grant suggested we set it up as a place where the owner could store all the small appliances and cooking equipment that doesn't need to be accessed regularly, as well as cookbooks. We are going to build it out with one large bookshelf, and the rest of the space with deep shelving that can easily hold more equipment than any passionate cook could collect in two lifetimes.

For the moment, it's just an empty room, but it doesn't have a window and seems to stay cooler than the rest of the house, so it seems the perfect place to let the rolls rise, and I'm arranging the pans on the seats of the chairs.

"Um, Betty Crocker? You working today?" Liam asks, as I go to place the last tray of rolls on the last chair.

This causes me to throw the tray directly up in the air as I shriek in terror. Liam, quick as a cat, albeit one without a bell, reaches over my head and snatches the tray out of the air, rolls intact, and hands it to me sheepishly.

"Oops. Did it again, there."

"Liam, if you do not learn to make your presence known AS you are approaching someone, I am going to FUCKING KILL YOU."

"Got it. Really. What's all this? We starting a soup kitchen?"

"We're making rolls."

"Yes, obviously. Are we also repairing the plaster in the master bedroom today, or is this the only thing we're mixing up?"

"Relax. I've already got the plaster stuff up there."

"Good. Where's your better half?"

"He went to pick up Juan."

"The cabinet guy?"

"Yeah. I want him to refurbish the drawers and doors on those dining room hutches we installed, and fix and key the locks."

"We could have done that."

"I know, but he's a master, and offered to do it in exchange for me doing a recommendation letter for his kid for college, you remember Jose? The one who interned with me last summer? Anyway, I thought it would be good for Jag to watch him work and learn some stuff." Lucky for me, Juan's desire to see his kid get into a good college makes the risk of working with me worth it, despite Murph's embargo.

"Smart."

"I'd appreciate your not mentioning it at the office." I presume Liam is aware of Murph's program where I am concerned, and equally sure that Murph has no idea Liam is partnering on this project.

He winks. "Of course. And where is the lass?"

"Sent her on a dog walk slash coffee run."

"Very useful, that slip of a girl. So, shall we plaster, milady?"

He offers me his arm and I take it and curtsy. "Absolutely."

Luckily, the plaster is in fairly good shape, considering. Sometimes when you see cracks in old plaster it means that big sections of the wall have come loose from the underlying wood lath, and can't be saved. In this case, the cracks are just cracks; we use box cutters to gently cut away the part of the plaster around the crack that is loose, about an inch on either side, and ensure that the remaining plaster is secure. Then we mix a paste of plaster that includes horsehair, for strength, and work it into the cracks. We'll come back when it's cured to sand it down. Then we'll do a thin scratch coat over the patch, and a smooth surface plaster, and when we're done, we'll be able to repaint the room and hopefully not see the patchwork.

With both of us working, and working quickly and with small batches of plaster so it doesn't seize up on us, we're able to finish the largest wall in just a couple of hours. It seems silly to stop when we're on a roll, so we decide to postpone lunch and just keep going. By two o'clock the whole room has been patched up. We head all the way downstairs to the mudroom to clean up the buckets and our tools, passing by Jag and Juan in the dining room, drawers strewn about the room.

"Come see!" Emily says excitedly, coming over to grab my hand and take me to one of the hutches. I wink at Juan and Jag on my way by, and Liam goes to shake their hands. "Look. At. This!" Emily reaches over and with one finger, gently opens the top drawer. It slides out like magic, with full extension. Then she takes her fingertip and subtly touches the front of the drawer, which glides right back into place slowly. But I can't see the mechanism; the sides of the drawer are still just wood.

"Did you do that?"

"I did." She is beaming.

"I'm terribly proud of you."

"Thank you. That's not all. Look at this." She reaches above to the glass door, turning the small skeleton key. The door opens smoothly, and closes flush, and the key has easy action.

"Oh, honey, that's terrific."

"Hey, one drawer and one door and the kid's an expert," Juan says sarcastically. "Why don't you keep installing those slides, protégé." Juan gestures at the drawers lying all over the room, the new undermount slides in small piles.

"Gotcha, boss." Emily salutes him, golden hair dusted with wood shavings; she reminds me of when I was a teenager, working at Joe's side, so thrilled when some new technique was revealed to me. Joe, for a simple guy, was fairly profound about certain things. I remember he said to me once, when I was at a low point, having gotten a horrible haircut that would take months to grow out, between boyfriends with no prospects, that self-esteem is fine, it is nice if you can like yourself, but that will ebb and flow almost daily. And that he could tell me every day that I was smart and beautiful, and some days I would believe him, and some days not. But the one thing he felt he could give me that I could rely on every day was a sense of self-efficacy. Because even on a day when I didn't like myself, I would still unflaggingly believe that I was capable, that I could do things, do them well. He thought in the long run that that was the most important thing. And if the past six months have taught me anything, it is that he was dead right. Because even in my lowest moments, I do still feel like I am generally competent at the things I do. I realize that if I didn't have that, I would have given up on learning to cook ages ago, but my deep-seated knowledge that I can actually do things keeps me moving forward.

"She's a natural," Jag says. I kiss him on the cheek and let them get back to work. I pick up the buckets and tools Liam and I have been using and schlep them to the mudroom to fill them with hot water so they can soak for a bit. Then I grab the lava soap and the stiff nailbrush we keep down here, and set to work getting the plaster out from under my fingernails.

"Anneke . . . I'm headed your way!" I hear Liam call from down the hall, and can't help but laugh. He appears in the doorway.

"Thanks for the warning. Much appreciated."

His face looks a little worried. "Um, I think the dog might be a wee bit under the weather."

"What do you mean? Did she have an accident?" Schatzi, for all her annoying habits, would no more shit on the floor than Grand-mère would have. And in all the time I've known her, let alone lived with her, she's never been sick. Ever.

"No, um, I think you should come."

I dry my hands on my pants and follow Liam back through the dining room to the front stairs and head up a level. We go through the dog gate, and he leads me back to the kitchen, where Schatzi is lying on the floor, panting. And which is scarier, her little gray belly is oddly distended, making her look weirdly pregnant.

"Oh my god, poor pupper, what's wrong? What happened?" I get down on my knees next to a clearly miserable Schatzi, who raises her head and then lets it flop back down.

"Well, this might have something to do with it." Liam is standing in the doorway of the Kitchen Library.

I get up off the floor and walk over to see what he is looking at, and find that two of the five pans of rolls are on the floor. But they no longer contain rolls.

"Shit," I say.

"Well yes, I do believe she'll need to do a lot of that," Liam says.

We walk back over to the dog. She makes a small noise, and then a smell that can only be described as monkey-house awful wafts up from her general area. "Jesus, Mary and Joseph, please tell me that came out of the dog," Liam says, covering his nose with his shirt. I smack his arm and go to grab my phone.

I put in a call to the emergency vet, just as Schatzi gets up, wobbles a bit, walks over to her empty food bowl, and vomits copiously and noisily into the bowl. This is both disgusting and impressive. Figures the dog would manage to not get a drop on the floor. Liam waves at me that he's got it, picks up the bowl of soupy foaming dough and bile and heads for the bathroom with it, when the nurse finally answers.

"My dog ate two pans of raw bread dough."

"How long ago?"

"I'm not really sure. She's been alone with access for about five hours."

"Hold for the doctor." In a few seconds, the doctor comes to the phone. He has a kindly voice, very Mr. Rogers, and it immediately soothes me.

"Well, a naughty pup got into the bread dough, hmm? What kind of dog?"

"She's a miniature schnauzer."

"How is she behaving?"

"She has horrible gas, her stomach looks bloated, and she just threw up."

"Was the vomiting difficult or easy?"

"How can you tell?"

"Did she struggle to get it out? Was there any gagging with no production? Was there a lot of volume? Did her breathing change after?"

"She didn't appear to struggle at all, she just sort of leaned over and let it all out, and the volume was sort of shockingly large given her size."

"That's actually good, it means that she didn't get any of the dough lodged in her throat. What is in the dough?"

"Um, flour, water, shortening, salt, yeast, butter . . ." I'm trying to remember the recipe.

"How much shortening and butter, would you say?"

"A lot. At least it seemed like sort of a lot."

"Good, that's good, the fat in the dough will mean that it will be slippery for her to get out. Is it a kneaded dough? Stiff?"

"No kneading at all, just sort of mixed together. It's pretty soft, actually."

"Okay, that's great, a nice soft dough without a lot of structure is better. So here are our concerns. One, you don't want the dough to block the esophagus, which usually would happen after vomiting or attempting to vomit, and now that your dog has vomited once without problems, we don't have to worry so much about that part, which is great."

"Okay. That's good."

"Based on how much you know she ate, what do you think is a rough percentage that she would have thrown up?"

Because this is the math everyone longs to do. "Not sure, probably somewhere between a third and a half maybe?"

Liam comes back into the kitchen with the now-clean bowl, places it down, and then picks up the water bowl and empties and refills it. Schatzi comes over to it and gives the new water three halfhearted laps, and then schlumps back down.

"Okay, okay, that is also good. The second problem is that the warm environment of the dog's stomach can make the bread continue to rise for a bit until the stomach acid finally shuts it down. How far along in the rising process was your dough?"

"It was in the final rise."

His voice sounds like he is smiling. "This is terrific, all good, so between the vomiting and the stage the dough was in, the rising is probably done. So the last thing we have to worry about is ethanol poisoning. The sugar in the dough will start to ferment, essentially making alcohol in the dog's stomach, and if it makes too much, the dog can basically get alcohol poisoning, like a tiny little sorority sister."

This makes me laugh despite myself.

"Good, I like that little joke myself. Here's what I think we should do. Watch the dog closely for the next few hours. You can expect more vomiting, either mixed with or leading to diarrhea. The distension of her stomach will likely remain for a day, but shouldn't continue to get bigger. She will probably have copious flatulence, which we want; it means the gasses are moving through her system, and nothing is blocked. She may begin to act, for lack of a better word, drunk. All of this is normal, and means the dough is working its way out. If she starts vomiting or having diarrhea in a manner that seems uncontrollable, and if she won't take in any water, bring her in so that we can be sure she doesn't get dehydrated. If her stomach continues to bloat and get bigger, or feels hard to the touch, bring her in. If her breathing appears labored, bring her in. I'm going to pass you back to my nurse, and she is going to take your information. I'll give you a call to check up on her in about an hour. In the meantime, just don't leave her alone. And if anything about her behavior scares you, just bring her on in. But I'm hopeful that we can let her work through this at home where she's comfortable. Okay?"

"Okay, Doctor, thank you so much."

I give his nurse my cell phone, and then fill Liam in. We

decide that if the dog is going to explode from both ends, we'd better let her do it outside, so I take her water bowl while Liam gently picks her up, cradling her like the delicate thing she is, and we walk out to the front yard. There is a nice patch of shade and we put her down in it.

"I'm going to go grab her little bed," Liam says, sprinting back into the house.

"Oh, Schatzi, I'm so, so sorry." I can't believe I left such a temptation right in her path.

Emily comes running outside. "My god, it's all my fault, I went in to look at your beautiful rolls when Schatzi and I came back from our walk, and I must have left the door open, I'm so sorry!" She starts crying and petting the dog's head.

"It's okay, Emily, you didn't do it on purpose."

Jag comes out. "Liam told us, how is she doing?"

"Not good."

"How are you?"

At this, I burst into tears. Jag takes me in his arms, murmuring to me that she'll be fine, it will all be okay. He rocks me gently, and when I stop hiccuping he takes my face in his hands, wiping my cheeks with his thumbs. And then he leans in and kisses me very gently. It is the friendliest thing I can imagine, and I throw my arms around his neck. Over his shoulder I see Liam, standing in the doorway, watching us, with Schatzi's bed in his arms, and an oddly uncomfortable look on his face.

He walks down the stairs, dropping the dog bed in the shade, and then pats Emily's back. "She'll be fine, lass, don't you worry." Emily begins to cry even harder, and throws herself into Liam's arms, sobbing into his chest. He cradles her head in his hand, murmurs into her hair, and everything in my stomach clenches. I remember what that felt like, to be anchored there, to have a place to unload my anguish, and while I tell myself I just hate the idea of Liam having his hands on my sister, there is a part of me that doesn't want to think about the fact that it might in fact be the reverse.

Emily and I take turns all afternoon keeping Schatzi company in shifts, while the boys work, poking their heads out every once in a while to check the progress. She throws up and shits explosively all over the front half of the lawn, tastefully away from where we're sitting, but unfortunately close to the street where passersby are understandably horrified. Talk about your dirty bombs; it's a minefield of ghastly out there. At one point, she staggers around, clearly drunk, falling over her own feet, and wandering in circles, which despite her obvious discomfort, cracks us up. The vet calls every hour on the hour to check her progress, and by six thirty says that he is fairly certain she's over the worst of it. He recommends no food at all till her stomach is back to normal and she hasn't vomited in at least four hours, which hopefully will be tomorrow morning. Then I'm to start her on a diet of cooked chicken breast and white rice for at least two to three days to let her system fully recover.

At seven, Liam runs out to pick up some food for us. He returns forty minutes later with seventy pounds of Chinese food from Orange Garden. "I didn't know what everyone liked. Plus none of us had lunch." He shrugs, unpacking egg rolls, pot stickers, barbecue ribs, pork lo mein, vegetable fried rice, sesame chicken, beef and broccoli, ma po tofu, cashew chicken, shrimp with peapods and water chestnuts, combination chow fun, and mushroom egg foo young. White rice, plenty of sauces, and about forty-two fortune cookies. A six-pack of Tsingtao beer. "I asked them to cook up a couple orders of plain steamed chicken breast and got a couple extra pints of the white rice so the dog should be covered for the next few days." This is such a touching gesture; it literally makes my heart stop.

"That is just the sweetest thing," Emily says, looking up at him like he's wearing a halo. And a thong.

"Thank you, Liam, that is most kind," Jag says.

"Well, I figured we didn't want this one cooking for her again anytime soon." He tilts his head in my direction.

"Even I can't argue with that," I say, too moved by his kindness to be affected by his gibe.

Thankfully, it's a beautiful night, balmy, hinting at the summer that is right around the corner. We set the spread out on the porch and sit on the steps, and armed only with chopsticks, we tackle the feast together, trading containers back and forth. We don't talk much, focused on the hot food, the cold beer.

"Wait!" I jump up. "I almost forgot!" I run inside and up the stairs to the kitchen. I grab a plate off the counter, and scamper back downstairs. I burst through the front door with my prize, and place it reverently down on the top stair. "Ta-da!"

Liam and Jag look down at the plate of burnished golden rolls, and then at each other, and then at me. And then the four of us burst into laughter. What? I wasn't going to let the whole thing have been in vain; besides, they just needed to be baked.

Jag, being a good husband, is the first one to reach for a roll when our hysterics subside. "This is really delicious. Good job."

Emily picks one up and takes a small bite. "Yummy. So good, Anneke, really. Where's that barbecued pork, I'm making a sandwich!"

Liam reaches over and eats half a roll in one bite. "Vry gud," he says, still chewing.

I reach for one myself, the crust has a buttery crispness, the interior is tender. They have a simple goodness, and I completely understand why the family would have eaten them happily every night. I take Emily's cue and layer a couple of pieces of crispy pork into mine. We finish all of the rolls, all of the beer, and about half of the feast before calling it quits. By the time we're done, Schatzi hasn't had an eruption in nearly two hours and is snoring loudly on her little bed.

"Okay, me first," Liam says, grabbing a fortune cookie. He breaks it open and unfurls the little paper. "You are a constant surprise . . . between the sheets!" he says gleefully.

"Yep, as in 'Surprise! I have no idea what to do with this little thing of mine!'" Jag says wickedly, as I make a loud snorting noise. Emily blushes beet red.

"Nice one, bro," Liam says.

"BRRRRRRRAP." Jag belches deeply in response. "What? It's part of my culture, means we appreciate the food."

We're all clearly punchy. Jag grabs for a fortune cookie. "You have many people who love and respect you . . . between the sheets."

"Great," I say. "Who are these other people? Please at least tell me the multitudes of my competition are all women!"

We all laugh and Jag looks a bit sheepish.

"Your turn, lass," Liam says, tossing Emily a cookie.

"Happiness is just beside you . . . between the sheets." She looks sidelong at Liam. Sweet fancy Moses, the girl is so smitten her lust is coming off her like fumes.

"How about you?" Jag reaches over and hands me a packet.

I pull open the cellophane, and crack open the cookie. I look down at the paper in my hand. "There is a storm on the horizon, be careful how you weather it," I say.

Liam smacks Jag on the arm. "Old Stormy over here, huh?" he says with what weirdly sounds like forced jocularity.

"Uh-oh. Maybe I should sleep somewhere else tonight, hmmm?" Emily says, stealing a glance at Liam.

"I think we all need a quiet, decent night's sleep," I say.

"Uh-oh, no storming for you tonight, mate," Liam says to Jag.

"The honeymoon must be over," Jag says with a fake sad face.

"If you two keep it up, I'm going to start to get paranoid that you're falling in love."

"Boy, one gay fiancé and she sees boy-on-boy action everywhere," Liam says. "Don't you worry, little Annamuk." He throws his arm around Emily, whose jaw literally falls open. "I'm all about the ladies, as you well know. I won't steal your handsome husband from you."

"As if you could," Jag says, standing up and stretching.

Jag and Liam repack all of the containers, and Emily helps take them in to load up the fridge. It should feed us lunch for the coming week. I pick up my sleeping drunk dog in her bed like a schnauzer taco, and take her inside and up to our room. She can sleep in the hall when she's feeling better; tonight I want her with us. When I get back downstairs, Liam has left, and Jag and Emily have gone to the garage to get a couple of shovels and some lawn bags. We head out to the front lawn for the unenviable task of removing the offending deposits. It's like trying to wrangle soup. We decide that since we'll need to resod the lawn eventually anyway, it's easier to just dig around the bombs and remove the divots of grass with the toxic waste on top. It takes the better part of an hour for the three of us to remove all the ick, and Jag takes the bag out to the Dumpster while I survey a lawn that now looks like a flock of grenade-bearing gophers have attacked it.

"She'll be okay," Emily says soothingly.

"Yes she will. The lawn on the other hand . . ."

She laughs. "Yeah, this is pretty bad. I'm really sorry."

I hold my hand up. "This is not your fault, don't even think about it. The dog will be fine, the lawn will eventually be fine."

"I'll figure something out about a place to stay, I know it must be a pain to have me here."

"It's fine, Emily. You've been a big help. I know I'm not good at it, but I want you to know that I appreciate it. You're a hard worker, and you're doing a good job, and really being helpful."

She grabs me in a bear hug. I will never get used to all of this wild affection. "Thank you, Anneke, that means just everything to me. But aren't I in the way, I mean, with you and Jag?"

"We're doing just fine." I don't know why I'm not agreeing with her, I really should just take this opportunity to tell her that it is fine to stay a couple more days, but that she definitely should find a new place soonish, but the words aren't coming. She smiles, nods, and follows me back inside. What can I do? And Jag is right, she is going to have to leave soon to head for school, it won't be that much longer.

I decide to indulge in a long, hot bath on the first floor with a large tumbler of bourbon. With some of the stress of the day finally leaving my shoulders, I get into my comfiest pajamas and head upstairs to check on the dog. She's still snoring, and luckily, hasn't left us any surprises on the floor, so I'm tentatively hopeful she's on the other side of it.

"Hey, you," Jag says behind me. I turn around, and he's standing there, two Chinese containers in his hands, chopsticks sticking out of the tops. "Rice or noodles?" he asks.

I smile. "Noodles, please." He hands over the lo mein, and I take a bite. It is that perfect place between warm and cool, and delicious.

"Always hungry again an hour later." He shrugs and digs into the fried rice.

"Yep."

"I'm glad she's going to be okay."

"Thank you for all your help today."

He winks. "I think I'm going to follow your lead and have a soak in that tub."

"I highly recommend it. Just don't leave rice in the drain."

"As long as you don't drop noodles in our bed."

Heeding Jag's warning, I finish the lo mein at the desk, flipping through the latest *Dwell* magazine. Just as I'm getting ready to go to bed, my laptop pings. I have an email.

From: arizonaanneliese@me.com
To: a_stroudt@gmail.com
RE: visit

Anneke—

Alan has been invited to do a brief midterm special course at Northwestern from November 19–30. He has asked me to join him, so I will be in Chicago as well, and would like for us to see each other. He would also very much like to meet you, so I hope you will be able to find some time for that as well while we are there.

Anneliese

How ironic. I would have thought that Schatzi was the biggest shitstorm of today, but apparently my fortune was accurate, if not fortunate. I think for a moment and reach for Gemma's journal. I let the heavy book fall open in my lap and close my eyes.

"My mother is coming, Gemma, what on earth do I do about that?" I let my finger fall onto the page, and then look down to see where it has landed.

"Sometimes, despite all your best efforts and deepest wishes and most fervent prayers, bad things just happen. And all you can do is try to survive your own suffering."

And for the first time, Gemma brings me no comfort. None at all.

26

All of our parents are coming at once. The actual fact of this begins to sink in, and both Jag and I fear that we may not survive. He's encouraging me to see them while they are here, but not to invite them to Thanksgiving, which I thought would be the easiest way to do it, so that there would be plenty of buffers. He says that might not be a great idea because he thinks things are likely to be tense with me and my mother, and because he fears his parents will be uncomfortable enough, and he wants the day to just go smoothly. The concept of parents and children having no relationship at all just doesn't compute for him, nor would it for his parents, and the idea of bringing Anneliese and Alan in on what will already be a pins-and-needles day really worries him.

In light of the impending parentals, we decided to go full steam ahead on the first floor, which is the formal entertaining space, and will have the most details and wow factor. We are hopeful that the place will be somewhat close to finished, since our new goal since Liam came on board is to have it listed quickly after the New Year, but we really want this floor on point, in case the rest of the house isn't quite there yet.

We got the dining room finished, and it looks spectacular. Both hutches are installed and all of the doors and drawers are functioning beautifully. The restored coffering is stunning, and we installed small pin lights at some of the junctions to supplement the two antique chandeliers. It now has two cased archways, over six feet wide each, trimmed in wood we salvaged from other areas of the home. Since the space will accommodate a table of up to eighteen feet, having two ways to access the space ensures that none of the future guests will feel trapped. Liam and Jag both thought I was insane for wanting to paint the space in a high-gloss deep poppy orange, but when I pointed out that two whole walls are built-in hutches, and one wall has five large windows, the actual amount of orange in the room becomes more of an accent and not overwhelming.

I know it's a risk, but I think many developers and builders make a mistake with spec spaces by keeping things too homogenous, assuming that future buyers will be scared by strong design choices. They paint the whole place white or off-white from basement to attic, they pick the most neutral colors and styles for fixtures and finishes, and as a result, their places show as very boring homes. They don't know that by ignoring their own personal aesthetic and trying to keep things generic, they end up with houses that lack any aesthetic whatsoever. But when you ask people who aren't buying new construction what drew them to their home, they say it was the special uniqueness that got them. It's the art nouveau tulip tiles in the fireplace surround, or the deco fixtures in the bathroom. It's the stained glass, or the built-in hutches or shelving units. I know one woman who convinced her husband to buy their shabby fixer-upper solely because of the original his and hers bathrooms and dressing rooms that flanked the master bedroom . . . His was all black marble, with black tub, toilet, and sink, and leather handles on all the drawers and doors in his dressing room. Hers was all pink and gray marble with pink tub and toilet and sink, and fully mirrored fixtures, like a 1930s Hollywood dream. The rest of the place they effectively gutted, but those bathrooms and closets didn't change a bit. One of my favorite home improvement bloggers, Victoria E. Barnes, says that she fell in love with her house because of the exquisitely detailed 1890s door hinges.

MacMurphy never did spec builds; god forbid they would lay out their own money up front. But Chicago has some amazing developers who believe enough in the quality of their design choices to simply build beautiful homes and know that they will find the right people to buy them. My personal hero is Andy Bowyer, who started his company Middlefork Development with a simple commitment to elegant artistry and quality. Essentially, if you were going to build the Palmer house from scratch today? Andy is the guy to do it. He makes strong design choices, and his houses are spectacular. They have a very European old-world feel, with total twenty-first-century functionality, and the combination is magic. I firmly believe it's because he brings his own personal taste and design sense to his projects, and doesn't shy away from letting them take center stage. And as a result? None of his projects stay on the market for more than a month.

That is the kind of builder I want to be. I may not want to do as much with new construction, but I want to find places like this and honor their history and make them shine and help them realize their full potential and find their forever family. So when I had the vision for this dining room—the deep chestnut brown patina on the hutches and woodwork, the inside of the glass-door hutches upholstered in camel-toned leather, the ceiling between the coffering in pale linen paint, and then the pop of the orange in fabulous, polished high gloss bringing warmth and elegance to the room—I had to go for it. I can just picture the Rabins in this room, having one of their famous dinner parties, the buffets covered in Gemma's delicacies, a long table set elegantly with white china and silver and sparking crystal. I think the room feels like a hug. If Cary Grant were hugging you. In his best tuxedo. On Valentine's Day. After proposing.

Of course it was a huge pain in the ass. Nothing is worse than high-gloss paint. You have to sand the walls to make sure there isn't the tiniest blemish. You have to do a zillion layers of the paint, sanding between each one to keep that smooth surface. And you have to be uber-careful to not let the tiniest particle of dust or piece of hair get embedded in the surface while it's wet. The paint? Took Emily and me three full days to get right, while Jag and Liam worked on the third floor. I give the girl credit, she has great attention to detail and was amazing with the meticulous and mind-numbing work. Of course, she also never shut the fuck up, babbling incessantly about everything from television programs to music to vacations she took with her dad and Anneliese. I eventually figured out that if I brought in music, she didn't feel the need to fill the silence, so I invested in a Bluetooth speaker that I could connect to my iPhone and created some fun playlists, heavy on the '70s rock and '80s pop.

The oasis on the third floor is still very much a work in progress. The bathroom fixtures need to go in, the walls all have to be repaired and replastered, the crown molding and baseboards stripped of layers of paint and stained to match the rest of the house. The laundry room and back bonus room and bathroom haven't even been touched.

"So, girls' night tonight?" Jag appears in the bathroom door.

"Yep. Have to prove to them I haven't completely fallen off the face of the earth."

"It's good, you should go out more." Jag has boundless energy. He can finish a long day of hard labor with me, and then head out for the evening to socialize. I try to participate at least once every other week or so, just to keep up appearances, and the evenings are always fairly enjoyable, despite always feeling shitty for deceiving them. But mostly? I hang at home with my best friends, bourbon and Netflix. I just don't have the oomph at the end of a workday to get myself out and about. I've been sticking to lunches and brunches with Marie and Caroline; Hedy has spent the last three months commuting between Palm Beach and the Hamptons, where she has clients. But now that she's home, she's organized a dinner out for the four of us, even convincing Caroline to come downtown for a change. We're going to Del Frisco's, a huge, loud, scene-y steak house, the opposite of what we usually do, but Hedy decided we needed a little noise and sparkle, and promises that the people-watching will be spectacular, and the food is good. She's even insisted on treating "to celebrate her new jobs," which I have a sneaking suspicion is more because the three of them still don't want me to feel badly about not wanting to go to such an expensive meal, and it isn't quite close enough to my birthday to use that as an excuse.

"I'm just not the social butterfly you are, husband."

He comes up behind me, putting his hands on my shoulders. "You are wonderful. Don't change a bit." He kisses the top of my head, and winks at me in the mirror. "Have a great time and give my love to the ladies."

"I will. You going out?"

"I think so, probably just dinner, maybe a movie."

"Well, say hi to the gang for me."

His face looks a little puzzled for just a flash, and then returns to impassive. "Will do."

I put on a little bit of lip gloss, and look in the mirror. It is kind of nice to be in real clothes, to be going out for a change. Maybe Jag is right; maybe I need to resurrect my social life a bit. Before I met Grant, I went out a lot. With the girls, with vendors or subs, occasionally with clients, or with the guys I was dating and their groups of friends. I wasn't a party girl, but I had an active social life.

"Schatzi? Perhaps I need to rethink my homebody thing, what do you think?"

She tilts her head at me, as if thinking it over, and then gives what looks like a definitive nod, which cracks me up.

"Should we consult Gemma on this?"

Schatzi nods again, and follows me back to my bedroom. I

grab the journal and open it at random, closing my eyes. "Gemma? Should I get out more?" I let my finger fall and look down to see what her advice will be.

"Whip the egg whites until they are foamy and white but not stiff."

Guess even Gemma can have an off night.

S o wait a minute, it made her DRUNK?" Marie asks, passing me the sweet-chili-glazed calamari.

"Yeah. And horrifically explosive out of both ends. I did not know it was possible for one twenty-pound dog to create forty pounds of vomit and liquid poop." I hand Hedy the cheesesteak egg rolls.

"We. Are. EATING. Good lord, people, can we not have a single meal without body parts or effluvium?" Hedy waves off the egg rolls, and sticks a fork in Caroline's crab cake.

"Help yourself, dear." Caroline leans back to give Hedy easier access. "For once I agree, perhaps we can shift the subject."

"My mother is coming to visit."

Three heads turn to me, forks paused in midair.

"And E. F. Hutton says . . ." I say, not sure how else to respond to their shocked silence.

"Are you okay?" Marie asks.

"When?" Hedy says.

"Why?" Caroline pipes in.

"Oy . . . Okay, Alan has some course he is doing at Northwestern end of November, so she is coming with him. She asked to see me and Alan wants to meet me, so I guess we'll figure all that out. It overlaps when Jag's parents are here; he doesn't want me to invite them to Thanksgiving."

"Are you okay?" Marie asks again, noting that I ignored that part.

I think about this for a second, and take a sip of my wine. "No, not really."

"Does she know you're married?" Hedy asks.

"Nope. I haven't even replied to her email yet to tell her that I will see them."

"Do you want to see them?" Caroline asks. "You know you don't have to."

"How would that work?" The idea never occurred to me.

"Honey, you are a grown-ass woman. She has been a non-entity in your life for as long as you've had a life. If you don't want to see her? If you don't want her in your life? Opt out. Tell her you're sorry, but the time they are here isn't convenient for you, and you hope they have a fine trip." Hedy takes another bite of Caroline's crab cake, and Caroline picks up the plate and places it in front of Hedy.

"She's right, you know, Anneke," Caroline says. "If you don't want to see her, don't see her."

"She's my mother. How do you say no to family?"

Marie gets a dark look on her face. "There's a difference between relatives and family. You can be related to someone; that is an accident of genetics. Relatives are pure biology. But family is action. Family is attitude. That woman . . ." Marie's voice drips with venom. "Is NOT your family. WE are your family. That woman is just your relative."

Hedy's mouth drops, and Caroline's eyes fly open so wide I think they might get stuck.

"Don't hold back there, Marie," Hedy says, finding her voice.

"I'm sorry, but . . ." Marie's eyes fill with tears.

"Oh, no!" Caroline leans over and takes Marie's hand.

Marie shakes it off. "I hate her. I hate that she had the best daughter on the planet and never appreciated her and wasn't ever there for her and never once did anything for her. You guys don't know. She was the most self-absorbed narcissistic cold person . . ."

"She gave me Joe."

"But . . ." she says.

I raise my hand. "She. Gave. Me. JOE. Whatever other bullshit happened, the most important thing in my life growing up was Joe. He made me who I am, he helped me find my calling, he was a gift, and everything else is just beyond my ability to get upset about."

"You could get a little upset," Caroline says.

"It takes nothing away from Joe, and how important he was to you, to acknowledge that your mother failed you in almost every way," Hedy says.

"I think you should tell her to go fuck herself," Marie says, leaning back in her chair and crossing her arms like a petulant child. I don't know that I've ever seen her so furious. "You guys don't get it, I was THERE. I MET HER. Wanna know how she screws in a lightbulb? Holds it up in the air and lets the universe just revolve around her."

This makes the three of us bust out laughing. "Oh, Marie, I love you. Thank you for being so on my side." It does mean the world to me that my oldest friend is so protective. "But I do think I have to see her. At the end of the day, if for no other reason, to prove that I am who I am in spite of her and what she did or didn't do. I frankly think that telling her to fuck off would be the easy thing, and maybe it's what she wants. I certainly get the sense that this is all Alan's doing, wanting to meet me, taking this job in Chicago for two weeks. I'm sure if she could have figured out a way to avoid it, she would have. So I'll see her, I'll be polite, I'll be a grown-up, and then she'll leave."

"I still think she probably just needs a kidney or something," Marie says, refusing to be placated.

"I promise. I will give her a minimum amount of my time. My kidneys stay with me."

"That's all I'm saying," Marie says, finishing her glass of

wine. Caroline raises an elegant hand, and our waiter appears in a flash.

"We'll need another bottle," she says, and he heads for the glass-enclosed wine storage in the center of the restaurant.

"I'll be right back," I say, getting up and heading for the bathroom. Marie gets up to come with me, taking my hand and holding it tightly as we wend our way through the throngs of people.

"I love you," she says.

"I love you back."

"I still hate her."

"I know. And that makes me all wiggly with adoration for you."

We go to the bathroom, and Marie touches up her lipstick while I pee. Then we head back out, and walk by a couple who are essentially having stand-up sex in the hallway where the bathrooms are; all we can see is long blond hair on top of a tiny black dress, and a pair of male hands grabbing a tight tush. The left hand has a thin scar down the back, and the middle finger is somewhat shortened. I know that hand. I know the back of that hand like I know the back of my own hand.

"Grant?" I say.

Grant's head emerges from the curtain of blond hair, and the hair turns to look and see who is talking to him. She can't be more than twenty-five, with that bland prettiness that is mostly makeup and a body that is mostly boobs.

"ANNEKE!" Grant looks like he is going to throw up.

"Hi! I'm Crystal!" the blonde says.

"Of course you are," Marie mutters.

"Well, this is a surprise to say the least," I say. "Gregg working tonight?"

Grant blushes beet red. "I, um, I . . ." he sputters.

"Yeah. Exactly," I say. My heart is a tight little fist in my chest. I want the floor to open and swallow me up. "Interesting to see you here," I say, since Grant was always very snobby about places like this.

"Anneke?" A voice behind me makes me jump nearly out of my skin, and I turn to see Liam, who has just come up the staircase.

"Je-SUS!" I shriek, in an octave somewhere between dolphin and Mariah Carey.

"Grant," Liam says, taking in the scene.

"Hi! I'm Crystal!"

"Yes, dear. Good for you. Anneke? A moment?"

Marie looks stunned, like she doesn't know what to do. "I'll meet you back at the table, Marie," I say, while I half swallow my tongue. She looks relieved, and turns to head back to the dining room.

"Grant, good to see you. Crystal," Liam says, and takes my arm, moving me forcefully down the hall toward the bar, finding us a corner that is shockingly empty. He waves over the bartender. "Two Knob Creek, neat." The bartender pours two generous shots, and hands them over, and Liam and I both take them down in one gulp. "I thought I'd better get you out of there before you said something you'd regret."

"You mean like asking Crystal if she has a penis? Or if she plans on introducing him to anyone who has a penis?"

Liam smiles. "Something like that. You can't give him the satisfaction. You win. You dodged a bullet with him, and because of that you found Jag. I know it hurts your pride, and makes you angry, and that is totally understandable. But if you make a scene here, if you show him that it hurts you, he wins."

"I want to go home."

"You can't go home."

"I'm a grown-ass woman." I think about what Hedy said earlier. "I can do whatever I want."

"You are indeed. And a grown-ass woman doesn't run away. A

grown-ass woman knows that she is more powerful than any idiot like Grant. You are going to go back to your table and have a great meal and a fun time, and when you leave, if he's still here, you are going to go right to his table and kiss him on the cheek and tell him it was good to see him. And THEN you can go home."

"I don't know if I can."

"Stay here one second." Liam leaves me and heads halfway down the bar to a small group of people, talks to them for a moment, and then comes back to me. "C'mon. Where's your table?"

He places a hand on the small of my back and guides me through the restaurant to where the girls are sitting. "Hello, ladies, so good to see you, any chance a bloke could crash your party for a while?"

"Of course, you're very welcome," Caroline says. She raises a hand and within moments another chair has been added to our table, right next to me, and a place setting appears like magic.

"So you must be Caroline." He winks at Caroline, who actually blushes prettily. "Hedy, Marie, nice to see you both again."

"Indeed," Hedy says, implying just the opposite, and raising an eyebrow at me.

"So, I'm sure Marie has filled you in on what just happened," Liam says.

Hedy tilts her head across the room, where we see Grant and Crystal being taken to their table. He still looks like he swallowed a hot coal.

"Ah, yes, now, ladies, everyone laugh. Now."

We all start to fake giggle, awkwardly at first, but when it sinks in, we actually laugh for real. "Showtime," Hedy says, knowingly.

"Let's make this fun," Marie says, with a wicked glint in her eye.

"Fuck that assomelette," Caroline says.

"Did you just say ASSomelette?" Hedy says. And the five of us burst into genuine laughter.

"What did you order?" Liam whispers in my ear.

"Bone-in rib eye," I say.

"Perfect. We'll share," he says and winks at me.

For the next hour Liam is charming, funny, self-deprecating. The girls are all buzzing like bees in a hive. He compliments Caroline, trades barbs with Hedy, is sweet and sincere with Marie. And the whole time he stays right by my side, telling them stories from MacMurphy that make me sound like a rock star surrounded by idiots. And while I know he is pumping up my ego a bit and trying to keep everything light, there is something in the stories he chooses and the way he is talking that actually makes me believe him. Within ten minutes, I stop looking over at Grant's table and just focus on having fun. Liam splits my steak with me, and then finishes Hedy's lamb chops, Caroline's veal, and Marie's tuna, not to mention the mac 'n' cheese, onion rings, brussels sprouts, and creamed spinach we've ordered for sides. I have no idea where he puts it. Then he orders their signature lemon cake for all of us to share.

By the time the meal is over, I feel a million times better. I'm full of good food, and good wine; we've laughed heartily.

"Ladies, I thank you all for letting me crash your girls' night, and letting me steal all your food. It was a pleasure to finally get a chance to know you all, and I hope to see you again very soon. But I don't want to overstay my welcome, and I know that you all want some time together, so I will take my leave. Besides, I've had the lemon cake and don't think you're going to want to share it with me." He kisses all of our hands, and crosses the restaurant to Grant's table, where he leans over and whispers something in Grant's ear, making Grant blanch white, before clapping him on the back and walking away. I would give my left arm to know what he said.

"Well, Anneke, that was an unexpected pleasure," Caroline says.

"We thought he was a douche?" Hedy says, shaking her head.

"Did you see his shoulders?" Marie says almost absent-mindedly.

"MARIE!" Caroline says.

"HA!" Hedy says, as Marie turns beet red.

We are all laughing, when my phone vibrates in my pocket. I pull it out and see a text from Liam. Thanks for letting me crash. Don't forget to kiss him good-bye. See you tmrw. L.

"Well, despite his history, I have to admit, that is a pretty good guy in my book," Hedy says.

"Yeah, he has his moments," I say.

After we devour the lemon cake, our waiter comes over to inform us that Liam has taken care of our bill, and to thank us for our patronage, and we get up to leave. I'm absolutely overwhelmed with his generosity, both emotional and financial. It felt actually sort of wonderful to sit with him at my side, sharing a meal.

"Just a sec, guys, I'll meet you at the elevator." I walk purposefully over to Grant's table.

"Grant, great to see you, hope you are having as much fun as we did. Crystal, nice to meet you." I lean over and kiss his cheek, and then walk away without a backward glance. And for whatever flaws he has, Liam was right about one thing. It would have been a pity to run away. I head over to the elevator where my posse is waiting for me, grinning at my chutzpah, and we ride down, laughing at the complete ridiculousness of the night. We head out the door onto Oak Street, and it is a beautiful balmy night.

"C'mon. Let's go somewhere for a nightcap," I say. And the four of us link arms, and head off to keep the fun going.

Walter drops me off just after two, having dropped Marie off first, and then left Caroline to sleep over at Hedy's. I've got a good buzz on, but I'm not sloppy. We ended up at the Drawing

Room, where we continued to have drinks and fun, and I was able to let it all go. It felt great, and I have to say that I'm feeling awfully warmly toward Liam. There is a note in the kitchen that Emily walked the dog around ten, and is sleeping over at a friend's house. I'm just making a cup of tea when Jag tiptoes into the kitchen.

"You're still up."

"Just got home. Tea?"

"Sure. How was your night?"

"Lovely, actually, as it turns out. How about yours?"

"Lovely as well. But complicated."

"Complicated in what way?"

Jag strokes his shiny beard and takes a deep breath. "I have to say something I never expected to be saying."

My stomach drops. "What's that?"

"Wife, I have fallen in love."

Oh no. I never even considered this. "Jag, it's just the circumstances making you confused." I adore Jag, but he feels like a brother, or what I think a brother might feel like if I'd ever had one. I can't even remotely consider him in a romantic way.

"No, darling, I don't think so. It's very unexpected, and I know it makes things much more difficult than we had anticipated, but perhaps it is just that the situation has made some things clear to me, and at least made me feel like it is worth taking risks to get what you want."

"Jag, I don't know what to say, I adore you, you know that, your happiness is very important to me, not just professionally, but obviously personally."

He smiles tenderly. "I know. It's why I know you will approve, even though it meant that I had to break our pact."

Now I'm confused. "What pact?"

"To not tell anyone about our arrangement."

Wait a cotton-picking minute. "Who exactly did you tell about our arrangement?!"

"Nageena, of course."

"Why of course?"

"Because she is the one I've fallen in love with."

I am such a fucking idiot.

"I know it is a shock, Anneke, it is a shock for us both as well, but we had, for lack of a better word, a moment at the lake house over Memorial Day weekend, and when I realized not only what I've been feeling but that she was clearly feeling it as well, you must understand that I had to tell her. I couldn't have her thinking that I was some unfaithful horrible person."

"Not at all. You're a fucking prince. You just impose this horrible restriction on me and my life and my relationships, and the moment you get a little itch that needs scratching, you throw it out the window for your own convenience."

His eyes narrow. "That's not fair. This couldn't have been anticipated."

"It couldn't have been anticipated that it would be really hard for me to not be honest with my best friends while living this farce? Hard for me to not date? I made a commitment to you, to this, and you barely even lasted FOUR MONTHS before putting the whole thing in danger? We have TWO YEARS to get through here, both of us. No, Jag, it isn't fair, not one little bit."

He shakes his head. "Look, she understands, she wants to help us however she can. For what it's worth, when I told her what you did for me, she cried and said she knew you were a truly extraordinary person. She's so grateful to you, Anneke, and so am I."

"Well, bully for me. And congrats, husband, I'm glad your mistress loves me so much."

"Please, Anneke, don't be angry. I know that when you fall in love with someone you would absolutely need to tell him, and I will completely support you in that. I know it's hard for you right now with your friends; it's hard for me too. For us. But

Nageena is committed to making sure none of them find out. It's just not the same with friends as it is with the person you are in love with, surely you can see that."

Yeah. When I fall in love. Not likely. "Emily's out for the evening. Sleep in your own room tonight."

And with that, I take my cup of tea, and head upstairs.

I get into my pajamas, and into bed. I hate everything about this. I hate being mad at Jag, I hate feeling like other people just get what they want and everything is so hard for me. I hate that it bothered me to see Grant with another woman, even more than it bothered me to see him with another man. I hate how much I enjoyed being with Liam tonight. I hate that I can't shut my head off, so I get back up and go to my laptop.

From: a_stroudt@gmail.com
To: arizonaanneliese@me.com
RE: RE: visit

Anneliese—

I'd be happy to see you while you are in town, and to meet Alan. I'd also like very much for you and Alan to meet my new husband, Jagjeet Singh. We are having a small group for Thanksgiving at our house, and hope the two of you will plan on joining us. The rest of the visit we can figure out when it gets closer. I hope you are well.

Anneke

There you go, hubby of mine. You want to throw some wrenches into the works? I've got one of my own.

27

From Gemma's Journal:

Time moves so fast sometimes, I can hardly believe it. It seems like barely a few weeks have passed since Martha married Mr. Rabin's brother, and today they are coming for tea to visit and to celebrate their son's third birthday, and introduce their new baby girl, just twelve weeks old, to her cousins. The tyke is adorable, but somehow manages to leave sticky handprints on everything, and their last visit meant that the satin-covered settee in the parlor was positively ruined. Mr. Rabin refers to his visits as the Reign of Terror. I've made three kinds of biscuits, cucumber sandwiches, and salmon croquettes. There are the first strawberries of the season, with custard sauce, and all that is left is to bake the scones. It always makes me think of my mother; scones were the first thing she ever taught me to cook. So simple, and yet so satisfying.

It took a few days for things to get back to some semblance of normal with Jag. I spent all my days working with Emily, and left him alone dealing with plaster issues on the third floor. But we finally had to deal with it when Emily poked her nose in.

"I think I should try to find another place to stay," she said last night. "I feel like my being here is causing a lot of strain on your relationship, and things seem a little tense, and what kind of family therapist am I ever going to be if I'm actually causing trouble with your marriage!"

"Don't be ridiculous, Emily, we're fine," I said.

"Of course we are, don't be concerned at all," Jag added.

"YOU ARE NOT FINE. Something is wrong. You aren't joking at all, Jag goes out every night after work and comes home late and you never go with him. You barely talk about anything except work and you are both being excruciatingly polite! And I know for a fact he slept in my room the other night, because the pillow smelled of his cologne. Now, I've ordered you some dinner, and I'm going to sleep at a friend's tonight. Get your mojo back, and tomorrow I'll start thinking about a plan to stay out of your hair."

She flounced out, and we looked at each other and began to laugh. "Guess we're in trouble, huh?" he said.

"Guess so."

Emily had ordered us sushi from Hachi's Kitchen, and we sat in the kitchen eating and trying to figure our shit out.

"Look, Jag, I'm sorry I blew up like I did; that wasn't fair. I'm clearly not good at serious relationships, real or fictional. And it isn't that I'm not happy for you and Nageena, I am, truly, thrilled for you both. It's all just so complicated."

"No, I should apologize. This whole thing is my fault. I should have just sucked it up and stayed in school."

"You would have been miserable, and you and Nageena never would have gotten together."

"Why do you say that?"

"Because I might be bad at relationships, but I know one thing: You aren't attractive if you aren't happy. Why do you think you guys just figured this out now? Because you have the security of knowing you can stay here, and a job you love that you are really, REALLY great at. You're happy and feeling good about yourself, and that, with all your other wonderful qualities are what made her fall for you now instead of before."

"You're probably right. What are we going to do?"

"What we have to. We have to ramp up our happy marriage for Emily's sake, at least for the next month before she leaves to go back to school. Then you can move back to your room permanently, and we can finish this stupid house, and find a place to live."

"I don't know what I've done to deserve you, Anneke, and I'm truly so sorry for making your life so difficult."

"You're worth it, you ass."

"Well, then, I'm eating the last gyoza."

"Over my dead body." I snatch the final dumpling out of the container and stuff it in my mouth whole.

It's very attractive when I laugh so hard it pops back out and lands on the floor, where Schatzi snatches it up and runs away with it.

It feels good to be back on good terms with Jag, which is why I haven't told him yet that my mom and Alan are coming to Thanksgiving. Emily came back in the morning, to find us in a tableau we set up just for her benefit, both of us in our robes looking rumpled, feeding each other pancakes and bacon. She beamed, very proud of herself, and agreed to keep staying here, but promised to spend the night out at least once or twice a week so we could have some privacy.

We're taking a step back from the fun finishing work to refocus our energies on the basement, finally getting the new HVAC system installed, if for no other reason than we desperately needed the air-conditioning up and running. We are much less stinky over here now that it isn't a thousand degrees in the house. Liam has fully embraced the industrial vibe Jag suggested so many months ago, and the two of them set about polishing the concrete floors, which glow like stone. Emily and I cleaned up the steel beams, stripping off the paint and putting an oil seal on the metal. The bathroom is completely finished; we installed the tub in the stonework nook with a foot-deep ledge around for candles or bath products, as well as a large trough sink with two faucets in lieu of his and hers side-by-side sinks, which is a look I particularly detest. I have converted many a couple to either totally separate vanities on opposite walls when they have the room, or single long sinks with double faucets when they don't. The shower floor we did in a variegated slate tile, a gray base with hints of copper running through it, with a simple floating glass-panel door. We hung a vintage silver light fixture, small sconces in the tub nook, two antique mirrors side by side over the sink.

It's been reasonably low-key, and with the small exception of having accidentally roughed-in a left-side drain for the tub, which, as it turns out, actually has a center drain, without rehab drama. Ever since our night at Del Frisco's, Liam has almost entirely stopped ribbing me, not to mention calling me by the wrong name. He still won't tell me what he whispered in Grant's ear that night, just said it was something he needed to say out loud. Lord knows I won't get it out of Grant, who emailed me last week to say he was trying to figure out who he is and that he was sorry if running into him that night upset me in any way. I replied that since I was blissfully happy in my marriage, there were no hard feelings in the least and that I wished him a long happy life with the genitals of his choice.

Which is why I didn't think twice about answering my phone when he calls.

"Hey, whassup?"

"Hi, Anneke, how are you doing?"

"Great, actually, things are really coming together over here."

"That's fantastic, really, that makes me happy. But, um, we have to talk about the money thing again, which makes me feel like a total ass."

"It is what it is, Grant, I don't know what to tell you. I'm working as hard and as fast as I can, and we are pretty sure we will be able to list it right after the New Year. So if we get a quick sale, you're looking at about five to six months."

"Well, the thing is, the lawyer, he called me back. And now he's offering to buy me out at a ten percent profit."

"What do you mean?"

"They're offering to give me 220K for my stake, even though I only put in 200."

Fuck.

"Anneke, I know this whole thing sucks, but I don't know what to do."

I know what to do. You don't cheat on your fiancée. You be the stand-up guy. You don't pull the rug out from under people. "Me either."

"I still have a little time on my end, but not six months. And I don't need it all, but I do need something, at least enough to do the earnest money for the restaurant deal."

"How long do I have, and how much do you need?"

"I need a minimum of 50K, and I need it in six weeks latest."

"Fine."

"Fine?"

"What do you want me to say, Grant? I get that it is bad timing for you, it's certainly bad timing for me. But I can't let you just sell your share in this house out from under me, and I don't have enough cash liquid to buy you out completely. I'll have to figure it out, but yes, if I have to start hooking on the side, I will get you your fifty grand in six weeks, okay? Just don't sell to anyone."

"Okay."

"I gotta go, Grant."

I hang up the phone, and punch the wall. When I look up, Emily is staring at me with her jaw hanging open.

"Oh, ANNEKE!" She comes at me with one of her patented bear hugs.

"How much did you hear?" I say into her shoulder. She releases me, looks deep in my eyes.

"Enough."

"How much is enough?"

"You owe Grant fifty thousand dollars in six weeks or he is going to sell his stake in the house to someone else."

"Yeah, that's enough."

"What does Jag say?"

"Jag doesn't know, Emily, and you are not going to tell him."

"But . . ."

"But NOTHING. Jag isn't to know. This is my mess. I have to figure it out."

"He's your husband, Anneke, your mess IS his mess."

"This predates him. It's grandfathered mess."

"Doesn't work that way."

"If you tell Jag about this, I will tell Liam you have a phone full of pictures of him that you take when he isn't looking."

Her jaw flops open.

"You're not that sneaky, kiddo, but unless you want him to know about your little personal Liam porn collection, you'll keep your mouth shut." She looks mortified, and I realize what I have to do. "Besides, isn't that what sisters do? Keep each other's secrets? You are the only person who knows, Emily. Just you and me."

She smiles a little, and I can see how happy it makes her that I just called us sisters. I feel a little bad using it in such a manipulative way, but not bad enough not to do it. "That's true. So it's just a sister secret?"

I nod. "Just a sister secret." I hold out my pinky for her, and she breaks into a full-on blinding grin, links it with her own, and we shake.

"C'mon. Go do a quick coffee run, and when you get back, come find me."

Today we'll be in the butler's pantry, while Jag and Liam figure out the puzzle of the wine cellar. Liam found a restaurant in the burbs that was going out of business and bought their lightly used wine racking, and their practically new Vinotemp temperature and humidity control unit for about a quarter of what it was going to cost us. There is plenty of light oak racking, mostly for single bottles, but also some shelving for cases and some spaces for larger-sized bottles like magnums, but obviously it had been custom built for that space and now needs to be repurposed in the old canning room under the front porch, which is something of an odd shape. When they get it all in, they will give it a light sanding and then a slightly darker finish, since the very blond wood is not exactly our taste.

Emily and I finished up the building out of the butler's pantry over the course of this week. We took the kitchen cabinets I salvaged from Liam's old Fremont job, and installed them in a U shape around the room. The lower cabinets alternate between deep spaces with shelves and double doors, and sets of drawers, and the uppers are all glass-front with shallower shelves. We had to build a couple of custom pieces to match, to make everything fit properly, but it was fun to figure those pieces out. We had a narrow eighteen-inch space to fill on one wall, and Liam had the brilliant idea to create a single tall cabinet with a rod, where someone could hang their tablecloths instead of folding them up in a drawer. And under the one window, instead of leaving the space open, we created a window seat on top of deep, long shelves, so that someone can organize their largest platters. The upholstered seat actually flips up on a piano hinge to reveal a solid wood top, so that the future owners can get a bit of extra usable square footage when they need it for organizing or setting up for parties.

The butler's pantry opens to the dining room with wide double pocket doors, so I want the space to serve as storage, but also as a space the new owners can use as a bar during parties. We installed a small brass bar sink, and an undercounter set of freezer drawers for ice storage. Since we saved so much on the cabinetry, we splurged on zinc countertops, which look fantastic, and as they patina will only look better. Today we're upholstering the insides of the upper glass-front cabinets with the same leather we used in the dining room hutches. It's a tedious job, the cutting of the pieces has to be insanely precise, and we have to make sure not to get any of the very sticky glue that we're using to attach it anywhere on the surfaces, since it would never come off. These cabinets will be slightly more complicated than the ones in the dining room, since they have a small plate rail in the back, which will require a certain amount of patience with the leather.

I've brought in one of our folding tables to be a work surface, and take the time to cover it with a fresh sheet of butcher paper to have a clean surface to work on. I have my sheet of measurements for all the pieces of leather, and I have the whole hides rolled up and lying on the counter. We'll just go cabinet by cabinet, cutting the pieces and then getting them installed. There are nine upper cabinets in here; if we work well today, I'm hoping to get at least four of them finished.

Emily returns, handing me a latte, and Schatzi jumps up lightly onto the window seat and curls up in the little bit of sun that is coming through the window. I love how it brings out the reddish undertones of the chestnut finish on the cabinetry in here, the patina of over one hundred years is a glow you just cannot fake or replicate. I accept the coffee gratefully, and walk Emily through the process for the leather. She wasn't here when I did the dining room hutches, so I'm a little nervous to let her help; we have almost no extra leather and can't afford to make any mistakes. I want her to watch me do a couple before I let her jump in. She sits down and waits patiently for me to walk her through my process. With the first piece of leather, I flip it over and carefully mark off the cuts I need to make on the back side with a fine-tip Sharpie. With a leather knife and a metal straightedge, I make the cuts slowly and carefully. When all of the pieces are cut, I dry fit them into the first cabinet, to make sure they are perfect. Thankfully, they are, and I'm able to use a small foam roller to apply the glue to the back of the hides, and to the inside of the cabinet. We'll have to wait a half an hour for the glue to dry, so that when I go to apply the leather, the two glue surfaces will create an instant bond.

"I've got lunch plans, if that's okay?" Emily says, checking her watch.

"Of course, I'll be doing this all day. Have fun." Emily heads out for her lunch, and I stand in the room just letting its beauty sink in.

"Lunch?" a voice says right behind me, making me yelp.

"LIAM! For the love of all that is holy can you PLEASE stop sneaking up on me like that?"

"Sorry, lass." He grins, which lets me know he isn't sorry in the least. "Just came up to check the plans about something."

I take a deep breath and wait for my pulse to slow. "What do you want for lunch?"

"Jag and I were talking about maybe needing a little Persian fix. What do you think?"

"I think I will do an order to Noon O Kabab, and then take the dog for a walk. Can you keep an ear out for the doorbell?"

"Will do."

I grab my iPad and log in to the restaurant website and place an order for hummus, baba ghannouj, spicy pomegranate wings, and skewers of chenjeh, koubideh, and lamb. The combination of grilled marinated rib eye, minced spiced beef, and tender lamb should be plenty for three hungry worker bees, with Persian rice and grilled vegetables, chunks of feta, and their delicious large pita breads. I log out and grab Schatzi's leash, ignoring that keeping her waiting has put the ultimate look of disapproval on her face. I open the front door, and am hit with a blast of hot air. August in Chicago is just miserable. If you can't be inside with air-conditioning, or lying in a cold pool, there is no point.

"Good lord, dog, let's make it a quick one, okay?"

We head across the street to the park, where Schatzi finds a sprightly Boston terrier to strike up a conversation with. The two of them are playing happily, as I find a bit of shade under one of the large trees that line the park.

"Is he yours?" I turn to find myself facing directly into a torso. I look up the seemingly endless length of person to finally find a kindly face somewhere a long expanse above my head.

"She. Is. Yes. And her new friend?"

"Mine. Beanie." He is probably fortysomething; there are a few glints of silver in the dark hair that clings to his well-shaped head. He has got to be six five or six six, and I am proud of myself that I resist the urge to ask if he plays basketball, which my girlfriend Amita once told me was a truly horrible borderline-racist thing to ask a tall African American gentleman.

"Your mother named you Beanie?" flies out of my mouth without warning.

He laughs. "My mother named me Jacob. I named the dog Beanie."

I can feel my face turning red. "Right. I'm Anneke. She's Schatzi."

"*Sehr schön zu zwei schönen Damen zu erfüllen,*" he says.

"Excuse me?"

"Anneke, Schatzi? I went with German."

"You'd be right, but I don't know the language. You seem to speak beautifully. Did you just order the sauerbraten?"

"I said it was nice to meet two lovely ladies."

I think I must be blushing purple by now. "Well, it is nice to meet you too, Jacob. How do you come to speak such beautiful German?"

"My grandmother is German." I must have a blank face, and I'm sure he has answered questions about his heritage forever. "My granddad was a GI in World War II, Tuskegee Airman, and he became friendly with a German family while he was there. Turns out the nanny for the family was actually a young German Jewish girl that they were hiding in plain sight. They fell in love, he married her, and brought her back to Chicago after the war."

"Wow. That is amazing. My family were also German Jews, but they got out before the occupation. We could be cousins!"

"Anything's possible, are you part black?" he says with a wicked grin.

"Couldn't you tell?" I fluff my hair at him.

We laugh, and Schatzi and Beanie come running over to where we are, clearly overheated from playing in the brutal sun. Jacob takes out a bottle of water and kneels on the ground, pouring water into his large hand and letting both dogs get a drink.

"Thank you, I didn't think to bring water for her. It is horrific out here." I can feel sweat trickling down my back.

"My pleasure. So are we neighbors?"

"Depends. Where do you live?"

He gestures down the block, about eight houses from mine, a gorgeous redbrick building that appears to be the same era as my old girl.

"We're in the little castle right across the way."

"I love that building."

"I'm actually a builder, we're converting it to single family, will hopefully be flipping it sometime later this year."

"Very interesting. I'm actually a real estate broker; when

you're ready to get it on the market, I'd be delighted to help." He reaches into his pocket and pulls out a business card.

"I don't have a card to offer you right now, I'm afraid, but I will call you for sure when we are ready to list."

"Wonderful. I'll look forward to it." He leans down and attaches Beanie's leash, rubs Schatzi's head. "Maybe Beanie and I will see you in the park again."

"We'd like that."

He reaches out his hand, which completely engulfs mine. I can't help but be aware of how clammy my hand must be; I'm sweating from every pore.

We walk across the street together, and Schatzi and I go into our yard as Jacob and Beanie keep heading up the block. Schatzi has a little spring in her step, and I feel bad.

"Don't get too attached, little girl. Our days here are numbered."

When I get back in the house, I'm shocked to hear raised voices coming up from the basement. Schatzi and I stand at the top of the stairs, listening to the latest British/Irish hostilities.

"I saw you! I was at the movies the other night, and saw you with that girl," Liam says.

"It's not what you think," Jag says. "She's a friend. Anneke knew I was out with her, she was invited to join us."

"Well, if it's not her, it's something. I was upstairs this morning; I saw that pullout bed open in the den. You can tell me it's because you snore all you want, but there is something shady happening here, man, and I will not be in the middle of it."

Crap. Emily slept out last night; Jag must have forgotten to pack up his bed.

"Then perhaps you should stay out of it altogether."

"I can't stay out of it. Anneke has been my friend for almost ten years. She had the rug pulled out from under her with that idiot Grant, she's dealing with this house and her future, and you came along in her most vulnerable moment and swooped her up. You married her in like ten minutes for chrissakes! And she really loves you, man, I can tell. So all I'm saying is you had better be up for that. Because as much as I like you, I will fucking kill you if you hurt that girl." I can't help but smile at this, listening to Liam stick up for me, even though my heart breaks for poor Jag having to be on the receiving end.

"It isn't my intention to hurt her. I promise that nothing bad is going on between us, and I'm not doing anything that would be hurtful for her."

"Okay."

"Liam? Thank you for looking out for her; it makes me happy to know she has you on her side."

"Fine."

Then I hear what sounds very much like muffled slapping, and I assume some sort of bonding ritual is going on down there. My two protectors.

The doorbell rings, and I yell down that the food has arrived. But when I open the door, Jacob is standing there holding the bag. "Delivery," he says.

"Now that is a surprise."

"I was heading back this way, and hijacked your lunch. I thought maybe you'd give me a tour."

"You real estate moguls, you're relentless."

"Yep."

On the one hand, I sort of don't want Jacob to leave. But I realize that I'm not quite ready for this step. "It's lovely of you to want a tour, but I'm not totally feeling ready for it. And now is a bad time anyway, I've got some time-sensitive stuff on the docket today. Will you take a rain check?"

"Absolutely. I didn't mean to be pushy, I just love old places like this, and the minute you said you were fixing it up, I just couldn't wait to get a peek."

"I promise, if you can be patient just for a few weeks, you can come look."

"Deal."

"How much was the lunch?"

"My treat. For the intrusion."

"I couldn't possibly."

"You can, and I hope you will. Beanie and I are in the park pretty much every morning around eleven. Maybe we'll see you."

"Sounds good. Thanks for lunch."

"My pleasure."

Jacob leaves just as Liam and Jag come up the stairs.

"My favorite wife!" Jag makes a point of coming over to me and giving me a big wet kiss right on the mouth. I play along, but can't help but notice when we pull away that Liam is looking at Jag with barely concealed distrust.

"My goodness, are you boys sure you've been installing a wine cellar and not just hiding in the basement drinking wine?"

"Sober as a judge, boss," Liam says. "And starving." He takes the bag from me, and Jag and I follow him upstairs to the kitchen. And within minutes, the three of us are elbow deep in spicy meats and perfumed rice, and things are peaceful.

I'm just mashing the potatoes when Jag comes downstairs after his shower. Thankfully, I got to the place in Gemma's journal where she explained the need to handle potato mashing delicately so that they don't go gummy, and ever since, while they aren't the magical pillowy, fluffy, buttery spuds that Caroline produces, at least they are no longer a substitute for Spackle. I've got the salmon steaks in the steamer, and broccolini on the stovetop cooking in chicken stock with shallots and lemon.

"Smells delicious, Anneke, you're really becoming a good cook," Jag says, sticking a finger in the potatoes. "Mmm."

I swat at him with the spatula I'm about to use for the fish. "I heard you and Liam get into it earlier." Even though I know Emily is downstairs in the shower and we'll hear her heavy clomping tread way before she could overhear anything we say, we still speak in hushed tones.

"Oh. Sorry about that. He showed up early while I was still in the shower and hadn't made up my bed yet; never occurred to me he'd go up there. And apparently he spotted me and Nageena at the movies last week."

"Well, I think you handled it fine. I'm just sorry he got in your face about it."

"He was right to. He doesn't know about our arrangement; all he sees is someone who might be using his friend or potentially being deceitful to her. I'm glad he poked at me. The more people on your side, the happier I am."

I grab the plates and serve us each up a salmon fillet, a scoop of potatoes, some spears of broccolini. We each grab a paper napkin from the pile on the counter, forks and knives from the pint glasses where we keep them, and sit down at the breakfast bar.

"Maybe we should spend more time together, especially when Liam is around. He's here a lot of evenings; I guess he is just noticing how separate our social lives are, how many nights I stay to work and you go out. And you and he are usually working together, instead of you and me. I think for the time being we should pair up more, at least when he is here."

"Yeah, I never really thought of that."

"I'm sorry that bringing him on is creating an issue."

Jag smiles at me with a tilt of the head. "I've got a green

card, a job, and a very good friend. And thank god, a girlfriend who totally gets it. Besides, with my parents coming in just three months, I should probably focus on being here and working more nights anyway."

"I think for starters we should have a regular date night. Maybe Saturdays, when Emily is out anyway? That way when Liam is here all day we can casually mention that we are getting ready to go out together, or I can be prepping for a romantic dinner, put on a good show."

Jag's face falls for the briefest second, and then he nods. "You're right, that is a wonderful idea."

"Will Nageena be horribly disappointed?"

"She gets it. She'll be fine."

"Maybe this week you could start to teach me some of your family dishes; we can practice for Thanksgiving."

"Good idea. Maybe sweet potato masala curry? You mentioned that you hate the cloying candied sweet potato dishes; that would be a good substitution."

"Perfect! Would it go with roast pork? I've got a simple recipe I want to try."

"Absolutely."

I hold up my bottle of beer, and he clinks it with his. "It's a date, husband."

"I look forward to it, wife."

"Now dig in, and I'll see if I can get the brat out of the shower before the salmon is cold."

You met Jacob Lewiston?" Caroline says reverentially.

"Yeah, he lives up the block, we were walking our dogs."

"Is he still with Jameson?"

I look at Jacob's card. Lewiston Realty. "Looks like he opened his own shop."

"Good for him. Is he still deadly gorgeous?" Caroline whispers in a way that makes me think Carl isn't far away.

"He certainly makes an impact," I say, thinking of the cheekbones, his blinding smile, the sheer elegant length of him.

"Goodness, he was in my five forever," Caroline says, sighing.

This makes me laugh. The very idea of Caroline having a "five" list is like Martha Stewart admitting to sexting on Andy Cohen's show. It isn't that I don't believe it, I just find it incongruous.

"He seems nice. I think he just wants to be the one that gets this listing when we're ready."

"You can certainly feel comfortable doing that; he's very good. I wonder if he's still dating that anchor from WGN?"

"Oh no, should I warn Carl?"

"No, I actually thought he might be a good fix-up for Hedy."

"But he seems like such a nice guy, would we really want to foist Hedy on him?"

"He'd be great for her. But regardless, befriend him for sure, he's a very good broker. And if you get a whiff of singledom, don't be shy about mentioning our girl; something tells me they might spark. Speaking of handsome boys, how goes everything over there?"

Liam completely won over the girls at Del Frisco's, even flipped the script on Hedy, who was still harboring a hair-related grudge, and now they can't stop teasing me about "being the meat in the handsome-boy sandwich." I always remind them that anything that involves two men would give me PTSD flashbacks. "Good. Tedious but good. On budget, which is a miracle. Almost on schedule, which is an even bigger miracle." I get a small knot in my stomach thinking about Grant and the huge clock that keeps ticking in my head.

"That's good. The impending storm of parents not freaking you out too much?"

"I'm trying not to think of it too much. Jag is worried, of course; breaking the news to them about school and his new career path makes him very nervous. And I really want to make a good impression on them. I want them to think that it wasn't a terrible mistake to marry me."

"They couldn't possibly think that. What about your mom?"

"She emailed that she and Alan look forward to meeting my husband, and that they would be delighted to join us for Thanksgiving."

"Did you tell Jag yet?"

"I'm working on it."

I can almost hear her swallow down the advice she is dying to give me, and the way she forces herself to change the subject.

"Did she send anything like Jag's parents did?"

"Hah! I haven't had a birthday acknowledged since I was fifteen. She certainly wasn't going to send a wedding gift."

"Since you brought it up . . ."

"No."

"Anneke."

"N.O. No. I will allow a girls' night dinner. You can cook, if you want, I never say no to that. But I do not want some big thing."

"Anneke, it's thirty-five."

"I know you won't let me ignore it completely, but let's please not make it a big hairy deal, okay?" My impending birthday is just a reminder that nothing is what I thought it would be. My thirty-fifth was supposed to be a big party at Grant's new place. It was supposed to be an awesome prequel to the wedding festivities, and happily ever after, and a big bright future. I don't want to celebrate where I am right now, or the uncertainty of what comes next.

"Okay. I hear you. But can we at least do plus-ones? Carl and John and Jag and someone for Hedy? Maybe even Jacob? Emily and anyone she would want to bring? Don't you want to celebrate with your husband? Maybe even include some of his friends?"

I think about this, and realize that it would look very weird to not celebrate my birthday with Jag, and that if we do it right, it might allow us to put a good face on things. "Okay. Plus-ones, and Jag's gang. Essentially the wedding all over again."

"Good. Leave everything to me."

"Fine. And Caroline? You will make the chocolate cake with the vanilla icing, won't you?"

"Of course, sweet girl. With plenty of rainbow sprinkles."

Which is good. Because if I have to turn thirty-five at all, there had better be sprinkles.

28

From Gemma's Journal:

In the spring, it is time for list making. The housekeeper makes the list of all the spring-cleaning chores needed to get the winter doldrums out of the corners. The houseman explores the house and makes his list of necessary repairs; the landscaper assesses the property to see how everything fared over the long winter, and to plan the small kitchen garden for the backyard. I take stock of the root cellar to see how the stores have been depleted, and give the kitchen a full scrubbing from top to bottom. The under housemaids will help me do a full polish on all of the silver. The houseman will give the wood floors in the kitchen a scraping, and then reseal them with mineral oil and beeswax. The mattresses will all be fluffed and restuffed as necessary, the heavy velvet drapes of winter will be taken down, cleaned, and stored, replaced with the cotton drapes for spring and summer. The rugs will all be taken outside for a good beating, and the winter clothes and shoes cleaned, repaired and packed away in the attic, the spring and summer clothes brought down and aired out. It is a time of enormously hard work, long days. The windows are thrown open to the fresh air, and everything seems bright and possible.

Punch list time. Like Gemma's annual spring cleaning and refreshing, you get to a point in a job where you move from an endless series of lists to one master list, the punch list. Joe used to go very old school with his, actually using an antique hole punch to check off the items on his lists, and I still have his punch, but I don't use it. I prefer the satisfaction of the black Sharpie line-through. To ensure that we don't miss anything, I asked both Liam and Jag to take their own tours of the house to make their lists, so that the three of us can compare notes. Between our sets of eyes, we should be sure we don't leave anything undone.

Now that the stultifying heat of summer has abated some-what with the imminence of September, we can do the outdoor work, installing the decking material on the top of the garage roof, along with the privacy fencing. With the new AC up and running smoothly, we can finish the painting in the rooms that haven't been done yet, without fearing that the humidity in the air will prevent a clean job. Most of the heavy-duty work has been finished, so we can make a schedule to strip and reseal the wood floors on the second and third levels. We'll save the stair-case for last, stripping and then re-staining and sealing only after we know we're ready to put it on the market.

Over the weekend Liam helped Jag and Emily and me shift all of our stuff down into the basement bedrooms, freeing up the second floor for finishing. I have to say it's been a total treat to be able to use that bathroom; I've become a total bath junkie, taking a nightly soak in the deep tub when Emily takes Schatzi for her evening walk, and Jag showers on the first floor.

As much as the baths are wonderful for my body, they are the time I'm most plagued by my head. I still don't know what I'm going to do about Grant and his money, and my time is ticking away. I keep going over the finances, and as far as I can tell, if I want to get him his fifty grand without telling anyone, I'm going to have to cash in some of my retirement savings, which also will carry a penalty and additional tax burden at the end of the year. At least Emily will leave next week to go visit her dad before heading to school, so Jag and I won't have to tiptoe around, and we can get our sleeping arrangements back to normal. I have to grudgingly admit that she's been a big help, but having her living here these past months has been exhausting. Her boundless energy is fine when we're working, but the chatter during dinner and her constant need to try to poke at the recesses of my brain, asking a zillion questions about my past, telling me the endless stories she invented about us and the years we supposedly spent together, it's exhausting. She quizzes me about vacations we never took, memories I don't have, games we played and parties we had. The whole thing is just weird, it's not like I'm going to bump into one of her Harvard professors and have to get through an interrogation. But it's just a few more days, and the free labor has been a godsend, so I suck it up and play along.

Jag and I are very ready to stop sharing a bed, which started off sort of friendly, but now feels strange in light of his relationship. Once Emily is gone, he'll be able to sleep over at Nageena's without raising eyebrows. The three of us had a very lovely dinner at her house last week, they are truly adorable together, and I feel shitty for being so petulant with him about the whole thing. Nageena pulled me aside to tell me how much she appreciates what I've done, and promised to be as helpful as she can in assisting in maintaining our cover. I promised to not be a jealous wife, and she laughed and hugged me hard, and I felt lighter. Which made my annoyance even worse, because not only does he get to be in love with a wonderful woman, he also gets another confidante and co-conspirator in our charade, and for some reason, it just makes me feel even more alone. I'm not sure why it bothers me, since being alone is the thing I crave more than anything these days. I never really thought about how much time I spent on my own when I was with Grant, but with his long hours, his travel schedule, and my work on the house, I had long, luxurious stretches of time without anyone else around. Now with Jag and Emily living here, and Liam coming in at least two evenings a week, plus all weekend, I feel like I never get any significant time just for me.

Of course, I'm not terribly good company for myself these days, so perhaps it's not the worst thing in the world to have other people keeping me from getting too much in my own head. Which is probably why, with Jag and Nageena having a hooky day at the movies in the far north suburbs where no one will see them, and Emily indulging in a beach day with her friends, and Liam dealing with a Manning issue, I faced a blissful stretch of total me time, and panicked.

The doorbell rings, and I jump up to answer it.

"Hello, Anneke, good to see you," Jacob says when I open the door. We saw each other a couple of times in the park right after we met; he remembered Caroline fondly when I mentioned the connection. So far I haven't been able to figure out if he is single or not. I hadn't seen him since; until yesterday, he had been out of town visiting his parents in North Carolina, but thinking about today and the endless time with just me and my worries, I invited him for a tour just so I could fill some time.

"Thanks for coming, Jacob. Hello, Beanie!" The pooch jumps up and down excitedly, and Schatzi comes skittering around the corner joyfully to greet her boyfriend.

Jacob comes in, and tosses a couple of treats to the dogs, who are now romping together happily in the living room.

Jacob makes a low whistling noise. "Wow, Anneke, what a space!"

I grin. "Yeah, it was love at first sight for me."

"I can see why. How do you want to do this? Top down?"

"I thought so, if you don't mind, I think it makes the most sense."

"Lead on, Macduff."

I'm enormously conscious of the fact that he is face-to-face with my substantial butt as I lead him up the staircase. "We'll be refinishing the stairs last," I say over my shoulder.

"Makes sense, keep them pristine."

We head up to the third floor, where I take him through the special small French doors we've installed to the bedroom. The narrow doors close flush into the wide, detailed jamb with magnet closures, so that they become a seamless part of the hallway when opened, but when closed, provide some light and sound protection for the bedroom, so if one partner is an earlier riser than the other, they can have full access to their closet and bathroom without disturbing whoever is still sleeping.

"These are a great detail."

"Thank you."

He has a small Moleskine notebook open, and takes some notes as we go, noting the light in the master bedroom, the special details in the walk-in closets, and the stunning bathroom.

"I love that you have a laundry room up here. Makes so much sense."

"We have two more, actually: one in the basement for big jobs, towels and linens and such, and a small stackable on the second floor in the bathroom closet, but figured that having one up here too was just logical."

"So smart."

We head through the matching French doors at the end of the bathroom and into the back bonus room. "We thought a young couple might want the option for an adjacent nursery space, or an older one might like the idea of a caretaker's bedroom back here. Or it can be a home office."

Jacob scribbles. "Good thought to give it a three-piece bathroom."

"There was already a bath back here, so we figured we'd use it to our advantage."

We head down the back stairs to the kitchen, where Jacob takes a quick inhale of breath. "Anneke, this is just the most spectacular kitchen I think I've ever seen."

"It is the heart of the home."

"It will sell this house."

"That's what I want to hear!"

For the better part of the next hour, Jacob looks at every room, every detail; wherever things are unfinished, I take him through our plans. He's appreciative of the design and layout, offers a couple of wise suggestions, and seems very certain of his ability to do a quick sale for us.

"I do want you to be realistic. If it were in Lincoln Park or Bucktown, you'd get three times as much as you will here. Other Realtors will use the location and the transitional neighborhood to haggle down a lot on price. So I want to manage your expectations about how things will go. Can I ask, what's your bottom line?"

I've been running the numbers forever. When it is all done, we will be about six hundred grand out of pocket in all. I need to clear at least a hundred thousand just for myself to move and try to start some sort of business. There is the Grant issue, and Liam will get his cut, and Jag doesn't know it, but I've set aside a percentage for him as well. "I really don't want to take less than 1.2 million."

"I'm comfortable we can get you that. I'm glad you aren't expecting two million in this neighborhood, even though the house certainly warrants it! What is most important to you, quick or maximum money?"

I think about that. "Quick, I think. If the first offer we get is 1.2 or more, let's take it and be done. Rip the Band-Aid off."

"Good to know. When do you think you'll be ready to list?"

"Mid-December if all goes well."

"I will make it my mission to give you a great Chanukah present."

"Thank you, Jacob."

We head to the living room, where the dogs are curled up in a tangle, napping. Jacob whistles for Beanie, who leaps up, and they head for the door. We promise to meet them in the park tomorrow, and watch from the porch as they head for home. And for some reason I feel my chest get tight.

"Schatzi, it's going to be over soon. We're going to have to let someone else live here."

Schatzi tilts her head at me.

"I'll tell you something I never said out loud to anyone else. I always sort of dreamed, deep down, that when it was finished, Grant would just say, 'Surprise!' and we'd move in." Until today I hated to admit even to myself that what I was building here is my absolute dream house, and now that it is almost finished, the idea of having to leave just breaks my heart.

I wake up to a smell that can only be described as amazing. I get up and put on my robe and slippers, and head up the stairs to the kitchen.

"HAPPY BIRTHDAY!!!" Emily grabs me in a hug, bouncing up and down.

"Good morning, my love, happy birthday," Jag says, coming around from behind the stove in an apron to give me an appropriately deep kiss.

"Happy birthday, Anneke," Liam says, sitting at the breakfast bar. I'm suddenly awfully aware of the nest that is probably my hair, the fact that the girls are unfettered beneath my pajamas, and I pull my robe tightly around me, hoping it will provide some much-needed support.

"What's all this, then?"

"We decided if you were going to be working on your birthday, at least you should have a special breakfast," Jag says.

"Eggs, bacon AND sausage, toast, muffins, and something called a hash brown casserole."

"It's my specialty," Liam says.

"I made the muffins!" Emily says.

"Well, that all sounds wonderful. Do I have time to change?" I have never wanted to put a bra on more in my life.

"Of course, we are about ten minutes out."

"And I already walked the dog," Emily says.

"You guys are the best." I head back downstairs to the basement and quickly get dressed, pull my hair into a bun, and follow the scent of delicious pork products back up to my celebration.

Liam's hash brown casserole can only be described as so over-the-top ridiculous I fear Paula Deen is sitting somewhere cackling about it. I can tell that there is cheese, butter and sour cream in there, and do not want to know what else. It is delicious, as are the perfectly fried eggs, crispy bacon, buttery toast, and juicy sausages. The muffins are banana chocolate chip, otherwise known as breakfast cake. Liam stopped at Intelligentsia to see my girl Rainn and came well stocked with caffeine, and there is fresh-squeezed orange juice to boot.

We feast, all of us slipping bits of egg, toast, and meats to Schatzi, and talk about where we stand. We are now all operating off the master punch list, and have been trying to divide and conquer as much as possible. Today we are going to install the fixtures in the second-floor bathroom, which will officially take plumbing off the list. Jag did a great job at the salvage yard, finding us a perfect small-scale claw-foot tub that will allow us to have both a tub and a stall shower in the space. He also found a lovely antique tall chest of drawers missing its legs, and convinced us to install it on a tiled riser to appear built-in, which I think will be a very cool look.

"We have a birthday surprise!" Jag says.

"Wasn't breakfast plenty?"

"Oh, wife, you're going to love this." Jag takes my hand and leads me over to the pantry. It takes me a moment to see what is different. Against the far wall, there is a small door. I walk over and open it carefully.

"You rescued the dumbwaiter!" Behind the door is the restored unit, a lovely generous size, with its mini-elevator-call-button mechanics. "However did you do it? And where does it go?"

"We upgraded the electrics, everything else was in pretty good shape. And it opens on the first floor in the prep kitchen." Since there was a small kitchen in the back of the first level, we thought it made sense to keep it for the owners to use as a catering kitchen for large parties. Having the dumbwaiter available to shuttle dishes from the primary kitchen here on the second floor down to that space is going to be a huge selling point. And I'm deeply touched.

"Thank you, both, so much, what a lovely way to start my birthday." I kiss Liam on the cheek, and Jag on the mouth, and they both look chuffed and proud of themselves, high-fiving and winking up a storm.

"And I have a birthday surprise too!" Emily says, literally clapping her hands.

"Do tell." I can't help but laugh. I'm actually weirdly going to miss her when she leaves in two days.

"I called Harvard and they are going to let me defer for a semester so that I can stay and help finish the house!"

Holy shit. "Emily, that is very sweet, but you need to go to school." Good GOD she needs to go to school. For the love of everything that is holy she needs to go to school.

"When I told them what I've been doing here, they completely understood why I need to stay and see it through."

"Emily, this is, um . . ."

"Wonderful, Emily, it's very lovely of you to want to stay, and to be willing to postpone your education to help your sister," Jag says, coming up behind me and putting his arm around me, squeezing hard, forcing me to do the right thing, as opposed to the thing I want to do.

"Of course, Emily, I'm sorry, I was just surprised, thank you for wanting to stay."

"I couldn't leave now, it's just getting good!" she says.

"I suppose I get out of doing dishes today?"

"Of course!" Emily says. "Go take a little break or something. We got this." And the three of them start to tackle the insane mess they've created in the kitchen.

I go back downstairs to calm my nerves. She's staying. To the bitter end. Which means that Jag and I are going to have to have a conversation with her about the real state of the marriage. I was counting on her leaving, on getting some normalcy back, and if I have to put up with her for four more months, he is going to have to understand the need to bring her into our confidence.

I'm shaking with frustration. Birthday surprise indeed.

Jag heads out after he finishes cleaning up to go pick up the chest that Juan graciously refurbished for us to thank us for helping his son, who got accepted early decision, and Liam and Emily and I head to install the tub and shower.

"Big birthday plans tonight?" he says, taking a large wrench to the old showerhead.

"Caroline is having a small dinner party for me."

"Nice. I'm not much of a birthday guy myself."

"I'm not a birthday girl either, but it's a reasonably big one; they wouldn't take no for an answer."

"Aren't you coming? You have to come; it's an odometer birthday! Caroline said that I could bring someone, you can be my plus-one!" Emily gushes.

"I wouldn't want to crash the party, especially if it is just the nearest and dearest." He looks straight into my eyes.

Emily smacks him lightly on the arm. "Silly goose, who is

nearer or dearer than you? You must come. We insist, don't we, Anneke?"

What the hell, I didn't want the party anyway, might as well. "Of course, Liam, you should absolutely come, the more the merrier."

"Well then, lass, I guess it's a date. Dress code?" Emily is looking like she just won the lottery.

"Casual," she manages to get out. I can practically hear her heart race from here.

"Casual like dark jeans, or casual like my zebra-print Speedo?" he teases, and Emily looks down at his crotch reflexively, and then blushes beet red.

"Jeans would probably be more appropriate," I say, hoping he didn't notice her ogle. "I am thirty-five, you know. Speedos are so early thirties."

"Ah, thirty-five is nothing. I'm rounding the bend toward forty myself."

"You wear it well." And then, just to underscore things for both of them: "Emily, doesn't he look good for being nearly twice your age?"

She just nods, and I know she isn't listening at all, she's just figuring out what to wear tonight.

Liam gives a mighty groan and a big push, and with a loud grinding noise the showerhead gives way. In moments we are both being doused with icy cold spray.

"AHHHHH!" I say, trying to block the blast with my hands.

"Crap!" Liam says, trying to get the fixture reattached. "I turned the water off to this space."

"I beg to differ!" I say, water filling my mouth.

"EEEEEEEEEEEKKK!" Emily shrieks, with more joy than annoyance.

Liam, unable to get the showerhead reattached, starts turning the knobs frantically. Both of which come off in his hands. "FUCK!"

The bathroom is rapidly flooding; we are all soaked to the skin.

"Emily! Remember where the water shutoff is? Go shut it off!" And she runs off down the stairs. Liam finally gets the wrench reattached to the showerhead. "Okay, I'm going to hold this on; you turn with all you've got, okay?" he sputters at me. The only way to get hold of the end of the wrench is to duck under Liam's arms. He holds the wrench head, and I take the free end and push up as hard as I can. I feel it twist and soon the water stops. Liam lets his arms down around me, resting his chin on the top of my head.

"You okay?" he asks into my sopping hair.

"Yeah. You?"

"I think so." I can feel the full length of his body pressed against my back, and then he starts to laugh. And then I start to laugh. I'm not sure which of us moved first, but whoever it was stepped wrong and slipped in the water puddled on the shower floor, and we both went down in a tangle, me landing on top of Liam. We're still laughing, and suddenly Liam is brushing my hair off my face and holding my head in his hands, and then he leans up and kisses me. His lips are firm, and then his tongue is in my mouth, and I've never felt anything so unbearably sweet in my life. Every fiber of my body is suddenly alive, and we are devouring each other's mouths while water from my hair drips into our eyes. I can feel him moving beneath me, and all I want is to give myself over to him, to the pleasure that is building so rapidly. And then, unbidden, I get an image of Grant and Gregg in the shower, and despite my body crying out for more, I pull myself away. Liam looks stricken.

"Anneke, I . . . I'm sorry, I . . . I don't know what . . ."

"Stop. Get yourself together. Clean up the water. I'm going downstairs to dry off, and when Jag gets back, the two of you should deal with the bathroom, I'm going to work on the wall-paper in the vestibule."

He looks like I stole his puppy. "I'm an ass, Anneke, I can't believe . . ."

"It's fine, no biggie, I know you can't be near any woman without at least trying to get in her pants, it's just a reflex. For-gotten already." And as quick as I can, I leave, carefully drip-ping my way downstairs all the way to the basement bathroom. I'm shivering, and I don't know if it's from being cold and wet or hot and bothered, but I run the hot water into the tub regard-less. I peel off my sodden clothes and get into the filling tub, curling myself into a ball with my head resting on my knees. I'm still shaking, and I don't know what is worse: that I have never before in my thirty-five years ever had anyone kiss me in a way that electrified my whole body and briefly made me understand why sex can be so obsessive, or that Liam was the one to do it. The past months are flashing before my eyes, every nice thing he's done, every time he's made me laugh, his rescu-ing me at Home Depot, his support when I ran into Grant. And suddenly it occurs to me that for all of my protestations that he is the most hateful specimen of manhood, I know that just like I wasn't fully aware how much it would hurt me to leave this house, I have some feelings where Liam is concerned that have nothing to do with annoyance or distaste.

When I stop shivering, I get out of the tub and wrap my towel around me, leaving my soaking clothes on the floor of the shower. I go to my room, pull out fresh clothes, and get dressed. I sit on the bed and reach for the journal.

"Oh, Gemma. What on earth am I going to do?"

The book falls open and my finger finds the page.

"Your body will always tell you what you need. If you crave sweet things, your energy is flagging. If it's meat you want, your

iron is low. When you want potatoes above everything else, there is something not grounded with you. Whatever tricks your head may play on you, however fickle your heart, your body will tell you very specifically what it is you need, and it is up to you to listen."

Crap. I was counting on Gemma for wisdom about not letting your guard down, or avoiding things that are bad for you, or trusting your first impression. Because if I were to listen to what my body says it wants? That means Liam Murphy on a platter. And I'm not exactly sure what on earth to do with that. Except maybe plan on eating my weight in cake tonight while trying desperately to erase the taste of his kisses.

D id you have a good birthday, lovely wife?" Jag asks as we walk into the house.

"I did, in spite of myself."

"You did very well, I think everyone had a good time. Caroline certainly knows how to throw a party." I follow him into the living room, where we both collapse on the couch.

"She certainly does." The evening was perfect. Caroline is a genius at entertaining, and really thinks about her audience. Some people throw dinner parties to show off their skills, or set an example of some kind. Sort of like the people who buy you presents that they think you should want as opposed to the presents you actually want. But Caroline is all about delivering pleasure. So instead of doing one of her classic elegant dinner parties with many courses of beautifully plated food, she set up her kitchen with a series of stations inspired by the foods I like best. There were mini Vienna hot dogs with all the classic Chicago toppings. A macaroni 'n' cheese bar with all kinds of fun add-ins. Cold sesame noodles in tiny white cardboard Chinese take-out containers, sliders served with small cones of skinny fries. Fried chicken legs, barbecued ribs, mini gyros in tiny three-inch pitas. All of it the most delicious and perfectly pre-pared elevated junk food, complete heaven, and just what I love. She gave us each a bamboo tray with a piece of parchment paper on it to use as plates, and large kitchen tea towels instead of napkins. There were cold beers in a tub, endless bottles of rosé, and a massive birthday cake, chocolate with fluffy vanilla frosting, and rainbow sprinkles. And then, after coffee, mini ice-cream sandwiches on chocolate chip cookies.

"I may have to have her host my birthday party."

"She'd be delighted. When is it?"

Jag makes a face of mock horror. "WIFE! This is something you should know!"

"I'm too full to remember."

He laughs. "January twenty-seventh."

"I'll put it in my book. And I'll tell Caroline. She'll start learning traditional Indian recipes immediately."

"I bet she would. Well, between the wedding and tonight, I think my friends would be delighted to go to Caroline's any old time."

"Everyone did seem to have fun."

"Especially Emily."

"Indeed."

Liam was perfectly charming, connecting with all of the girls in the same way he did the night at Del Frisco's, cementing his place in their good graces. He schmoozed all of Jag's pals, praising Jag's skills in ways that made Nageena glow with pride, and made me feel even worse that her love had to spend his whole night doting on me with extravagant affection. I caught her eye whenever I could, and squeezed her arm or shoulder whenever I walked by her, just to let her know I was there and I got it. I wish someone had been able to do that for me. Watching Liam being an attentive date to Emily was like a punch in the gut. He kept leaning over to whisper things in her ear, making her giggle. She was wearing a light loose summer sundress that managed to be sexier and somehow more revealing of her perfect willowy body than if she had been clad in spandex. Her golden hair was pulled off her face with a clip, little wispy pieces escaping. Liam, in his dark jeans and crisp white linen buttondown shirt, looked like an Abercrombie ad, and the two of them together made for a sickeningly stunning couple.

Every time I looked over at him, he would catch me, and smile or wink or raise his beer bottle, and the kiss would come right back to me, and my knees would weaken and my breath would catch.

"How are you doing with her staying?"

This seems as good a time as any. "I'm okay, or at least I've decided to try to be okay, but we have two problems. One, my mother is coming. And while that wasn't an issue when Emily was going to be in Boston, now she'll be here and I don't really know what to do with that. On the one hand, it might be good closure for Emily to see her, to see her with a clearer eye, to confront her. On the other hand, Emily's memories are so overwhelmingly positive, do I want to be the one to take that away from her?"

"That's a tough one. But if you think you shouldn't tell her, don't tell her. She'll be at her dad's for the long holiday weekend anyway, and as long as we keep your mom away from the house, it should be a piece of cake. What's the second thing?"

"I think we should tell her. About us. The truth. It's been so difficult having her living with us and being on edge all the time, I don't know if I can go another four months. I think we can trust her, and if you approve, I'd really like to have us both sit down with her and lay the whole thing out."

"I dunno, Anneke. I get why you want to, I do, but she's so young, and the young are impulsive. What if she slips, what if she tells one of her friends? You know how romantic she thinks our whole fictional love story is, I can only imagine what fantasy she'll create around the truth."

"I know it's a risk, but I feel like it might be one we should at least consider. I mean, think about four more months of having to sleep with me, and not sleep with Nageena."

He nods. "It would be nice not to have a snoring wildebeest stealing all of the covers for a change."

"Hey, it's my BIRTHDAY."

"Not anymore," he says, checking his watch to confirm that it is after midnight.

"Fine. Will you at least think about the Emily thing?"

"As long as you are willing to admit that it is a bigger risk than telling Nageena, and we should tread lightly. After all, if she and Liam are getting closer, what if she told him?"

"Liam is just being nice to her."

Jag pauses.

"Do you know something?"

"It's probably nothing."

"WHAT?"

"I just overheard Caroline saying to Emily that she was glad she was going to sleep over there so that you and I could have a nice night, and Emily said she had made other arrangements, but she was so thankful for the offer."

I feel like I could throw up.

"Maybe she is just going to her girlfriend's house, I mean, that's where she goes on our 'date nights,' right?"

But I know in my gut that isn't where she's going.

"Liam wouldn't, would he?"

"I told you about him, he isn't what he appears to be." He's a lying, womanizing, evil pile of poop. And I really wish that I were more worried about the impressionable, starry-eyed young woman who calls me sister than I am about the fact that mere hours ago Liam Murphy was kissing me and waking up some dormant part of myself, and might now at this very moment be doing the same to her.

Jag is silent, and it speaks volumes.

"What?"

"She's a grown-up. So is he." He shrugs.

"She's a child, and he's an ass."

More silence.

"WHAT?"

My husband puts his arm around me and pulls me close. "Methinks my wife doth protest too much. It's okay to be jealous."

"HA!" I say too loudly. "As if. Jealous? Of what?"

"Of Emily. Of the idea of Emily and Liam. Of the idea of Liam, I suppose, at the end of the day."

"So what, now I'm supposed to want to be with Liam? I'm pretty sure they don't make antibiotics strong enough for that." Even I can hear the false bravado in my voice.

"I think you like him more than you want to, I think you are attracted to him in ways you would prefer not to be, and I think you aren't interested in admitting that you're lonely."

"How can I be lonely when I'm never alone?"

"It's not the same, and you know it."

I do. And the very idea makes me insane.

Jag and I head downstairs and spend our individual time in the bathroom. We get into bed and turn off the lights.

"I'll think more about telling Emily if you think more about what you need in your life. I'm not saying it's Liam or that it should be, but it's okay if it's someone."

"Fine."

Jag leans over and kisses my forehead. "Happy birthday, Anneke. I, for one, am very glad you were born."

"Well, you might not be for long."

"Why is that?"

"I invited my mother to Thanksgiving."

For a moment there is silence, and I'm waiting for him to blow up at me, and then the bed starts shaking, and then he barks in laughter and then I laugh, mostly in relief that he's not mad at me. We both crack up, just lying there in the dark, and my husband drifts off, and I wait all night for the images of Emily and Liam to stop flashing in my head, until finally, I can sleep.

29

From Gemma's Journal:

The Master is taking the Missus to a fancy-dress party. They are dressed like a milkmaid and shepherd, and are both near giddy with the freedom the disguises are giving them, reminding me of masked balls at the big house when I was a girl. The cook who trained me told me that all of the upstairs folks wore masks every day, the importance of a certain public face that often hid the private faces that we saw. The outwardly imperious dowager who loved to sneak belowstairs to play cards with the footman. The ever-proper lady of the house who was having a torrid affair with the stableman. The charitable older daughter who volunteered with the orphanage and visited wounded soldiers in hospital, and once beat her lady's maid within an inch of her life with a silver hairbrush for laying out the wrong dress. We all have the mask we show to others, and our secret hearts, and rarely are the two at peace.

It took a week for Liam and I to be relatively normal around each other. Another until we stopped avoiding working together. And just this week things are starting to feel back to normal. At least on the surface. I'm doing my best to keep my mask on, to focus on the work, on scratching things off the list one by one. But inside? I'm a hot mess. I can't stop thinking about the kiss, and the way it made me feel. Like we were inventing kisses. I've tried to convince myself that I'm just lonely, starved for physical affection, in need of some sex with another human being, but even I don't believe me. And, which is worse, Emily has attached herself to Liam's hip, the two of them suddenly have all sorts of inside jokes, and little looks, and every time I see them together I want to hit him in the balls. With a sledgehammer. Covered in fire ants. Twice.

Part of me wants to tell Emily to stay away from him, but since I still don't know if they've slept together, I can't take that risk. It's one thing if it's an unrequited crush that I could help her move past; it's something else if they've actually been together. I wouldn't do that to her. Part of me wants to tell Liam that Jag and I aren't real, see what he says, how he reacts, but I know that ship has sailed, and Jag would never approve. We've been putting on a very good show; our Saturday date nights are a major topic of conversation with Jag and Liam, and we're physically affectionate whenever he's around. I don't have the words or energy to confess, despite the fact that a part of me believes that telling Liam might be the unlocking of a door I never even knew was in my heart, let alone knowing I should look for the person with the key. Every time I think this, I shake it off and try to just think about work. There's no time to entertain flights of romantic fancy where Liam is concerned; work has to be everything. The house is really beginning to shine. We are less than five weeks away from the Thanksgiving Invasion, and feeling very comfortable with where we'll be by then. If we stay on pace, we may actually be pretty close to finished when everyone arrives.

It took me a whole week of painstaking work, but I managed to get all of the wallpaper off the vestibule walls and revealed the original murals in surprisingly good shape. A friend of Marie's from art school who does conservation accepted a piddling amount of money to restore it, and it makes the entrance so special. The gilded background with its chinoiserie landscape design is just the perfect thing, and every time I come in the front door it makes my spine straighter. At least until I have some insane vision of Liam slamming me up against the wall and kissing me until the glass in the front door fogs over and then I schlump over again.

Lucky for me, tonight I can actually distract myself with the girls and chocolate. Halloween in this neighborhood is spectacular and insane. Somewhere in the arena of eight hundred kids will stop by tonight. Hedy, Caroline, and Marie volunteered to help man the door as the endless hordes descend. Jag is going to Nageena's for a rare date night; we told everyone he was doing something at the Sikh center. I splurged at Costco, buying enormous bags of the mini bars of my favorite candy, putting it all in a huge plastic cauldron I found in the clearance rack at Jo-Ann Fabrics. I've got hot apple cider spiked with rye to keep us warm, and various bags of salty snacks to balance the sweets. Caroline is bringing sandwiches so that we can picnic on the front porch, and luckily, while it is brisk, it isn't bitter, and no rain is expected for a change.

For now, the rest of today, I'm focusing on the floor in the prep kitchen. When we went to strip the original floors, we discovered that the soft maple had already been sanded one too many times; nailheads began to appear everywhere. We pulled it all up, and reinforced the underlayment where necessary. I realized that the original flooring in the downstairs kitchen had once been end-grain wood tiles. Often used at the turn of the century for warehouse and factory floors for durability, it seemed a natural way to bring a special touch to a small space. When I'm done, the floor will look much like a huge cutting board. I found salvaged large six-inch square red oak beams from an old barn, and had them cut down into one-inch-thick tiles, and sanded smooth on one side. I'll install them directly onto the plywood with heavy-duty adhesive, and then effectively grout them with wood putty to fill any gaps or small holes or cracks. When the putty is dry I'll sand the whole thing, and seal it with a combination of mineral oil and beeswax, which will bring out the natural grain and color in the wood. Hopefully when I'm done it will look essentially like Gemma's kitchen floor would have.

I've put down a pair of chalk lines crisscrossing the space, so that I can begin at perfect center. Too many people start flooring flush against one wall and work to the other wall, which often makes for awkward cuts, or a floor that just feels slightly "off" to the eye. I'll start in the middle and work my way out, disguising the cuts at the outer walls and under cabinets. Once the baseboard molding is reinstalled, it should look fairly perfect. I get my heavy-duty kneepads, and bring the first box of tiles into the small kitchen. Working in two-foot-by-two-foot sections, I lay down the ultrasticky adhesive, and scrape it with a quarter-inch notched trowel. I carefully lay in the wood tiles, getting them butted up against each other as closely as I can. I'm glad I found the salvaged beams; new wood would never have had this beautiful tight grain.

I love how work like this can absorb me completely. The noise in my head, the worry about what I may be feeling for Liam, or what he may be feeling for Emily, the fact that my mother is coming, the dwindling days that I get to live in this special house before I have to let it be someone else's home, it all goes away. I lose myself in square by square. Put down the adhesive, lay the tiles, keep them even and tight, check my level. The work is precise and meticulous and doesn't leave room for examining your life. And let's be clear. Socrates may have said that the unexamined life isn't worth living, but I think that it is precisely that type of thought that has led us directly to reality television, and I'm pretty sure if Socrates ever met a Kardashian, he'd have gone into the first bar and ordered himself a double hemlock straight up with a twist.

It takes me four hours to get the center of the floor done, and another hour to mark the first set of cuts needed to do the far wall under the windows. I've not only marked each tile for its precise cut but also numbered them in case they get out of order while I'm cutting them. I load the tiles into an empty box, and take them down to the garage, where we've set up the chop saw and other bigger equipment. I'm just finishing the cuts when Jag comes to the garage.

"The floor is looking stunning. What a wonderful and unusual idea."

"Thanks. How is the painting going up there?"

"Third floor is officially done with taping and priming. I'll start painting tomorrow morning."

"That's awesome!"

"You want me to help you for a bit? I've probably got an hour and a half or so before I have to take a shower and head to Nageena's."

"Sure, that would be great." I hand him the box of tiles and we head back inside. The wall goes quickly, with Jag handing me the tiles in order as I install them. I show Jag how to measure the end tiles for the wall underneath the cabinets, and he goes to cut them in batches, bringing them back to me to install while taking the next batch to go cut. We set the final tile just as Jag's phone alarm goes off.

"That is what I call good timing," I say, standing and stretching.

Jag stands next to me and puts his arm around my shoulders, kissing my temple. "Now that is a floor."

"Yes it is. And you stink, husband; it's like you're smuggling old meatloaf in your pits. Go shower."

"Oh, wife, how you talk to me." At which point he sniffs at

his own armpit and pretends to swoon. I smack his tush, and he heads downstairs to get ready for his party. I tidy up in here, wash my trowel off, and pack up all the remaining tiles and half tiles for the garage. I always leave my homeowners with their extras; in case of future damage, they can pop out a single tile and replace it with one from the same lot, or cover a wall stain with the original paint.

I take Schatzi for a quick walk, and by the time we get back Jag is done with the bathroom, so I jump in for a quick shower. Since it is just the girls tonight I toss my wet hair in a bun, throw on some ratty jeans and a thick fisherman's sweater full of holes that had been Joe's, and my old K-Swiss sneakers that I've had since high school. Emily jumps in the shower after me, very excited to get into her costume, a cowgirl getup that at least is going for cute and not sexy. I head upstairs and feed Schatzi, and send all the snacks and the cider downstairs in the dumbwaiter. I always race it down the stairs, trying to be waiting for it to arrive, but so far it always beats me. And I'm pretty sure one of these days I'm going to break my neck flying down the stairs.

I put the pot of cider on the stove in the prep kitchen, with mismatched mugs next to it on the counter. The bags of chips and pretzels and cheesy crunchies I take out to the table I set up in the vestibule, which we'll take outside when everyone gets here. I go back to the kitchen to see how the cider is getting on; I want it to be warm, but not scalding. It's barely steaming, and I turn the heat down, and ladle a bit into a mug. I bring it to my mouth, inhaling the fruity boozy steam, and take a large sip.

"How is it?"

I immediately spray the mouthful out in a spectacular arc, much of which, to my horror, heads in the direction of the uncovered pot.

"LIAM!" I spin around to see him red-faced and suppressing laughter behind me.

"Oops," he says.

"Now look what you made me do." I peer sadly into my beautiful pot of cider, cinnamon sticks and allspice berries bobbing merrily.

"I didn't see a thing," he says, walking over, and pointedly taking a ladle, pouring it in a mug, and taking a big gulp. "Delicious."

My knees turn to pudding.

"There's plenty of booze in here to kill any cooties you might have. And I won't tell. Julia Child always said what happens in the kitchen stays in the kitchen."

"I can't serve SPIT to my friends."

"Would you give any of them blood? A kidney?"

"Of course. They can have the organ of their choice." This makes me think about Grant's friend Jenna, who gave her best friend part of her liver, sadly to no avail. Grant and I used to double-date occasionally with Jenna and her husband Elliot, and I loved them both. They live not far from here, but I didn't tell them when I moved into the Palmer house. They were his friends, not mine, and I'm sad to have lost them in the split. Although they do have the worst-behaved dog on the planet, who slobbered all over Schatzi the one time we tried to meet at the dog park, and ate my purse the last time they had us over for dinner, so maybe it isn't the worst loss.

"Well, then they can suffer a tiny bit of your spit. It isn't toxic." He says this with a knowing glance, which immediately makes me blush, and makes other areas dampen.

"Well, it does seem wasteful to throw the whole thing out . . ."

"That's my girl."

"What are you doing here? You know we're not working tonight."

"I know, you're doing the trick-or-treating thing."

"Right."

He looks sheepish. "Is it not okay? Emily said people were coming to help."

"You want to help with the trick-or-treaters?"

"Yeah, if you don't mind. No one really comes to my place."

"Of course, you're very welcome." Which he isn't, but what else can I say?

"Thanks, Anneke. I love seeing all the kids in their outfits."

"Don't you mean all the ladies in their myriad slutty costumes? I'd have thought for sure you'd be at a bar on Rush Street or somewhere in the Viagra Triangle." This comes out meaner than I intend it. But Liam just laughs.

"Please, I got an eyeful today at work. We had a slutty nurse, a slutty kitty, a slutty French maid, and a slutty pirate wench."

"So it was Thursday."

"Exactly! But at least they were so focused on prancing around in their costumes they managed to not break the copier, lose my blueprints, misfile my invoices, or spill coffee on my laptop."

"Well, that is something."

The bell rings and I find the girls mugging on the front porch. They pile in, and ooh and aah over the changes in the house. We take the sandwiches and other treats that Caroline has brought into the kitchen, where the girls greet Liam warmly. He agrees to man the door while I give them the tour, just as Emily comes upstairs looking like Jessie from Toy Story, and after hugging all the girls, she quickly announces that she will stay with Liam to hand out candy. Because of course she would.

"Oh, honey, this place is spectacular," Caroline says as I show them the dining room and butler's pantry. "It's going to sell in a hot minute."

"I want to decorate it sooooo badly," Hedy says, when we get up to the second-floor den.

"I would live here forever," Marie says when I show them the master bathroom.

This is when I burst into tears.

The three of them rally around me, hugging me and rubbing my back and telling me it will all be okay. Soon the four of us are sitting on the floor leaning against the big freestanding tub, and everything pours out of me. How much I want to never leave this house. How scared I am about my career and my future. My mother coming and everything that dredges up for me, and the fact that now that Emily is staying, what do I do about that? The whole time I'm disgorging my secret sorrows, the doorbell is ringing off the hook, and I think about Liam downstairs giving away candy because he likes to see the kids in their costumes, and knowing he is there with adorable Emily, and I want so badly to tell them about my fake marriage, and Grant and the money, and the Liam kiss and my confusion, to get everything out. But I can't go that far, and having to carry the weight of those secrets feels like a space between us that will never close, and my heart aches even more.

So I say the last thing that I can. "And I spit in the cider." I finish, throwing my hands in the air, completely spent. Truth telling is completely draining, especially when it's incomplete.

"I'm sorry, you spit in the cider? On purpose?" Marie asks.

"THIS is the thing you're worried about?" Hedy shakes her head.

"Well, it is a valid question," Caroline offers. "Why exactly did you spit in the cider, darling?"

"Stupidhead Liam snuck up behind me and scared me and I accidentally sprayed the cider in my mouth out like a *Three Stooges* episode, and mostly it ended up back in the pot."

"Good lord, none of us care about drinking your spit," Hedy says. "What are we going to do about the rest of it?"

"Bird by bird," Marie says quietly.

"We don't really know what that means, dearheart." Caroline pats Marie's arm.

"It's a book I read. Anne Lamott. It's like, her brother had to do a report on birds and had all the encyclopedias around him and he was totally paralyzed by how to do it and where to start, and their dad was like 'just take it bird by bird, buddy,' you know, don't look at the whole picture, just take it piece by piece. Like that old joke, how do you eat an elephant? One bite at a time."

"That actually makes a weird bit of sense." Hedy bites her thumbnail. "You have to sort of think about the problems in order of magnitude, you know? Like, the Mom visit thing is the most imminent, right, because she's coming in a few weeks, and that is connected to the Emily thing. And then the house, because once you sell it you are unemployed, and have to see what that is going to mean."

"That's smart." It's all I can think about managing.

"We'll have dinner next week. Put our heads together on the Mom thing, see what you need from us," Hedy says.

"Okay."

"It'll all be okay, sweetie," Marie says.

"I need some spit cider," Hedy says, hauling herself off the floor.

"Me too," Caroline says, offering me a hand to help me up.

"And lots of chocolate," Marie says.

"Thanks, you guys. You're the best."

We do one more group hug and head downstairs to soothe our souls with fun-sized chocolate bars and cider. Because sometimes all a girl needs is the kind of friends who will drink your spit. And for now, I'm ignoring that Liam is, like it or not, in that category.

When we come downstairs, Liam and Jacob are drinking beer on the porch, and entertaining the huge groups of kids that come in an endless flood, while Beanie and Schatzi romp in the front yard. They're bro-bonding hot and heavy when we arrive, but once introductions are made and Caroline and Jacob play Real Estate Six Degrees of Separation, she deftly leads him to the seat next to Hedy, and the two of them stop talking to anyone else. Caroline grins like a fool every time she looks over at the two of them, since you can practically see cartoon electric bolts flying between them. Liam is amazing with the kids, can recognize most of the costumes, especially the super-heroes and cartoon characters. He jokes with the older ones, gets down on one knee for the shy ones, tells the princesses that they are the most beautiful in all the land. Emily watches him with a sappy look on her face, and for the first time, I really just completely get it, her longing for him, the way she looks at him, and I hope like hell that I don't look at him that way. A family arrives with a very shy little boy in a Walter Payton jersey, hiding behind his mom's legs, and Liam drops into a squat, and starts telling him with total sincerity that he is his favorite Chicago Bear of all time and asking for an autograph, until the kid is giggling and trying in vain to convince him that he isn't actually the REAL Walter Payton. I can totally see him as a dad, and for the first time in my entire life, my womb aches.

I always thought that I would never be a mom. I know a lot of people who have a shitty childhood choose to have kids to right those wrongs, but for me, I just figured that I wouldn't bother. Wouldn't risk becoming my own mother. Considering Grand-mère, and Anneliese, it isn't unlikely that the damage is on a cellular level. Plus I never really connected with kids, not even when I was a kid. Anytime my friends with children assured me that even if you don't like kids as a group, you always love YOUR kids, that it happens instantaneously, I can't trust that. After all, it's clear my mother never fell in love with me. But I look at Liam and the way he is so easy with these tiny people, and out of nowhere, I suddenly wonder.

I've had a tremendous amount of boozy cider, and the turkey sandwiches Caroline brought and the eleven zillion chocolate bars I've eaten are not exactly soaking it up entirely. I'm shy of drunk, but happily tipsy, just pleasantly fuzzy around the edges, and despite my earlier meltdown, I'm having a good time. Also, I have to pee like a moose. I head inside, and avail myself of the bathroom. When I come out, I decide I can risk one more little nip of cider and go to the kitchen.

"Hey," I say to Liam, who is putting the remaining sandwiches in the fridge.

"AHHHHHH!" he yells, dropping the platter on the floor. "Jesus, Mary and Joseph, you've stopped my heart, girl."

"Serves you right."

"I promise to try to be louder in future."

And before I even know what I'm doing, I cross the room and stand in front of him. "I promise to try to keep your heart from stopping."

"You'll have to stop dressing so provocatively for a start." He gestures up and down over my fabulously dowdy outfit.

"Well, we can't all be Emily."

"Nor should you be."

"Did you sleep with her?"

"What on earth?"

I know it's not my place to even ask, but the cider in my veins has taken over my mouth. "The night of my birthday party, did you sleep with her? She was supposed to stay over at Caroline's, but she didn't and she didn't come home and she's so into you, and you were her date for the evening. Did you sleep with her?"

He shakes his head. "Of course not." His voice gets husky. "She's not what I'm interested in." His eyes tell me the rest.

And then the cider takes over my arms as well, and I reach up and pull him down to me, kissing him with everything I have. His hands grip my hips, and pull me into him, the kiss matching and then exceeding the one from my birthday. My hands slide into his hair, as my tongue explores his mouth, sweet with recent chocolate. Every cell in my body is sparking with electricity, I've never wanted anything this badly. The first one wasn't a fluke, Liam is the best kisser on the planet, and all I want is more. And then his hands come up and pull mine away forcefully, and he stands up straight, breaking the exquisite connection.

"I should go," he says, his voice low and ashamed.

"Liam, I . . ."

"No. We can't. And we won't. Last time was on me, and I'm sorry for that. But this was you, and I need your word you won't. Not again. Full stop."

My heart cracks in two, and my eyes fill, but I nod.

"I'm going to go. I'll see you Saturday. And for what it's worth, everything else aside, I would never do anything with Emily. She's like a little sister to me."

And then his hands drop mine, and he is gone. I'm left in the kitchen, sandwiches exploded all over the floor, fridge gaping open. I hear a noise behind me, and turn to see Emily, standing in the shadows looking utterly brokenhearted, and everything is completely ruined.

Can I come in?" I knock on Emily's door after everyone goes home. She gets major points for keeping it together and rejoining the gang on the porch after leaving me to clean up the kitchen, but as soon as they all left, she stomped downstairs and slammed the door.

"It's your house," comes the muffled reply. I turn the knob and enter. Emily looks like she's packing up. Her clothes are exploded all over the room, and she's still in her cowgirl getup.

"Can we talk, please?"

"Don't worry, I won't tell Jag. But you should. It's just so unfair and horrible to him."

I sigh. Now I know how much she actually saw. "I'm not worried about Jag, I'm worried about you."

"Nice. What is it, like the seven-MINUTE itch? YOU JUST GOT MARRIED!"

"Emily, please, sit down, you need to let me explain."

She plops on the edge of the bed, and I feel her pain, and it cuts me to the core. The good thing about having no family is that you don't have to worry about being a disappointment to them, but I'm slowly beginning to understand what Caroline struggles with, why she says that there is no worse feeling in the whole world than disappointing or hurting your family.

I take a deep breath. "Emily, first off, I'm so sorry that I hurt your feelings. I know that you care for Liam, and you must think I'm the worst person on the planet right now."

She shrugs. I look at her, and around the room, and I think for a second. This could be the answer to everything. She'll be hurt, but she'll get over it. And she'll move out, so Jag and I can get the house back, and not have to worry about my mom coming and what to do about that whole mess. It would solve a million little problems, and help things get back to some semblance of normal. She is sitting next to me, hands fidgeting in her lap, her hair still in pigtails and fake freckles painted across the bridge of her nose. I know what I have to do. I know I need to rip the Band-Aid off fast so that we can all move forward.

"I need to tell you some things, and I want you to know that I'm taking a huge risk, I'm putting many people in jeopardy by sharing this with you, but I'm doing it because I trust you, and because I care about you, and because I don't want you to leave."

This makes her look at me with a little less animosity, and I keep going. I tell her about Jag's visa problems and my decision that we should get married because I didn't really believe I was someone who needed a romantic partner. I tell her about him falling in love with Nageena. I tell her about my history with Liam, and the switch that happened that day at Home Depot, and the kiss and everything it meant to me, and how worried I was for not only her feelings, but for my own. I tell her how completely fucked up I am about everything, and that for the first time in my life I feel like I have to admit that I don't know my own heart, but that I want so badly to figure my shit out, and I feel like now I've dragged everyone I really care about into my mess. I tell her how scared I am about the whole Grant business, and she's still the only one who knows. I tell her that I haven't been able to tell the girls, and I feel like the only friendships I really can count on in my life are now going to be irrevocably damaged by the lying, and I've never felt more alone or more lonely.

She listens like a champ and I watch her angry glare slowly dissipate and become a soft look of sympathy. She tells me that Liam just reminds her of her ex-boyfriend who broke her heart and that she just wanted to be with someone who was a grown-up, even though she knows it probably means she has some unresolved daddy issues since he never dated after my mom left him, and she sort of became as much a wife as a daughter, not in an icky romantic way but just in a keeping house and cooking and taking care of him and being his primary companion and playing hostess at his parties kind of way. She says she understands about the Jag thing and promises cross her heart not to tell a soul, and that I'm a really, really good person to make that sort of sacrifice for a friend, and that she is sure the girls will understand. She says that she is still hurt about the Liam thing, but more because she's embarrassed by her own obvious behavior, and that she totally forgives me, and pretty soon we are both crying and holding each other.

I call Jag and tell him that it is okay for him to sleep over at Nageena's and I'll explain in the morning. Emily and I wash our faces, and get into our pajamas, and I make popcorn, and we crawl into her pullout bed and watch *Ferris Bueller's Day Off*. When it's over, she asks me to stay and have a slumber party, and we lie in the dark and talk about Liam, and her ex, and Grant, and boys in general, and she snuggles into my shoulder like an overgrown kitten and the last thing I think before I fall asleep is that whatever else happens, I have a sister.

30

I tell Jag everything as soon as he gets home the next morning. Well, almost everything. I still can't tell him about the Liam kissing stuff, not until I figure out if I have feelings FOR Liam, or just ABOUT Liam. Not until I figure out if the physical connection is because it is *Liam*, or if it is just because I've had the very bad luck to go thirty-five years without ever being with someone who was a good kisser, or maybe the right kisser. He was mad for a moment, saying he didn't understand why I would just jump in and do it without finishing our discussion first, without making the decision together, but I tell him that Emily overheard me asking Liam if they had been together, and his response, and how hurt and embarrassed she was, and that she was packing up and going to leave us. That's when he finally smiled and hugged me and said that he understood why I told her.

He's proud of me for wanting to keep her, for acknowledging that despite being unexpected, she's been good for us, for the project, for me. And while he's still nervous, he's on board. He made a huge stack of pancakes, and when Emily came upstairs he gave her a big hug and the three of us had an easy breakfast, figuring out our strategies. Emily offered to move to one of the rooms upstairs so that he could have the pullout couch again, but he said he thought downstairs should officially be girl quarters. Now that we don't have to hide the truth from Emily, he'll spend most nights sleeping at Nageena's, and will rock the blow-up mattress upstairs on the nights he stays here.

So far it has worked pretty well, and contrary to Jag's concerns that Emily might tell Liam, she has decided that if he wants to think of her as a little sister, she is going to act like one, making fun of everything from his hair to his accent, and being generally bratty. It's been delightful to watch.

Today Jag took Emily to Salvage One to look for some lighting fixtures. We're in need of wall sconces for the long hallways, a couple of chandeliers, some flush-mount ceiling lights for bedrooms. I'm working on the front room on the second floor, refinishing the French doors that lead out to the balcony. I'm just finishing what I pray is the final coat of stripper when my phone rings.

Oy. "Hi, Grant, how's it going?" I try to force joviality.

"Okay, busy, stressful."

"I know the feeling."

"Yeah. How is everything with you?"

"Great, really, things are coming along over here."

"I'm glad, Anneke, that sounds good, you sound good. I, um, hate to do this but I sort of need to know where we are with the money. The guy called again and now they're offering 235, all cash."

My stomach turns over, pancakes becoming a lead brick. "I can get you the fifty in two weeks." I sucked it up and asked my financial guy about cashing in some of my retirement savings, and he said he could make it liquid in three business days, but that he strongly advises that this is a one-time deal, and I not think of my accounts with him as a savings account. Every time I dip in there are additional fees and penalties, and ultimately I'd almost be better off putting things on high-interest credit cards. I hired him because he is so conservative. When we first started working together I was a single girl with no plans to either wed or have children. I needed to make sure that my retirement savings would be there for me. I carry the highest amount of both long- and short-term disability coverage; I've always planned for future that only relied on me.

"That's good, really, great, and I appreciate it, but it doesn't solve the bigger issue. I would still need the rest pretty soon, and if you're still talking about a sale after the New Year, I won't be able to float it that long."

"I'll figure it out, Grant, please, I just need a little more time. And if you can figure out how to wait till the sale, I'll beat their offer, you can have 250 total."

It kills me to be having this conversation. My feelings about Grant are so up and down. I'm still so hurt by his betrayal, and confused by his recent behavior. Cheating on me with a man, shitty, but almost somewhat understandable, questioning his identity, his sexuality, presented with temptation he hadn't expected, okay. Showing up to stop my wedding? Stupid, but I guess maybe romantic, in a rom-com kind of way. But between catching him sucking face with a random woman in the hallway of a restaurant he wouldn't usually have been caught dead in, and now suddenly pressing me about money? Deep down I could strangle him.

"You know it isn't the profit issue, it's just the circumstances." I hate him for using that "woe is me" tone. As if it's just killing him to even ask me for the money. The fact that he is daring to come to me with all of this just underscores that whatever else came of his infidelity, I clearly dodged a bullet relationshipwise.

"Please, just let me figure this out for a few more weeks."

"Okay."

I hang up, and head to the bathroom to splash some cold water on my face. I suddenly have a horrific case of heartburn, probably my conscience heating up. I like being the strong self-sufficient broad. I hate women like my mother, who survive entirely at the mercy of generous men. When Joe died, I discovered that he had paid her alimony for two years, until she remarried. The very thought turned my stomach. After abandoning him, to take money from him? Unconscionable. And yet, standing here right now, there is a part of me that wonders what would happen if I sued Grant for breach of promise and palimony. I know deep down I could never go through with it, but a tiny delicious shiver runs through my body at the image of some oily little process server showing up at one of his fancy investor meetings and handing him papers. Or maybe selling the story of finding him in the shower with Gregg to one of the sleazy tabloids. "Fan Favorite Chef Heats Things Up in the Kitchen . . . AND the Shower!" This makes me giggle.

I go back to the doors, where the paint is bubbling and puckering. So far I've removed three layers of various browns, one horridly garish yellow, and a bright Kelly green. This pale blue is hopefully the last of it, and if I get lucky, the wood will be good enough to stain. I use a soft plastic scraper to pull off the paint, carefully revealing the red oak underneath. I wash off the last bits of stripper, and give the doors a light sanding so that they'll take the stain. One of the first things I came up with when I bought the house was a custom stain blend that matches the color of all of the existing woodwork. That way I can both stain new wood to match and refinish old wood as we go. With the new wood we use on cased openings and places where moldings and things had gone missing, I prep it with an aging solution I make by soaking steel wool in white vinegar, and then use my stain blend once the wood has cured a bit. On these doors, which are original, I just need to stain them and then I'll seal them with a UV-protective polyurethane coating on the outside. Luckily the porch is north facing, and protected by the massive trees that line the boulevard, so I don't need to worry about much sun damage.

I put on the first coat of stain and then carry all the stripping gear down to the mudroom to wash it while the stain sinks in. I'll ultimately do five coats of penetrating stain today, with an hour between coats. It should have been a relaxing day, the time between coats is too short to jump into anything else, so my plan was to just hang out in the room, read Gemma's journal, maybe do a power nap. But after speaking with Grant I know I won't be able to focus on her spidery violet handwriting, won't be able to drift off. Instead I go to my desk to get the legal pad that has all of the numbers for the rest of the job on it, to see if by some miracle I'll be able to pull this all off, to see if some magic has happened that makes it all possible.

Hedy, Marie, and Walter pick me up at six on the dot. It's been a good long time since we had a regular girls' night, and despite Caroline's attempt to lure us to the burbs with promises of homemade food and Carl's wine, we've decided to go out downtown instead. I've been craving Italian, and Marie has never been to Piccolo Sogno, so we overrode Caroline, and we're making her leave the enclave for a change. Despite the low-grade headache I'm sporting, the result of a day both breathing stain fumes and squinting at numbers, doing endless math, I'm actually looking forward to tonight. After the Halloween meltdown, I feel a little bit like maybe things are getting easier with the girls, and even though there is still so much I can't tell them, Emily has begun to convince me that when the time comes, they'll understand, and forgive. I don't really know that I believe that, but what I do know is that the time to come clean is far away, and if it's possible I'm going to lose them eventually, I need to stop pushing them away now and instead get as much of them in my life as I can stand.

We order a bottle of prosecco to start, and suddenly appetizers begin to arrive. Tony, the chef, comes out to the table to let us know that he will be taking care of us for the evening. He and Grant are great pals, and he and I always got along well. One of the waiters spotted me when we came in, and let him know I was in the house. He leans over to kiss me on both cheeks, and whispers in my ear.

"I was sorry to hear about you and Grant, but I also hear that congratulations are in order. I'm happy for your happiness."

"Thanks, Tony. It's all for the good." He nods.

"Well, tonight you let me help you celebrate with these beautiful ladies!"

"Absolutely."

"And you bring your new husband soon? I need to make sure he is good enough for you." This makes me blush.

"Of course."

"It's nice to be with the queen," Hedy says, raising her glass to me and winking.

"There goes my diet," says Marie in a tone that says that she is both delighted, and probably not really on a diet to begin with.

"I should have worn an elastic waistband!" Caroline says, taking a sip of her bubbly.

I fill my plate with crunchy calamari, favoring as I always do the tentacles over the rings, a crispy stuffed zucchini blossom oozing cheese, and a large spoonful of panzanella salad. "Dig in, ladies, or it will be gone."

Caroline delicately takes three rings of calamari, picks the onions out of the panzanella, and cuts a zucchini blossom in half. Hedy rolls her eyes, picks up the half Caroline leaves behind, and pops it in her mouth whole while filling her plate with panzanella and calamari, just as a platter with prosciutto and figs arrives. We feast as course after course descends on us, three kinds of pasta, an impossibly thin and crispy pizza, grilled meats and vegetables.

Marie tells us about the very cool new artist that has joined John's shop, a young woman who is specializing in classic pinup girls, and custom portraits. Caroline talks about the plans they are making for their time in France, and that she has joined the board for Writers Theatre. Hedy talks about her newest client, a woman who received her Winnetka home and her Gold Coast pied-à-terre in an acrimonious divorce, both properties having been in her ex-husband's family for generations, decorated by her former mother-in-law. Apparently the husband's infidelities meant that not only was it important that she gain ownership of his inheritance, but that she completely undo every choice that had been foisted upon her during the course of her twenty-year marriage, so she is doing a complete gut on both spaces and donating all the family heirloom furnishings to local women's shelters.

"So, let's get down to brass tacks, shall we?" Hedy asks.

I chew a featherlight ravioli. "Tack away."

"Anneliese is coming," Marie says, wrinkling her nose as if she is smelling something rotten.

"Yep."

"And Emily doesn't know," Caroline says.

"Correct."

"Have you thought any more about the best way to handle that?" Hedy asks, pulling the leg off of the whole duck Tony sent out with her fingers, and tucking in like she's at a family picnic.

"I can't really decide. On the one hand, Anneliese isn't coming anywhere near the house except for Thanksgiving Day, and Emily will be safely on the East Coast, spending the holiday with her dad. So I don't think it would be at all hard to just not tell her at all. On the other hand, a part of me really wonders if it wouldn't be the best thing for her, to meet her again, to see her for what she is, take the rose-colored glasses off."

"And this is about protecting Emily, and not yourself?" Marie asks.

"Meaning?"

She takes a deep breath. "Anneliese was the crappiest possible mom to you. But Emily remembers her as a great mom."

"Who left."

"As she always does. But still, who was a great mom for long enough that after all this time she remembers her more fondly than not, true?" Caroline says.

"Fair enough. What's the point?"

"The point," Marie says, "is that I think it's only fair to be certain that keeping Emily from a reunion is about believing that Emily is better off not seeing Anneliese for who she really is, and not about being afraid that the two of them will have some lovey-dovey reunion, and reinforce your deep-down belief that it was your fault she never loved you."

Harrumph. "I hate that you know my secret shit."

"Oh, honey, that is not a secret," Hedy says, dropping the perfectly cleaned duck bone on her plate. "That is some right-upfront-on-your-shoulder, written-all-over-your-face shit."

"You know it's not true, deep down, right? Your mother's inability to be a parent to you is not your fault and completely her own problem." Caroline's eyebrows are reinforcing this opinion emphatically.

"Yes, bitches, deep down I know that my mother is a cold-hearted, sociopathic ice queen incapable of actual love, and I was a perfect child who deserved better."

"Sing it, sister," Marie says.

"This does not help with the Emily thing."

"I think you should tell her," Caroline says. "She's a big girl, let her have some face time, let her try to get some answers, or at least some closure."

"I'm with Caroline, although I think you just tell Emily and let her decide if she wants to see the old bag."

"I hate to disagree, guys, but I'm leaning toward not," Marie says. "The chances are just so much better that it will just be horrible and hurtful. After all, Emily didn't come here looking for a mother; she came looking for a big sister. And a big sister protects you. She doesn't send you into the lion's den."

"Look, Emily is a sweet kid. She's managed to figure out how to not be bitter and angry about Anneliese's abandonment and ruination of her darling dad. I'm with Marie; I think maybe the best thing is to just let the visit happen and not mention it, and if Emily ever asks me about contact information for Mommie Dearest, I'll give it to her and let what happens, happen."

"You do what you think is best; we'll take our cues from you," Caroline says, and for the first time since I left Grant, I actually think that she believes I'll make a smart decision, and that is all that matters.

"What I need to do at the moment is hit the bathroom." We've gone through a bottle of prosecco and almost two of red, plus a couple of bottles of sparkling water. I have to pee like a racehorse.

"I have to check in with John; he might want me to meet up with him after dinner," Marie says, and heads toward the front door to make a call.

I go to the bathroom, grateful that my girls are not the sort who all need to hit the bathroom together, and blissfully the room is free. I settle into a stall, and let her rip. Then I hear the door open and clicking heels enter.

"Did you see that Annaconda girl here tonight?" Holy shit, it's Disco Barbie.

"I know! Crazy. Did you see how much they ordered?" Looks like Pinky Tuscadero Barbie is also in the house. "She should eat up while she has the chance. Sounds like Liam sure seems to have her where he wants her, and she's not long for her project." My pee stops midstream.

"Serves her right."

"Murph said that he is buying out her other investor on her stupid house, so that between him and Liam they'll have majority control."

Disco Barbie laughs. "What an idiot. You'd think she'd have known better than to open her mouth like that. Carmex is a bitch." And I'M the idiot.

"I dunno. It seems kind of mean. They already told all the workers to not work with her anymore. And I know that Murph called all his friends at the other firms to say not to hire her." Great, not just blacklisted with the subs, but with all the other high-end design/build companies as well.

"Well, whatever. I just wish we could see her smug face when she realizes that Murph and Liam have totally fooled her. Murph wants to come in and tell her that she's out, and then they can finish it quick with all their guys and sell it fast." That absolute SHITSTAIN.

And Liam. After everything he's done, after everything I was beginning to believe about him, the fact that I was even thinking that I might really have feelings for him. I could strangle him. And Grant. Selling me out to Murph? All these phone conversations about his financial needs, and never once telling me it was MURPH trying to buy him out. My blood is boiling.

"Where are we going next?"

"I dunno. The boys want to go to some bar."

I can hear their heels clicking as they leave the bathroom, and when the door closes, as if a switch has been flipped, I start to pee again. I've never peed angry before, but I wonder if I am literally blasting the finish off the porcelain. I hope Tony is planning on a lot of desserts for us, because if I'm going to manage to get through the rest of dinner without telling the girls about Grant and the money, and Liam, and now this little Murph wrinkle? I'm going to need an enormous amount of sweetness in my face. And definitely more to drink.

Hey, Grant, it's Anneke. I know you are probably finishing up service, which is good, because I think if I heard your voice right now I might lose my shit completely. So let me make something clear. You let Brian Fuckhead Murphy buy out ONE CENT of my house? And I will bring a shitstorm down on your head of biblical proportions. After everything, the IDEA that you would even ENTERTAIN an offer from him just makes me sick. You aren't half the man I thought you were, and I hope you know that if you push me, I will protect myself. By any means necessary. You spectacular ASSHOLE."

Right before I fall asleep in my clothes I momentarily think that perhaps I should have waited till morning to make that particular call, but what the hell. Done is done.

The doorbell rings awfully early. I throw on my robe, and go to make my way upstairs, waving off Emily, who pokes her face out of her room to see what's up. I go upstairs and wrench open the door.

"Figured you'd need this." Grant proffers a large cup of coffee. Instinctively I reach out and take it. "Can I come in?"

I step aside so he can enter. Schatzi comes skittering down the hallway and launches into his arms, and the two of them have a very slobbery reunion.

He whistles, still snuggling the dog. "It's looking amazing, Anneke, everything you said it would be and more."

"And?"

"And I got your message." Schatzi nibbles his earlobe.

"Clearly."

"I didn't know."

"Right."

He puts the dog down and looks deep into my eyes. "Anneke, I did not know it was Murph. The calls were all from a lawyer, he only ever referred to his client, no names. I had no idea it was him. You have to know I'd never do that to you, no matter what financial shit I was going through personally. Don't you?"

I shrug. "Never thought you'd cheat either, never thought you liked boys, there's a lot of stuff I never would have thought and yet . . ." I wave my arms around. "Here we are."

"I deserve that. Can we sit? Please?"

I motion him over to the couch. "Thank you for not selling to him."

Schatzi leaps up onto his lap, and he scratches between her ears. "You don't need to thank me, I'm here to thank you; I would have hated to sell not knowing and then find out later. I'm grateful you saved me from myself."

"I live to serve."

"Can I ask where you are getting the fifty grand for this week?"

Tears prick my eyes, but I blink them back. "No."

"Fair enough. I'm going to ask the investors to hold off on the rest till end of January. Do you think you can really sell this place by then?"

"I hope so."

"I'll make them wait. If you can get me the fifty, I'll make them wait. And no profit sharing, okay, just the fifty and then the remaining one-fifty, and we're done, like I promised."

"Thank you."

"Well, it's the least I can do. Especially if I want to avoid some biblical repercussions." He smirks.

"I was a little drunk. And a lot mad. Sorry."

"You were more than entitled. I've been a spectacular ass."

"True enough."

"Can I come back and see it when it's done?"

"Of course."

"Can I come back and see you?"

"I don't know. Maybe."

"I'll take it. And Anneke?"

"Yeah?"

"Whatever happens, I'll always be glad that we were what we were, for the time we had."

I think about that. I can't say it in return, but I can't leave him hanging. "Thanks for that," is all I can manage. "I'll send over a check by Friday."

"Great. Talk to you later." He gives the dog one last smooch, and then heads out. I sit on the couch, nursing my coffee and my headache.

"What check?" Jag says, coming down the stairs.

Crap. "Nothing, sorry we woke you, thought you were at Nageena's last night."

"She had an early morning. Didn't sound like nothing. Sounded like Grant."

"Yeah. He had an offer to buy out his share of the house. From Murph."

"Wow, that's shitty."

"Not as shitty as the fact that he and Liam were colluding to get more than half so they could push me out."

"Liam said that?"

"I heard it."

"I don't believe it."

"I wish I didn't. Anyway, Grant isn't going to do it, but . . ."

"But you have to give him money?"

I nod. "A chunk now, the rest when we sell."

"How much is a chunk?"

"Fifty grand."

"Whew. That's not a chunk, that's a gouge."

"Yeah. But it's worth it. I'll recoup it when we sell."

"We."

"We what?"

"WE will recoup it when we sell, wife. You remember the whole 'richer/poorer' thing we said in front of all of our friends? We're in this together. Good and bad. I've got thirty liquid, so that is something."

"I can't let you . . ."

"I've got ten," Emily says, coming up the stairs. "My dad deposited it, he thinks he's paying my rent and expenses here, but you aren't letting me pay anything, so it's just sitting there."

"No, guys, it's very sweet of you, but it's okay, I'm going to cash in some of my stocks, it's all good."

"No it is not, and no you will not. You know that is the dumbest way possible to raise capital. Emily, that is very generous of you, and we would love to have you as an actual partner, lord knows you've done enough hard labor. You put in your ten, and you'll get a smidge of the profits when we sell." Jag is very sure of himself, and for the first time, it feels sort of good to have someone taking charge, solving a problem. "Anneke, that just leaves ten grand. Do you have that much without having to liquidate anything?"

I think about this, and nod. "I have just the thing." Looks like the earrings are going to go after all. Seems fitting.

"Alright, that is the first problem solved. Now we just have to talk to Liam."

"What does Liam have to do with anything?" Emily asks.

"Anneke thinks he was trying to steal the house from her."

"He wouldn't, he couldn't." She looks stricken.

"We're not talking to Liam," I say, taking back a little control. "Look, the big sneaky plan is foiled, we win. But we have to sell this place by end of January or we are going to have to come up with three times this to pay off Grant. So I say we don't say a thing, because frankly, we need his sweat equity for the final push. We just let him keep working and then when it is all done we can call him out on his duplicitous crap."

"But what if he isn't duplicitous?" Emily asks.

"He's been great this whole time, I really find it hard to believe that he would be capable of something so underhanded."

I can't tell them that it just feels good to hate him again. To have reason to want him out of my life. I don't want to believe he was doing this, but I'm hard-pressed to imagine he didn't have a hand in it, and if I'm going to be having feelings for Liam Murphy, it is so much easier for them to be bad ones. "I think it is possible. I've known him longer, guys, I tried to tell you. But regardless, it's nipped in the bud, so let's just keep him working."

"Your call. We'll follow your lead," Jag says.

"Thank you, both of you, I don't know what to say. Your generosity is just overwhelming."

Emily walks over and gives me a hug, pulling Jag in with her enormous wingspan. "That's what family is for."

31

My stomach is in knots as I wait at Toast, nursing my tea, waiting for my mother. She and Alan have been in town for a week, with many social obligations connected to his work at the university. But they asked for Sunday brunch, so I felt obliged to humor them. I would frankly have preferred that they blow me off and just come for Thanksgiving, when I'll have the buffers of Jag and his parents, Caroline and Carl, Marie and John, Hedy and Nageena.

And Liam.

Apparently his sisters and cousins arranged a Thanksgiving family cruise in the Caribbean, but we are so close to finishing the house he couldn't afford to leave for a week. Or at least that is the excuse he gave them. When Jag found out Liam would be a Thanksgiving orphan, he insisted that he join us, much to my chagrin. He still doesn't believe that Liam was part of the whole buyout plot, but I've embraced my newly rekindled distaste for him, and luckily, after the Halloween debacle, Liam has avoided me almost entirely, choosing to either work alone or with Jag, much to my relief. I'm not really sure why he even said yes to Thanksgiving, but for once he won't be the person I hate the most in the room.

I'm of course completely mortified by my behavior, especially now that I know about the sneaky business. I don't have time to dwell on any of it, I just have to focus on the plan the girls and I cooked up to survive this week. We're doing the meal potluck-style, with Caroline providing the turkey, gravy, mashed potatoes, and pies. Jag and I are making sweet potato masala curry, steamed green beans, and the yeast rolls, keeping a very watchful eye on Schatzi when we do it. Marie and John are bringing her famous stuffing and his cranberry sauce. Hedy is bringing corn pudding. Nageena is bringing some Indian desserts and mini samosas for appetizers. Liam is bringing the wine. I pulled in a favor from Cort furniture rentals, who agreed to furnish the living room and dining room for the event in exchange for being able to take pictures of the rooms for use in their marketing materials. I had to give them a fairly substantial deposit, but as long as we don't damage anything, we have a fully and beautifully furnished living room and dining room, and I have to say, it is bittersweet to see the place looking like a home and knowing it won't ever be mine.

Emily is leaving Thursday morning to join her dad for Thanksgiving, his family does their big dinner on Friday so that no one conflicts with in-laws or exes, and will be back Sunday night. Since my mom and Alan are leaving Saturday, we should be safe on that front. I decided in the end not to tell her, and Jag agreed that it just would add too much stress and complication to a time that needs none. He is almost as wigged out at seeing his parents as I am about seeing my mother, and the two of us are jumpy and on edge.

But for now, I just have to survive today, which I've opted to do without the Xanax Hedy gave me, or the brandy Jag offered to put in my coffee this morning. I've decided that whatever it is, it is, and dulling my senses won't do much for me.

The door opens, and I look up. My mother, looking chic and elegant as always, her figure trim, her blond hair perfectly coiffed. Behind her, a tall handsome man with a shock of white hair. I stand and go to greet them.

"Anneliese," I say, accepting the brush of my mother's lips on my cheek.

"Anneke, it is so nice to finally meet you," Alan says, coming forward and giving me a hug that feels at once genuine, and terribly awkward. I hope my cringe isn't felt.

We sit at the table, and our waiter takes their coffee order, and they look at the menu, asking for recommendations. Alan decides on an omelette, as do I, with hash browns and sides of bacon. Anneliese of course orders a single poached egg and wheat toast with fruit.

"So, Anneke. Your husband couldn't join us?" my mother asks in a way that implies she disapproves.

"He's picking up his parents at the airport and getting them settled at their hotel. He looks forward to meeting you Thursday."

"How wonderful, we look forward to that. Are they coming in from India?" Alan is either the cheeriest person on the planet or heavily medicated. But at least he picked up on Jag's last name.

"London, actually. Jag's father is in the diplomatic corps."

"Well, isn't that exciting, Annie?" He turns to my mother, who nods over the rim of her coffee cup.

Annie? This guy must be really rich. In my whole life she's only ever been Anneliese. "How has your class been going, Alan? Anneliese said something to do with city planning?"

"Indeed. It's been quite nice. It's sort of a continuing education program for graduates of the business school. We have a good group, wide range of ages and people, so that's always interesting."

I like this guy. He's very open, kind. I'm enormously relieved. And I feel bad for him, wondering how much longer he has before she takes off on him. We make the usual small talk, I fill them in on the house project. The food is delicious, and we focus on eating.

"I have to say, I'm looking forward to a traditional Thanksgiving dinner!" Alan says. "Annie seems to schedule vacations for us in tropical locales during the holiday. I think it's so that it isn't even a discussion. I'm sure I don't have to tell you that cooking is not among your dear mother's wide and varied skill set."

"I'm sure I wouldn't know."

Anneliese glares at me, and I wonder exactly what she told Alan about me, and my unconventional upbringing. He doesn't seem to notice my barb, and we continue to eat and talk of nothing. And then Alan excuses himself to go to the bathroom, and I'm left alone with my mother.

"You seem well," she says.

"And you." What else can I say? "I like Alan."

"He's a very good husband." Which is not the same thing as being a good man, or a great love, I think, but for my mom, being a good husband is an actual quantifiable attribute. "Is yours?"

"Depends on the standard. By your criteria? Probably not."

"And what do you think you know about my criteria?"

"He isn't rich. He doesn't lavish me with presents or fancy vacations, for starters."

"I see. So my relationships are purely financial. Of course you would think that."

"What on earth would make me think different?"

She sighs deeply, as if wounded. "What indeed. You don't know my life, Anneke, and never wanted to. So let's not pretend that we know each other."

I'm gobsmacked. You'd think she was the injured party. And then I realize, in her mind, she must be. Otherwise, how could she live with herself? I take a deep breath. "Jag is a loving husband, a good friend, and makes me feel safe and loved. We work well together and are starting our own business. He gets along well with my friends, and I trust him. So yes, he is a good husband."

"Well, I am glad for you, Anneke," she says in a way that implies she is nothing of the kind.

"And I'm glad for you." Which weirdly, I am. Of course I

feel badly for Alan, I think he could do a lot better, but he seems happy enough.

"Will you and Jag have children, do you think?" she asks.

"Doubtful. I never really wanted them. Guess we have that in common."

She sighs as if I'm desperately obtuse. "Want is tricky, Anneke. Sometimes we want what we can't have; sometimes we want what we shouldn't have. Neither is particularly healthy."

"Well, you never had others." I know I'm digging, just to see if she'll even mention Emily. There is still time; if she admits to having been close to someone in her past, to missing a little girl she once left behind, even if it wasn't me, I can still reconnect them. I realize I actually want her to wax poetic about a little blond doll she used to love very much, which must mean that the whole sister thing has really taken hold.

"Well, as you say, I was never really cut out for it."

"None of the other husbands came with progeny?"

"Not in a way that impacted me materially."

And with that, my decision is completely validated.

Alan returns, and fills the better part of the next hour with stories and asking questions about my work, and keeps Anneliese and me from having to have any more "real" conversation.

You've got to be fucking kidding me," Marie says, peeling the paper off her second cupcake. I called her from the car on my way home from brunch, and she immediately ran over to Maddiebird Bakery and got six cupcakes for us.

"Oh no! Not kidding. You'd have thought that I abandoned HER for her whole life. She was all pouty and petulant and 'you don't know my life and never wanted to' blah blah blah."

"She's a cunt," Marie says, in such a matter-of-fact way, I

almost don't notice that she has used her own professed least favorite word.

"I'm sorry, did you just turn into Hedy?" Hedy loves the word. She thinks it's endearing. Whenever she says it Caroline looks as if she has been poked with a cattle prod, and Marie puts her fingers in her ears.

"Well, she is. How on earth can she imagine that she's the one who is entitled to be hurt? You don't know her and never WANTED to? When were you given the opportunity? The ten minutes she was around between men?"

"Who knows? She's clearly delusional. And we were totally right about not telling Emily; I gave her the perfect opening, and she essentially said that she never had any other children in her life. But you'll like Alan. He's shockingly normal. And there will be plenty of people around to keep things easy for Thursday, and then she can go away and hopefully never return."

"I want to spit in her food. I want to pull a full-on *The Help* on that woman."

Marie says this and takes a huge bite of delicious cupcake, getting frosting right up her nose, which cracks us both up. And by the time we each finish our third, my day is fairly saved.

I change for the third time, going with dark gray velvet pants, and a simple scoop-neck black sweater that has a tiny bit of shimmer in it. Black ankle boots. Little gold hoops, now that my diamond earrings are safely at Steinfeld's, being polished up for a future in someone else's ears, and a pewter leather wrap bracelet Hedy gave me for my birthday. My hair has actually reached a length that makes for a decent ponytail. I slip on my wedding band, and slick on a bit of lip gloss. I'm meeting Jag and his parents for dinner, and I'm even more nervous than I was having brunch with Anneliese and Alan. Apparently Jag's parents are both completely debilitated by jet lag when they travel, so even though they got in two days ago, this will be our first meeting. They've spent the past forty-eight hours holed up in their hotel, sleeping and ordering room service. But Jag says that they are feeling good today, and very excited to see us. We have to tell them about Jag dropping out, and I don't know which of us is dreading it more. But we realized that we couldn't just wait till Thursday when everyone is around; that wouldn't be fair. And while we would have preferred to not spring it on them the night they first meet me, apparently the Sikh community is ridiculously tight, so tomorrow they have plans for breakfast, lunch, and dinner with friends or friends of friends. Lucky for us, the fact that we are hosting on Thursday gets us off the hook for joining them.

We're heading up to a Pakistani place on Devon called Masti Grill that Jag and his friends all love. The owner, Tanveer, is a friend of Nageena's, and apparently we are going to get the royal treatment. Jag promises that the karaoke is optional. It's BYOB, so I'm stopping to pick up the beer and meeting the three of them there.

DAUGHTER!" Jag's dad says as I come into the restaurant, his arms wide and a huge smile on his face. I receive the hug, immediately struck by how different he and Jag are. Bahal is maybe only an inch taller than me, round and jolly, like Winnie the Pooh with a beard in a turban.

"Let me see you." Jag's mom pulls me out of his embrace. She holds both my hands, pulling my arms apart to look me up and down. She is the tiniest of women, probably under five feet and delicate like a doll, in a gorgeous deep orange sari, with large gold chandelier earrings, and an armful of bangles. She smells almost spicy, like cardamom. "Beautiful!" she proclaims, grasping my face in her hands.

"Hi, honey." Jag comes over and kisses me, eyebrows curled as if to say, "I warned you!"

Nageena has clearly called ahead, because we're never given menus. Food just starts to arrive. Chicken and vegetable pakoras, chickpea fritters with delicate spices. Aloo samosas filled with spicy potatoes, peas, and cilantro, with a fiery green sauce. Goat curry. Tandoori chicken. Mutton biryani. White lentil dal with onions and spices, potatoes and eggplant fried with onions and tomatoes, and four kinds of bread, naan, tandoor roti, chapati, and paratha. All of it delicious, and surprising. The three of them are easy together, and loving; Bahal tells all the funny stories that embarrass Jag a little, and then Bahula follows up with the ones that make him sound like the smartest child that ever lived. It is fun, and it kills me.

I hate that we are lying to these lovely people. I hate that we are going to break their hearts, not just once, but many times over in the years to come. And I am so very jealous that Jag got to grow up in the embrace of these amazing, warm people who adore him. I'm usually pretty Zen about my upbringing, it was what it was, and I never lacked for food or shelter, I wasn't abused, I got a good education, and I did have Joe. There are so many who had it so much worse, it's always felt stupid and whiny to complain about not being doted on. But every once in a while something just hits my heart, and it shatters along old fault lines. I'm probably so much more sensitive because I saw my mom two days ago, and have been generally in a tender place this past ten months, but whatever it is, my neck just clenches up.

When a vat of beautiful spiced rice pudding arrives with a platter of small fried milky doughnuts dusted in pistachios, along with some tea, I look at Jag, and he nods.

"Amma, Appa, I have something to tell you that I hope you will understand," Jag starts, and a cloud falls over their faces. He presses on. "I've thought long and hard about this, and I know it will disappoint you, but I've left school." He starts to speed up as Bahal's brow furrows and Bahula's mouth drops open just a bit. "I just realized that it isn't what I want for my life. I love working with my hands, making things, and I'm good at it. I've been helping Anneke remodel the house, and wait till you see how beautiful it is, how good we are at what we are doing. We want to start our own business, I want to do this for my career."

"We thought this house was for you, for you to raise your family in?" Jag's mom seems gutted.

"No, Amma. It's Anneke's work, and now mine. When it is finished next month we will put it on the market and take the profits to buy the next building to fix."

"So this is your doing?" Bahal looks at me, all warmth and "daughter" and happiness drained from his face. "You take my son for cheap labor? Any uneducated fool can swing a hammer."

"Appa, please. That's not fair."

"No, son of mine, it is not fair. Years of sacrifice to raise you to be a professional, thousands of pounds in education, all the support you could have wanted, for what?"

"Appa, this is what I want. I love it. What we do is beautiful. And I am using my education; it makes me very good at this. Building homes, real homes for real families, that makes me happy. I have a good eye for design and function, and my education gives me a solid foundation to grow from. Anneke is also at the top of her field and is a wonderful teacher."

"Your father just means that it seems strange to have moved halfway around the world to finish your education, only to get married and quit and find a whole new career all in the span of a few months."

"I know, Amma, it seems sudden. But frankly I wasn't happy from nearly the moment I arrived here, and I had already started to pursue this sort of work when I met Anneke. And when it turned out that she was an accomplished builder and designer, that bonded us, and that bond was a big part of why we got married."

"But why not finish the degree, son? In case this doesn't work?"

"Because the degree does not do anything to move me forward in the life I want. Because my place in the program would be wasted on me, and prevents someone who is passionate from getting their chance. Because this is what makes me happy."

"I'm very tired," Bahula says quietly, and this seems to be some sort of code among the family that the conversation is tabled and it is time to leave. And I realize that they want to continue the conversation, just without me. Poor Jag. He'll have to face the tribunal alone.

"Mr. and Mrs. Singh, I know it's a lot to take in and a surprise. But I want you to know that your son is very gifted. He has wonderful design sense, and a real natural feel for the work, and has learned so quickly it makes my head spin. I think it a true calling for him, and for what it is worth, I believe he is going to be enormously successful in this business."

"Well, you'd better hope so, hadn't you?" Bahal says in a way that implies I have somehow trapped his son into marriage in some sort of gold-digger way, which, considering my mother and her propensities, really puts my hackles up.

"I do hope so. Because I think that is what will make him happiest, and all I want is for him to be happy."

"Of course you do, dear, we are all just tired. Very tired," Bahula says pointedly, which is tantamount to telling her husband and son to get her the fuck out of here.

Jag pays the bill, and gives me a hug. "I'll see you at home. I might be late, there is some lecturing in my immediate future."

"Stay strong, husband. They're only here till Friday."

He winks at me. I receive hugs that are far less warm and welcoming than the ones that greeted me, and I head home, hoping that Jag isn't in for too much hassle. I get the feeling that there is a lot that wasn't said due to my presence that is about to explode all over the inside of his Honda.

I get home, and Schatzi and I head out for a quick walk. She disappears behind a tree to do her business, ever the delicate flower, and suddenly I hear familiar voices behind me.

"Well, hello there!" Hedy says, with more than a little joy in her voice.

"Hello, Anneke, so nice to see you," Jacob says, leaning down to let Beanie off his leash, and laughing as he takes off to tackle Schatzi just as she is finishing kicking dirt over her mess. The two of them run off to play.

"Hey, guys. How are you?" Hedy and Jacob have been having a very nice time, much to Caroline's smug delight.

"Good. Just had an insane dinner over at Fat Rice, and trying to walk it off a bit," Hedy says.

"And getting in some quiet before the storm," Jacob says. "I leave in the morning to go to my folks' in North Carolina for Thanksgiving."

"That sounds good, can I come?" Suddenly the idea of being anywhere but here is a nice one.

Jacob laughs. "You'd be most welcome. But I tried to get this one to come with me and was told in no uncertain terms that you needed her here." He puts his arm around Hedy's shoulders and gives her a squeeze. She grins, and it makes me so touched to think that as happy as she is in her new relationship, she still made having my back a priority.

"I'm not facing that quite yet, Mr. Man. Let's see if we're still together come Easter and we can talk about it."

He kisses the top of her head. "Yes, ma'am."

"I almost forgot! How'd the dinner with the in-laws go?" Hedy asks.

"Great. Right up until it wasn't. Jag is still with them, getting an earful, I'm sure. I believe I went from 'fabulous future

grandbabymama' to 'gold-digging manipulative hateful American who corrupted our perfect son' somewhere between the
biryani and the dessert."

"So about as good as your brunch with the egg donor." Hedy
hates to refer to Anneliese as a mother.

"About that good, yes."

"Thursday is going to be quite the event," Hedy says, shaking her head.

"Not exactly sorry I'm missing it, but I can see why you
might want to come with me!" Jacob says. "Makes me grateful
for family far away myself. But you'll be fine. And then they
will be gone."

He whistles for the dogs, I wish him a good holiday, and we
make plans for the four of us to have a recovery double date
Sunday night when he returns. Hedy gives me a strong hug,
and whispers that it is all going to be okay, and the three of us
head back across the park for home.

I get a text from Jag that he is going to Nageena's for drinks
to recover from his parental tongue-lashing, and not to wait up,
he'll fill me in tomorrow. This seems like a good idea, and once
I'm in my pajamas after a long, hot bath, I pour myself three
fingers of bourbon with a single ice cube, and head downstairs.

"Oh, Gemma. Do you think there is a magic potion to get us
through this week?" I pick up the journal and let it fall open. I
don't even need to drop my finger; there is only one thing on
the page.

Recipe for Hot Cocoa with Buttered Cinnamon Toast

"Now that is the best advice you've given me in a long time,
lady!" And I jump right back out of bed and go to fire up the
cauldron.

I'm just buttering the bread when Emily comes in from her
movie night. "How'd it go?" she asks, kneeling to pet Schatzi.

"Not great. Want some hot cocoa and cinnamon toast?"

"YES PLEASE!" She claps her hands. I'm really glad she doesn't know Anneliese is in town, or that she isn't remembered fondly. I'm glad she can leave in a couple of days and have a great fun family holiday, and then come back after our dust has settled and never have to know that the woman she thought of as her second mom, never thought of herself as a mom for a second.

"Toss me the bread." I take out three more slices of bread, and following Gemma's instructions, butter them liberally, coating them with a combination of cinnamon and sugar, and panfrying them till they are browned and crispy on both sides. I ladle us each up a cup of the steaming chocolate, and we tuck in while I tell Emily all about my evening and Jag's parents, and in the sharing it becomes less horrible and more funny, and by the time the cups are empty and the plate is just crumbs, I'm feeling better. Gemma may have the right recipes, but I'm learning that they work their magic best when you have someone to share the results with.

32

From Gemma's Journal:

There is nothing like a holiday to create an atmosphere that is at once giddy with excitement, and rife with disaster lurking around every corner. Belowstairs we are run ragged keeping everything as smooth as possible. While I adore the challenge of these weekends, and the praise that the Rabins and their guests are so generous with when they are over, the older I get the less the praise and satisfaction can balance the crush of work. But the one consolation remains that remembering the bickering and shouting and discord of holidays with my own family, I'm grateful to be here working and not back home participating.

"You have everything you need?" I ask Emily on the way to the train. I offered to take her all the way to the airport, but she insisted that with the weather and the traffic, there was no point in losing the time at the house before everyone arrives. She did accept a ride to the blue line, since it is pissing rain.

"I'm just gone for three days," she says, smirking.

"Whatever. If you are missing something, you'll just make your daddy buy you a new one."

"Exactly."

"Emily?"

"Yeah?"

"Have a safe trip, and a good time, okay? And call when you

are getting close Sunday night; I'll come get you at the train again."

"Will do. Have a really good Thanksgiving, Anneke, I'm sure it will be fine." Little does she know.

"I'll try."

"And Anneke?"

"Yeah?"

"I'm very thankful for you." She grabs my neck in an awkward hug, and jumps out of the truck into the rain and is gone with a wave.

"I'm grateful for you too, you brat," I say to the space she left behind, and pull the truck back onto the road and toward what promises to be the longest day of my entire life.

I'd like to propose a toast," Alan says, when we are all reconvened in the living room, after-dinner drinks in hand, leftovers stashed in the fridge, having decided to take a break between the meal and dessert to digest a bit. "To our wonderful hosts, to all of the chefs, and to all being together on this special day."

We all raise our glasses, and clink around the room. I wish I were thankful. The dinner was delicious, everything turned out beautifully, and the combination of the upstairs main kitchen and downstairs prep kitchen with the dumbwaiter worked brilliantly, just how I hoped it would. But it was the most stilted meal I've ever attended. Jag's parents seem to have resigned themselves to his decision, and are cordial, but not especially warm. Alan continues to be easy and charming, but Anneliese clearly thinks that Jag was not the right choice for me, and keeps asking him pointed questions about whether he thinks it is a good idea for us to work together. Nageena was unusually quiet, Carl and John sat together and kept very much to themselves, and the girls did a lot of quick-thinking subject changing. Liam did his best to be charming, seated smack between the two sets of parents, but it became quickly clear that no matter how much he praised Jag to his parents and me to Anneliese and Alan, no one was really buying it, including me.

"Perhaps, if anyone wants to stretch their legs, I can lead a tour of the house," Liam suggests, as we sit with our drinks, no one saying anything.

"Yes, actually, I'd like to see this house that means so much," Jag's dad says, clearly wanting to get some more ammunition.

"What a wonderful idea!" Alan says, ever the gamer.

"I'll pass, thank you," says Anneliese, as usual, not remotely interested in me or what I'm about.

"I don't know . . ." Jag's mom is clearly torn; she wants to go see the house, but I think she probably feels strange going off with all the men.

"Oh, please come, don't leave me alone with them!" Nageena jumps up and reaches a hand out to Bahula, and I'm grateful for her saving the moment, and glad that they can have a little bonding time. It makes me a little wistful knowing that eventually she will be the right daughter-in-law for them, and won't be such a disappointment.

Jag, Carl, and John join the tour party, and the girls stay to protect me from my mother.

"I'm sure it's lovely, dear," Anneliese says, patting her flat stomach. "I'm just too full to go gallivanting about." This is surprising, since she ate about two ounces of turkey breast with the skin pulled off, three green beans, and nothing that remotely resembled a carb. And sighed audibly when I got up for a second full plate.

"That's alright," I say, not wanting to engage.

Marie glares at me. "That's too bad, Anneliese, the house is really spectacular. Anneke is a true talent."

"It will be a new standard-bearer for the neighborhood," Caroline says.

"I have no doubt," my mother says in a way that implies the opposite. And I? Snap.

"You have every doubt, although I can't imagine why. Exactly what did you want from me, except for me not to exist? I'm sorry I'm such a disappointment, but for the love of god, why on earth did you even come here? Surely with all your experience over these many years and many husbands, you have figured out how to avoid me, why did you come this time? Why did you not just tell Alan I wasn't going to be in town and save us all the fucking painful charade?"

Hedy reaches out and holds my hand, giving it a squeeze in a way that clearly says, "You go, girl." And not "You might want to shut up now."

"This is why I avoided coming here, to face your accusations. You never wanted me, Anneke, not from the moment you were born. You wouldn't take the breast; I had to bottle-feed you from day one. You never wanted to be near me, always running off, playing by yourself, going into other rooms when I came near. When I would travel, never a card or a letter. Never once did you ever tell me you missed me when I called or when I returned. I did the best I could, Anneke, but it was never good enough."

And then I start to laugh. Because the whole thing is so ridiculous. "I didn't take the BREAST? You're mad at me because I didn't SUCKLE? You didn't travel, Anneliese, you LEFT. For months and years on end. You left me with your bitter, judgmental mother to go off with an endless string of men, and always made clear how uncomfortable you were on your rare visits home. Even when you married Joe and we were together for those three years, you weren't really there, were you? Not like a real mother. Do you know why I may never have kids of my own? Not because I can't or don't want to, but because

I'm so afraid of being like you. Of being another in a long line of self-absorbed, cold, aloof bitches who are incapable of providing a loving home. And I will never forgive you for that. For making me think I shouldn't be a mother. But you know what? I'm beyond it. I'm beyond needing your approval or validation. So let me be clear about something, *Mommy*. Take whatever you need from this evening, because it is the last time you are welcome in my life. Fuck you."

"Hear, hear," Hedy says under her breath. Marie is grinning sheepishly. Caroline looks quickly over my shoulder. I turn and see the rest of the party all standing on the stairs, looking shocked, and I wonder how much they all heard.

"Anneliese?" Alan says, looking like someone just told him there isn't a Santa Claus.

"My word," Jag's mom says, clutching the top of her sari, and looking horrified.

"This is the sweet girl you couldn't live without? Who disrespects her parents in this way?" Jag's dad turns to look at him. "This is the girl so magical you give up your career and schooling to work like a slave, this foul-mouthed creature?"

"That is enough, Appa, you have no idea what Anneke has done for me."

"What has she done, besides ruin your chances at a decent future?" Bahal throws his hands in the air.

"Because your son is such a prize," Anneliese mutters.

"Excuse me?" Bahula spins and looks at my mother.

"She was perfectly happy with a good job and a fiancé who was a world-class famous chef, and your son comes along and suddenly she has quit her job and is living in this monolith, supporting him financially, as far as I can tell. Who are you to pass judgment?"

My mouth falls open. I realize that of course she assumes that Grant, whom she met at Grand-mère's funeral, was displaced by Jag. That I left MacMurphy at Jag's behest. The very idea of her defending me is laughable, but weirdly nice.

"Stop, Anneliese, that is not how things happened. Jag is the most wonderful man I've ever known. And nothing about my current situation is his fault."

"I'm sure you'll figure out how it's all my fault," she says petulantly.

"Anneliese, could you please just shut the fuck up," I say. "None of this is your business. These people are the most wonderful loving parents, they are concerned for their son, and they have every right to be. Because they have always been there for him, they have earned his love and his respect. They get to have an opinion. You on the other hand are a sack of vanity and self-absorption, and you have never ever been there for me, so you don't get to say ANYTHING."

"My word," says Bahula, clearly shocked by my outburst.

"Mr. and Mrs. Singh, I'm so sorry you had to be here for this. The truth is that my mother was never really a mother to me, and I don't really know why she is even here. But I regret that I invited her, because I truly like and respect you both, and would have loved to have this opportunity to get to know you in a calmer situation. But for what it's worth, know that you have raised the most amazing and spectacular son, and just knowing him has brought a tremendous richness and joy to my life."

Bahula beams in spite of herself, and Bahal strokes his glossy beard thoughtfully.

"I'm sorry, Alan, I'm sure this is all very mortifying, and I'm sure you're a really nice guy."

"AUGH! That's it," Jag yells. "Sit down, all of you. Right now." The forcefulness of his voice makes almost everyone comply. Carl and John come over to stand behind their women protectively. Jag takes a deep breath. "This was a mistake. We thought we were doing the right thing, but clearly we have made a huge mistake. There will be no more dishonesty. Amma? Appa? Anneke and I are not in love. We did not get swept away by romance. I had already quit school when we met, to pursue my dream of becoming a homebuilder, and was standing in the parking lot of a home improvement store trying to work for a pittance as a day laborer just to be near the business, and being ignored day after day. Anneke took pity on me and hired me, and when she saw that I wasn't unskilled, took me on as a full-time apprentice."

Jag's parents are looking confused, and Alan is concentrating so hard I think his head might explode. My mother, of course, is checking her perfect manicure. The girls are looking agape. Jag doesn't stop.

"When I found out that since I wasn't going to be going to school my student visa was going to expire, Anneke married me so that I could get my green card and stay here to do the work I love. She sacrificed so much to make my dreams come true, and I am blown away by her generosity and kindness. She put my name on the deed to this building, and has invited me to be a partner in her new firm, despite my inexperience and lack of reputation. And, beyond that, by staying here and marrying her, I was able to realize my own deepest heart. Nageena and I are the ones who are in love. And as soon as she is naturalized, I will be able to give Anneke her freedom and marry the woman who is the true love of my life."

It's like a soap opera. The girls are just sitting looking shocked, except for Marie who is looking slightly smug. Carl and John look like they want nothing more than to run away. I can't even make eye contact with any of them, as Jag keeps talking.

"Amma, Appa, we didn't want to tell you because of Appa's job, we thought it could reflect badly on him for work if you had to keep such a secret. We didn't want you to have the burden of it." He turns to the couch where Marie and Caroline and Hedy are sitting with John and Carl behind them. "Or to you all.

You've been so generous and welcoming of me, and I want you to know that it was only at my absolute insistence that Anneke didn't share the truth with you. Not telling her best friends has been the hardest thing for her to bear, and she only did it because of my fears. So please be as angry at me as you like, but do not be angry with her for acquiescing to my wishes." Marie is crying, Caroline looks pained, and Hedy looks pissed.

Jag turns back to his parents. "We are sorry, we wanted to tell you, but we didn't know how. I dearly wish that you could have met both Anneke and Nageena under different circumstances, my best friend and my true love, but that just cannot be. Whatever you think of me for abandoning the career you wanted for me, I will not let you blame Anneke for your disappointment, or make her feel bad for her unselfish act of friendship."

Nageena blushes deeply, and I smile at her and mouth, *I'm so happy for you.* Which makes her smile back at me. I wait for them to explode, or to storm out, but then the most unexpected thing happens.

Bahula bursts into tears and comes over to me. She reaches out her hands and I take them, and she pulls me into her embrace. She's very strong for a wee little thing, and I receive the hug gratefully and return it genuinely. "You are an angel, sent from heaven to help my son, and so you will always be my daughter." She holds my face in her hands and beams. Then she turns and reaches a hand out for Nageena, who comes to take it. "And you will be my other daughter." And she pulls both of us into another deep embrace. I look over her shoulder at Anneliese, who is entirely unmoved by the whole scene, and simply looks gassy.

Bahal walks over to Jag and holds both his shoulders. "I'm so sorry, my son. I was wrong to be so full of judgments. Clearly this is what you want to do, and I'm happy that you found the right job and the right woman and the right friends to make it possible. I wish you had spoken with us, taken a less complicated path, but there are far worse crimes than marrying a wonderful woman, whatever the legalities or motivations. Anneke, my deepest apologies, dear girl, I hope you can forgive us for our small-mindedness." He walks over to hug me, and I hug him back.

"Don't think twice, most parents are concerned about what is best for their children," I say.

"Don't miss an opportunity for a dig," Anneliese mutters under her breath.

"Shut up, Annie," Alan says, and every head in the room spins in his direction. My mother's mouth snaps open, and then closes quickly into a straight line. Methinks Alan heard plenty of my earlier rant, and there is going to be some serious conversation later. I start to walk over to the couch to see if the girls are even going to speak to me, but they all have a look of shock and dismay on their faces as they look past me. I turn to see Emily, soaked to the skin, lips blue, shivering in the cold as she stands in the doorway.

"My flight got canceled, and I called but you didn't answer, and I just . . ." She looks around the room and finally lands on Anneliese. "Mom?"

Anneliese looks around, as if Emily is addressing someone behind her.

"MOM?" Anneliese looks at her again, recognition slowly coming over her face.

"Emily?" she says.

"What are you doing here?"

"I believe the better question is what are YOU doing here?"

I walk over to Emily, grabbing the lovely throw blanket I've rented from Cort off the arm of the couch and throwing it over her shoulders, pulling her into me to help warm her. "She's my sister. And this is her home."

"I don't, I just . . ." Anneliese throws her arms up in the air.

"Alan, we should go." She won't even look at Emily, and I can feel her start to shrink in my arms.

"It wasn't real, was it?" Emily says, as much to the air as to me.

"No, honey, it never was. I'm so sorry," I whisper to her.

"Excuse me, I need to get out of these wet clothes," Emily says with a tremendous amount of poise, and turns and heads downstairs.

"We'll go," Caroline says, grabbing Hedy and Marie to go down and take care of Emily, and while I fear that they are going to be very hurt and disappointed with me for a long time, I'm grateful that they are still being so kind. Carl and John head back to the dining room to be out of the line of fire.

Alan shakes his head, and then stands up very straight. "Anneke, it was lovely to meet you and have this beautiful meal with you in this very special home. I know you will have much success with it. I think this is a time for some family privacy, so we will take our leave." He walks over to me, deep concern on his face, and gives me a hug. "I hope you will stay in touch, with me, at least." He whispers into my ear, and I feel a business card slip into my hand. I look at him and nod. And he goes to offer a hand to my mother, who follows him silently out the door without saying good-bye.

Jag walks over to me. "I hope it is okay, dear wife. I just couldn't let it go on."

"It's more than okay, husband. I'm really happy for you. Your family is amazing and Nageena deserves to be the one by your side when you are with them."

Then, suddenly, I spot Liam's back, headed in the direction of the kitchen, and my heart leaps. Now that he knows, we are free to be together. I forget that I currently hate him, that I think he was plotting against me, and all I can think is that I want him. I want his arms around me and his lips on mine. I follow him, letting Jag and his family and Nageena take over the living room.

And as I get to the kitchen, my brain racing to see what words I can find to open myself to him, I see only his shadow as he heads out the back door.

I don't try to follow him, knowing that he can't be my priority right now, and I slowly walk down the back stairs. Everyone is in Emily's room. She is curled in a fetal position around Schatzi, weeping into the dog's fur. Caroline is rubbing her back, and Marie is stroking her hair with a small towel. Hedy is sitting on a chair, looking constipated.

When I walk in, Caroline and Marie look at each other and nod, and get up so that I can sit down next to Emily. I reach out to them, but Marie shakes her head and motions to Emily. *Later*, she mouths at me, and the three of them leave. I have no idea what any of them are thinking, but I also can't worry about them right now, I have to focus on the soggy mess of girl in front of me.

"Em, sweetie, I'm so sorry."

"She didn't even . . . she just stood there . . . and then her eyes, she just . . ." Emily hiccups and sniffles, and sobs even harder.

"I know, it's why I didn't tell you she was coming. She's a horrible selfish person, Emily, she never deserved you, and you deserved so much better than her."

She looks up at me. "I never believed you."

"Why would you? From everything you said, she was awesome to you."

"But she was awful to you."

"Always."

"I should have believed you."

"It's okay; for what it's worth, I wish I had been wrong about her, at least for you."

Emily shakes her head, and wipes her tears forcefully. "She gave me you."

I smile. "You got me all on your own."

"Are there leftovers?"

"Buckets of them."

"Is there pie?"

I nod. "So much pie."

She wipes her nose on her sleeve. "I need pie. And stuffing," she says.

I stand up and hold out my hand.

33

"Anneke! Good news." Jacob sounds very pleased with himself, and lord knows I could use some good news after the past three weeks.

The upside is that the house is finished. And, if I do say so myself, it is spectacular. It's turned out even better than I ever expected. It took just two weeks of putting our heads down after the Thanksgiving Massacre, as Hedy refers to it, to get all the bits and bobs checked off the punch list. We've tested and double tested every appliance and feature, gone over the whole place with a fine-toothed comb to make sure there is nothing left undone. I hate to admit how much Liam made all of this happen. His cash infusion, not to mention his ability to sweet-talk discounts out of every vendor on the planet, means that our finishes are spectacular. We were able to triple the amount of millwork, doing custom wood wainscoting up the staircase, floor-to-ceiling shelves in the library, paneling in the foyer.

Jacob came over the other day to give it a thorough once-over, and for Jag and me to sign the listing agreement. We're listing it for 1.25 million to weed out the people who aren't serious, and would come looking to lowball. Jag and I went over the final numbers, and were pleasantly surprised. With all of the salvage products we found, and the discounts Liam managed to finagle for us, even with the flood we ended up coming in a decent chunk under budget. Which means that we can actually afford to take 1.1 million and still clear the right amount, although obviously we'd rather get more.

"I'm very ready for some good news."

"You have an offer."

"Is it a great offer?"

"That depends on how you look at it. I know we talked about getting you 1.2. And I do think that is a realistic price. But we also talked about speed being an issue for you, so I want to present this offer to you even though it is a little low."

"How low?"

"One million even."

"That's a little disappointing."

"Well, let me present this to you. It is an offer with no contingencies. The buyer doesn't need an inspection, no sales contingencies, no special requests. The buyer is preapproved for a mortgage for that amount, and you and I both know that mortgages these days are often the deal killers. Just the property as is, closing right after the New Year, which is as fast as you could ever hope for. And even with an early January closing, they would be willing to let you and Jag live there rent-free until February first to give you time to find a new place. They have no agent, and I'm not taking a commission on this, this is just something I'm doing for a friend, so no arguments. With all that, you'll net out pretty close to where you wanted to be, and it rips off the Band-Aid fast for you. This is an awkward time of year to list a high-end property, everyone is thinking about holidays, and no one wants to even imagine moving in Chicago in the dead of winter, so while yes, I do think we could get a higher offer, I also think it might not come till spring, and you need to think about whether that is worth it for you."

"I don't understand, when did they see it? I thought the listing wasn't even live yet, and unless you've been sneaking around behind my back, you haven't shown it to anyone."

"I have a habit of sending a pre-listing email to some key people in the industry to give them first crack at special properties. One of them had a personal friend who was planning on buying, and made the decision based on the pictures and descriptions I sent."

"Wow. That's amazing."

"A rare thing, but sometimes it does happen."

It isn't all of what I want, but it also does seem to make a lot of sense. And no commissions on either end of the deal puts an additional fifty grand in our collective pockets. "I have to talk to Jag and Liam. How long do we have to make the decision?"

"They'd like an answer before Christmas, does that seem reasonable?"

"Five days. We can do that."

"Think it through; whatever you decide is the right decision, and if it's yes, we'll get it put to bed fast for you, and if not, we'll get it sold as soon as we can for more."

"Thank you, Jacob, it means a lot to me."

"It's my pleasure. And for what it's worth? This offer? I'd be happy to have them as my new neighbors, even though I'm going to miss having you guys up the block."

"We're hoping to stay in the neighborhood, maybe not on this street, but fingers crossed we can find something nearby."

"I hope so."

"Do they deserve her?" I have to ask. "Will they be good to her?" This means as much to me as the money.

Jacob pauses. "Yes. Of that I am completely certain."

Jag and Nageena and I spend the afternoon looking at rentals in Logan Square and Palmer Square. When we find the three-story redbrick building on Sacramento, it seems like maybe our luck is turning after all. There are two large apartments on the second and third floors, three bedrooms and two bathrooms each, and a commercial space on the first floor, big enough to have two good-sized offices, with some reception space and a conference room. Jag and I are in the process of incorporating Palmer Custom Homes, and will be hanging out our shingle right after the New Year for home renovation projects and quick flips while we look for our next big spec home build. Since he and I still have to be married while we wait for Nageena's naturalization process to finalize, we figured the best way to handle things was to look for a place for all three of us to live together. Finding a place that also had an office space available seems too good to pass up, and the landlord offers us a rent break if we sign a three-year lease and take all three spaces, so we are hopeful that they will approve our application.

Jag thinks we should take the offer. It will make it easier to get ourselves settled in the new space, should we get it, get the business up and running, a bird in the hand and all that, but he also thinks it should be entirely my decision. Or rather, mine and Liam's. Which means I have to see Liam. He's managed to effectively spend almost no time here since Thanksgiving. He blames the Mannings, family obligations, the usual holiday season pressures on his time. But I don't think it's a coincidence that the only days he has been here to work since then were on the weekend Jag and Emily and I spent scouring the Kane County Flea Market for last-minute salvage items and bits and pieces.

I've written seventeen emails that I've deleted. I've asked Gemma at least twice a day what to do, and she has told me, in no particular order, to go for it, let it go, love him, lose him, bare my soul, batten the hatches, find someone else, become a nun, and make salmon croquettes. Each of these makes a weird sort of sense in the moment.

And the croquettes were shockingly delicious.

Tonight is my first face-to-face with the girls since Thanksgiving, and my bowels are in an uproar. I've got serious stress runs. There have been a couple of brief phone calls with each of them, long enough for me to apologize and ask to get together for me to fully explain in person, but luckily this time of year is so busy for everyone, I can convince myself that the almost complete radio silence is just due to holiday season crazies. And for the first time since I left Grant's apartment, I'm hosting.

Gemma may have been falling down on the life guidance lately, but at least she's still my best plan for cooking. For tonight I've made the Rabin family brisket recipe, braised with root vegetables in a thick, oniony gravy. I'm making buttered egg noodles to serve it over, and some steamed green beans. And I've got a classic sticky toffee pudding for dessert. Jag and Nageena and Emily are at a movie at the Logan Theatre followed by a late dinner to give us some space. I'm just putting out cheese and crackers when the doorbell rings.

"Hey," I say to the three faces on the doorstep.

"Hey," they all say in near unison. I let them in, and hang coats in the newly finished front hall closet. Caroline admires the way the magnetic doors pop open to reveal the closet, which is invisible in the paneling. We head upstairs to the kitchen, where I've got the nibbles laid out on the island, and the three of them perch on the bar stools while I open a bottle of champagne.

"To the most forgiving friends a girl could ask for." I raise my glass hopefully.

"To the biggest pain-in-the-ass friend anyone could be saddled with," Hedy says, clinking my glass and scowling at me.

"To the most annoying friend on the planet," Marie pipes in, eyes narrowing.

"To a friend who tries one's patience," Caroline says with an opinionated head tilt.

I knew I wouldn't get off lightly. "Okay, can I get the groveling portion of the evening under way?"

"Absolutely," Hedy says.

I take a deep breath. "I'm a shit."

"Hear, hear," Marie says.

"I'm a horrible, terrible, no good friend, and I've been spectacularly assholey and dishonest and disagreeable, and I don't begin to deserve any of you. I wouldn't have survived the past year without all of you, and I've repaid your overwhelming kindnesses with lies and deceptions and pouting and whining, and sneaking about and being a general twat and I truly, truly could not be sorrier. I love each and every one of you with my whole heart, and I know you may not be able to forgive me for a very long time, that you may hate me for a while yet, but I hope you'll let me work to win back your trust and love." I let the tears run freely down my face; if nothing else, my insane life path has put me well in touch with the soggier emotions and I've decided to just embrace it as a new reality.

"Oh, good lord, woman, quit your weeping," Hedy says, handing me a napkin.

"Did you really think we wouldn't forgive you? Would stop loving you? Silly goose." Caroline hops off her perch to come hug me.

"Jesus, Anneke, you can be angry with someone you care about for something they've done; it doesn't mean you hate them, you're just disappointed in their behavior. You hate the thing they've done, not the person."

"After everything you've been through, don't you get the whole family thing YET, you idiot?" Hedy asks, exasperated.

"I'm working on it." I sniffle.

"You better be," Marie says.

"Yes, you hurt our feelings, and yes, we forgive you," Caroline says.

"But you have some serious 'splaining to do, Lucy," Hedy says, cutting off a small chunk of cheddar and popping it in her mouth.

"I know. Everything will be revealed."

I wipe my face, and drop the beans in the steamer and the noodles in and begin my saga. By the time I've drained the pasta and dressed it with melted butter and chives, and tossed the green beans with a little bit of garlic oil and lemon, I've told them how hard it was to feel like such a charity case, and how much of a loser I felt like here by myself. By the time I've pulled the brisket out of the oven and everyone has made their plates and sat around the small table, I've told them about my decision to marry Jag, and how much it was related to my belief at the time that I just wasn't cut out to be in a real long-term relationship. They mostly listen and nod, and Marie and Caroline add the occasional "oh sweetie!" or "poor thing" and Hedy periodically snorts. I fess up about Grant and the money, which prompts Caroline to smack me in the back of the head most uncharacteristically. "What on earth is the fucking point of being stupidly rich if you can't help your friends???"

"Um, Caroline, chill," Hedy says. "You know that we'd all call you for bail money, and we're delighted to receive your generosity, but none of us would ever borrow money for our day-to-day life. It's not how we roll. That part, at least, makes sense to me."

"Thank you," I say.

"The rest is fucking twaddle," she says with a smirk, and I know that everything is really going to be okay. We finish our meal, which is really delicious, while I confess to the hardest of all, my kisses with Liam and my conflicted feelings and the whole Murph-trying-to-steal-my-house business.

"Okay," Marie says as I dish out the sticky toffee pudding, generously dousing each bowl with caramel sauce, while Caroline adds scoops of vanilla ice cream. "Knowing you, I do get almost every part of how it all went down. I could still fucking kill you for not telling us the Jag thing was a fake, but by the same token, I know how seriously you take keeping a promise and holding a secret, and he certainly made clear that he had made you swear not to tell."

"I'll totally pay you back for the wedding, Caroline, I know you spent a ton making it so wonderful . . ."

"You'll do no such thing. It was a lovely party, and apparently for a very noble reason. It was my pleasure to do it, and I'll kill you if you don't let me do it again should you ever decide to give a real marriage a go."

"The Liam thing, that's a lot trickier," Hedy says. "I mean, I get that he sparked something major in you, but that might just be that you've never been with a great kisser before. Or maybe you're just a late bloomer. I mean, they always say that a woman reaches her sexual peak in her midthirties; maybe yours was an all-at-once peaking, and not a gradual thing like with the rest of us."

I think about this for a minute. "So you think that maybe I'm not having emotional feelings for Liam, but instead it's just a chemistry/physical attraction/loneliness thing."

"I think you're in love with him," Marie says.

"That seems extreme," says Caroline.

"I think that's ridiculous. Her kitten is ruling her head at the moment." Hedy waves her hand dismissively at Marie.

"I think the last ten years have been foreplay. I think all his poking at you all this time is like the boy in kindergarten who pulls your hair. And frankly, in all this time you've never once been able to say one truly horrible thing he has ever done to you specifically to warrant how intensely you disliked him. It's *Moonlighting*. It's Sam and Diane. It's Scully and Mulder. It's Ross and Rachel. He's Mr. DARCY for chrissakes. It's the classic you hate each other because you love each other and you're perfect for each other." Marie says this as if she is reciting the findings of her doctoral thesis.

"Holy shit, Nipple Girl could be right. You might actually love him," Hedy says.

"She does make a couple of good points," Caroline admits.

"Great. Now what? And what if he was in cahoots with his cousin? If Grant hadn't been at least partially honorable, I could have lost this project."

"Deep down, do you believe he did it?" Marie asks.

I nod. "That's the problem. The way he swanned in, kept pushing to get his foot in the door even after I said no at first. The amount of time he put in, even though he wasn't getting paid for the work beyond the eventual profit on the house. He and Murph are like brothers, so yes, I can see him doing it. And you're right, Marie, it would actually be the first thing he did to me specifically to warrant hating his guts, and even though I think he very well may have done it, I still want him."

"Then it really is love, because if it weren't, and you thought he did it, you'd want to cut them off, and not cup them," Hedy says.

This makes us all crack up, and we dig into our desserts with gusto. At the end of the day the girls all agree that I need to talk to him face-to-face. To ask him point-blank what his part was or wasn't in the whole Murph debacle. To explain my behavior and see what it is that he feels, and prepare myself for the fact that he may indeed have orchestrated an attempted takedown, and that he may not have feelings for me that emanate above his waistline. I'm not sure how I would deal with either of those eventualities, frankly. But I know one thing. My girls have my back, and my conscience is clear. And for the first time since this whole ridiculous turn my life has taken began, I feel free and light. Our evening ends with a round of hugs, and promises from me to never ever do any of this shit ever again.

I clean up the kitchen, take Schatzi for a walk, and think about my next move with Liam, since that is the final piece of this puzzle to put in place. With the offer on the table, and the need to be proactive about moving out and moving on, I have to fight my instinct to put my head in the sand, and just do the grown-up thing. So I text him.

> We have an offer on the house. Need to discuss. Can you come over sometime in the next couple of days to meet? A.

He replies quickly.

> Will be there after work tomorrow, if that is convenient. L.

> It is. See you then. A.

Let the countdown begin.

A re you sure you don't want me to stay?" Jag asks.
    "I desperately want you to stay, but I think I'd better face the music alone." Emily has gone to visit her dad for Christmas for a few days, and the house is weirdly quiet without her.

"For what it's worth, I just think his feelings are hurt."

"I know. But I'm not really sure what to do about that."

"I tried to tell him it was my fault, that I was the one that told you we couldn't tell him."

I hadn't realized that they had been in contact. "Did he buy it?"

"Not really. He sort of said that he was pretty sure if that was true it was because you told me that he wouldn't be trustworthy."

"He's not wrong. I appreciate your trying to take the fall, though. You're a mensch."

Jag comes over and gives me a hug. "Is this just about mending fences with a friend and colleague, or do you want to admit that there is something more going on here?" It's the first time he's ever come close to prying into my personal life.

"I don't know for sure."

"For what it's worth? I think you guys would be good together. And I really don't believe he would have plotted against you with his cousin."

"I wish I was sure of that. It would be so much easier to be confident."

"Whatever happens, I'll be pulling for you. And tell him if he's mean to you, your husband is going to kick his ass." He grins.

"Thanks, hubby. Give my love to your mistress." I wink and he laughs.

I have a lot of nervous energy, so I take Schatzi out for a walk. When we get back, Liam is just coming in the back door, and Schatzi pulls the leash out of my hand and becomes a heat-seeking gray blur, launching herself about four feet off the floor and into Liam's arms, licking him all over his face, and biting his nose like he is a disobedient puppy.

Liam laughs and snuggles with her, muttering about how much he misses her.

"You can have her, she clearly likes you better than me."

"Well, who can blame her?"

"Want a beer or something?"

"No, I'm fine, thanks." We stand awkwardly, not really making eye contact.

"Should we go up to the kitchen to talk?"

"Fine."

I lead the way up the back stairs to the kitchen, and sit at the breakfast bar. Liam sits beside me, and I am powerfully aware of the physical presence of him, his scent, the warmth of him so close to me.

"So, we have an offer?" he says, all business.

"Yes. Jacob got an offer, so I wanted to talk to you about it." I quickly run through the details, and give Liam a copy of the bullet points that Jacob pulled together for me, along with the spreadsheet Jag and I did when going over all the financials. Liam looks it all over carefully.

"If you want to take it, you should take it, it's your project."

"It's our project, you are an investor, you did a tremendous amount of work, you got us amazing bargains on a lot of the finishes and fixtures. I want to know what you think."

He sighs. "I think if you feel comfortable with the numbers, then I do too, and you should feel free to say yes."

This pisses me off. You'd think he was some pouting teenage girl. As if I've done something so horrible. He kissed me first!

"Fine. I think I'm going to take it."

"Fine. Is that all?"

This unbelievable bastard. "Well, if you are going to be some petulant ass, then yes, I suppose it is. We close in January, I'll get you a check as soon as I can."

"You're mad at ME, little Annamuk? That's rich."

This pierces. He hasn't called me by the wrong name since the night at Del Frisco's. "What did you want from me? It may shock you, Liam Murphy, but the world does not revolve around you. And based on your behavior, what choice did I have? I couldn't risk the arrangement Jag and I had, certainly not in the beginning, and then the lie was so, you know, THERE, even when I realized we could probably trust you, I didn't know how to . . ."

"PROBABLY trust me? My word, you are hard as nails, lass, impenetrable."

"But I'm NOT. And you know that more than ANYONE you enormous cockcrumpet."

"Is that an apology? If it is, you are very bad at it."

"AAAAGGGH! I'm SORRY. Do you get that? I am. I never wanted to hurt you."

"But you also never wanted to like me. Isn't that at least part of this? Because if I'm not the world's biggest shitheel, then your high horse isn't so high, is that it?"

"No. Liam. I never wanted to like you. And I sure as shit never wanted to want you. And yet I do. And I don't know what to do with it all. You were in a box, and I knew what label to put on that box, and then you went all rogue and kind and knight on white horse, and I? Have no idea how to manage what that dredges up for me. So yes, I am horribly sorry. And scared. Because I don't know specifically what I feel or how to contain it, and I have so much I need to do to get my life together, that having all of this in my head is like trying to climb a huge, uncertain mass of Jell-O."

"Cockcrumpet?"

I can feel myself blushing. "It just came out."

Liam runs his hand through his hair, and rubs his eyes. "Look. I get it. More than you think. I know what you've been going through, at least a lot of it, and obviously a lot more became clear at Thanksgiving. I think you need to figure out your life and your future with you. I can't be a part of that, and I shouldn't be. I'm sure part of why I was so upset, why I'm still a bit tender about it, is that I know that a lot of who I have been, a lot of the Liam you knew, warranted being treated like that. It makes me not like who I have been very much, and I have to think about who I want to be and how to get there. And that is what I have to deal with. On my own."

I take a deep breath. "I just need to know, did you make a plan with Murph to try to steal this project from me?"

"What on earth are you talking about?!"

"I'm talking about your asshole cousin making Grant multiple offers to buy out his investment in this property because between that share and yours the two of you would have controlling interest and could push me out."

"He didn't."

"He most certainly did."

"And you think I was in on it."

"I don't know what to think. I want very much to believe that you wouldn't have done that. Certainly my feelings for you underscore the depth of my desire to believe that. But I also know that he is like your brother and you owe him a lot, and at least when you first came in here I certainly hadn't treated you in a way that would make you loyal to me. And I have no idea how he would know about Grant and the money on his own. I knew he had blacklisted me with all the subs, and I know he's called all the big firms to tell them not to hire me, and none of that really surprises me, but trying to get this project . . ." I trail off.

Liam runs his hands through his hair. "That ass. I'm going to fucking kill him."

"You told him."

"I told him I was coming in on your project, as an investor. I told him you and Grant had split and you needed a new investor because you weren't going to take more cash from him. He must have hatched a little plan on his own and run with it, but I swear, Anneke"—he uses one finger under my chin to force me to look into his eyes—"I never was a part of a plan like that, and if he had been successful in buying out Grant, I never would have sided with him over you on this project."

My heart unclenches, and I believe him. "I'm really glad to know that. So where does that leave us?"

He pauses. "At the bottom of the Jell-O."

"What do we do?"

"Climb."

"But not together." It sounds like he is saying we can't even be friends, and I can feel my throat get tight.

"I think we'll like ourselves and maybe even each other more if we do it alone."

"You kissed me." It's the only thing I can get out.

"So I did, lass. And you kissed me. So I think, for now, that makes us even."

"So what, are we friends? Or just, done?"

"Oh, Anneke. Of course we're friends. Always that, no matter what else happens. I don't mean that we can't . . ." He shakes his head. "I just think that we both have a lot to do, internally, and we shouldn't complicate it unnecessarily."

"Okay." But it doesn't feel okay. "I, um, well, Jag and I thought maybe we'd do a quiet New Year's Eve here, sort of a good-bye party to the house. Just small and low-key, good food, some champagne . . . do you think, I mean, would you want to come?" Which we totally have not even discussed, but suddenly I feel the need to put at least another meeting on the books, and I'm sure Jag won't mind.

"I would. But I have another engagement."

Of course he does. "Okay, then."

"Okay. We did good work here. For what it's worth, it's the best work I've ever been part of, and I will always be grateful for that."

"Me too, Liam. It wouldn't have happened without you."

"Of course it would, lass. You can do anything. I was just along for the ride." He reaches over and squeezes my shoulder. "Congrats, Anneke, on your first project. Sold before getting to market. That should look good on a brochure."

I laugh. "Yeah. Go me."

He stands, slips back into his coat, leans over and kisses me lightly on the temple, leaving a mark that I can feel long after he is gone.

34

⌒

From Gemma's Journal:

Everything is abuzz with the coming of the New Year, especially such a monumental year. 1920. Seems impossible, as if the distant future snuck up on us all. The Rabins have decided to host a classic dinner party, a nod to the old world, sixteen people, fourteen courses in the old Victorian style. The table in the dining room is extended to its full eighteen feet; a new linen cloth and napkins have been sewn for the occasion. I've hired in two extra cooks, and a pastry chef to assist, as well as three young men to serve. Starting Monday, we will begin preparing in earnest, and hope that a week will be enough time to get everything perfect. In the meantime, tomorrow is the annual servants' Christmas dinner. Since the Rabins don't celebrate, they always go out for dinner on Christmas Day so that those of us who have family nearby can spend the holiday at home, and those of us without can make a party here at the house. They give me free rein to put out a feast, and we eat in the dining room and pull crackers, and decorate a tree belowstairs. It always touches my heart that they embrace the celebration of a holiday that isn't theirs in their home, and they always return in time to join us for Christmas pudding and biscuits, and Mr. Rabin will bring a bottle of port up from the cellar, and the family gives us all gifts, small handmade things from the children, personal items from the Missus, and envelopes

with bills from the Master. It is probably the happiest day of
the year, and one of the days I am most delighted to be me.

"Okay, pooch. A very merry Christmas to you, I'll be home
before bed." I lean down and give Schatzi a head scratch, which
is met with a sharp nip. The more things change. I call out to
Jag. "Hey, husband, get a move on, would you? If we're late,
Marie will eat all the sweet and sour meatballs."

"Sorry," says Nageena, her pretty round face appearing in
the stairbend. "My fault entirely."

Nageena and Jag mostly stay at her place, but she has been helping him pack for our upcoming move. I think they pack one box
and then make out for the rest of the night, and I'm very grateful
both for the soundproofing insulation we installed, and for the fact
that they will be cohabitating a floor below me in the new place.

"No worries. I just like to give him shit." I think for a moment.
"You know, we got into the habit of calling each other husband
and wife, but we can stop if it makes you uncomfortable."

She laughs. "Not at all. Frankly, I like being reminded that
you cared enough about him to keep him here so he could
finally see me in front of him. And being the mistress makes
me feel deliciously wicked and femme fatale." Turns out
Nageena had her eye on Jag from the moment they had met,
and had confessed her feelings to him one night after a gathering when I had been conspicuously absent again, and she suspected things were not all rosy at home.

"Well then, Mistress Nageena, go tell that husband of mine
to shake a tail feather."

Holy CRAP this is yummy," Marie says, rolling her eyes.
Caroline has outdone herself, with a huge pork shoulder
cooked with dried cherries and port, a ridiculously creamy Par-

mesan polenta, sautéed spinach, glazed carrots, herb bread dressing, creamed onions, and buttery garlic knot rolls.

"It's a miracle you have any room, considering how you hit those meatballs," Hedy says.

"You're just mad she didn't make the pigs in blankets," Marie counters, not insulted in the least.

"Well, even Caroline can make a mistake," Hedy says with mock disappointment. She doesn't love the meatballs the way Marie does, but she can eat forty-seven little pigs in blankets if no one is watching.

"So sorry to have let you down, I was a tiny bit busy, and the piglets are fussy and time-consuming," Caroline jumps in, mock defensive.

"Not if you make them like a normal person, Martha," Hedy says bluntly. Because of course, Caroline makes them with sausage meat she makes herself, and homemade puff pastry instead of a package of cocktail franks and a can of Pillsbury Crescent dough like the rest of us.

"Well, I for one think the whole meal is a triumph," Carl says, raising a glass.

"Hear, hear!" we all chorus, clinking. I try not to feel like the odd girl out. Caroline and Carl, playing Mama and Papa Bear. Marie and John, feeding each other bits off their plates. Jag and Nageena with their heads together, flush with love that is at once still new and yet has the obvious comfort of permanence. Hedy and Jacob, emitting nearly visible sparks of electric passion. And me. Sitting at the end of the table with plenty of elbow room.

How goes it?" Hedy says, handing me a platter to dry. She's at the smaller of the two sinks in Caroline's kitchen with me doing serving pieces and pots while Marie and Nageena flank Caroline at the big sink, Marie drying silver and Nageena loading the dishwasher with plates. The boys, all of whom offered to help and were solidly rebuffed, are off in the den watching football.

"It goes. We're picking up the keys to the new place this week, and will start to move stuff over. The mover can't come for the really big stuff till the second, but we should be able to do a lot with my truck and Jag and Nageena's cars."

"Want to borrow Walter?" This is as close as Hedy would ever come to helping someone move.

"Maybe. I'll let you know. Thanks."

"I may have a job for you."

"That would be good. What is it?"

"A client just called, empty nester moving back to the city from the burbs, just bought a pretty spectacular penthouse space on Lake Shore Drive, but it needs a total gut. You should see the kitchen. The wallpaper matches the Formica countertops matches the freaking CEILING. Some blue-on-white Dutch china pattern. It is so insane I actually weirdly love it, but it cannot be kept. Lots of very good custom woodwork that needs refinishing, new layout. Not as vintage as you would normally want, but they have pretty old-school style, so I think it will be a good fit aesthetically. I showed them the pics of the Palmer house that Jacob took, and they want to meet you. They have plenty of bucks, and are strangely non-annoying. I think you'll like them, and I think they will love what you and I will come up with."

"Oh Hedy, that would be amazing." We haven't worked on a project together in years, much to our chagrin.

"We'll schedule something once you are settled after the move." She hands me a sauté pan. "How about the Liam thing?"

"I dunno. It's weird. He says we're friends, that it will be what it should be when it should be, but I feel weird reaching out to him, and so I'm just kind of waiting for him to get in touch. If he even wants to."

"Do you think maybe you should be just thinking about letting that whole thing go and maybe consider looking at other options?"

"Nunnery?"

She laughs. "I'm thinking more just, you know, normal dating. Jacob has a friend from college who recently moved here; I've met him, very nice guy. Maybe the four of us could go out?"

"Oh, honey, I don't think so. The one thing that Liam said that actually made sense was that I needed to figure my shit out. I want to move, close the house, get the new business open, land the first client. I want to start to research new places that night be good for our next big thing. I want to process everything that I went through this year, and put it well in my rearview mirror before I even think about dating."

"So return to the back burner."

"Yeah. At least for a while. Talk to me in the spring. If Jacob's pal is still single, we can make plans."

"Will you promise me one thing?"

"Of course."

"If you meet someone organically, no fix-ups, no Internet dating, just random meeting, will you at least be open?"

"I will promise to try."

"That's all I can ask."

We finish the cleanup and bring out all the desserts to the now-clear dining room. Caroline made a steamed fig pudding with brandy hard sauce. Hedy and Jacob brought a platter of dense, moist gingerbread squares studded with chunks of candied ginger and frosted with a lemon cream cheese icing. John and Marie brought a flourless chocolate soufflé cake filled with chocolate mousse, glazed with chocolate ganache and decorated with white chocolate swirls. Jag and Nageena brought a really interesting dessert called halwa that is made with carrots. And I brought Gemma's shortbread. We make a buffet of all the sweets, and call the boys in. We all fill plates with tastes of everything, Caroline pours coffee and Carl pours Madeira, and there is warmth and joy and laughter. One thing is for sure, I may not have a man in my life or any prospect thereof, but I have good friends and there is sweetness, and for now, that has to be enough.

O kay, dog, happy New Year," I say, putting some cut-up chunks of steak into her bowl. I look at the spread on the counter. I took Jacob's advice and went all out on the classic Southern good luck New Year's foods. In addition to my medium-rare porterhouse, there is hoppin' John over buttered Carolina gold rice, slow-cooked collard greens, corn pudding. The black-eyed peas are good luck in the Southern tradition but also in the Jewish, albeit not usually cooked with bacon the way these are. The greens are supposed to represent money, the corn represents gold. We're closing on the house this week, and I'll take whatever good luck I can find to start the New Year, hoping for a career resurrection and some personal clarity. There is a pan of three-layer slutty brownies sitting on the counter, chocolate chip cookie on the bottom, a layer of Oreos in the middle, brownie batter on top with swirls of cream cheese.

Jag and Nageena are spending their first New Year's in the new apartment; I insisted they have a nice romantic night there before I move in day after tomorrow. Nageena got all her stuff moved in earlier this week, including her bedroom set, and I think Jag was thrilled at the prospect of a quiet couple of bonding days with Nageena, not having to spend one more night on the blow-up mattress. Most of my stuff is already moved; we've got a guy coming on the second to pick up my bed, Jag's old pullout couch, and the furniture I inherited from Joe that is stored in the garage. Between the three of us, we'll be fairly well furnished for starting out.

"Everything smells good, sis." Emily comes into the kitchen. We are having a quiet night just the two of us, slumber party time with some John Hughes movies and a bottle of champagne from Carl's cellar. She is leaving in two days for Boston to start school. She has a cute little apartment in Cambridge waiting for her.

I'm shocked at how good everything is. And I realize that for the first time, there is nothing of Gemma's here. All the recipes either came from Jacob or Caroline or the Internet. I followed them, and they are delicious. The steak is seared crunchy on the outside and meltingly tender inside, pink and juicy. The corn pudding is crispy on top, moist within. The beans are perfectly cooked, not mealy or mushy, the rice grains are fluffy and separate and al dente. The greens, with their rich pot liquor, are spicy and vinegary and smoky from the smoked turkey wings I used when I couldn't find a ham hock. I think about when I moved in, all the boxes of Kraft mac 'n' cheese and frozen pizzas, and I'm suddenly very proud of myself for how far I've come.

I promised myself when I turned down invitations from all the girls that I was not going to spend New Year's reflecting on all I've lost this year, but that it would be a night of hopeful reflection on what I gained, most especially Emily. I can't mourn Grant, the apartment, or my job, or my security, or my mother, or even Liam. I have to go forward knowing that I built a beautiful, special home. That I met a man who may not have been my soul mate romantically, but is my soul mate professionally, and we are embarking on an exciting new adventure together. That I have my friends around me, and now a sister, and that is the only family I really need.

And I learned how to feed myself, and anyone else who might eventually come along.

No one can take any of that from me, and so tonight, I celebrate the New Year, and the new me, with a heart that is ready to be truly hopeful, and maybe, someday, happy.

I've decided to leave the journal for the new owner. I think it belongs in the house; I just can't bring myself to remove it. And I have to trust that whoever is coming to make this place their forever home, will understand why I left it behind.

And I have one more important thing to let go of.

"Em?" I ask as we are cleaning up the dinner dishes.

"Yeah?"

"You mentioned that when you went to look at your apartment that your upstairs neighbor had two puggles?"

"Yeah, Flotsam and Jetsam. So freaking cute."

"So the place takes dogs."

"Yes . . ."

"If you want, if it wouldn't be a pain in your ass, I think maybe you should take Schatzi with you."

"But . . . she's your dog!"

"You and I both know that this dog hates me. She is more your dog than mine, and to be honest, she's lost enough this year. She loved Grant, and she lost him. She had doggie friends in that neighborhood, and she's lost them too. She loved Liam . . ." I don't even want to finish that sentence. "The bottom line is that she adores you and has from the moment you first arrived, and I know you love her too. I think it would be great for both of you."

Emily throws her arms around me. "You are the best sister in the world."

"I think you are the best sister, I'm just trying to catch up."

"You're doing an admirable job. And we'll be back for the summer."

Emily finally did some fessing up of her own when she was home with her dad for Christmas. He knows the whole story, including the use of his purported rent money to invest in the house, where he will realize a very decent 50 percent return. And Emily got to meet the lovely woman he has been seeing, so everyone appears to be moving on at last. Emily still wants to be a family therapist, but she has also fallen in love with Chicago and houses, so she is planning on spending her summers here, doing internships as she can get them, and working part-time for Jag and me, and staying with me. I've agreed to come out to spend a long weekend over spring break with her and her dad and his family; they all want to meet me.

And for the first time in my life, I think I'm actually ready to be met.

Epilogue

~

Jag and I finish our walk-through, and then give each other a big hug. We've just bought a redbrick three-flat on the corner of California and Logan that was gutted by fire and left vacant. The previous owners took the insurance money and ran. Because of the damage, it has been on the market for nearly two years. But the foundation and shell are solid, it just needs a complete redo on the inside. Jag and I are going to convert it into two duplex condos. We'll have to excavate the basement to get the ceiling height we want, but we think it will be worth it to be able to gain the square footage. We've got a long haul ahead of us, but we're both eager to get started. The fact that it is walking distance on a lovely June day like today is a bonus.

Last week we finished up our work on the Lake Shore Drive project, and it turned out beautifully. Hedy will take the next month to get it fully furnished and organized, but the clients are thrilled and have already recommended us to their friends, one of whom is considering hiring us to redo a kitchen and dining room, and another who wants us to create a bigger master suite now that the final kid is off to college, so our income, while not extravagant, is at least steady. And Bahal and Bahula insisted on investing in our company, and their seed money paid for the new Logan property. And in the best possible twist, we have a meeting next week with Oliver Jacobsen, who says that he had an opportunity to tour the Palmer house, and the owner referred him to us for a big project he is looking to do in the neighborhood.

"What time is he picking you up?" Jag asks, as we lock up the front door and head back toward home.

"Seven."

"Are you nervous?"

"I dunno. A little."

"It'll be good."

I'm having dinner with Liam. He and Jag have kept in touch, they get together about once a month to have a guys' night out, so we've kept up a bit on each other, but hadn't seen each other in person until last week when I ran into him at Home Depot. It was awkward for a bit, but we talked about work. He told me he had just finished the Manning job and before I knew what I was doing I said we should celebrate, and after a deadly pause that made my stomach knot, he said that we absolutely should, and was I available for dinner tonight. He insisted on picking me up, which makes me think that maybe it's a date, but then I figured that we were probably just going to some big popular place and he wouldn't want us both to have to deal with parking.

"I hope so. I hope maybe it will just break through a bit so we can be normal."

"You don't hope that it is a first step toward something more?"

I think about this. There's no one else in my life right now. I've been on two dates with very nice, very boring guys that I didn't spark with, but at least it got me back out there and got Hedy off my case. Sometimes, late at night when I'm alone, I remember Liam's kisses and wonder where he is and who he is with, but not as often these past few weeks.

"I think I'm just going to see what it is, and whatever that is, I'm ready for it."

"Good girl."

"And I still have bourbon at home, right?"

He laughs. "Would I leave my wife without an ample supply of brown goods?" The three of us are in and out of each other's apartments and pantries and fridges like the gang on Friends, but we do try and not completely deplete someone's stash.

"No, my husband, you would not."

"If nothing else, Emily gets here next week, so that will be good."

"That will be great. Except she's bringing the hellbeast with her." My spring reunion with Schatzi was much as I would have expected. She bit me twice, shat in my suitcase, and ate one of my shoes.

"Well, you could always make yeast rolls . . ."

The bell rings promptly at seven. I take a deep breath, steel my shoulders, and open it. Liam is wearing dark jeans, and an untucked white linen button-down shirt, with the sleeves rolled up.

"Hi," he says.

"Hi."

"Shall we?"

"Of course."

He opens the door of a brand-new, red Ford F-150, which makes me smile. "Thought you should be the first one to ride in her, since I know how you love that new-car smell." He grins.

"Of course. I'm flattered." This cuts the tension a bit, and I settle in. We talk about the new project, we talk about the Mannings, he catches me up on the doings at MacMurphy. Apparently Disco Barbie finally snagged Murph, and they are getting married at the end of the year. We drive around for about fifteen minutes before Liam stops the car and parks. I look up. We're in front of the Palmer house. I've walked and driven by now and again since I moved out, but I try not to go that way. Jacob says the new owner is very happy, which makes me happy, but I asked him not to tell me anything else; there is something about it that still stings. I know I'll probably meet them eventually, since apparently they have become friendly with Jacob, but he and Hedy know better than to discuss it with me or try to arrange a get-together.

"Why are we here?"

"Dinner. C'mon."

"I don't understand."

"I know the owner. Thought you might want to come see what the old place has become."

That is the last thing I want, frankly, but clearly Liam has some sort of agenda, and I don't know what it is about, so I follow him up the stairs to the front porch. Liam opens the door, and we go inside. The place looks amazing. The living room is furnished with oversized couches and chairs that cry out for a gathering. The dining room, much to my delight, is still orange, and is now home to a long, antique table with mismatched chairs, old pottery and knickknacks in the hutches.

"I thought we'd eat in the kitchen, if that's okay."

"Sure."

I follow him up the stairs, and to where delicious smells are wafting down the hall. There is a gate across the entrance, which Liam moves aside for me, and there is a scrabbling noise as a red blur comes zooming across the room. Liam reaches down and picks up the dervish, who licks him frantically. "Hello, girl. Nice to see you too. This is Anneke, she's a friend of mine. Anneke, this is Kerry. Like the county." I can finally see that she is an Irish setter, maybe four or five months old, and I reach out to pet her, and Liam drops her unceremoniously in my arms. She is soft and warm, and immediately snuggles cozily against me.

"Cute pup."

"Yeah. I have to say, she has stolen my heart."

"That's just because she's Irish."

"That might be it. Always did have a thing for redheads." This makes me blush, and I focus on cuddling the puppy to cover my discomfit. He goes to the fridge and pulls out a bottle of wine, which he opens deftly and pours out two glasses. "To being back where it all started." We clink.

"What smells so good?"

"Braised short ribs. I know it's a little heavy and off-season, but I've been learning to cook, and my teacher says that you can always lean on something braised if you are worried about timing, because it is very forgiving."

This sounds awfully familiar to me. "Who's your teacher?"

He looks right into my eyes. "Her name is Gemma. She's an awfully good coach, and terribly wise." I look over his shoulder and see the journal, open on a stand next to the stove.

"I don't understand." Except I do. In an instant, I understand completely. Liam doesn't say anything. "May I?" I hold my hand out for the book, and Liam hands it over silently.

I run my hand over the smooth leather cover, the thick pages. I let it fall open and look down at the familiar violet script. It is the introduction to her recipe for soufflés.

There is nothing wrong with believing in yourself, in your heart. It always knows the path you should take, and often, the more you fear it, the more that is probably what you should try. Even if there is the likelihood of failure. Our failures prepare us for our successes, and you never know when you start which it will be.

I look up at Liam, who is smiling at me.

"I've always found that braises are quite delicious if you let them go longer than the recipe says," I say.

"Do you?"

I stand up, and reach for his hand, which he allows me to take. "I do."

"So, perhaps a more complete tour before we eat?"

"If that's okay with you?"

"It is."

"Shall we start in the bedroom?"

"If you like."

"I know the way." And we head back to the stairs, and this time, go up.

We eat dinner at midnight. It is delicious. And we are very hungry.

Recipes

Anneke might not be a gourmet chef yet, but Gemma would approve of her progress. Because at the end of the day, cooking is as much about the process as the product, and there is always a pizza nearby.

One-Pot Pasta

SERVES 4

Grant may be a fine-dining chef for a living, but it is simple, heartfelt meals like this that show his ability to convert that passion into just dinner. This is the one meal that is guaranteed to save you from takeout, even when you are feeling exhausted. It is literally fifteen minutes from start to finish, and delicious enough to serve to company. You can even substitute drained canned whole plum tomatoes without a worry.

Adapted from Martha Stewart

12 ounces linguine
16 ounces cherry or grape tomatoes, halved or quartered
1 medium onion, thinly sliced
½ teaspoon red pepper flakes
2 sprigs basil
1 clove garlic, crushed (optional)

2 tablespoons olive oil

2½ cups chicken stock

2 cups water (may need more depending on pasta brand)

Salt and pepper to taste

Grated Parmesan, chopped fresh basil, and extra virgin olive oil
    to garnish

In a large, straight-sided skillet, combine all ingredients except garnishes and bring to boil over high heat. Boil, stirring frequently with tongs until pasta is al dente and liquid has nearly evaporated. If you taste for al dente and it isn't there, but the liquid is almost gone, just add a little more water, maybe half a cup, and keep going. The dish is done when the pasta is cooked and the sauce has reduced so that the dish is not soupy, but not completely dry. Remove basil sprigs and discard. Season to taste with salt and pepper, garnish with grated Parm, torn fresh basil, and a drizzle of oil.

Caroline's Girls' Night In

She may not be a professional chef, but Caroline knows how to lure her girlfriends to the burbs: an amazing dinner.

Pan-Roasted Sea Bass with Soy-Miso Butter

SERVES 4

1 tablespoon olive oil

4 (8-ounce) sea bass steaks, skin removed

Kosher salt and black pepper

4 tablespoons unsalted butter, softened

1 tablespoon white miso paste

1 tablespoon soy sauce

Preheat the oven to 400°F, and put a large, oven-safe nonstick skillet over high heat with the olive oil. Pat the fillets dry and season well on both sides with salt and pepper. When the oil is shimmering and almost smoking, put the fish in the skillet and time one minute. After 1 minute, the first side should have a nice golden-brown sear. Flip the fillets carefully and cook one minute on the other side. After 1 minute, slide the entire pan into the oven and set the timer for 10 to 12 minutes depending on the thickness of the fillets.

While the fish is in the oven, mix the softened butter with the miso and soy.

Pull the fish out of the oven and place each fillet on a plate with 1 tablespoon of the miso butter on the top.

Smashed Roasted Duck-Fat Potatoes

SERVES 4

2 pounds baby Yukon Gold or red-skinned potatoes

¼ cup duck fat

Kosher salt and black pepper

Leaves from 4 sprigs fresh thyme

Put the potatoes in a pot and cover by one inch with cold water. Put over high heat and bring to a boil. Cook uncovered for about 15 to 18 minutes until a fork pierces easily all the way to the center. Drain and let dry completely. Melt the duck fat. (You can substitute olive oil or chicken fat or bacon fat if you like.) Preheat the oven to 400°F.

Arrange the potatoes on an oiled sheet pan and use the bottom of a jar or drinking glass to press down on each potato until it smashes open and is about ¾ of an inch thick. They should still hold together as individual potatoes. Drizzle with the duck fat, season with salt and pepper, and sprinkle the thyme leaves around. Roast for 25 to 30 minutes until very crispy and golden brown.

Green Beans with Lemon-Chive Oil

SERVES 4

2 tablespoons extra virgin olive oil
2 tablespoons finely minced chives
1 tablespoon lemon zest
Salt and pepper to taste
1½ pounds thin French green beans, stems removed

Mix oil, chives, and zest in a bowl, and season to taste with salt and pepper. Steam the green beans over boiling water for 4 to 6 minutes until tender but still al dente. Drizzle the lemon-chive oil over the beans and serve hot.

Gemma's Rice Soubise

SERVES 6 TO 8

When the daughter of the house is feeling both peckish and picky, Gemma knows just how to soothe her. The fact that it is a simple dish Anneke feels brave enough to tackle is just a bonus.

Adapted from the New York Times

4 tablespoons unsalted butter

3 pounds Spanish onions, 2 cups diced and 12 cups thinly sliced

Kosher salt and freshly ground black pepper to taste

½ cup rice

½ cup grated nutty cheese like Swiss, Gouda, Gruyère, Appen-
   zeller, or Emmenthaler

⅔ cup heavy cream

Preheat oven to 300°F. Melt the butter in a large Dutch oven set over medium heat and, when it foams, add the onions; season well with salt and pepper. Cook slowly for 15 to 20 minutes, stirring often, until the onions are soft and translucent. If it looks or smells like it is going to scorch, turn the heat down.

As the onions cook, bring a small pot of water to a boil and add the rice to the pot. Cook the rice for 5 or 6 minutes, then drain it. Add the rice to the onions and stir to combine.

Cover the Dutch oven tightly and place it in the oven. Allow to cook, undisturbed, for 35 minutes. Remove from oven and allow to sit for 30 more.

Before serving, remove the top of the Dutch oven, stir the rice, and place over a medium-low flame to reheat. Stir in the cheese and the cream and cook, stirring occasionally, until the dish is hot.

Grand-mère's Hoppel Poppel

SERVES 2 (OR ONE VERY HUNGRY SAD GIRL)

She may not have been the coziest grandmother, but this tradi-
tional German dish was handed down from her mother, and
adapted to include a classic Chicago substitution: hot dogs! If
you don't have a great-quality hot dog available, you can use
the original chopped ham.

2 tablespoons butter
½ small onion, chopped
1 cup leftover potatoes, chopped
1 hot dog, sliced into ¼-inch coins
6 eggs, beaten
Pepper to taste
½ cup shredded Swiss cheese

In a large nonstick skillet, melt the butter over medium-high
heat. When the bubbles subside, add the onions and potatoes.
Cook, stirring occasionally, until the onions are soft and
golden, and the potatoes have begun to get a crust. Add the
hot dog slices, and cook until they get a little color on them.
Pour the eggs over the whole thing, and stir gently until they
have cooked through. You should have a pan of what looks like
scrambled eggs, with chunks of hot dog and potato and bits of
onion. Taste for seasoning; you probably won't need salt
because of the hot dogs, but ground pepper will bring some
life to the party. Sprinkle the cheese on top and let it melt.
Serve hot with buttered toast.

Emergency Chocolate Cake

SERVES 6 TO 8

This cake is like a little miracle. It is vegan, can be made entirely with pantry staples, and is about 45 minutes from "I want cake" to "cake."

Adapted from Food52

1½ cups all-purpose flour

⅓ cup unsweetened cocoa

1 teaspoon baking soda

1 cup sugar

½ teaspoon salt

1 cup cold water

5 tablespoons neutral oil (like corn, canola, or vegetable)

1½ teaspoons vanilla

1 tablespoon cider vinegar or white vinegar

½ cup chocolate chips or chunks, dusted with 1 teaspoon flour
  (optional)

Confectioners' sugar (optional, for dusting)

Heat the oven to 350°F.

Mix together the flour, cocoa, baking soda, sugar, and salt. Sift. In a separate bowl, whisk together the water, oil, vanilla, and vinegar.

Whisk together the wet and dry mixtures. If lumpy, whisk until smooth, or pour through a strainer into a bowl and break up lumps, pressing them through.

Mix again, stir in chips if you are using them, and pour into a greased 9-inch round cake pan. Tap the edge of the pan against the edge of the counter, or drop from 6 inches to the floor several times to pop air bubbles. Bake for 25 to 30 minutes, or until the top springs back when pressed gently.

Cool before removing from the pan and dust with confectioners' sugar, or frost if desired.

NEW YEAR'S GOOD LUCK FEAST

Hoppin' John

SERVES 6 TO 8 AS A SIDE DISH, 4 AS A MAIN

Anneke needs all the good luck she can get, and starting the New Year with hoppin John is one way to invite it.

⅓ pound slab bacon, or ham hock
1 celery stalk, diced
1 small yellow onion, diced
1 small red pepper, diced
2 garlic cloves, minced
½ pound dried black-eyed peas, about 2 cups
1 bay leaf
2 teaspoons dried thyme
1 heaping teaspoon Cajun seasoning
2 cups long-grain rice
Salt
Scallions or green onions for garnish

If you are using bacon, cut it into small pieces and cook it slowly in a medium pot over medium-low heat. Once the bacon is crispy, increase the heat to medium-high and add the celery, onion, and red pepper, and sauté until they begin to brown, about 4 to 5 minutes. Add the garlic, stir well, and cook for another 1 to 2 minutes.

Add the black-eyed peas, bay leaf, thyme, and Cajun seasoning and cover with 4 cups of water. If you are using the ham hock, add it to the pot and bring to a simmer. Cook for 30 minutes to 1 hour, or longer if needed, until the peas are tender (not mushy).

While the black-eyed peas are cooking, cook the rice separately according to package instructions.

When the peas are tender, strain out the remaining cooking water. Remove and discard the bay leaf. Taste the peas for salt and add more if needed. Ladle the peas over rice and garnish with scallions or green onions.

Collard Greens

SERVES 6

A traditional Southern favorite, and a delicious way to start the New Year, even if you are on your own.

2 tablespoons unsalted butter

2 tablespoons olive oil

2 medium onions, chopped

12 cups collard greens (or the green of your choice), stemmed, washed, and chopped

1 cup chicken stock

1 smoked turkey wing or leg

4 teaspoons cider vinegar

Salt and freshly ground black pepper to taste

Hot sauce (optional)

In a large pot, melt the butter with the oil. Sauté onion for about 5 minutes, without it coloring.

Stir in the assorted greens and cook over medium-high heat until the vegetables are wilted and tender, about 8 to 10 minutes. Stir in the chicken stock, add the turkey wing or leg, reduce heat to low, and cover. Let simmer at least 2 hours. If it begins to get dry, add more stock or water.

At least 30 minutes before you serve, stir in the vinegar, and season with salt and pepper to taste, and add hot sauce, if desired.

Corn Pudding

SERVES 6 TO 8

A classic recipe, simple and delicious. And its golden color cannot help but put you in a good mood.

1 can creamed corn
1 can whole kernel corn (do not strain or drain)
8 ounces sour cream
1 stick butter, softened
1 box Jiffy corn muffin mix
1 egg
Pinch salt
Pinch ground white pepper

Mix all together and bake in a square buttered baking dish for 45 minutes at 350°F. Serve hot.

Don't miss

Big Delicious Life

Stacey Ballis's Most Awesome Recipes

One hundred and fifty simple and scrumptious recipes from
Stacey Ballis's hit novels *Recipe for Disaster*, *Out to Lunch*,
Off the Menu, and *Good Enough to Eat*, as well as forty new,
never-before-seen recipes!

Stacey Ballis is not a professional chef. She is, however, a
foodie novelist, meal innovator, family cook, memory
maker, and brussels sprout advocate who believes that
delicious meals can be simple, fun, and creative. Her
love of all things culinary has made her "foodie fiction"
irresistible. Now all of the best recipes featured in her
novels are available in one mouthwatering cookbook,
including forty "lost" recipes that were not included in
the original printings.

With dishes for every occasion, designed to appeal
to both experienced cooks and kitchen newbies, this
easily transportable digital collection will make every
meal a happy moment and a special memory.

Available now from InterMix
www.penguin.com/book/big-delicious-life
-by-stacey-ballis/9780698154032